Hoofbeats

Katie and the Mustang

Book Four

by KATHLEEN DUEY

PUFFIN BOOKS

PUFFIN BOOKS
Published by Penguin Group
Penguin Young Readers Group, 345 Hudson Street,
New York, New York 10014, U.S.A.
Penguin Books Ltd, 80 Strand, London WC2R ORL, England
Penguin Books Australia Ltd, 250 Camberwell Road,
Camberwell, Victoria 3124, Australia
Penguin Books Canada Ltd, 10 Alcorn Avenue,
Toronto, Ontario, Canada M4V 3B2
Penguin Books (N.Z.) Ltd, 182-190 Wairau Road,
Auckland 10, New Zealand

Published simultaneously in the United States of America by Dutton Children's
Books and Puffin Books, divisions of Penguin Young Readers Group, 2004

1 3 5 7 9 10 8 6 4 2

Puffin Books ISBN 0-14-240093-9

Printed in the United States of America

My childhood memories are set to hoofbeats:
a fog-softened gallop on a lonely morning; the joyous
clatter of friends pounding down the Canal Road;
a measured, hollow clop of a miles-to-go July afternoon;
the snow-muffled hoofbeats of wintertime; the squelching
rhythm of a close race with a rainstorm. These books
are for my dear friends, the horses of my childhood—
Buck, Ginger, Steve, and Cherokee Star.

Thank you all.

CHAPTER ONE

The little one walks beside me every day. Her soft feet
make almost no sound in the dust. We have passed through
good grass into badlands. The scent of sage is stronger
every day. When will we see the mountains?

*W*e stayed at Fort Laramie three days. The
McMahons were fussing with a sore-hoofed
ox, Andrew Kyler had a broken water barrel, wheel
rims were loose—the troubles went on and on.

Mrs. Kyler and I spent two days washing every
single-bingle piece of clothing in the wagon,
cleaning the dirt and bugs out of the jockey box,
sharpening knives, rearranging the tangled mess of
her belongings, beating the dust from the feather
bed, her blankets, and the quilts. I washed my blanket in the Laramie River, leaning out over the water
with Mrs. Kyler holding my ankles so I wouldn't

fall in. We did all the things we hadn't had time or strength to do while we were traveling. I reread two stories from my mother's book in the evenings.

Mrs. Kyler had hoped to buy a few things at the post store, but the prices were too steep—ten to twenty times more than the cost of the same goods back in the other towns we'd passed through. She had hoped to sell a few of her extra things, as well, but the post trader wasn't buying anything from anyone. People with overloaded wagons had only had one option left. Weight was killing the oxen.

I heard the Craggetts arguing over leaving behind a caned rocking chair that had belonged to her grandmother. Their oxen were wearing thin already—Mrs. Craggett had packed all her household treasures. I wondered about Mrs. Stevens. There was no way to know if she and Mr. Stevens were behind us on the trail or ahead of us—or if they had decided to turn back long ago. Had they found a big party to travel with? Had Mrs. Stevens tried to bring all her things?

The guide we thought about joining turned out to be a man of hard opinions, determined to take a wagon cutoff he'd heard about from a friend of a friend of his. He said it was brand-spankin' new, just discovered, and that it'd cut a hundred miles off the journey.

Not even Mr. Silas thought that was a grand idea, chasing down some route the guide himself didn't know. So Mr. Kyler thanked him and sent him back to the party he was leading.

New wagon parties arrived once or twice a day while we were at Fort Laramie. Most were Mormon folks. Some barely stopped. Others circled their wagons and camped as we had. When I walked the Mustang out to graze, I saw people standing beside their wagons in the mornings, stretching and talking, enjoying a morning without the constant hurry to keep moving.

On the afternoon we left, we could see wagons lined up before us on the trail, like beads on a necklace. Looking back brought the same view. The menfolk stopped arguing about getting a guide. From here on, at least until Fort Bridger, there would be help in sight in any direction and no doubt at all about where the best route lay.

"There are only fourteen of us," Mrs. Kyler said to me that afternoon. She was walking behind the wagon as she did sometimes to stretch and get away from the endless jolting of the wooden wheels.

I looked up at her and nodded. She ticked the names off on her fingers. "Six wagons full of us Kylers, then one for Mr. Silas and his partners, one each for the Craggetts, the Heldons..."

And as she went on down the list, I thought about the odd combination of people who had decided to go on together. Starting at the front of the wagon line, there were six Kyler wagons with me walking somewhere alongside, ranging wide to find grass for the Mustang whenever I could. Andrew came behind, usually, herding his stock. Julia, Polly, Hope, and the younger Kyler girls usually walked together behind one of the Kylers' wagons.

Then there was Mr. Silas and his three partners, bearded, rough-spoken, and private. They pretty much kept to their own campfire at night, talking in low voices about business and cattle and the war in Mexico and who knew what all else. I listened to them when I could, but if they noticed me grazing the Mustang nearby, they'd wave me off.

There were our mileage keepers—the Taylor family—with their four children, their pale daughter

Mary riding inside the wagon, often lying down, the rest walking. I felt so sorry for Mary. She smiled at me when she saw me, gentle as spring rain. I always smiled and waved back, but I never really talked to her much. I wish I had.

The McMahons were next—big, comfortable folks with a funny and adorable little son named Toby. I loved the way they talked about everything, the way Mr. McMahon always let his wife speak her mind. Then came the Craggetts. Mrs. Craggett was so proper that I knew she would hate Liddy McKenna forever for being different from most women she knew, no matter how many times Liddy and her big draft mare pulled a wagon out of deep sand or offered some other neighborly help.

Then came the Heldons—Grover and his parents. I hated Mr. Heldon for the bruises on Grover's face. And I was afraid of Grover, because he was the meanest boy I had ever known. I wished, more than once, that they would find another wagon party to travel with, but they stayed with us.

Miss Liddy McKenna's three wagons came last. She drove one, a Negro man drove the second, and an odd-looking man with big hands and feet drove the last one. There was a third man with blond hair pulled back in rawhide tie like a trapper. I had noticed the Negro man limping at Fort Laramie. I didn't know how he had gotten hurt, and I hadn't heard anyone else talking about it, either.

People acted like the circus folks weren't there, bringing up the rear, camping separately—unless help was needed. Except for Miss Liddy McKenna, I didn't know their names. I wasn't sure anyone did. They'd been around fever deaths before they'd joined us, and no one wanted to associate with them, but no one had objected too much. It was a comfort to have three more wagons, even if they weren't proper, covered wagons and carried loads of circus-show costumes and cracked corn for their fancy horses instead of farm tools and quilts.

Mrs. Kyler had fallen silent when I looked up from my thoughts. She was watching me.

I smiled. "I was just thinking about everyone." I made a wide gesture with one hand.

"It's an interesting batch, all right." She smiled. "I admire that Miss Liddy, but don't tell my husband that." She lowered her voice. "Women can do lots more than most men like to admit."

"I keep hoping they'll decide to give us their show," Mrs. Kyler said.

I smiled at her. "I would love that!"

She nodded. "We all would, I think. I wondered why they didn't offer to back at the fort. There would have been quite a crowd. Maybe because Mr. Le Croix twisted his ankle."

"Mr. Le Croix?" I echoed.

"Mr. Pierre Le Croix. He said it rhymes with 'the boy.' Le Croix! He came here from France," Mrs. Kyler said. "I didn't know there were Negroes in France." She smiled. "Of course I can't think of anything I do know about France except that they gave old Ben Franklin enough money for troops and food so we could win our revolution."

I stared at her. "Mr. Le Croix," I said, as much to myself as to Mrs. Kyler. "Do you know the other two men's names?"

She nodded. "Miss Liddy got to talking to Andrew about horses one day at the fort. I was close by, so I asked. The blond-haired man is Mr. Jacob Swann, and the tall man is James Dillard."

I sighed. Miss Liddy and I had only spoken the one time, when she asked about the Mustang, and had said she was an orphan, too. I wanted to talk to her. But truth was, it scared me to be around her, to be around any of them. Fever terrified me. I couldn't think about it without remembering my family, how fast they had gotten terribly sick, how quickly they had been gone.

"Are you all right?" Mrs. Kyler asked me again.

I nodded.

"Thinking about your family?"

I glanced up. I had never talked to anyone about losing my family except Hiram a little—and the Mustang. I couldn't see that it would do any good to share my troubles with Mrs. Kyler. She had enough of her own. So I shook my head. She reached out and patted my arm.

All that first week out of Fort Laramie, we had parties of Mormon folks close behind and before us. I saw the men pushing the harness bars of their odd little horseless carts day after day. I was amazed to imagine their weariness and suffering; watching them ford the Platte River worried me, but all made it safely, as did we. There was a makeshift ferry but the water was low and we didn't use it.

We headed southwest to find the Sweetwater

River, then followed it, keeping enough distance between the parties to let the dust settle a little. It was terrible. Sometimes it was so thick Mrs. Kyler would loan me a linen kerchief to tie over my mouth and nose. We'd wet the cloth. It helped, but our eyes itched and watered constantly from the grit. The wagon canvas turned brown with it; it rimmed the Mustang's nostrils.

He and I had it better than most. I could walk away from the wagons to where the dust thinned out a little. I pitied the wagon drivers. And I pitied poor Mary Taylor most of all. I could hear her coughing at night.

The Sweetwater River had clean, clear water that was cold in the mornings and still cool in the hot afternoons. With the good water, there was better grass. I kept the Mustang grazing every second of the day that I could. He was thinner, but seemed fresh and ready to travel every day at dawn, calling to the mares when I led him away from our little half circle of wagons. We didn't have enough to make a full circle anymore.

"You keep an eye out for snakes," Mr. Kyler warned me one morning.

I looked at him. "Rattlesnakes?" I asked. There had been some in parts of Iowa, I knew. But I had never seen one.

"The rattlers get thicker as we go, a man at Fort Laramie told me. They like the sage and the rock."

I swallowed hard and nodded. Snakes. Why hadn't I thought about it myself?

"A big enough rattler can lame a horse so's he needs to be shot. It'd kill you. I wish Hiram and Annie could have come," he added, as though thinking about snakes somehow led to it. I knew what he meant, though. He liked me, but I was one more child to worry about, and he had no time to look after his own granddaughters the way he wanted to. If Hiram and Annie had come, Hiram would have been responsible for me.

"I'll be all right," I said evenly.

He smiled wearily, then Mr. Silas shouted his name and he turned to go see what was wrong.

Sixty long, sun-stricken miles along the Sweetwater River, traveling through brittle grass and leathery sage, brought us to Independence Rock, a shapeless mound of brownish stone. The boys and men swarmed over it like ants on spilled sugar, looking for places to carve their names.

I led the Mustang closer, reading the letters gouged into the rock with knives and chisels and pry bars. There were messages that made my heart ache. *"Margaret died,"* one said. *"I am going home."*

Others were almost funny. *"Oregon, by gum"* someone had written. The first *"O"* was four times as big as the other letters. I wondered if the person who inscribed it had started off with big intentions, then realized how hard the rock really was and made the rest of the letters smaller.

I could hear voices coming from all over the rock, people were reading inscriptions aloud, calling out names and places, reading messages left for relatives and friends.

After Independence Rock we came to a pair of stone gates—or so it looked to my fanciful mind. The Sweetwater had worn a narrow opening in high cliffs of stone. People called it Devil's Gate. We couldn't go through it; there was no bank along the riverside to follow. We went around it instead, and soon saw the tracks of those who had come before us, marking the way. The ground was rough and sloped.

Coming back up the hill on the far side, one of

Andrew's herd mares slid sideward and fell, squealing in pain. She struggled back upright, then stood, trembling, holding one back leg at an odd angle, her hoof not touching the ground.

When a horse ruins a leg, it is impossible to save its life. It cannot heal, and it will only be in terrible pain as it starves to death, unable to walk and graze. I know that is a terrible thing to say, but it is true, even on a farm when there was not the pressing need to keep moving that we had.

I remembered my father shooting a horse because it had broken its leg, and as much as it upset him, that's what Andrew Kyler had to do.

I led the Mustang away when I saw Andrew walking back to his wagon for his gun, running as fast as I could over the rocky ground. By the time we heard the shot, it was dimmed by distance. I still flinched. I saw Andrew later that day, and his eyes were deep and sad. The mare had been a favorite of his, a sweet-natured animal.

After the Devil's Gate was behind us, we passed onto a sage desert so dry that my lips dried, then cracked. I had a fissure in my lower lip that broke open and bled a little most mornings when I yawned.

The earth beneath the oxen's hooves turned to sand as we traveled. There were rocky ridges, steep-sided ravines and bluffs as far as the eye could go—and beyond that, almost at the horizon, were bluish mountains peaks jutting skyward. We all stared. None of us had ever seen mountains.

It just seemed impossible to me. How could dirt and rock get piled up like that? I was amazed at how the peaks got a little bigger with each day's progress, too. One day we could see clearly that the tops were white.

Miss Liddy noticed my staring at them one day during dinner break. I had eaten, and I was leading the Mustang past her camp to go look for grass.

"It's snow," she called to me.

"Not in the middle of July," I corrected her. I stopped a good ways back, uneasy being so close to her camp.

She smiled and nodded without coming nearer. I was grateful. "What else could it be, Katie?"

I shrugged. "White rock? Or salt? Like the lake where the Mormon people are building their city?"

She grinned. "Want to bet?"

I shook my head, flushing. "Betting wasn't allowed

in my family. No kind of gambling was."

Miss Liddy laughed aloud. "But you're taking a big risk coming west. That's a gamble—you're betting that everything will come out all right."

I shrugged, knowing my parents would scold me for even talking about gambling. It seemed to me that Miss Liddy was right in a way, though. Anyone who came west was willing to take chances or they would have stayed home.

"They all say the worst part is the last," Miss Liddy said quietly.

I had heard the same thing. The Mustang was holding up, healthy and sound. But looking around at the heat shimmers already rising off the dry soil, I wondered if we would all make it to Oregon. Some days I was so weary and discouraged that I wondered if any of us would.

CHAPTER TWO

🙞 🙞 🙞

*The land is dust dry, and the scent of sage covers
all others. Sometimes on the wind I can smell
pine trees. I try to travel faster, but the little one
holds me to the pace of the oxen.*

"Never saw a stallion as tame as that one is,"
Mr. Taylor called to me one morning as we
broke camp.

I looked at him. "He's not all that tame. He just
trusts me, I guess."

Mr. Taylor shrugged. "You ought to let one of the
men break him so you could ride. He wouldn't be
much burdened, a little thing like you."

"I don't mind walking," I said, and I meant it. I
was so used to walking that when I did have to ride

in the wagon for a stretch, the jouncing made my stomach sick. I told him that.

"You'd like riding a horse better than being in the wagons," he said, laughing.

I smiled at him so that he wouldn't think I was rude, but I wanted to walk away because I had just noticed Grover on the far side of the wagon, walking with his head down. Was he listening? I watched him for a few seconds; he wasn't looking in my direction as he went back to his chores.

"Would you look at that," Mr. Taylor said, smiling, and he waved one hand at Miss Liddy's wagons, then walked off to help his wife finish reloading their wagon.

I followed the direction of his gesture and saw Miss Liddy McKenna, mounted on the huge mare, riding astride in her trousers, without bit, bridle, or saddle. I stared. I had seen her ride the big mare this way many times now—everyone had. It never lost its charm for me, to see the horse cooperating out of respect and love like that, not fear of leather whips or metal bits. I sighed. Riding a horse like that, with trust and respect...

I touched the Mustang's cheek, and he turned

toward me as he usually did, to nuzzle my shoulder. "Would you *let* me ride you?" I asked him, then blushed when I heard Grover laugh out loud.

"Nooo, I doooon't want you to ride meeee," he answered, making his voice into a quavering whinny sound. His face was twisted into a taunting grimace.

I led the Mustang away without a word to him. I was furious with myself. The truth was that I *did* talk to the Mustang like he was a person. I was so much in the habit of it that I didn't even realize I was doing it.

"I have to be more careful," I said to the Mustang, then I blushed and glanced around.

Polly and Julia were together as usual, standing near Polly's parents' wagon, sorting through a basket of berries they had picked along the river the day before. Polly's tiny mother was sitting on a log, mending, her needle flashing in the early sun.

No one was looking toward me. They rarely did. Nothing had changed. They weren't ever mean to me. It was more like I was invisible to the Kyler girls. I slid my hand beneath the Mustang's mane and felt the warmth of his coat against the palm of my hand.

I had thought about it a lot. I knew part of the

reason none of them had bothered to become my friend was that they had one another. They had all known one another all their lives, and they were as close as peas in a pod.

Another reason was that I was rarely without the Mustang at my side. I had to take care of him—not play silly games. From the time I'd met them, I'd had to spend most of every day finding grass for the Mustang. I couldn't race between the wagons or have contests to see who could find the most firewood or buffalo chips. I couldn't play hide-and-seek on our dinner stops, either. I was busy helping their grandmother make supper, then clean up. Their mothers let them go play together before bedtime. That was when I was helping Mrs. Kyler ready the wagon for morning, repacking the jockey box and getting the stallion settled with the mares and Andrew's horses for the night.

The Kyler girls were playing and giggling less than they had at the beginning of the journey, though. They were tired in the evenings, wrung out by the heat of the day. We all were. The searing hot sun was affecting everyone's spirits.

As the days dragged past and the weather got

hotter and hotter, sometimes you couldn't hear anyone talking at all in our evening camps. Some nights, people just ate, then stared into the flames for five or ten minutes and went along to bed without saying a word to anyone.

Once in a while, Mrs. Kyler would notice that her granddaughters were ignoring me, and she would repeat her offer to speak to them on my behalf. I always begged her not to. I wasn't sure I wanted them for friends at all—but even if I did, having her say something to them would hardly help. If anything, it would make them dislike me.

I envied all the Kyler girls. None of them had lost their parents and a sister like I had. None of them had ever had to live with cruel strangers. The closest misfortune had come to any of them had been Annie's accident. And as awful as that had been, Annie was probably on the mend, and she had Hiram's love to see her through. As always, when I thought of Hiram and Annie, I hoped that they were both well and that Annie's burns were completely healed.

"I hope I can see them again someday," I whispered to the Mustang. He breathed along the side of my neck, and his breath smelled like sage.

I glanced back at the wagons. No one could hear me talking to the stallion. "The Kyler girls have to be called over and over for supper," I said, and I knew it sounded like a petty and ridiculous complaint. But it bothered me when they chased back and forth through the camp, giggling, when I was helping Mrs. Kyler fix supper. They had no sense. One night Hope had kicked dirt into the bean pot. Mrs. Kyler had used a spoon to get most of it out, but I could feel it gritting between my teeth when we ate.

Toby, the McMahons' little boy, was better behaved. So were all the Taylor children. The Kylers all doted on their daughters, and they weren't exactly spoiled, but they were kind of silly-headed, maybe because nothing bad had ever happened to them.

That thought bothered me. I didn't *want* anything bad to happen to them. "Maybe I'm just jealous," I said aloud, and the Mustang flicked an ear to hear me better.

I led the Mustang farther away, settling into my everyday routine of grass finding. The Mustang wasn't pulling a heavy load or working, but neither were most of Andrew's horses, and they were all getting thinner.

Every day that we traveled, grass got scarcer. A number of times we saw some kind of antelope with pronged horns at a distance.

Twice the Kyler men rode out with their guns to try to kill fresh meat for the party. The first time they came back tired and grumpy; but the second time, they came back with two of the antelope slung over their saddles.

That night everyone in the party gathered around Mrs. Kyler's fire. I could tell that she loved it, that the commotion and the laughter—and a good supper that contained no bacon—were a balm to her sore spirits. She loved having people around, she loved joking and laughing and making each one feel welcome.

My mother had been like that—always ready for company. Watching Mrs. Kyler made me miss her so badly that I had to keep myself busy to keep from crying.

I didn't want to spoil Mrs. Kyler's happy evening. She didn't have all that many now. I knew she was constantly worried about Annie, left behind in

Council Bluff with Hiram. How could she not be worried? Annie's hands had been burned so badly. And it would be a least a year before Mrs. Kyler would find out how Annie was doing—and probably closer to two years. Letters to and from the Oregon country were slow and uncertain at best.

I sent a little prayer for Hiram and Annie's welfare and wished they could have come. Annie had been right that day back in Council Bluff. Hiram was kind. He was the best sort of man—and a good friend. I missed him.

CHAPTER THREE

*It is full summer now, and the grass is sparse
and dry. We do not stop even a day to rest.
There has been no shade.*

"The prairies are behind us," Mr. Kyler said
one evening. "We will have nothing but hills
and rocks for quite some time—and a pass through
the Rocky Mountains after that."

I sighed. Rocks and ravines were all I had seen
in every direction every morning for a week or
more—except to the west. In that direction, the
Rocky Mountains rose up out of the earth, blue
and misty with distance—and with every passing
day they looked bigger.

The Mustang seemed uneasy one morning,

prancing sideways as we veered off from the wagons as we always did, searching for grass. I found three or four clumps right off that still had some green blades—most was hay brittle from the summer heat. I let the Mustang graze until the wagons had rolled past, then I ran to catch up, the Mustang trotting beside me.

The lead rope, as always, was slack between my hand and the Mustang's halter. We had walked so long, so close together every day, that it was as though as soon as I *thought* about slowing down, he responded by *doing* it.

Most of the time, I didn't think twice about him being with me—in fact, it felt odd to me when he wasn't. In the evenings, sometimes, I had the strangest feeling that I had forgotten something, that something was missing, and then I would realize that it was the Mustang, off with Delia and Midnight and the rest of the horses.

I pulled in a long breath, appreciating the cool morning air as the Mustang grazed. When he had leveled the patch we were on, we ran to catch up, then repeated the process. It felt good to run, the air was almost chilly.

I watched the ground ahead of us for snakes, but I didn't see any—nor did I expect to, at least not until the sun was enough to warm their cold blood.

The day passed slowly, the sun sliding upward in the sky until the midday heat settled against the land. After our dinner stop at noon, the wagons moved through a haze of heat and dust, the oxen plodding onward as though they had forgotten any other kind of life and would plod onward until they dropped dead.

I squinted, trying to spot patches and pockets of grass, as always, but the heat made it harder to see—the air shimmered up from the ground in waves. Grass was greener and darker than the sage, but the heat blurred the colors and the shape of the land ahead.

I saw what I thought might be grass and headed toward it, following a downward slope. There was a slough, I discovered, as I got closer, marshy and wet. There was no river, not even a creek—and the ground around the slough was dry as old bones. It had to be spring-fed, the water just bubbling up somewhere close by.

I glanced up at the Rocky Mountains in the

distance as I followed along the edge of the slough. They looked a deeper blue as we got closer, darker than the sky but not by too much. They were crowned in white.

"That's snow, Miss Liddy says," I said to the Mustang as I spotted a tiny stream flowing from the earth. The water looked clear enough, and I stepped in it to cool my bare feet—then jumped backward. The water and the mud around it were icy cold!

My reaction startled the Mustang, and he shied sideways, half rearing. I stood aside, leaving the lead rope loose, waiting for him to calm down; then, when he had, I put my foot closer to the spring. I hadn't imagined it! The ground felt like frozen soil in the middle of winter, not like sun-heated earth in the hottest part of summer.

I looked back toward the wagons. I was too far away to shout and be heard. I would go tell them in a minute. But first, I wanted to explore the slough a little. What in the world could cause such icy water? I waded into the little creek. It was so cold that I began to shiver, in spite of the hot sun. In places, there was a skim of ice on the surface. It seemed impossible. I had to reach down and touch it to believe it. I drank a little of the water. It tasted a little like moss, but it was good and cold as December icicles.

The Mustang lowered his muzzle, then lifted it, as surprised as I had been. Then he took a long drink from the shallow rill, and turned to face me, nuzzling his dripping cold muzzle against my neck.

I laughed and stepped back from him. He came with me, reaching out to nibble at my hair.

"Hey!" I scolded him, still laughing. "You'd better stop that!"

He shook his mane and tilted his head, and I turned to run, knowing he would canter a stride or two, then settle back into a trot I could keep up with as he always did.

Moving easily together, the lead rope loose in my hands, the Mustang and I played along the side of the strange ice-cold slough. It was amazing to find this little bit of winter in the oppressive heat of summer. Even the soil felt cold beneath my bare feet.

The stallion seemed to feel exactly like I did, a little giddy from the strange surprise, and just plain happy to be happy...we had had so many long, weary days on the journey.

I turned suddenly, knowing the Mustang would follow my lead perfectly. He did, tossing his mane. I ran in long strides, making him extend his trot into a spanking, staccato cadence to keep up.

Then I saw the rattlesnake, coiled and still, beside a sharp rock that jutted up out of the soil. But I saw it an instant too late. My right leg was already in motion, lifting, my left knee straightening as my weight came off my foot. The snake raised its head, rattling, a sound like steam chattering a pot lid, an ugly hissing.

Time stopped for me. I knew my foot would come to earth within inches of the snake's head and there was nothing I could do about it short of learning to fly. Then, quicker that I could think, the Mustang shouldered me aside. I was thrown a few feet, far enough, landing stumbling and stunned, the lead rope no longer in my hand.

I watched, terrified, as the Mustang reared. The snake coiled tighter and lifted its head.

"No," I shouted. "Just stay away from it!" I made a grab for the lead rope, but I couldn't get close enough.

The Mustang reared again, and I had to jump back to stay clear of his hooves. He squealed and

pounded the earth a few inches from the snake—
it recoiled, slithering backward against the rock
to shelter itself. Then it coiled again and lifted its
head. It was not going to flee, it was going to fight.
I looked around, frantic to find a stick, a rock, anything to help the Mustang.

I glanced back toward the wagons. Through the
glaring heat, someone was walking toward me. Maybe
one of the Kyler men had seen the Mustang rearing. I waved both hands above my head and screamed
"Help!" Then I turned back to the Mustang.

He was rearing once more, his head tucked into
his chest, half turned, to keep one eye on the snake.
There was no doubt that his hooves could crush
the rattler—but it might manage to strike, its fangs
pumping venom into the Mustang's foreleg—before
it died. The rock it was backed up against was the
same sharp black rock we had been traveling past
for a week. If the Mustang missed by even an inch...

"Stand back!"

I whirled, startled, and saw Grover's face, flushed
from running, his eyes on the snake.

"Get back, Katie!"

I stumbled out of his way, watching transfixed

as the Mustang dropped to all fours, danced backward as the snake slithered toward him, then reared again, even closer to the rattler. Grover cocked his arm, and I saw the rock, balanced, perfectly at home in his hand. Then he threw.

The stallion was in the air, his front hooves poised to strike. The rock smashed into the snake's skull an instant before his forehooves hit it. The Mustang drove all his weight downward, one front hoof pinning the snake to the ground for an instant, then he reared again. The second time he struck at the rattler's head, hitting hard.

But it didn't matter. The snake was already dead. Grover's rock lay beside the crumpled rattler, as though it had been there through the ages, still and solid and the same color as all the rocks around it.

I turned to face Grover. I was shaking. "Thank you..." I managed. It felt like I should say something else, but I simply could not make my mind work for a long moment. I stared at the snake, its muscles still writhing, even though its life had ended.

Grover jutted his chin at the Mustang. "You better catch him."

I looked up, my heart skipping a beat when I

saw that the Mustang was a little ways off, snorting and pawing at the earth, the lead rope trailing on the ground beside him.

He was shaking, too, but with anger, not fear. His eyes were wide and wild, and he shook his mane, hard, then reared again, striking the ground as though he was imagining the fight again, convincing himself that he had won.

"It's dead," I told him, "You don't have to worry about it anymore."

He stood steady at the sound of my voice and lifted his head sharply. He watched me walk toward him. I kept talking quietly, telling him how strong and brave he was, how he had saved my life.

He came toward me, and I reached out to gather up the lead rope as he nuzzled my cheek, blowing out long, windy breaths against my skin. "It's all right now," I told him again.

Then I bit my tongue. I was talking a blue streak to the Mustang. Grover would never stop taunting me now.

"He sure does trust you," Grover said quietly.

The soft, nearly gentle tone of his voice caught me off guard. I stared at him, waiting for him to sneer, to say something mean. But he didn't. "You saved his life," I said. "I am forever grateful. If he had been bitten...if he had died..."

I couldn't finish either sentence, and Grover just ducked his head anyway. Was he trying not to laugh? I was pretty sure he would lift his chin, grin his mean grin, and start to make fun of me any second. Before he did, I wanted to explain; I wanted him to understand.

"The Mustang has been my only real friend," I managed. "You laugh when I talk to him, but he listens, Grover. He really does." I knew that sounded foolish, but I knew I couldn't do any better now or later. It was true. Grover could taunt me all he wanted. I was still grateful. He had saved my best friend's life.

Grover didn't say anything for so long that I thought he was so completely disgusted with me that he'd just turn and head back to the wagons, without saying anything at all. I started to hope he would do that, rather than make fun of me.

"I didn't mean to," he said finally.

His voice was flat, full of pain. It took me a long moment to figure out what he was talking about. He just waited until he saw in my eyes that I understood.

"I only meant to scare that cat," he said in a low, pained voice. "I never meant to kill it." He sighed. "Did you tell them it was me?"

I shook my head. "I was afraid to have you mad at me. I was afraid you'd hurt the Mustang."

His eyes were glossy with tears. "Last thing I want is to be cruel like him."

I understood what he meant instantly this time. He was talking about his father. "You aren't. You never will be."

He smiled, a thin, uneasy smile that faded, then disappeared. But he met my eyes. "Andrew Kyler said you can tell a person's heart by how they treat a horse—and how the horse treats them."

I didn't know what to say to that, so I didn't say anything.

"Can I pat him?"

I held the Mustang's lead rope tightly and nodded. "Just come up slow."

Grover walked toward us, and the Mustang stood still, then let Grover pat his neck. Grover backed away, smiling, another thin, awkward little smile.

I looked past him at the slough and remembered. I pointed. "There's a skim of ice on that water. The ground is frozen, too."

His face went tight; he thought I was baiting him. It was a hundred degrees out, easy, the heat distorting the very air. "There is," I said quickly, "there is. Just come look." I led the Mustang back to the slough.

Grover touched the water and looked up at me, grinning. "No one will believe us."

We gathered up as much of the ice as we could carry and tried to get it back to show Mrs. Kyler. It melted halfway back, all but a sliver or two. But that was enough to get them to follow us. Most of the party came to look, drinking the cold water out of cupped hands, splashing their heat-flushed faces.

This was the oddest place I had ever been; impossible things had happened here. There was ice on the water in late July, and Grover Heldon had turned out to be sad, not mean.

CHAPTER FOUR

✹ ✹ ✹

*I could smell snake for two days until the sage finally
washed it away. We were headed toward high country.
I could scent pine trees on the wind sometimes. I traveled
as fast as the little one would let me.*

A week after Grover killed the snake, we
started the long climb over South Pass.
The name had made me picture a narrow gorge or
a steep-sided valley that curved between the high,
jagged peaks. But it wasn't like that at all.

South Pass was *miles* wide. It was like a giant hand
had smoothed out the mountains the way a woman
would smooth the soil in her kitchen garden before
she planted beet seed.

For a while, we could see peaks in every direction,
and the air got thin because we were so high, people

said. I noticed it some. I got out of breath quicker when the Mustang and I ran to catch up to the wagons, and at night I was so tired I felt sick.

Now that I wasn't afraid of Grover anymore, I began to notice how seldom he was with his own parents. He helped Andrew Kyler herd the stock most days, and when he wasn't doing that, he'd walk with the Taylors and help count the wheel turns to figure how many miles we had come, or he'd just walk by himself.

"We left the United States today," Mr. Taylor announced when the slow upgrade of South Pass leveled, then started downward.

Mr. Kyler rubbed his chin. "Are we past the divide?"

Mr. Taylor nodded. "Highest point is behind us now."

I wasn't sure what they were talking about at first, but, listening, I figured it out pretty quickly.

The Continental Divide was the high land that separated the rivers. In many places, it was a band of sky-piercing mountain peaks. Here it was a gentler slope. But the result was the same; rain that fell on the east side flowed east. Rain on the west side would run into the creeks and rivers that flowed west.

But no one in our party cared much about that part. This was what mattered to all of us: The Continental Divide was the boundary of Oregon country. So even though we still had a thousand miles to travel, we were in Oregon already. We all cheered and whooped that night, our voices rising with the campfire sparks into the dark sky. I have never seen stars as bright as they were in the Rocky Mountains.

The days passed, blurring as they often did as we traveled. We filled our water barrels from cold, clear creeks and walked through cooler, sweet-scented air. I had never seen a mountain before, nor a forest that went on for miles, so the whole place was like a magical land to me.

On the far side of the pass, we came to the Green River crossing. There were ferries, and we took one, each wagon paying the astounding price of sixteen dollars! It was outrageous—a man could buy an ox for that—but the river was deep, rocky, and swift, and no one counted a life cheaper than sixteen dollars. Everyone had heard too many stories of Green River drownings to try to save money.

After we crossed, we followed the parties we

could see in the distance ahead and turned south-west for a time, heading through barren hills toward Fort Bridger. I will never forget that part of our journey because a wonderful thing happened. Miss Liddy and her partners began to practice their show every evening that they had the strength to do so.

The first evening, they caught us all off guard. The sound of Miss Liddy laughing as loud and hearty as any man ever did made Mrs. Kyler and me turn to look. Miss Liddy was sprawled on the ground.

"Oh dear," Mrs. Kyler said. "Is she all right?"

I nodded. "She's laughing. I think she just stumbled or something and..." I trailed off because I noticed the big mare cantering away—no, not really away. She was cantering in a circle. Miss Liddy stood up, brushing off her trousers. She whistled and the mare slowed, then stopped and turned to face her. As usual, there was no tack at all on the mare. Miss Liddy made a gesture with her right hand, and the mare cantered back toward her again. "That'll teach me to keep up my work better!" Miss Liddy called to the men.

Mrs. Kyler and I were nearly done cleaning up supper and we stood side by side, neither of us speaking as the mare passed Miss Liddy and Miss Liddy whirled to run along beside her, leaping onto her back.

I blinked, not quite sure how it had happened. Miss Liddy had been on the ground one second, then, the next, she was riding, her knees bent at a hard angle, her bare feet set firmly on the mare's broad back—standing up.

The mare had a slow, collected canter, and she veered into in a wide, easy circle. Miss Liddy stood for a long moment, then dropped to her knees, straddling the mare, but with her legs bent backward so she was more or less kneeling. Then she stood again, spreading her hands wide, gathering herself. All at once she leapt backward, turned a summerset in midair, and landed on her feet.

There was a scattering of applause, and I realized we weren't the only ones watching. Miss Liddy bowed grandly and called out, for all to hear, "Thank you all very much. You're all welcome to come to our first show in Oregon City. I make all my mistakes in practice, of course."

Everyone laughed. I grinned at Mrs. Kyler, then turned to watch Miss Liddy go through the routine a second time. I was breathless. It was like watching an eagle fly high like they do sometimes, without flapping its wings. It looked impossible. I had never seen anything so wonderful in my life.

The next evening, we rushed around and finished our chores, both of us keeping one eye on Miss Liddy's wagons. She rode the big mare for a while more, practicing the summerset a few more times, then Mr. Le Croix took a turn.

He didn't do the summerset trick. He rode backward and sideways and leaned down off the mare to pick up a stone off the ground. He turned on his side and pretended to be asleep while the big, wide-backed mare cantered in her smooth, balanced way.

While Mr. Le Croix rode the mare, I saw Miss Liddy standing with Mr. Dillard and Mr. Swann. The men were holding odd club-shaped objects that made no sense until they began to toss them up in the air.

"That's called juggling," Mrs. Kyler said in a hushed voice, as though she might somehow startle the men if she spoke too loudly. "Have you ever seen it before?"

I shook my head, then realized she wasn't looking

at me, she was staring at Mr. Swann and Mr. Dillard as the wooden clubs flashed between them, faster and faster.

"No," I whispered, astounded. How did people learn to do such things? Who in the world had ever figured out how to do it in the first place?

Mr. Swann changed the rhythm, and Mr. Dillard followed perfectly. They reached high above their heads, then low, then spun around between catches. It was beautiful, like a dance. Mr. LeCroix dismounted and went to watch them.

Mr. Swann shouted a warning and threw Mr. Le Croix a club. In an eyeblink, the men were standing in a triangle, the clubs going round from one to the next. They each did tricks of their own, spinning, catching the clubs behind their backs, all without missing, even once.

I exhaled, feeling something I had never felt before. I didn't just want to watch all the amazing things Miss Liddy and her friends could do, I wanted to learn *how*.

I began to time my chores, rushing through supper cleanup, doing more than my usual share, just to be sure to be finished by the time Miss Liddy and the others began their evening practice. I wasn't the only one. By the second week, most of the party was hurrying through their evening work. On days when the road was rough or the weather turned bad and Miss Liddy and her friends decided not to practice, there was a dimming of spirits in every camp.

One morning, just before we reached Fort Bridger, I took the Mustang out to graze early, as usual. Without thinking much about it, my sleepy thoughts still circling aimlessly, I led him toward the rear of the wagon line. I had seen patches of good grass a ways back up the trail. I knew I would have time to let him graze before the Kylers were packed and ready to leave.

As we passed the last wagon, Miss Liddy's big mare whickered, and the Mustang answered her. His whinny brought answering nickers from Delia and Midnight, too. I smiled and patted his neck. "You're so handsome that all the lady horses think you're grand," I told him. He tossed his head and pranced a few paces.

"Morning!" Miss Liddy called. "Off to find grass for him?"

"I am," I called back without moving any closer.

Then I realized that I was standing fifty feet from her for no good reason. There hadn't been fever among her party or ours for all this time, and I was still acting as though I had to stay clear of her.

Then I realized something else. No one else was. I was the only one still behaving as though it was dangerous to be around Liddy and her friends.

Mrs. Craggett and Mrs. Taylor and the younger Kyler wives still barely spoke to them—not even Polly's mother. The rest of them had given her heck for speaking up that first day. But it had nothing to do with being afraid of fever.

I walked forward a few steps, and the Mustang moved with me. "It's so wonderful, the way you can ride," I called.

Miss Liddy smiled so broadly that it was as though the whole morning had brightened, ahead of sun-rise. "Thank you, Katie!"

"Is it hard? It looks impossible." I walked a lit-tle closer so she could lower her voice.

"I remember the first time I saw someone trick ride," she said. "I was as amazed as you are." She pushed her hair back from her face. "I can tell you this. The only thing better than seeing it is doing it."

"Would you teach me?" The words were out of my mouth before I knew I was going to ask.

Miss Liddy frowned, and my heart sank.

"I know it would be an imposition," I said quickly. "None of us has but barely enough time to sleep as it is, and they say the worst part of the journey is ahead of us and—"

"No, it isn't any of that," she interrupted, raising one hand to stop me. "It is just dangerous, and I can't think why you would want to risk it. You are almost certainly going to end up with your uncle or the Kylers on a farm, and trick riding will be the last thing you need to know."

I had no answer for that, even though I searched hard inside myself to find one. "I don't care," I finally said. "I just want to learn."

She digested that for a long moment, then pointed at the Mustang. "On him?"

I was stunned to silence; I hadn't for one second thought about riding the Mustang. "No," I said quietly. "I don't want to ride him."

Miss Liddy tipped her head to one side.

I took a long breath, fighting the strange flood

of feelings inside myself. "I don't think he would want me to ride him," I said finally.

"Are you scared that he wouldn't let you?" she asked me in a gentler voice.

I nodded. I had never managed to explain it to myself, but she was right. I was afraid. What if he tried to buck me off, what if he shied and tried to get away? He trusted me. We were friends, but my trying to ride him could change that.

"Well," Miss Liddy said, "it's up to you. Can you finish chores a half hour earlier than usual?"

It took me a few seconds to take in what she had said. Then I nodded so hard I could feel my hair swing against my back.

Miss Liddy smiled. "Give me a few days. I'll let you know when we can start."

CHAPTER FIVE

※ ※ ※

We have found a good meadow, but there are too
many two-leggeds here. We are heading toward
the mountains, and I am glad. I can smell the pine trees
a little stronger each day.

*F*ort Bridger was in the middle of a green
oasis of creeks and trees. There were twenty
tipis, leathern tents shaped like tall funnels. Indian
women and their trapper husbands lived in them,
Mr. Kyler said.

There were children everywhere, running and
laughing or somber-faced and concentrating on
work of some kind. I saw a boy no older than five
scraping the hair off what looked like deer hides.

The women were busy like we were, from early
light onward. Once, when I took our plates to the

creek to wash them properly, I knelt down, then, after I got started, I saw an Indian woman a little upstream. She held a heavy iron stew pot and waited politely until I had finished so she wouldn't muddy the water. Her eyes were merry and her mouth curved into a lovely smile. I tried to talk to her. She answered me, but in her own language. We could only smile at each other.

Mrs. Kyler bought soft leather slippers for all her granddaughters that the Indian women had made. And she bought a pair for me, too. I was so touched to have the present that I wept, and she hugged me.

Everyone stopped and rested a day or two at Fort Bridger—the Mormon party in front of us and the one behind us camped not far from our camp while we were there. But when we packed up our wagons and headed northwest, they all joined into one big company and turned south.

We all waved farewell to them. I wondered what their city would be like, if it was in a place that had forests and green grass, or the kind of dry, rocky kind of land we had seen so much of on the way to Fort Bridger. For their sakes, I hoped the salty lake hadn't killed all the trees.

I asked about letters in the post store. There were a few, all tossed into a cracker box. There was no sign of any more of mine and that was a relief. But there was no answer from my uncle Jack waiting for someone to carry east, either.

I was blue for the rest of the day. But maybe he had sent an answer two years before, and it hadn't reached me. That happened all the time, I knew.

So I stopped moping around and got my chores done early, just in case Miss Liddy wanted to start teaching me that evening—but she didn't. Everyone in her camp was kneeling, looking at the axle on one of the wagons. I saw them talking to the joiner at the fort the next morning. Mr. Le Croix and Mr. Dillard carried a new axle back to camp around noon.

That same day, I spent a long time brushing the Mustang while he stood with Delia and Midnight off to the edge of Andrew Kyler's herd. I pushed my hands up beneath his heavy mane and pressed my palms against the warmth of his coat.

I kept watching Miss Liddy and the men in her company as they changed the wagon axle. I felt scared and at first I thought I was just nervous about the trick riding. Maybe I would fall off so many times that I would have to give up. It would be embarrassing.

But that wasn't it, I admitted to myself as I left the Mustang that evening and went to lay out my bedroll beneath the Kyler's wagon. I was worrying about finding my Uncle Jack. What if I *couldn't*?

🐾 🐾 🐾

The evening after we left Fort Bridger, we camped on a wide level place with grass closer than usual and a creek nearby. Miss Liddy waved at me and gave me a little nod as she jumped down from her wagon bench. I settled the Mustang with the mares and Andrew Kyler's herd, then I worked at a furious pace, cleaning up after supper.

"You excited about something?" Mrs. Kyler asked me, smiling.

I nodded, then hesitated so long that I blushed. I didn't want to tell her. What if she tried to forbid me? It was dangerous; that was perfectly obvious.

"Miss Liddy promised..." I began, then I stalled.

Mrs. Kyler was watching me carefully. "Promised you what?"

I flushed red but could not make another word

come out of my mouth. It was silly—the whole camp would know. They would *watch*.

I made a weak gesture in the direction of Miss Liddy's wagons and took in a breath. "She said she would teach me."

Mrs. Kyler's eyes went wide. "To ride like that?"

I nodded, waiting for her to go get Mr. Kyler so they could forbid me. But she didn't. Instead, she looked wistful. "If I were still light and young and graceful..." She grinned at me. "Oh, I am jealous, indeed. Everyone will be. How in the world did you talk her into that?"

I smiled, relieved. Then I shrugged. "We were just talking, and I asked her straight out."

Mrs. Kyler was nodding. "I remember that first day, the way you two called out to each other, discovered you'd both lost your parents."

I had forgotten, but Mrs. Kyler was right. Maybe that was why Miss Liddy had agreed.

"I hoped once you got over being scared of the fever, you two might be friends," Mrs. Kyler said. "Go on. I can finish up here."

I hugged her. "I thought you would try to talk me out of it."

"Mr. Kyler will, but we'll work on him."

I smiled at her again, then started running toward Miss Liddy's wagon. They had camped a little farther off as they had been doing since they had started practicing. It took extra room for the big mare to canter in her perfect circles.

"Are you ready?" Miss Liddy said when I got there.

I stood up straight. "Yes, ma'am."

"First of all, you need to meet Genevieve."

I started. "Genevieve?" I echoed, trying to pronounce it right. "Is that the mare's name?"

She smiled. "It is. It's an old name, French, I am told. The man who raised her knew all sorts of interesting things about horse training." She gestured for me to lead the way. I walked toward their picket line. The horses were all standing quietly, grazing.

Genevieve stood so much taller than the rest that it looked odd, like a real horse had been set next to toy horses. The closer I got, the bigger she looked. When I stopped in front of her, I stared down at her hooves. They were as big as Mrs. Kyler's pie tins.

"She's big," Miss Liddy said.

Her voice was so flat and wry that it made me laugh.

"Genevieve is the most gentle creature to walk

this earth," Miss Liddy added. "She would break a leg before she stepped on me—or you. So it is your duty to protect her from having to hurt herself. Ready to work a little?" she asked. I nodded, then saw that she was talking to the mare, not to me.

We walked a little ways from camp, the big mare following Miss Liddy as she always did, without any tack at all. Once we had found a level place, Miss Liddy stopped.

"This will do," she said. "How much riding have you done?"

"Never anything like what you do," I said timidly.

She laughed her loud, mannish laugh, and I felt suddenly shy around her. As used as I was to seeing her striding around in her trousers from a distance, she was so different from any woman I had ever known that she made me uneasy this close up.

She smiled and apologized for laughing. "I meant, can you ride a horse at all?"

I nodded, then I shook my head. "I rode when I was real little, sitting on the plow horses and sometimes behind my father on his horse."

"Never alone?"

"A few times in the pasture. I was only six when..."

"And you didn't ride much after you went to live with the farm couple?"

I stared at her, caught completely off guard. I guess it showed on my face because she apologized again. "Mrs. Kyler has told me a little about you. How mean those people were. She heard it all from your friend Hiram."

I nodded, wondering why it bothered me so much to know that Hiram had talked about the Stevenses to Mrs. Kyler. "Are you all right?" Miss Liddy asked. "I didn't mean to upset you."

"I'm fine," I said, even though it wasn't quite true.

"Let's just start with a walk and see how it feels to you," she said.

I watched her position herself by the mare's side. She bent down, facing me, her hands clasped together. "Left foot. Step in my hands like a stirrup, and I will lift you. Then swing your leg over. You can hang on to her mane; she won't mind. She won't much notice anything you do, in fact. She will be listening to me."

I took a deep breath and stepped into Miss Liddy's hands and reached upward to get a handful of mane. I was afraid I would fall off before I ever got on, but I didn't. I swung my leg over the mare's back and sat, feeling like I was astride a barn roof. The mare's back felt that high and that wide.

I heard a little round of cheers from the wagons and I twisted around to look. They were all watching. I saw Grover grinning at me. I buried both hands in the mare's mane, getting even more nervous.

"Circle, Genevieve," Miss Liddy said. The mare swayed into motion, picking her own path. "Trick horses are trained to keep a steady pace and an even line, no matter what," Miss Liddy told me. "If they slow or swerve, the rider would come flying off in the middle of a stunt. So don't worry if you flop around a bit."

I sat still and tried to square my shoulders and lift my chin the way Miss Liddy did when she rode.

"Head up, but pull your shoulders down, not back," she said quietly. I obeyed and felt the difference in my posture. It made balancing a little easier, too.

"You look very nice up there," Miss Liddy said.

I felt myself blushing—I was that pleased.

"Now let go of her mane," she said. "Spread your arms. She is only going to walk. She's trained riders before; she knows you need her help."

I lifted my arms and let my fingers curl gently, my palms down.

Miss Liddy nodded. "You have been watching carefully. That's good."

I blushed again and pulled my shoulders down. There was something wonderful about sitting on top of that tall, gentle mare. I couldn't wait for the day I could stand on her back, my arms out, amazing anyone who saw me.

"Head up," Miss Liddy said, and I lifted my chin. I wanted to look as graceful as she did, to feel like I was working magic. I concentrated, focusing on every word Miss Liddy said to me and the big mare's movements. Shoulders down, head up, eyes straight ahead. It felt *wonderful*.

CHAPTER SIX

❧ ❧ ❧

The spring smelled very strange. The little one led me
close to it, but we moved away quickly. Some of the
two-leggeds drank the water, but I would not.

The next week or two was hard traveling, and I
only got to practice on Genevieve twice more—
we were all too tired to do much once we stopped
for the day.

There was a hill so steep the men had to line
up behind each wagon, gripping a rope, dragging
their weight to hold the wagon back, to keep it from
rolling out of control. Then they all had to walk
back up and do it over again. It was frightening,
how steep it was. Mr. Taylor said it was just called Big
Hill. I would have named it something far worse if

anyone had asked me. It took us all day to get everyone down it safely.

One morning after that we came upon something I knew I would remember forever. There was
a long, narrow patch of steaming rocks—or so it
looked from a distance. As we got closer, we could
smell sulfur and phosphorus and we saw water spurt-
ing up into the air.

I walked the Mustang closer. The ground was hot
in places under my feet, and the steam floated along
the ground like some enchanted fog. People got
buckets and tins and we all tasted the soda water—
just to prove to ourselves that it was real, I guess.
Who would ever have thought there was a place on
earth where soda water just shot up out of the rocks?

We dragged into the grounds around Fort Hall
tired and worn. It seemed as if we were tired most
of the time, now. Even the Kyler girls had settled
down. Their running and giggling was rare now at
suppertime or any other time.

Fort Hall wasn't much compared to the other forts
we had seen, but it was a place to rest, to feel a little
safer than we did on our own. We had come so far
without a guide of any kind, but now there were many

fewer people on the trail with us, and sometimes we couldn't see anyone ahead of us at all. At the forts, there were usually several parties at once. Fort Hall was no different, and it was a comfort.

I asked everyone I met if they knew my uncle. No one had heard of him. I tried not to let it frighten me.

"Want to practice?" Miss Liddy called to me the second evening we were at Fort Hall.

"I do!" I called back.

Mrs. Kyler winked at me. "I'll finish up. You can clean up breakfast to pay me back."

I stuck out my hand, and we shook to seal the bargain, then I ran to make sure the Mustang was all right before I went to Miss Liddy's camp.

This was the first time we had practiced where there were other people. I hadn't been up on Genevieve's back more than five minutes before I noticed that Grover was sitting a little ways off, watching. The second time I looked, three or four boys I had never seen before had joined him.

"I want to have her canter," Miss Liddy said.

"I'm not sure I'm ready," I began, but she interrupted me, speaking quietly to Genevieve. The mare suddenly rose beneath me as she lifted her front legs and leapt forward into a canter. I sat as steady as I could, my hands gripping her mane.

"Find the rhythm of her gait," Miss Liddy reminded me. "It's like a rocking horse with her, almost."

That made me smile, but a few minutes later, I realized it wasn't a joke. The big mare lifted her front legs high, then came down smoothly with every stride.

"Head up," Miss Liddy said as Genevieve brought me around the circle again.

I lifted my head and loosened one hand from the mare's mane. Miss Liddy noticed.

"Good. Free both hands when you can. Get them up."

I wanted to say I wasn't ready again, but I didn't. I refused to look down or to think about how far I would fall if I lost my balance.

"Breathe," Miss Liddy reminded me. "She's going well for you. She has come to trust you. Just relax and lift your arms."

I loosed my grip and let my arms rise. It felt wonderful, only a little scary—I was used to the position at a walk and this wasn't too much different, not really.

"Perfect!" Miss Liddy said, and I felt my cheeks flush. "Twice more around, Katie, then I'll have her halt in front of me."

"Yes," I called back without turning my head.

"Be ready," Miss Liddy said. "When I tell her to stop, she'll turn to come toward the center of the circle, then she will slide to a halt, she won't drop back to a trot."

I steadied myself and concentrated on keeping my posture correct for the next two rounds. Then, when Miss Liddy called the command to Genevieve, I leaned with the turn and curved my back slightly when I felt her stiffen her front legs to stop. I leaned forward just enough to keep my balance as she plunged to a halt. I kept my arms up and my head high, the way I had seen Miss Liddy do it.

Grover was on his feet instantly, clapping. The boys I didn't even know shouted and cheered. Mr. Le Croix, Mr. Dillard, and Mr. Swann whooped, all of them grinning. I heard a whistle from the other side of the camp and saw Mrs. Kyler waving; past her, I saw a group of folks from another wagon company. It was obvious that they had been on their way to the fort and had stopped to watch.

For some reason, all this made me feel strangely wonderful. My eyes flooded with tears and I blushed as I swung my right leg over the mare's withers and slid down from Genevieve's wide back the way Miss Liddy sometimes did—facing out, my head high and my arms out for balance.

Genevieve lowered her head, and I reached as high as I could to pat her broad jaw. Miss Liddy was grinning. "You're a natural. I thought you might be and you are." Then she looked over my head at her companions. "If any of you have an ounce of energy, we could use traveling money." She gestured at the crowd that had gathered to watch Genevieve and me. The men got down from the wagon bench and got out their wooden clubs.

It was amazing to watch the three men juggle— really juggle, not just their practice routines. The clubs were heavy, and still they threw them high overhead, over and over, their hands flashing too fast to follow.

They stood in a triangle and tossed the clubs back and forth in an intricate pattern that changed, then changed again. Once Mr. Le Croix ended up with all the clubs, holding them in rows beneath both arms and six in each hand. The crowd laughed when he made a face. Then he tossed the clubs back out one by one. With Mr. Dillard and Mr. Swann catching them neatly, soon they were moving in a rhythmic circle again.

"It's like magic," Grover murmured. I nodded without looking away.

When they finished juggling, there was more applause, and I turned to see that the crowd had grown—there were at least two hundred people watching.

Miss Liddy stepped forward with Genevieve at her side. People gasped to see the big mare so obedient, so well trained, without a single strap or rope on her. Miss Liddy vaulted up and sat with her arms extended. Then, moving to music that only she and Genevieve could hear, they began their act. Miss Liddy was as graceful as anything as she rode standing up, with her arms out at shoulder level. Then she dropped down, threw one leg across Genevieve's withers, and sat sidesaddle at a canter. I stared. How could anyone balance well enough to do *that* without a saddle?

Miss Liddy rode backward, hung down to pick

up a stone from the ground, then threw it into the air. Mr. Le Croix caught it and tossed it back. She stood up again, the stone in one hand. She vaulted upward suddenly and turned a flip in the air, landing on her feet.

The people cheered and clapped, making a din that brought even more of a crowd out of the fort to see what was going on.

As the crowd noise subsided, Mr. Le Croix and Mr. Dillard began shouting at each other, spitting insults back and forth. My stomach tightened until I saw the smile on Miss Liddy's face. Looking for all the world like two men about to fight, Mr. Dillard and Mr. Le Croix circled each other. The crowd stared.

Then Mr. Le Croix drew back a fist—and the motion seemed to lift him off his own feet and set him spinning. The crowd inhaled, then I heard chuckling from a few of the men.

Mr. Swann came running to help, lifting his knees high and flailing his arms. He reached out to grab Mr. Le Croix by his shoulders and stopped the spin. Mr. Le Croix doffed his hat as though he was thanking him, then ceremoniously reached out to shake his hand. The instant Mr. Swann took it, Mr. Le Croix stepped forward and somehow lifted the much-bigger Mr. Swann off the ground and flipped him over his shoulder.

The crowd roared as Mr. Swann stood up, dusting his clothes and glowering. The mock fight went on, with both men using exaggerated gestures and pretending that gentle taps sent them flying. The crowd's laughter brought more and more people to watch.

Mr. Le Croix ran at Mr. Dillard like a furious bull. At the last instant, Mr. Dillard bent forward, and Mr. Le Croix jumped to his shoulders. Mr. Le Croix raised one finger to his lips, warning the crowd not to give him away. Mr. Dillard pretended to be confused, peering in all directions to see where Mr. Le Croix had gone. The crowd laughed so long and so hard that I thought they might never stop.

Finally, the sunset pinked the sky, and Liddy and her companions lined up to bow. Before the applause died down, they walked forward into the crowd, each one carrying his hat out upside down for people to put coins into.

As I walked back to Mrs. Kyler I could hear people joking and talking. Miss Liddy and her friends had changed a glum, weary crowd into a happy one.

Once I was back at the Kylers' wagon, I let Mrs. Kyler know I was there, then I ran to the herd and found the Mustang on the edge as usual, standing quietly with Delia and Midnight. I kissed him on the forehead, then told him about riding Genevieve.

"Did you hear people cheering? The first time?" I asked him. "That was for me."

"Katie?"

Grover's voice startled me. I turned, wondering if he was going to tease me about talking to the Mustang. He hadn't for a long time, but it probably *did* sound pretty funny to hear me talking to him like he was a person.

"Katie, do you think they would teach me?"

I looked at him. "To trick ride?"

He nodded. "Anything. I just wish I could go with them."

It took me a few seconds to understand what he was saying. "But your family—" I began.

"I know." He nodded. "My mother is sick a lot now. She needs my help." He looked up at me. "And my father would never let me go, anyway," he said. "Never."

I had no idea what to say, but he sounded so sad that I touched his arm. "I will ask Miss Liddy."

He looked so grateful that I felt awkward. "Grover, I don't know what they'll say, but I will ask, I promise." He thanked me, then ran off. I stood a long time next to the Mustang wishing things were not so hard for Grover or me, or anyone else.

The next day, I asked Miss Liddy what she thought about the men teaching Grover like she was teaching me.

"He can ask them himself, Katie," she said quietly. "I can't say what they would do. I won't put him up on Genevieve. Tell him I am sorry, but one student is all the mare and I can handle."

I told Grover that night, and he hung his head. "She didn't say they wouldn't," I repeated, "just that you should ask the men yourself."

He nodded, and I wondered if he would. He was shy, especially with adults. I had seen him taking to Mrs. Kyler a few times, but to almost no one else.

We were back in salt-dry sage country right after we left Fort Hall. The ground was rockier than anywhere we had crossed yet, dark, jagged rocks that cut my feet. I started wearing the leather Indian slippers Mrs. Kyler had bought me.

They were the best shoes I had ever owned, soft enough that I could still feel the ground, but strong enough to dull the rocks' edges.

The days were hot and dusty. I practiced riding Genevieve every evening that Miss Liddy would let me. I got better, a tiny bit each time, at holding the erect posture that made her riding so beautiful.

We crossed creeks and rivers, none so big as to be very dangerous, which was such a relief. I had heard the men talking about the Columbia River, which we'd have to cross some way or another toward the end. They compared it to the Missouri in size, but rougher, with circular currents and no ferry boats except tied-together Indian canoes. I tried not to think about it.

After one river crossing—no one seemed to know the name of the river—we passed a cutoff trail, a pair of shallow-rutted tracks, heading south into the California country. It was a faint trail compared to the one we were on. I saw Mr. Silas staring down it as we rolled past.

The oxen plodded slowly forward in the midday heat, and I spotted wagons in the distance. Some had turned off for California. They were headed southwest, raising so much dust that I couldn't see how many there were.

I hadn't met anyone who was going to California and I wasn't sure what drew them there instead of Oregon. There must be some reason.

I suddenly thought about my uncle Jack. Maybe he had started out for Oregon and had gone to California instead. Maybe that's where his family was—hundreds of miles south. Would he have gone to join up and fight in the war?

The thought made my skin prickle. I didn't think he would have done that without letting my mother know, but I had to admit it was possible. It would explain the returned letter at Fort Laramie.

My eyes filled with tears. How was I supposed to know what to do? How was I supposed to find him? I stepped back and hid behind the Mustang as we walked closer to the wagons so no one would see me crying.

I had been so sure that I would find my uncle Jack in Oregon country and I still thought I would be able to. But the truth was, back home in Iowa, I had never realized how big the Oregon country was—and I had never once imagined or understood how hard or how long the journey would be.

There was an enormous difference between thinking about walking two thousand miles and actually walking each mile, one by one.

As always, the Mustang kept turning to nuzzle at my face and shoulder when he heard me sniffling, trying to hold back the tears.

I tried, but the tears came anyway and rolled down my cheeks. Hurrying, I led the Mustang even farther away from the wagons and found a swath of good grass off the trail.

I stopped, and he dropped his head to graze. I stood so the Mustang was between me and the wagons and gave up on fighting the tears. I just wanted my family back. I wanted to see my mother and my father. I wanted to play with my beautiful little sister. I leaned against the Mustang's shoulder and just plain sobbed. As he had since the beginning, the Mustang stood still, reaching around to touch me with the velvet-soft skin of his muzzle, nudging at my shoulder.

I didn't start after the wagons until I was finished crying. I didn't want Mrs. Kyler to see me coming undone. She had enough to worry about with her own big family.

As we got close to the end of the wagon line, the Mustang lifted his head suddenly and drew in a long, shuddery breath. I let out the lead rope to allow him to shake his mane and prance a little to one side.

"Do you smell something?" I asked him. "Is there something dangerous up ahead?"

He shook his mane again. Then he danced a half circle and I had to follow him.

I held the lead rope without pulling on it. Something was really upsetting him. "What is it?"

He stamped a back hoof, hard. Then he whinnied, a high, squealing call.

"What is it?" I asked him again. "Oh, how I wish you could just talk to me."

He blew out a sharp breath and whinnied once more. We were close enough to Andrew Kyler's stock that the mares heard him and answered. But then, a few seconds later, I heard another whinny, from the other direction.

Indians? Trappers? It wasn't anyone driving any kind of a wagon, that much was sure. No wagon could make it up or down the hills on either side of the trail. Even the trail itself was full of rocks that the wooden wagon wheels jolted up and over.

I walked faster, and then ran until we caught up with the wagons. I kept my eye out for riders coming out of the rough country on all sides of us for the rest of the day, but no one did.

The next day I heard the whinny again when I was searching for grass for the Mustang. This time he turned, pulling me along with him, and squealed a long, high-pitched call, his head so high I had to reach up to catch hold of the halter. He squealed again and I heard a distant answer. It was then that I saw the horses through the trees, flashing past at a gallop, barely visible in the distance.

They were galloping in a group, strung out behind a big-boned gray. Behind them ran a horse that looked a lot like the Mustang. He had a thick, black mane that streamed out behind him. I waited to see who was herding the animals along, half expecting to see Indians. But the horses passed and disappeared, and even though I stared, I couldn't spot a single rider. It took me such a long time to figure it out that I blushed with embarrassment when I finally did. No one was herding them. They were wild.

I looked at the Mustang, at his arched neck. His eyes were as bright and alive as I had ever seen them. His nostrils were flared wide as though he had been running. For an instant, he surged forward, pulling at the rope so hard that I stumbled and nearly fell, hanging on to it. Then he looked back at me and slowed again, and I caught up.

I patted his neck, and we walked on together as we had been doing for months. I found a good patch of grass, and he lowered his head and ate hungrily. My stomach was fluttery. I would have to be more careful. If he ever saw wild horses up close, he would probably try to follow them.

CHAPTER SEVEN

❧ ❧ ❧

The rocks here are sharp, and the oxen go even slower than
before. The little one and I sometimes run a little
and I am grateful. In the cool of the mornings, I long
to gallop, but I know the little one could not keep
up. I heard a stallion and scented his mares. There are
horses here that do not walk with two-leggeds.

ot long after that we came upon the Snake
River. It was so beautiful to see water in the
middle of that strange and broken countryside, the
river curving in a long sinuous path across the broken,
rocky land. Its surface was smooth as a gray-green
looking glass on the cloudy day when we came over
a rise and saw it below us.

The river was some distance from the trail at first,
then the wagon tracks led us closer to the banks. The
river had worn away the soil to form steep-sided
bluffs. We saw many strange sights as we went. There

was one stretch of bluffs on the far side of the river that spouted roaring springs that flumed enormous waterfalls straight out into the air, splashing downward to fall into the river below. It was as if an underground river ended there, joining one that ran aboveground.

One fine morning, as it was just barely beginning to turn light, we all heard splashing in the water. We stopped our morning chores and turned to look. In the dusk we could just make out blurred silver arcs—fish were jumping!

Andrew and two of his brothers rigged up netting, using twine from the Taylors' goods. By midmorning, they had soaked themselves and caused their wives hours of worry, but they had caught ten of the magnificent fish.

"Salmon!" Mr. Kyler said happily when he saw them. "I've heard about this kind of fish."

No one even suggested traveling on until the fish were cooked and eaten. It was heaven, after all the months of beans and bacon, to eat the delicate, pink fish meat.

Mr. Taylor and Mr. Heldon made hooks from old wire corset stays that Mrs. Kyler gave them.

They used twine for line and baited the hooks with chunks of bacon. The salmon didn't seem to be as tired of it as we were, because they took the bait and were pulled in, hand over hand, to the rocky banks. This was much easier than stringing nets, and all the men endeavored to make hooks and lines.

We ate salmon whenever we could, and it was delicious every time. The bacon we carried had been half-rancid for weeks in spite of being salted until it was nearly intolerable and stung our mouths.

But even though we got a welcome change in our meals, our stock did not. One night after supper, Miss Liddy pulled me aside. She looked sad.

"I want to stop the lessons for a while."

I felt my heart sinking, but I knew why. "We shouldn't work Genevieve at all, probably," I said aloud.

Miss Liddy nodded unhappily. "She's losing flesh. They all are. This cursed sage," she said, taking a sideward kick at a clump of the gray-green plant, "doesn't nourish like grass does." She shook her head. "And you can tell they hate it."

It was true. "The Mustang curls his lip—and he is eating less," I told her.

"They only eat it because there isn't much choice," Miss Liddy said. "Ever wonder if you made a mistake by coming?" she asked me.

It caught me off guard. "Sometimes," I admitted. "If I can't find my uncle..." I trailed off because I couldn't think about it without feeling physically sick.

"Oregon City will have enough people to give our show," Miss Liddy said quietly. "So we'll make some money, enough to winter on, I expect." She pushed her hair back. "Come spring we might head south to Mexico City if the war is over and travel is easy. I've never seen Alta California. I want to."

I was astonished at the idea of her going where the war was being fought now, of talking about traveling an inch farther than we had to. I was also fascinated by the idea. Mexico City! What was it like just to go places because you wanted to see them?

"I'd like to travel one day," I said quietly.

Liddy nodded. "Then you should."

I looked at her. "The Kylers promised to get me to Oregon and help me find Uncle Jack," I told her. "I can't imagine that he'd ever let me go traveling on my own."

She smiled gently. "Circus life is hard work. And you're right, most people wouldn't let a girl your age go traveling. I did, but there wasn't anyone to tell me not to."

"Liddy? We need your help here!"

It was Mr. Le Croix, shouting from across the camp. She waved at him to let him know she'd heard, then she kissed my forehead, her hands gripping my shoulders. "You are going to have a fine home, Katie. You are a wonderful girl, and they will be lucky to have you."

I watched her walk away, feeling odd. The wagons would all separate when we got to Oregon City, I knew. The Kylers, the McMahons, the Heldons, the Craggetts, and the Taylors would be looking for land, I was sure. Who knew what Mr. Silas and his friends were thinking? They didn't seem like farmers to me. I wondered where we might all end up—if we would ever see one another again.

It made me sad to think I might not ever see Mrs. Kyler again. She had been so good to me. She was so funny, so patient; I knew my mother would have loved her.

I felt tears seeping into the corners of my eyes,

and I turned away, walking fast. I needed to graze the Mustang. Lately, no matter how hard I worked to find grass, he was getting thin.

Maybe he was sorry he'd allowed me to lead him all this way. Maybe he would have been better off if he'd just kept going that time he'd run off. The thought startled and hurt me, and I pushed it aside. I took good care of him, and I always would.

I led him away from the wagons, and after a half mile or so, I spotted a patch of grass that still had a little green in it. The Mustang veered toward it when I did, without so much as a tug on the lead rope. He walked beside me, not behind me, as always. It wasn't like I was leading him. We were just walking together.

CHAPTER EIGHT

❧ ❧ ❧

The river was wide and deep, and the water was cool.
It was hard swimming—the current was very strong.
We need to find better grass. The mares are weary
from all this travel and need to rest. The two-leggeds
must know this, but still they travel onward.

*M*rs. Kyler was cheerful as we cleaned up after supper every evening. But she was quieter than she had been a month before. She looked tired, too. As we walked along the rutted trail beside the Snake River, the wagons creaking and moaning over the rocks, I began to realize that a lot of people weren't doing all that well.

Poor Mrs. Heldon had terrible stomachaches that made her double over with pain, and sometimes she had to vomit. She would walk away from camp, but we could hear her, and we all felt sorry for her.

I noticed Grover doing the cooking for his father most mornings and at supper, too. His mother was lying down in the wagon every moment she could.

Andrew's wife, Hannah, was pregnant again—the rest of us could finally see what she must have known in Council Bluff. She looked nearly faint on the hottest days.

Mr. and Mrs. McMahon had lost their plump faces. She was thin as a scarecrow. Their little boy, Toby, was often weepy and whining, and I saw blood on his chin now and then.

For some reason, a number of people had dark, tender gums that bled when they ate. Andrew Kyler had had his left hand bound up in cotton rags for weeks—he had cut himself, and it hadn't yet started to close and heal.

Those among us who weren't hurt or sick were just plain tired. I was. Polly and Julia and Hope usually lay in one of the wagons reading to one another at night right after supper. I barely noticed them anymore, they were so quiet.

Mr. Kyler seemed tired almost all the time now, dawn to dusk. He looked older than he had when Hiram and I had met him, too. I heard him sigh a hundred times a day. And poor, pale Mary Taylor was too weak to walk to supper most nights.

Her father would carry her, setting her gently on an overturned apple box so she could get out from beneath the dirty wagon canvas and sit with us under the wide sky for a half hour or so each evening.

Mr. Silas and his friends kept farther and farther apart from the rest of us. They had never been much for socializing, but now they kept to themselves so much it was rare that any of them spoke to one of us.

I heard them arguing now and then, if I grazed the Mustang close to their wagon. From what I could gather, Mr. Silas had talked the others into coming, and they were all beginning to question whether what he had told them about the wonderful land of Oregon was true. One of them kept saying they should have turned off to go to California instead of heading into these treacherous mountains.

I led the Mustang away before they could notice me. The truth was, a lot of the families were having similar doubts and similar talks. We were all just so tired.

All the weary way to Fort Boise we traveled across dry country littered with sharp, dark rocks that gritted and ground at the wagon wheels. We stayed there only a day. As hot as it was, the menfolk were worried about being in the Blue Mountains when the snows began, so we pushed on. I asked after my uncle, but again, no one had ever heard of him.

The sun had felt like an enemy all through August, and, as we passed into September, the hot days ran one into the next. The country was so rough, so barren, that if the Snake River hadn't been there, we would never have made it through.

Finally, we got a few cloudy days and some relief from the heat. But the rain, when it came, pelted down in a flood and soaked us all, leaving the trail a mud mire. There was lightning, too, so loud and bright it seemed fit to crack the earth in two. Over and over it hit near enough to shake the very ground. The Mustang was terrified, and so was I. We stood by the wagon close together. He was trembling.

"Katie Rose, get inside!" Mrs. Kyler shouted at me more than once.

I pretended that I couldn't hear over the pounding of the rain, and she finally gave up. I knew she meant well and was only trying to take care of me, but I felt safer standing outside with the Mustang than

I ever felt huddled inside the canvas-topped wagon—
and he needed my comfort as much as I needed his,
I was sure.

It rained most of the night. Around midnight,
Mr. Kyler brought me a piece of canvas to wear like
a shawl and his own hat. I was already soaked, but it
helped some, and I was grateful. I leaned against the
side of the wagon, and I guess I fell asleep standing up.

At sunrise the next morning, I was startled awake
by a long, eerie, wailing sound. It was Mrs. Taylor.
Sometime during the long, violent storm, Mary Taylor
had gone outside the wagon for some reason. She had
been unable to climb back in and she was soaked to
the bone, shivering and feverish. None of the Taylors,
deep in an exhausted sleep and deafened by the rain
on the canvas, had heard her.

I could see the anguish in Mrs. Taylor's eyes from
that morning onward, and I felt sorry for her. She
and her husband took such good, tender care of
Mary. They were as loving as two parents could be,
and it broke their hearts to have failed her.

Not long after that, we had to cross the Snake
River. There were three islands in the river at the
crossing. We camped and watched another party

go over, and while we were camped, a big party of wagons caught us up and passed, going south rather than crossing the river where we were.

I heard some of the men calling to the other party, asking what they knew about the trail ahead. That set the menfolk to debating. It was another hard decision, like all the rest. Some wanted to wait and cross farther north. The men in the party that had gone past had thought it might be easier farther on.

Mr. Silas wanted to build rafts to float the wagons. Mr. Kyler liked the idea, but everyone knew it would take three or four days to cut trees and lash the logs together. And there weren't many trees close to on this side of the river. It'd mean dragging them with our already tired oxen.

I noticed Liddy's three companions joining in as the decision was made. Mr. Swann was strongly for crossing. We'd had cloudy afternoons the past two days, and, if it rained again, the river could rise. Mr. Dillard kept pointing out that the islands would let us cross in the wide spot, where the water would be at least a little less deep.

It became a shouting match. Mr. Le Croix argued

one side, then switched to the other, then back. Andrew Kyler liked the idea of the stock being able to rest on each island, but he wasn't sure about anything else.

In the end, we crossed. I think the men were too tired to keep arguing about it. It took the whole day, what with figuring the best way, then recaulking the wagons so they would float better, easing the load for the oxen to pull as they swam across the deepest places. We spent hours repacking, deciding who would ride where and how to get everyone over the water. It was past noon before we ever started.

I rode with Mr. and Mrs. Kyler again. The Mustang would stay with the mares and swim over, with the Kyler boys herding the whole bunch.

Mr. Kyler led the way, and I was glad. The only thing worse than crossing rivers was *waiting* to cross rivers, staring at the water, worrying. Mr. Kyler shouted and whipped the oxen forward, forcing them into the water until it was deep enough to swim, then he reined them toward the first island and shouted encouragement as they headed toward it.

I thought the current might push us too far downstream, but Mr. Kyler had figured it right. The wagon bumped against the bottom, and Mr. Kyler started a second fit of shouting and whip snapping to urge the oxen up out of the water and on up the bank.

Once we were on level ground, Mrs. Kyler gave me a quick hug, then got down to walk alongside, watching the wagons behind, concerned for her family. I got down to walk beside her, keeping an eye on the Mustang, still on the far shore with the rest of the horses.

Mr. Kyler guided the oxen the length of the little spit of land, then let them stand and rest for half an hour before he drove them into the water a second time. While we waited, two more wagons had come across. Mrs. Kyler went to check on Hannah, then came back. Hannah had insisted on driving her wagon while Andrew drove the stock as usual, even though her pregnancy made Andrew nervous and protective.

Andrew had the stock spread out and grazing. He would bring them across last. Mrs. Kyler and I got back up on the wagon bench. It made me uneasy, as always, to be separated from the Mustang, and I fidgeted so much leaning out to look back that Mrs. Kyler reached out and took my hand.

Finally, Mr. Kyler popped the whip and swam the oxen across an even deeper channel to the second island. The current was strong, and I gripped the wagon seat with both hands, staring at the rushing water.

We waited again, this time for nearly an hour. Then we led the way to the third island. It was the smallest, and it had steep banks. The wagon jolted, and I hung on to the edge of the driver's bench as the oxen staggered out of the water and onto dry land again. Mr. Kyler rested the team an hour or so before he asked the oxen to swim the last stretch back to solid ground.

They heaved and blew as they swam the last channel, their breath rasping when they touched bottom and began to pull again. The instant the wagon halted, I jumped down and ran back to watch the rest of the wagons come across. All came fine, except the Taylors'. The current tumbled it over and we all stood helpless, watching the oxen struggle to keep their muzzles above water, fighting their wooden yokes and the harness. I could see Mr. Taylor clinging to one wheel. His wife was washed downstream, but she wasn't far from the bank, and Charles Kyler jumped in to save her. Their other children hung on to the wagon and were dragged to safety when the oxen stumbled up onto the bank.

The one no one could save was poor Mary. Weak and ill with the fever she'd caught in the rain, she had been in the back of the wagon and had been drowned. From the instant we saw her limp form in her father's arms, the whole party went silent. He carried her alongside the wagon while Mrs. Taylor drove. Both looked stricken, and we all just watched them come ashore, unable to say or do anything to help them.

Last across were Andrew and his brothers with the horses. The Mustang swam at the rear as he usually did, a little off to one side, Delia and Midnight just in front of him. It was a wide, deep river, and I held my breath, but the horses all came across safe to the first island.

Andrew let them blow and shake and graze until they had all caught their breath and rested a little, then he brought them on across to the second island, then the third.

I ran toward the Mustang as he waded out. "Mary died," I whispered to him, and somehow that made it real. My eyes burned. I was standing too close when he shook the water from his coat. He spattered my dress.

I turned to walk beside him up the bank and saw Grover watching me. He had dark circles beneath his eyes. I had barely spoken to him lately. He had been busy dawn to dark doing almost all his mother's chores as well as his own. I was pretty sure her stomach had gotten worse.

"Poor Mary," he said.

I nodded and sighed. "Poor Mary."

Grover walked a little closer, keeping one eye on the Mustang. The stallion flicked his ears back and forth. I wondered if he remembered that Grover had killed the rattlesnake.

"She was always so nice to me," he said.

I nodded. It was impossible for me to talk much about Mary just then. I think he felt the same because he just nodded, then bit at his lower lip for a long time. "Mr. Swann showed me a little juggling trick," Grover said finally. "I've been practicing." He fished in his pockets and pulled out three round stones as we walked up the bank and followed the slow, sad parade of people in front of us.

"Look." Grover tossed one stone in the air, and caught it in his other hand. Then he tossed a second one. Then, for a few seconds, he had all three stones in the air at once before he got mixed up and dropped them.

"It looks hard," I said.

He nodded. "It is."

"How is your mother feeling?" I asked, patting the Mustang's neck.

Grover shrugged. Then his eyes met mine for an instant. "She can't eat. I think she might be dying." He said it so quietly that, for a moment, I wasn't sure I'd heard him right. But I could see in his eyes that I had.

I didn't know what to say. I just reached out and touched his hand. I thought he might talk about it more, but he didn't. I wanted desperately to say something to help. I took in a breath, and I even opened my mouth, but no words came out. Everything that formed in my mind sounded empty and useless in the face of Mary's death, and what he had just told me.

"I'm so sorry," I finally managed. My voice sounded stiff and brittle. But he wasn't listening to me; he was turning away. He walked slowly, like he had forgotten I was there. I watched him pass his parents' wagon and head off into the trees. I said a little prayer for him, then added one for Annie and one for Hiram.

Even though there was a grave to dig, no one wanted to go any farther than we had to after the exhausting river crossing, so we camped about a half mile from the river. I could see the oxen's legs trembling with fatigue as Mr. Kyler unhitched them.

They were thin and exhausted, and it scared me. What would all the families do if the oxen gave out? We could only hope to hit better grass country soon. The horses in Andrew's herd were all looking rough. Midnight's ribs stood out. Delia had kept her weight a little better.

The Mustang still had a bit of flesh over his ribs as well, but that was only because I did nothing all day except find him little clumps and patches of grass.

The women set to making camp in silence. The men found a place to dig a grave. The grave digging was terrible hard work, hampered by mud and sprinkling rain—and the rock. I stood back through most of it, busying myself with finding grass for the Mustang and with helping Andrew gather up the stock. He was stumble-tired, had gotten even less sleep than I had.

Once the grave was deep enough for decency, I heard Mrs. Taylor sing a hymn, her voice shaking and weak, but brave. Then Mr. Taylor read from the Bible. They had wrapped their daughter in a quilt and buried her in it. I could not watch the whole time. The feelings that stirred inside me were more painful than I could bear.

In the morning, the oxen walked slowly as we started off in the chilly predawn dusk. "How much farther do we have to go?" I asked Mr. Kyler when the Mustang and I came past his wagon. I smiled, waiting for him to tell me Oregon City was around the next bend.

"I don't know for certain, Katie," he said slowly. "I'd say three, four hundred miles."

I could only stare at him, it surprised me that much. He saw my reaction and gathered the reins in one hand so he could reach out and pat my head.

"It's a hard road, no doubt about it," he told me. "But we have to get along it now quick as we can to beat the snow. No time to rest."

I nodded and tried to smile at him; he looked so worn out that it worried me.

"Snow would be about the only thing that'd stop us now, though," he said, and chuckled as though he had said something funny.

I smiled and nodded. "It won't snow," I said, just to be cheerful, too.

He shrugged. "It will or it won't; no way to know. I hope not." He looked up at the sky. It was clear overhead, but there were a few clouds on the northern horizon. "Storms probably come in from the north out here, or maybe the west, coming in off the ocean."

I waited for him to say something more, but he didn't. I finally gave him a little wave and angled the Mustang off the rutted trail, to look for grass. I could tell Mr. Kyler was truly worried.

When I found a patch of dry, leathery grass, I stopped and the Mustang dropped his head to graze. I leaned against him and he lifted his head, turning to nuzzle my face, his mane falling like a shawl across my shoulders. I was so tired of traveling. I was so worried about so many things. But I didn't cry. I couldn't. Maybe a person had only so many tears in her, I thought. Maybe I had run dry. But, it turned out not to be true.

Later, walking some distance from the others, I cried for Mary and for myself and for Annie's poor burned hands and for Grover and for the mare that had broken her leg and for all the weary world.

The Mustang nuzzled at me and walked more slowly than he usually did, matching his pace to mine for the rest of the day. I put one foot in front of the other, and that was hard enough.

CHAPTER NINE

🐂 🐂 🐂

*I smell snow in the wind sometimes. It is out there, waiting
for its time to come. I would not want to be caught in
these rocky pine forests by the snow. The two-leggeds are
traveling hard. They must know the danger.*

*W*e were in the Blue Mountains now—the
part of the trail everyone had always said was
the worst. It was. There was one grade so steep that
I stood at the bottom and held my arm out, sight-
ing along my hand at the top of the rise. My elbow
touched my ear, it was that steep!

It took us two terrible days to get all the wagons
up. We hitched twelve oxen to each wagon. Even so,
it was hard.

At the top, the men would rest and unhitch one
team, then start back down, driving the six oxen

ahead of them. We went on that way until dark, each team pulling twice.

A few days later we came to another hill almost as steep, and it slanted side to side as well. Each wagon was double teamed again. We all lined up on the low side and pushed against the wagons, palms flat against the wooden bed rails. We had to walk sideward, crisscrossing our legs with each step, shoving with all of our strength to keep the wagons from crashing down the mountainside.

Every hand was needed. I left the Mustang with Andrew's herd and the mares so I could do my part. The Taylors' youngest son watched the stock with Grover's mother and little Toby. The boys were seven and five, and Mrs. Heldon could barely stand, but Mr. Kyler was so afraid that one of the wagons would tilt and wreck, rolling downward, that he asked everyone to help. Mrs. Heldon rode up in the last wagon, and Toby and I held the stock until Andrew and Charles Kyler could get back down.

A few days after that, there was a steep, rocky downgrade, and we used the heavy ropes as makeshift drags and brakes as we had before. One place was so steep that we had to unload every single-bingle wagon, lower it down by rope over a rock shelf, then lower the goods down to repack. One ox broke a leg and had to be shot. It was awful.

Mr. Silas butchered the poor animal and we all ate fresh meat for a few days. I was ashamed that we had driven the poor animal to its death, but like everyone else I was starved for fresh meat. Everyone's bacon was rancid, plain and simple. It stank. But everything else was long gone.

I had a dream one night, about eating a salmon supper. When I woke up I was so disappointed that it had been only a dream that I nearly wept.

One chilly morning, we woke to a ground frost that coated the pines and crackled beneath our feet when we started off. We had followed a deep rutted trail all the way. But more and more we were sure that whoever had run wagons down to—and over—that rock ledge had been lost. And so were we. We all kept walking, and no one talked about it much. I was grateful. Talking about it would have only made it worse.

We saw deeper ruts on a road we came upon, and so we turned down it. That must have brought us back on course, because we saw wagons ahead of us two days later. And Mr. McMahon had a name in his guidebooks for the big, lovely valley we came into shortly thereafter.

Grand Round was a pretty place. There was a wide valley surrounded by country as pretty as anything we had seen in the Rocky Mountains. The soil was dark and smelled like farmland. And the hillsides were covered with tall, stately pine trees. It was beautiful, and everyone slowed to breathe in the soft air and gaze at the hillsides.

I was walking the Mustang beside the wagon. "You have to wonder why this isn't far enough," Mrs. Kyler said, looking around. She climbed down off the wagon, jumping off the step as the oxen went on. Mr. Kyler frowned and watched to make sure she'd landed safe, then turned back to face the road ahead of the wagon.

"Why should we go another step?" Mrs. Kyler asked the sky, stretching, then pressing her hands against her back.

I nodded and stopped with her. It was a wonderful place. Even the air was fine, scented with the pine needles. I could see two creeks, looking down the wide valley.

The Mustang tossed his head and pranced a little. I pulled him off to one side. I shivered, and Mrs. Kyler noticed.

"You have a heavy jacket?"

I nodded.

"Does it still fit?"

I nodded again. "I think it will. Hiram bought it too big. I need to get it out, I guess."

Mrs. Kyler went silent for a while, and I wished I hadn't mentioned Hiram. Thinking about him could only make her think about Annie. All the hard and weary miles behind us lay between her and her daughter.

Mrs. Kyler finally turned to look at me. "I suppose we'll have to keep on all the way to Oregon City."

I smiled at the resigned tone of her voice. "I suppose we will."

She sighed and pressed her hands against her back again. "The menfolk talk about Oregon City like it is heaven on earth."

We both pulled in a deep breath at the exact same moment, then let it out as if we had counted ready, set, sigh! It made us laugh, and the laughter helped us keep walking. Sheer habit kept us going, too.

We were so used to it that it was hard to imagine stopping sometimes.

A few days later two men on horseback caught up to us. They had been visiting friends near Fort Boise and were on their way home to Oregon City. Mr. Kyler called a greeting, and they reined in. He handed the reins to Mrs. Kyler, then turned sideward and jumped off the bench without reining the oxen in. They plodded onward. Mr. Kyler lifted his knees high for a few steps, getting the kinks out of his muscles, then strode along, talking, walking alongside the strangers.

I was saw Mr. Taylor climbing down, too, then Mr. McMahon and Mr. Le Croix. Within a few minutes, all the wagons were still moving and all but three had women at the reins: Mr. Swann and Mr. Dillard kept driving Miss Liddy's second and third wagons, of course, and Mr. Silas had passed the reins to one of his men. No one stopped. We were all afraid to stop—we were racing the snow.

The men coming from the rear of the line trotted past, then fell in beside Mr. Kyler, listening and talking.

The men stopped when we did for noon dinner,

the sun straight overhead. They had their own food, and I saw that Mrs. Kyler was relieved. We had little to offer besides smelly salt bacon.

I led the Mustang close. "Do any of you gentlemen know a Mr. Jack Rose?" I asked quietly. They all glanced up, shook their heads, then looked back into their plates. My heart was beating wildly, as it always did when I asked that question.

"You get that horse from around here?" one of the men called after me.

I turned, puzzled.

"There are wild ones in this country that look like that. Folks say they're from the Spaniards' horses that got set loose or lost a few hundred years ago."

"I brought him from Iowa," I said, and watched the man's brows lift. I didn't want to explain anything to him. I didn't want to talk at all. I crossed the little clearing where we'd stopped. I found some low, tough-bladed grass for the Mustang and he grazed while I swallowed my disappointment and tried to reason with myself. I would find someone who did know my uncle Jack eventually. I would. I had to. I shoved the thoughts aside and focused on what the man had said about the Mustang.

"Was your great-great-great-great-granddaddy from Spain?" I asked him. The idea pleased me. It seemed fitting that a horse as wonderful as the Mustang had come from somewhere magical like Spain.

As the Mustang grazed, one of the men drew a map in the dirt. Our menfolk crowded around, and I saw them nodding. They had decided something. I walked the Mustang back to the wagon and stood beside Mrs. Kyler.

"We're going to Whitman Mission," Mr. Kyler said, coming back once the men had ridden on. He climbed up onto the wagon and Mrs. Kyler handed him the reins. "This road bypasses the place, but we've decided to take an extra day to get there and back."

Mrs. Kyler looked astonished. "Why, if we don't have to? Why not go straight on?"

He looked at her out of the corner of his eye. "They have crops. Carrots, potatoes, squash..."

"Squash," she echoed, and my mouth flooded with saliva.

The Whitman Mission was a neat, tidy place, and the Whitmans had made a regular paradise out of it. There were Indians, polite men who seemed comfortable enough with the Whitmans, both Mr. and

Mrs., and with us. They stared at the Mustang, though, so I kept back a little. One of the Indian men walked closer and pointed at the corrals, then back at the Mustang. I followed his gesture. Standing in the corral was a mare that could have been the Mustang's dam. She had the same dark honey coat and a black mane that fell thick and heavy down her neck.

I nodded, to let the Indian man know I understood and was glad to know there were horses like the Mustang here. I showed Andrew, and he bargained with the man who owned the mare, but she wasn't for sale. "I'd buy that stallion from you," the man said, spotting the Mustang. "We don't see many of the wild ones and almost never a stallion. They never tame down unless you catch them as colts."

Andrew shook his head. "He's not mine, but I can tell you he isn't for sale." The man shrugged and walked away.

The Whitman Mission was like a well-tended garden. They had squash and apples and even some good wheat flour that they would have given to us as gifts—but most people gave them something in barter or a few coins.

The fresh food tasted like heaven to me. Mrs.

Kyler made the squash into a soup that lasted three days. She tied the lid tight onto the pot with twine every morning so it couldn't slop much when the wagon lifted, then crashed down again as the wheels rolled over rocks.

I managed to get save a bit of the squash rind, and I fed it to the Mustang. He ate it with his eyes closed, like my mother used to drink her hot chocolate on Christmas Day.

Almost everyone seemed to gain a little health back every day from the food. We badly needed it. The Blue Mountains seemed to be determined to take the last bit of our strength.

Mrs. Heldon had been bedridden for some time, unable to eat at all. As we headed down the steep, rocky road, she got jostled and shaken, and we all heard her cry out now and then.

Grazing the Mustang one morning, I saw Grover helping her climb out of the wagon. She looked tiny and thin, like a sickly child. Neither she nor Grover noticed me, and I am ashamed to say I was relieved that I wouldn't have to call out a greeting and try to sound cheerful. I am ashamed because two days later she passed away, and I never had another chance to say anything to her at all.

We stopped for a few hours to dig a grave. Grover walked back and forth, gathering rocks and piling them on the little patch of broken earth that covered his mother. His father stood stock-still beside the grave, his hair a wild halo around his head.

I had left the Mustang with Andrew's herd, but I still stood back from the others. I watched, knowing I should say something to Grover, that I was the one, out of all of us, who should be able to say something to him. But I couldn't.

Staring at the mound of earth, listening to Mr. Kyler read from the Bible, I was lost in memories of my own parents' funeral and the weight of those memories very nearly crushed my heart. I swayed on my feet, biting at my lip, determined not to cry. My loss had no place in this wilderness beside the Oregon Trail. Poor Grover was in the first wounded day of his own grief. He had become my friend, and this was his time to cry, not mine. I stood, fidgeting, while Mr. Kyler was reading a Bible passage.

Then, on impulse, I picked up a rock so big I could barely carry it and walked, stiff-legged, to the grave. I set it down, then went to fetch another.

Grover shot me one grateful look, and I knew I had done the right thing, maybe the only thing.

Together we carried enough rocks to half cover the grave before the adults got done with their praying and Bible reading and joined in. The men carried bigger stones than we could, of course. Mr. Heldon carried a few rocks, then stood back, his face bleak and cold as morning ashes.

Mr. Taylor, Mr. McMahon, and Mr. Silas found a big black stone the shape of a wind blown storm cloud, flat on one side. Sweating and straining, they rolled and dragged it across the clearing. Then others took over and heaved at it, finally positioning it at the top of the grave for a headstone. By the time Mr. Kyler called out for everyone to get ready to go, the whole grave was well mounded with rock. Grover was still working, his eyes down.

As the wagons lurched into motion and Grover's father guided his oxen back onto the trail, I lagged behind. I kept an eye on Grover as I went to get the Mustang. When I came back, he still hadn't left the graveside. His father had taken his usual place in the line of wagons and was well ahead; he seemed to have forgotten Grover entirely.

I saw Mrs. Kyler leaning out to see around the canvas wagon cover. I waved at her and gestured toward Grover. She waved back and I knew we understood each other.

As I came closer, I saw that Grover was holding a fist-sized rock, balancing it in his hand. He looked up when he heard the Mustang's hoofbeats. His eyes were empty of everything. I wondered if I had looked the same way. He swung around, his arm tracing a wide arc, the stone leaving his hand with all the strength in his body, all the violence of this pain.

I stood with him, listening to the sound of the rock as it passed between two pine trees and fell, striking random stones, glancing off, then pattering to a stop in the pine needles. He hadn't aimed at anything at all, and he didn't look at me.

"He told her last night that he's not staying here, that he doesn't want to farm," Grover whispered.

I tried to imagine why Grover's father would tell his wife these things. To make her worry? What kind of cruelty would it take to say such a thing to a woman so sick and weak?

Grover glanced at me, then away again. "Katie,

I hate him. I won't stay with him. But what'll I do?"

"You'll make your own way," I said. "Mrs. Kyler says some of us just have to."

He knelt and kissed the stones that covered his mother and then stood up and began to walk. I trotted the Mustang to catch up and we fell in beside Grover. All that day we walked behind the wagons, neither one of us saying anything more. I just stayed close. There was nothing else I could do.

CHAPTER TEN

❦ ❦ ❦

The little one is weary now. She walks more slowly. We must settle for winter soon. It is time to find a valley with water and grass. It is time to stop traveling.

"Today ought to get us to The Dalles," Mr. McMahon said one morning, reading from his handbook. Then he lifted his head and shouted it out. I heard Charles Kyler holler the news to Mr. Taylor and, in seconds, everyone knew. A ragged little cheer went up from the wagons. I heard Miss Liddy's voice, high, happy, and *loud*. The Mustang shook his head and danced a little, then settled back into the long-strided walk that I had learned to keep pace with.

I had gotten into the habit of traveling not too far

from Mr. Heldon's wagon. Grover would sometimes come walk with me and the Mustang. That morning I heard Mr. Heldon's angry voice, and I angled closer.

"I don't care what you say," Mr. Heldon was saying. "If you'd taken better care of her..." He dropped his voice, and I couldn't hear the rest, but I could imagine it.

I caught my breath. It was the cruelest thing I could imagine anyone saying. And it wasn't true. No one could have done more to help someone than Grover had done for his mother. I slowed and started looking for grass for the Mustang before Mr. Heldon noticed me.

After a little while, Grover saw me and dropped back to walk with me for an hour or two. Then he drifted toward Andrew and the stock. I saw him helping herd the animals.

At noon, I went and got Grover, and he ate at Mrs. Kyler's campfire with me. He helped us clean up and then walked alongside the Kylers' wagon the rest of the day. His father didn't seem to know or care where he had gone.

We got to The Dalles before sundown. The town had been built near a narrow chasm that the mighty

Columbia River roared through. We could hear it from our camp—which was nearly a mile from town. We stayed back that far to find grass for the stock; closer to town, it was all grazed flat.

Most of us walked on once camp was made, just to see if the guidebooks were true. They were. There was a place where the wagon ruts simply stopped. Wagons could go no farther because of the river. We all stood staring at it.

The Columbia River was wide and deep, the color of a storm sky, and it muscled its way past, the currents swirling and twined. You couldn't hear anyone unless they shouted.

The sheer size and force of the river scared me. I could tell it scared everyone. We saw two Indian men walk past, carrying three canoes lashed together on their backs. Was that how people got across? No one said much walking back to camp.

We weren't the only ones there, and the next day we talked to other people. My fears were true. They were all waiting, camped out in a mile-wide circle outside the town, for Indian men who hired out their canoes as ferries to take them downriver and land them on the far side. We were told it could be a week or more, that it was first come, first across.

The next morning I left the Mustang with Andrew Kyler's herd, and Grover and I walked down to watch. The roaring of the wide river was enough to caution anyone about getting into a real, flat-bottomed, wide-decked ferryboat—never mind the swaying, makeshift canoe ferries.

Three and four canoes had been lashed together with planks fixed on top to make a platform. People were removing their wagon wheels so the wagon beds would lay flat on the platforms.

"Look," Grover said, pointing. I turned. As we stood watching, one of the ferries—a trio of canoes lashed together with a wheeless wagon perched on top—started downriver. The Indian men seemed incredibly skilled at maneuvering it, but when it went over a swirling set of rapids, it broke apart. The wagon tipped and we heard people screaming as they were thrown into the rushing water. No one drowned, thanks to the strength and wit of the Indian men, but the wagon was lost; seeing the accident made all of us even more uneasy.

On the way back, I told Mrs. Kyler I wanted to go into town to ask about my uncle. She nodded and asked if I wanted company. I told her no, that I was fine, even though it wasn't all that true. Every time I asked after my uncle, my hopes rose—and it hurt something awful when they fell again.

I was a long ways down the path toward town when I heard someone running behind me. Grover caught up, breathing hard. "Mrs. Kyler says I am supposed to keep an eye on you," he said between breaths.

"I don't really need anyone to come along," I told him.

"But do you mind if I do?" he interrupted. "Mrs. Kyler will be upset if I don't."

I sighed and shook my head. "I don't mind, Grover, I'm just scared." He nodded and I knew he understood.

"If I see my father, I am going to hide from him," he said quietly. "He'll be drinking by now."

I nodded and felt terrible for forgetting that my troubles were no bigger than anyone else's.

Grover gathered up his shirttails as we walked, shoving them down into his trouser waist. For an instant, I saw him as a stranger might. His hair was long and scraggly, his shirt had been patched, and a long tear crossed the left knee of his trousers. I looked down at my stained dress and thought about the picture we must make. Then, as we got closer to town, I realized that most of the people on the streets looked just like we did—weary, dirty, and ragged.

I glanced at Grover. "We'll just try in the shops."

He nodded and followed me, barely saying a word as we went from one end of the main street to the other, then crossed the street and started back up the other side. It was discouraging. Nary a soul had ever heard of Jack Rose. I started walking faster, my head down. I was trying not to cry. Grover just lengthened his step and tried to keep up as I hurried into—then out of—a half-dozen shop doors. No one knew anything about my uncle.

"It doesn't mean anything, Katie," Grover said as we neared the end of the street. "People just come through here—thousands of them. The shopkeepers don't get to know hardly any of them."

I took a deep breath. "I hope you're right."

He took a skip-step to come up beside me. "You know I am. It'll be someone in Oregon City who knows where he lives. Not here."

I nodded. "I just get scared."

"Let's try there before you give up," Grover said

as we neared the end of the street where we had started. He was pointing at a dry goods store. I slowed. He was right. No matter how upset I was, it was silly not to keep asking.

The shopkeeper was rearranging dusty bolts of cloth when we came in. He had never heard of Jack Rose. But he was talkative. He asked me a lot of questions about where we were from, how long it had taken to get across, how much farther we intended to go.

"All the way to Oregon City," I told him. "But I'm scared of the river," I admitted.

He grinned. "I wouldn't take one of them canoe ferries if there was gold on the other side. D'yer folks know about the Barlow Road?"

Grover and I shook our heads. Neither one of us had ever heard of it.

"There's a toll, and it's steep, but it keeps you off the river in those dang canoes."

"We'll tell the men in our party," Grover said, and thanked him.

I stepped back onto the boardwalk feeling a little lighter. It was finished. No one in The Dalles knew my uncle, and I could stop worrying about it.

Someone in Oregon City would. And I was glad to learn about the Barlow Road. Staying off the river made perfect sense to me, and I was pretty sure Mr. Kyler and the other menfolk would feel the same way.

They did. There wasn't even an argument about it. Everyone had seen or heard about the canoe ferry breaking apart. So we took the Barlow Road the next morning. We had to pay five dollars per wagon, and Andrew paid by the head for his herd. It was expensive, especially now when most people had spent too much of their savings already and wanted to put every penny toward tools and seed for their new farms. Still, no one balked.

The man in The Dalles had been right. It was a hard and terrible passage. The road was narrow and steep, barely a road at all. It was full of fist-sized stones that stubbed our toes and made the oxen and horses footsore.

We weren't the only ones on the toll road, though. A lot of people had decided climbing a mountain on a brand-new road was better than facing that river. We couldn't travel fast, but the people behind us never caught up or wanted to pass us. Everyone was weary. It was hard enough to keep moving.

Grover walked with me most days. He barely said a word. He was hungry all the time and would take food from Mrs. Kyler only when he couldn't stand it anymore. His father had no supplies, He had used the last of their money to buy whiskey in The Dalles. He swayed and slumped on the wagon bench and growled at anyone who tried to talk to him.

Mr. Kyler and Mr. Craggett had paid his wagon toll, and I was sure they had done it for Grover. The other men tolerated Mr. Heldon and his drinking only because they felt sorry for him, losing his wife, and because they knew there was so little distance left to travel before they could be shut of him forever. He had told everyone he intended to travel on as soon as he could.

Grover avoided his father entirely if he could, and the awful thing was that his father didn't even come looking for him when he slept night after night by the Kylers' campfire in blankets Mrs. Kyler loaned him.

Grover practiced juggling stones almost every moment he was awake—standing, walking, or sitting down. He was getting good at it. I saw him talking to Mr. Swann a few times, and it looked like he was learning different patterns. I was glad. He wanted to go with them, and I hoped they would let him.

Sometimes I dropped back and led the Mustang alongside Andrew Kyler and the stock. I liked being around Delia and Midnight, and sometimes I put halters on them and took all three horses looking for grass.

Delia was calmer than I remembered her being, and Midnight had somehow become really affectionate. She rubbed her forehead on my shoulder and nibbled at my fingers when I patted her. The rest of the horses seemed worn out and cranky. Delia and Midnight seemed content. I began to think that they had missed my company. I was sure they liked being around the Mustang, too, so I took them grazing as often as I could.

I found myself talking aloud to the Mustang more and more when I was off with the three horses by myself. I told him how scared I was and he stood close to me and blew his warm, windy breath across my face and down the collar of my dress. I was so glad to have him as my friend, so grateful he was with me. I told him that, too. He tossed his head and whinnied, long and loud, as though he had understood me. It echoed off the mountainside.

CHAPTER ELEVEN

✺ ✺ ✺

The earth softened beneath my hooves as we went.
The grass in the valley was good. The pine forests in the
mountains were green and thick.

s we came down into the Willamette Valley, everyone began to brighten a little. It was beautiful land. This was the place the Kylers had dreamed of farming. This was the land the Taylors and the Craggetts had wanted more than anything. The McMahons were smiling, even Toby.

Mr. Kyler dragged his saddle out of the wagon and began riding off to look for land. So did the other men. They'd ride back near sundown and tell the others what they had seen. It all sounded good. I began to get excited again. If the farmland was all good and so much of it still unclaimed, then there was a good chance that my uncle Jack was doing well, that he would be able to take me in. I kept an eye on Grover. He spent most days with Andrew Kyler now, helping with the stock. I knew he wanted to earn his suppers.

Mr. McMahon and Mr. Taylor hoped to be neighbors, and they began to ride the valley together as we traveled, too, looking for 640-acre plots that bordered on each other.

Mr. Silas and his friends packed up one morning and left. No one had any idea where they were going or why. We all stared after them. They headed southwest—that's all we would ever know.

The Craggetts had been quiet and grim for months, and they were thawing out now, chatting more with everyone and looking for land. Mrs. Craggett still walked out of her way to avoid talking to Miss Liddy.

I remembered the times that Miss Liddy had done more than her share for everyone's safety. I made myself a promise that I would never treat anyone like Mrs. Craggett treated Miss Liddy.

Miss Liddy and her friends weren't looking for

land—and they spent the time practicing their show. I got to ride Genevieve a little, and one evening I managed to stand on her back for a stride or two before I had to slide down and sit astride again. It was thrilling.

Oregon City was a bustling place the day we got there. The Willamette River was wide and deep, and the mill wheels for a sawmill and a gristmill turned steadily as we passed them. There were shops and stores up and down the long street we came in on. No one so much as looked up when we went by— until Miss Liddy's party drew close.

Genevieve, with Miss Liddy riding tall—and without bridle or saddle—led the way. The other horses were tethered behind the wagons, and people stared at their odd coloring and conformation. Mr. Swann, Mr. Dillard, and Mr. La Croix had changed into bright-colored shirts, and Miss Liddy wore a hat with an ostrich plume.

Grover and I watched the faces of the people on the sidewalks change as they spotted Miss Liddy. Some people actually gaped. We didn't laugh aloud, but we kept having to bite our lips.

The wagons had been draped with red and yellow

banners that read MCKENNA CIRCUS CO. I was sure they would give a show as soon as they could. If they waited too long, winter weather would set in. At least we would get to see that before they left.

We went through town, then kept going. We passed four or five other wagon camps and finally camped along a slough a couple of miles north of town at the base of a swale that led back up into the mountains. No one knew how long it would take them to find land to claim, and the stock would need water and grass.

The nights were getting chilly, and Mrs. Kyler insisted that Grover and I both borrow more blankets from her. The next morning, I wanted to go into town and begin asking about my family. I waited until after morning chores and went to make sure the Mustang was settled with the herd before I told Mrs. Kyler.

"It's about a half hour's walk or a little more each way," she said. "You make sure you get back before dark." She looked past me. "Grover? Will you go with her?"

He nodded.

She smiled at me. "Good luck, Katie."

As we walked toward town, I glanced at Grover. "I will have to tell my uncle about the fever, about my parents and sister."

Grover exhaled slowly. "That will be hard news to bring him, Katie."

We walked for a time without saying anything else. I thought about how I would say it, how I would explain. I would have to tell him about the Stevenses and Hiram, too.

Grover picked a grass stem and chewed at the sweet end, then sighed and turned to me. "He will be glad to see you. I wish I had an uncle." He was silent another long moment, then he said, "I'm going to run away, Katie. I have to get clear of my father one way or another."

I met his eyes. "Maybe my uncle Jack can take you in, too."

Grover looked at me, blinking, his face lighting up. "I'd like that, Katie. I'd work hard for my keep."

I nodded. "I know you would."

Grover smiled. I lifted my chin as we got to the outskirts of town. I would go into every place in town, then stop farmers on the road if I had to. My uncle Jack was here somewhere, and I intended to find him.

The street was full of people, and we had to thread our way through the crowds. The first place was a hotel. The owner there said he had never heard of my uncle. Neither had the desk clerk nor a woman who was cleaning the floor with lye soap.

The livery stable was next to the hotel. It was big and full of spent-looking horses. "Never heard the name," the man said. "But I don't go to the saloons, and I don't talk to all that many folks. Your party have stock to sell?"

"We'll let our folks know that you buy," Grover said. The man turned back to his work.

"Your uncle could be farming somewhere a ways out of Oregon City," Grover said as we went on. "Maybe he doesn't come to town much."

I nodded and smiled at him, determined not to scare myself any more. We walked into three more establishments, and no one had heard of my uncle in any of them. Then we talked to two men who were working at the blacksmith's forge.

One of them scratched his head. "Never heard of him." He rubbed his eyes. "No, wait."

My heart leapt. I glanced at Grover, and he smiled at me. I held my breath.

"That's the man got in trouble over a card game, ain't it, Pete? The one who owed Sam Preston all that money?"

The man pumping the forge bellows paused in his work. "Maybe so. Yes, I believe it was. Jack Rose. Head of black hair, blue eyes—tall fellow. I heard he went to California by wagon. I also heard he jumped a ship in San Francisco and went whaling. Either way, he hasn't been in Oregon country in more than two years, miss."

I felt Grover take my hand. I don't remember thanking the men or even walking back into the rutted dirt street. All I remember is that Grover walked me along until I was steady on my feet again. Then he let go of my hand and moved off, but not too far.

"I should have known," I said as we got closer to the wagons. "I just *wanted* him to be here so bad." I wiped at my eyes and drew a shuddering breath. I started to cry. "I wanted him to have a nice wife and two daughters about my age."

I shook my head at how silly it all sounded, even to me. I had been believing a daydream. And now, here I was, two thousand miles from Iowa and no closer to having a home than I had been when I lived with the Stevenses.

"You all right?" Mrs. Kyler called when she saw us coming. I knew my face was blotchy from crying.

"Katie? Did you find out something?"

I nodded and bit at my lower lip. "He isn't here. He got into some kind of trouble and went off to California two years ago."

"Ah, child," Mrs. Kyler said. "Oh, Katie, I am so sorry." Before she could say or do anything else, I ran off, picking up my dress hem so I could go faster. I heard Grover call me, but I didn't answer. I just kept running until I had the Mustang on his lead, then I ran again, with him trotting beside me.

I didn't stop until the Mustang and I were a mile above the camp. The wagons looked like toys in the distance, and I was breathing hard.

I told the Mustang everything. He grazed quietly, lifting his head now and then to nuzzle at my face and neck. There was a breeze rising, and it fluttered my skirt as I started off again.

The Mustang moved with me, as he always did. I kept on, walking stiff-kneed, my hands clenched. I was so angry with myself. I felt so stupid and so helpless. What could I do now? The Kylers were wonderful people, kind and good. But they were getting old, and they had a big family of their own, all grown up and married, and they had grand-children born—and unborn—to think about. The last thing they needed was an orphan girl begging for a place. And poor Grover. I had all but prom-ised him. Maybe the Kylers would take him in. I hoped so.

They had never once talked about my staying with them and why would they? Farming the first few years would be rough. There would barely be enough to eat for the people or the stock.

Andrew had offered to buy the stallion; he had never offered me a place in his family. He had one baby, and his wife was pregnant. Taking someone in meant sharing scarce food. The Mustang blew a long, warm breath along the nape of my neck, and I looked at him.

"If Miss Liddy will have me, maybe we can . . ." I trailed off. It would be a long time before I could ride well enough to add anything to their show. And maybe I would never get good enough. Miss Liddy was no one's fool. She hadn't offered me a place in her company, and there was no reason on the green earth why she would.

My thoughts were such an unhappy tangle as I kept walking uphill that I was wading through good, tall grass without even noticing it until the Mustang tugged at the rope. I stopped and he fell to grazing.

I wanted to cry, but I couldn't. I was beyond crying, and I leaned against the Mustang's shoulder, moving when he did, letting my thoughts spin because I could not stop them. I could hear birds overhead and the sighing of the breeze and the sound of the Mustang tearing grass off in eager mouthfuls. It was as though everything else in the world had disappeared.

Then the Mustang lifted his head so sharply that I turned, expecting to see someone or something coming toward us. Grover? But no one was there.

The Mustang lowered his head again. He was half starved from the hard miles in the sagebrush country and the mountain pass we had come over. He hadn't seen grass like this in months. "Good," I told him. I took a deep breath. "Tomorrow morning, we can bring the mares up here and—"

The Mustang struck at the ground with one hind

hoof and tossed his head, arching his neck. I fell silent. He turned away from me and faced the wind. I moved closer to him. "What?" He blew out a long breath and lifted his head to scent the air.

I tugged gently at the lead rope, but he didn't react. "If it's a wolf or something, we should start back now." I looked over my shoulder toward the wagons, expecting to see the tiny white dots of the canvas covers in the distance. But the swale had curved, and I couldn't see them.

The Mustang pawed at the earth. I couldn't spot whatever it was he had scented. But it didn't matter; it was smarter to go back. I turned, expecting the Mustang to turn with me, but he didn't. I was so surprised that I stumbled, jerking on the lead rope without meaning to. The stallion was startled into rearing.

I instinctively loosened my grip on the rope to keep from being dragged upward as I scrambled aside and waited for him to settle. But he didn't. He pranced a little, then shook his mane and reared again.

"Easy now. Just be easy," I singsonged, scanning the woods upwind. I couldn't see anything, but that didn't mean much. "Come on. Let's go." I tugged gently at the rope, but he didn't respond at all. "I'll bring you back here in the morning," I promised him. He refused to move.

I was nervous. I couldn't remember his ever acting like this. I had no idea how long it would take to gentle him into following me back, but I knew I shouldn't have come this far out of sight without telling someone. Mrs. Kyler would worry. So would Grover, I was sure. I'd just been so upset that all I had wanted was to get away from everyone.

"Please," I begged the Mustang, talking to him the way I always had. I explained that people would worry about us, that it was time to go back now.

He tossed his head and nickered.

It was only then that I heard a rustling sound and what sounded like footsteps in the trees below us. I held my breath and lifted my head. "Grover? Is that you?"

The Mustang nickered again, and I pulled hard at the lead rope. He turned to look at me, then faced the wind and nickered once more. "Grover?" I called. It was then I heard an answer. It wasn't meant for me, though. It was a whinny.

Now that I knew what I was looking for, I spotted the mare. She was a honey-colored horse with a long dark mane and tail. She eased back into the trees just as I saw a deep sorrel pass farther down the hill. Peering through the branches, I could see three more mares, all sleek and fit.

The Mustang shook his head hard and pulled at the rope. I tried to turn him toward me again. He dragged me forward a little ways. The mare whinnied again. He answered her.

There was no squealing challenge this time. For whatever reason, these mares seemed to be without a stallion. I saw two more threading their way through the pines, a gray and a tall chestnut.

The stallion turned, and I saw an expression in his eyes that had nothing to do with me. It was as though someone had lit a lantern inside him. I felt my eyes fill with tears. I might never find my home, but he had. This Oregon country was where he had been caught. All he needed was for me to take the halter off and let him go.

I began to cry hard. Everything that mattered to me was gone, had been taken away, all at once. But I knew what was right. I loved the Mustang. He had been my friend when I had no other in all the world.

My hands were shaking, and my vision was blurred with tears, but I knew what I had to do. I would not pay him back for his good heart by keeping him from *his* home.

Choking back sobs, I unbuckled the halter and slid it off over his ears. He turned to nuzzle my cheek, then he shook his head and rubbed his muzzle on one extended foreleg, scratching, erasing the marks in his coat from the leather straps.

He took a few steps, and I caught my breath. Then he stopped and looked back at me. "Good-bye," I whispered to him. "Thank you." He looked at me for a long moment, his eyes deep and kind.

Then one of the mares whinnied. Involuntarily, I reached out as the Mustang whirled around, reared, then lunged into a canter down the slope. I lowered my arm slowly, my heart aching as I watched him disappear into the forest. The hoofbeats and nickering got louder, then faded slowly into silence.

For a long time I stood, motionless, listening, feeling empty and scared and alone. I coiled up the lead rope and slung the halter over my shoulder and started back toward the wagons. It was the longest walk of my life. I stopped twice to weep, and I couldn't help turning back, over and over, trying to spot him, to hear him, but he was gone.

By the time I got back to camp I was pretty much past crying. I knew I had done the right thing. I knew it. And it still hurt like fire and weighed like stone on my heart.

CHAPTER TWELVE

≈ ≈ ≈

The little one brought me home. All that long, terrible way, she was leading me to sweet grass and pine trees. I will lead the mares far away from the two-leggeds and the oxen that graze the grass to the ground. Winter is coming. I must find a sheltered valley with good grass for them, a place where foals can be born and grow strong come spring.

I woke up the next morning and remembered that the Mustang wasn't there. A weight settled onto my spirits that seemed too much to carry. My daydream about living with my uncle Jack was gone—and so was my best friend. I felt sad and numb. I felt like I had left my own heart on that mountainside. Day after day, I plodded through my chores. Mrs. Kyler was watching me and so was Grover, but they left me alone, and I was grateful.

Life in the camp went on. Every family was looking for land. I helped Mrs. Kyler as always and waited for her to tell me I needed to make some arrangement in town, find some employment. I still walked the mares every morning, looking for grass. It helped me to be around them, as odd as that may sound, because I knew they missed the Mustang, too, in their way.

Most evenings, I helped Mrs. Kyler make supper, then walked out to visit with Midnight and Delia before I went to bed. I usually cried a little, and the mares seemed to understand. One evening, Andrew was going through the herd, checking the horses. He thanked me for taking special care of them.

"They eat every blade of grass I can find for them," I told him. "Delia's flanks are all filled in, and Midnight's almost are. They're both putting on weight faster than any of the others."

The instant the words left my lips, I heard what I had said and understood. I blushed. He grinned, and I knew I was right. I stared at him, delighted. "They're both in foal? How long have you known?"

He smiled again. "A month or two."

I was astounded. "Why didn't you tell me?"

He shrugged. "I probably should have. I didn't want you and my mother worrying about one more thing every time we had to come across rough country or ford a river."

I stood still, a weight easing off my heart. Two foals. The Mustang had sired *two* foals. Maybe one would look like him. Maybe both would. I grinned, picturing them playing, leaping and running on Andrew's farm, racing across his good grassland.

"It's such grand news," Andrew said. "I was hoping for one. I didn't ever think we'd get this lucky."

I met his eyes. "May I come to see them? I don't know where I will end up, but, please, can I just come see them sometimes?"

Andrew was studying my face, and he chuckled. "My mother made me promise that if we got two, I'd give you one once it was old enough. I know better than to cross my mother."

I stared at him as though he was speaking some language I had never heard before. He patted my shoulder. "Close your mouth, Katie. You'll catch a fly."

I whirled and ran back toward Mrs. Kyler's wagon. She grinned when she saw me coming, and I whooped like Miss Liddy did sometimes, high and loud.

"Figured it out, did you, finally?" she teased.

I stamped one foot, pretending to be upset. "Everyone knew?"

She nodded. "We're all so pleased about it."

"Why didn't anyone tell me?"

She reached out and patted my cheek. "I thought losing the Mustang was something you needed to get used to first," she said. "Was I wrong?"

I didn't know what to say, so I hugged her, hard. She smelled like wood smoke and soap, and, for a minute, I didn't think about anything except how kind she was, how much I loved her.

"I don't know where I will end up," I began, "but if I can't take care of the foal right off, will Andrew keep it for me until I can?"

She nodded solemnly. "I am sure he would."

I danced a little jig, hopping in a silly circle. She laughed. So did I. It felt both strange and wonderful at the same time. I noticed Julia and Polly watching me from a distance. They smiled and waved, and I knew they were glad for me.

The next evening, Miss Liddy came into the Kylers' camp. Grover and I were eating second helpings of Mrs. Kyler's beans when Miss Liddy pulled a cracker box close the fire to sit upon.

Mrs. Kyler sat across from her. "My husband and I have been talking. We have an offer to make you, Grover." Mr. Kyler was leaning against the wagon, and he nodded.

I glanced at Grover. He had stopped chewing and stared at Mrs. Kyler, his eyes full hope.

Mrs. Kyler leaned down and put a stick of dead-wood across the fire. It flared up, sparks floating upward into the ink-dark sky.

"And you, too, Katie," she added. "Miss Liddy and I have already made our bargain."

I blinked and looked at Miss Liddy.

She smiled at me. "Mr. Kyler is about to settle his land claim. In exchange for our help building cabins for the winter, tending stock, whatever needs doing, they will let us all winter on their place. Me, Jacob, James, Pierre—and both of you."

Grover and I exchanged another quick glance. My heart was racketing inside my chest.

"Andrew says you work miracles with the horses, Katie," Mrs. Kyler said, "and everyone knows how hard both you and Grover can work."

"And come spring," Miss Liddy said, "we can all talk again and decide what's best for everyone."

She winked at Grover. "You can practice all winter."
Then she looked at me. "And we'll work on your
riding when the weather lets us."

I turned to stare at Mrs. Kyler. Her face was
full of kindness. Tears were stinging at my eyes,
but I blinked them back. This wasn't a time to cry.
I was going to be all right. I hadn't found my own
family, but I had ended up with friends so close they
might as well be.

I exhaled slowly, taking it in. Hiram would be so
pleased when I wrote him. So would Annie. They
weren't really my family either, but...I glanced at
Grover. Having family was no guarantee of having
love.

"Yes?" Mrs. Kyler said, looking between us.
"Do we have a bargain?"

Grover and I both nodded.

"And you can come back whenever you like," she
said to Liddy. Then she looked at me and Grover.
"If you leave, you can always come back."

I smiled, breathing in the cool, soft Oregon
air. Grover shot me a look so full of joy and relief
that I grinned at him.

I looked up at the sky and knew that the Mustang

was somewhere under the same stars, standing watch and guarding his herd. He had found his home. And maybe I had found mine. Maybe I had.

Eric caught her hand. "Please don't. I don't have the strength to stop you."

"I don't want you to stop me. I want you to take me away from this insane place, even if it's just for a few minutes. Make me believe that this isn't reality." Rachel lifted her head and sought his lips.

"This can't happen," he said against her neck. "You don't want me. You just want comfort."

"I do want you. Please. I swear. I won't ask you for more than this."

He lifted his head, and Rachel saw the anguish in his eyes. He touched her lips with his thumb. "I understand. You're asking for an escape from the madness." He shook his head. "I can't promise you that."

His tone struck fear in her heart. She ignored the question that rose in the back of her mind. Instead, she pulled his head down so her mouth brushed his. "Don't promise me anything. Just love me."

Dear Harlequin Intrigue Reader,

Summer's winding down, but Harlequin Intrigue is as hot as ever with six spine-tingling reads for you this month!

* Our new BIG SKY BOUNTY HUNTERS promotion debuts with Amanda Stevens's *Going to Extremes*. In the coming months, look for more titles from Jessica Andersen, Cassie Miles and Julie Miller.

* We have some great miniseries for you. Rita Herron is back with *Mysterious Circumstances*, the latest in her NIGHTHAWK ISLAND series. Mallory Kane's *Seeking Asylum* is the third book in her ULTIMATE AGENTS series. And Sylvie Kurtz has another tale in THE SEEKERS series— *Eye of a Hunter*.

* No month would be complete without a chilling gothic romance. This month's ECLIPSE title is Debra Webb's *Urban Sensation*.

* Jan Hambright, a fabulous new author, makes her debut with *Relentless*. Sparks fly when a feisty repo agent repossesses a BMW with an ex-homicide detective in the trunk!

Don't miss a single book this month and every month!

Sincerely,

Denise O'Sullivan
Senior Editor
Harlequin Intrigue

SEEKING ASYLUM
MALLORY KANE

TORONTO • NEW YORK • LONDON
AMSTERDAM • PARIS • SYDNEY • HAMBURG
STOCKHOLM • ATHENS • TOKYO • MILAN • MADRID
PRAGUE • WARSAW • BUDAPEST • AUCKLAND

For the members of
Magnolia State Romance Writers,
who have supported me without fail,
and for Lorraine.

ISBN 0-373-88637-3

SEEKING ASYLUM

Copyright © 2005 by Rickey R. Mallory

This edition published by arrangement with Harlequin Books S.A.

® and TM are trademarks of the publisher. Trademarks indicated with
® are registered in the United States Patent and Trademark Office, the
Canadian Trade Marks Office and in other countries.

www.eHarlequin.com

Printed in U.S.A.

ABOUT THE AUTHOR

Mallory Kane credits her love of books to her mother, a librarian, who taught her that books are a precious resource and should be treated with loving respect. Her grandfather and her father were both steeped in the Southern tradition of oral history, and could hold an audience spellbound with their storytelling skills. Mallory aspires to be as good a storyteller as her father.

She loves romantic suspense with dangerous heroes and dauntless heroines, and often uses her medical background to add an extra dose of intrigue to her books. Another fascination that she enjoys exploring in her reading and writing is the infinite capacity of the brain to adapt and develop higher skills.

Mallory lives in Mississippi with her computer-genius husband, their two fascinating cats, and, at current count, seven computers.

CAST OF CHARACTERS

Rachel Harper—The young psychiatrist is the newest staff member at The Meadows. The child of a bipolar mother, Rachel grew up determined to defeat mental illness. Now, in order to survive, she must trust her life to a man who may be insane.

Eric Baldwyn—Profiler for the Division of Unsolved Mysteries, Eric's empathic abilities and odd dreams of the twin brother he believes is dead, have made him a loner. But the only way he can save Rachel's life is to expose his innermost self, even if it means losing any chance of her love.

Caleb Baldwyn—Eric's identical twin brother is schizophrenic, and has spent the past twenty years in a mental institution. Caleb claims Dr. Metzger's heinous experiments and mysterious injections are killing patients. Is Caleb telling the truth, or are his ravings the delusions of his insanity?

Gerhardt Metzger—Obsessed with finding a cure for schizophrenia, Dr. Gerhardt Metzger has used Caleb Baldwyn for his increasingly invasive and inhumane experiments for years. Will the controversial and world-renowned neurologist resort to murder to keep his best patient?

Rajid Patel—The Chief Medical Director for The Meadows private mental facility is desperate to hold on to his most valued staff member, Dr. Metzger. Is Dr. Patel involved with Metzger's cruel experiments, or is he just a pawn in the doctor's wicked game?

Chapter One

"Let go of me, Caleb. You know the rules." Dr. Rachel Harper tried to pry his fingers off her arm. She'd been on her way home when the night nurse in the acute neurological wing had buzzed her to tell her that Caleb Baldwyn was in the sunroom. He'd woken up while sleepwalking.

"You're in on it, aren't you?" His voice was harsh and shrill. His ragged fingernails scraped her skin as he tightened his grip. Fear and hostility emanated from him like body heat. "Frankenmetzger sent you to kill me."

Rachel studied the troubled young man. She knew a little about his case from his meager chart. Childhood-onset schizophrenia was a heartbreaking disease. He'd apparently been in mental institutions for most of his thirty-one years, since he was eleven years old. In the last few years he'd become less and less able to function independently, even on the newest drugs. His constant relapses didn't make sense. Given his young age and excellent physical condition, he should have been a perfect candidate for the new antipsychotic medications.

Rachel heard the sunroom door open.

"Dr. Harper, is everything all right?" It was the night nurse.

"I'm fine, Gracie. Caleb's going back to bed now."

"No!" he screamed. "Frankenmetzger's going to kill me. I have to get away."

Gracie stepped into the room and slipped a syringe from her pocket. Behind her, the Meadows's security guard appeared in the doorway.

Rachel sent Gracie a frustrated glare. She'd specifically told her not to call Security.

"Caleb," Rachel said calmly. "Walk with me back to your room."

"Room? You mean, cage?" Caleb snarled, pushing her away. "Why can't you see what's going on around here?" He pinned her with his bleak gaze. "Frankenmetzger's switching medications. What's in the chart is not what we're being given." He brushed at his neck, frowning. "He's a monster."

Darrell Freeman, the security guard, advanced. "All right, Caleb," he said. "Let's go."

Gracie started toward Caleb with the syringe.

Caleb's eyes darted wildly as he took a step backward.

"Darrell, don't crowd him," Rachel muttered,

keeping her eyes on Caleb. She didn't want him to panic.

Darrell grabbed Caleb, flipped him around and wrapped his forearm across his throat.

"Darrell!" *Damn it.* Why were they ignoring her?

Caleb used the leverage of Darrell's grip to rock backward and kick at Grace. Her syringe went flying, Darrell overbalanced, and he and Caleb tumbled to the floor, rolling over and over as they struggled. Darrell pinned Caleb with one arm and Rachel saw the flash of gunmetal.

"Darrell, no!"

A shot rang out and the two men froze in place. Then, slowly, they crumpled like a pair of rag dolls and the gun skittered across the tile floor.

A dark red stain began to spread across Darrell Freeman's shirt.

Gracie screamed.

Caleb staggered to his feet and his long fingers stretched toward the gun.

Rachel dove for the weapon, but Caleb was quicker. He grabbed it, then lunged for her, hauling her up in a chokehold. Tremors racked his lean frame and his pounding heart thudded against her back.

"He's dead, isn't he? I killed him," he sobbed as he pressed the barrel of the gun under her chin. "It was him or me. Him or me. You know that, don't you, Pretty Doctor?"

His arm was so tight around her throat she could barely breathe. Her pulse drummed in her ears as fear shuddered through her. She pulled at his arm, fighting for breath. "Caleb, don't make it worse."

A sharp laugh exploded from his mouth. "It can't be worse." He jerked her more tightly against him, cutting off her air for an instant. "I need to go home. I need Eric. He'll know where to find me if I go home."

Gracie edged toward the door. Caleb whirled, pointing the gun at her. "No! Don't move!"

Gracie recoiled and wrapped her arms around her head. "Don't shoot me, please," she begged. "I have children."

Caleb's body grew rigid. "So did Darrell!" he sobbed. The tremors racking his body increased. "Oh, God. I killed him."

A faint movement from the downed security guard caught Rachel's eye. Her pulse leaped.

"Let me check him. I don't think he's dead." Rachel strained against Caleb's forearm. Her throat burned and she coughed.

Caleb shook his head. "No. No. Too late. It's too late now!"

TOO LATE NOW!

Eric Baldwyn shot straight up in bed, gasping for breath. His heart galloped as he kicked at the tangled bedclothes and raked his startled gaze over his surroundings. Gradually the images came into focus.

He was in his apartment in Washington, D.C. Not holding a beautiful, frightened doctor as a human shield. Not gripping a loaded gun while a man lay in a pool of blood at his feet.

Eric shuddered and wiped both hands over his face. That'd teach him to bring his work home. He'd spent all evening studying grisly forensic photos from his latest case.

He pulled on jeans and grabbed a bottle of water from the refrigerator. Propping his arm on top of the refrigerator door, he gulped the water, shivering as a few drops dribbled onto his bare chest. Rubbing the cool liquid into his skin, he shouldered the door closed and flopped down onto the couch, still haunted by the frightened blue eyes and the trembling lips of the beautiful doctor from his dream.

He clicked on the TV, hoping for some distraction. He closed his eyes, barely listening to the news anchor's drone.

The elements of the dream clung to him like mist. He couldn't shake them.

Why a shooting? Why a beautiful hostage? And most importantly, why had he dreamed he was inside the killer's head? He laughed grimly.

"Rookie question, Baldwyn," he muttered. His brain had turned a metaphor into an image. After all, as the Division's criminal profiler, it was his job to get inside people's heads.

He flung his forearm across his eyes.

"—breaking story from the Meadows Psychiatric Facility in Longview, Connecticut. Less than two hours ago, a security guard was shot with his own gun by a patient, Caleb Baldwyn—"

The words hit Eric with the impact of a bullet. *Caleb Baldwyn.* He sat up and stared at the screen. That was his brother's name.

"Baldwyn escaped with a hostage, Dr. Rachel Harper, a psychiatrist at the exclusive, private, resort-like facility that caters to the rich and famous—"

On the screen a long shot of sprawling buildings and manicured lawns switched to a grainy photograph. Eric bolted upright. His pulse pounded in his ears.

It was her. The woman from his dream. Black hair, wide, crystal-blue eyes, pretty heart-shaped face. Surprise tingled through him. He knew her—knew the silken swish of her hair against his cheek, knew the feel of her firm, slender body pressed against him, knew the sweet melodic sound of her voice. But how? He'd never met Rachel Harper—had never been to the Meadows.

He pressed his palms to his temples. His dreams had always been vivid, some more nightmarish than others. But he'd never dreamed a real incident, at least not since his twin brother had died twenty years before.

"No!" he cried in denial, even as certainty settled over him like a hot woolen blanket. He gawked at the TV screen in disbelief. What was happening to him?

His brother's name, the dream. There could be only one explanation, yet every molecule in his body still tried to deny it.

Grief and horror beat a rapid rhythm in his throat. His breathing became erratic and his palms grew clammy as denial slowly morphed into dread certainty.

His grandmother had lied to him all his life. *Caleb was alive.* It explained so much—the dreams, the odd, frightening thoughts, the echo of Caleb's voice in his head.

He'd spent the past twenty years terrified of succumbing to the same schizophrenia that had afflicted his only sibling. But now—

"—more information as it becomes available. Back to you—"

Eric flipped channels, but no one else was covering the story.

He shot up off the couch and paced, spiking his fingers through his hair in agitation. The shooting and the beautiful hostage were real. He'd been inside his brother's head. He'd seen what Caleb saw. The strange link they had shared as kids was still there.

His eyes stung. How had he not known? The guilt he'd carried like a cross all these years weighed even heavier. Had Caleb been alone all this time—locked in that exclusive snake pit? Eric rubbed his pounding temples. No wonder he'd never been able to banish his brother's voice from his mind.

Caleb was alive. He needed him.

BY THREE o'clock the next afternoon Eric was in an FBI van with Mitch Decker, the Special Agent in Charge of the Division of Unsolved Mysteries. Eric had explained to Mitch about the kidnapping and asked for Decker's help. He had to go to his brother.

Decker had agreed that Eric was the obvious choice to negotiate with Caleb about releasing the psychiatrist, but true to his nature, he refused to consider Eric going alone. He'd insisted on accompanying him, to smooth the way with the local authorities and to lend support to Eric.

Decker pocketed his cell phone. "They're at your grandmother's house, just like you said. Dr. Harper's car is parked in the driveway," he told Eric. "The sheriff has set up roadblocks and they're waiting for us. Your instinct was right on."

Eric took a deep breath. "Yes, sir."

Decker shot him a questioning glance. "What's going on, Eric? What are you not telling me?"

Eric swallowed. He should have known better

than to give Decker only part of the story. "You know what people say about twins—how some twins seem to have a special link? Well, last night I dreamed about the shooting and the kidnapping." He hesitated.

"What do you mean, you dreamed about it?" Decker's voice was cautious.

"I can't explain it, sir. I don't understand it myself." Eric laid out the information the way he knew Decker liked it, simply and chronologically. He talked about growing up with his schizophrenic brother under the stern hand of their society-conscious grandmother. The monster-laden nightmares, the days full of odd thoughts his young brain had had no name for. The fact that even after his brother's death, the sensations had never completely vanished.

"I was afraid I was going insane." He laughed shortly. "You probably think I am."

Decker spread his hands above the steering wheel. "I have no idea how you get inside people's heads, how you can solve a case just by studying the victim. But I believe in you. So my position is that you know what you're talking about."

"Here we are." Eric's heart pounded as he saw the familiar road to his grandmother's house. The area was milling with armed officers and dotted with

Fairfield County police cars and an ambulance. "We're about three hundred yards from the house."

"George Ford, the county sheriff, has agreed to let us go in first."

Eric nodded. He couldn't see the house—it was around a long curve—but he felt its pull. He'd grown up there. He loved it—and hated it. Apprehension churned in his gut.

Together they walked down the winding, tree-lined road. When the huge Colonial mansion came into view, Eric halted. Memories flowed over him like a waterfall, eroding his defenses.

Decker withdrew his service weapon. Eric nodded, but didn't pull his own gun. He hoped he wouldn't need it.

He took a deep breath and squared his shoulders, then walked toward the temple-like entrance of the house where his brother had almost killed him.

RACHEL HARPER opened her eyes and immediately panicked. She was in the dark!

Mama, don't! Don't turn out all the lights. I'll be quiet, I promise.

Her heart pounded so fast and hard, her chest hurt. She cowered on the floor. The hungry blackness was about to devour her, just like when she was a child. She fought to breathe.

A door opened, letting in blessed light. Rachel jerked and pain shot through her wrists and ankles.

It was Caleb! He looked awful. His eyes were wilder than ever, his clothes disheveled. Redness rimmed his eyelids and his skin under his day's growth of beard looked sickly pale.

Memories came rushing back—Caleb shooting the guard, forcing her at gunpoint to drive her own car as he shouted directions. Then when they'd arrived at the deserted house, he'd dragged her up two sets of stairs, bound her with duct tape and locked her in the dark.

"Eric's coming," Caleb said, waving the gun in her direction.

"Eric, your brother?" Rachel couldn't take her eyes off the gun. She'd heard Caleb talking about his brother the secret agent, but his medical records mentioned no family except his grandmother, who'd recently died.

Working the night shift, Rachel had gotten to know Caleb fairly well, and had found him fascinating. From his ramblings about secret agents and conspiracies and murder, Rachel had realized just how ill the intelligent, handsome young man really was.

"Get up. He'll be here soon." Caleb stuck the gun in his pocket and reached for her. She cowered, but he grabbed her feet and ripped the tape off. Then he hauled her up by her bound hands.

She yelped in pain as he yanked the tape off her wrists. Then he pushed her ahead of him downstairs to the kitchen, where he shoved her into a chair. He was becoming more agitated by the moment.

"How do you know Eric's coming?" she asked him, hoping to get him to focus on her question. Maybe she could get through to him.

His fingers tapped an erratic rhythm against his pant leg. "I called him." His opaque brown gaze met hers. "He was shocked. He thought I was dead."

Despite her certainty that Caleb was having delusions, Rachel couldn't control the hopeful leap of her heart. "You called him? When?" Caleb didn't have a cell phone. "There's a phone in the house?"

Caleb laughed as he gnawed on a fingernail. "I don't need a phone. Eric is a secret agent. He can do anything."

"Yes." Rachel's stomach sank in disappointment. He was rambling. "So you said."

"You don't believe me. Nobody does. They think I'm crazy."

He was intimidating, standing over her, his eyelids twitching, his pupils pinpointed. "Misty believed me, and look what happened to her. She's dead."

"Misty?" Rachel assessed him, frowning. It had

been over twenty hours since he'd had a dose of medication. "Who is Misty?"

"Not is. *Was*. Who *was* Misty? She was Misty Norwood. We were going to get married." He hit the tabletop, then spread his shaking fingers. "She was having trouble breathing. They took her away. *He* told me she died." His face contorted. "I tried to protect her. I tried so hard. One of the patients said her parents took her home. But you can't believe crazy people, can you?" He smiled briefly. "Besides, she wouldn't have left without telling me. Frankenmetzger killed her."

"Dr. Metzger? I'm sure you're wrong. He's internationally renowned for his research. He's done a lot of good for a lot of people."

Caleb's face turned dark and he clenched his fists. "He is a monster."

Rachel eyed the bulge the gun made in his pocket and steered the conversation back to a safer subject. "Tell me about Eric."

Hope fluttered in her chest, even as she scolded herself. There was no secret agent brother. She was in danger of buying into Caleb's psychosis, just as she'd done with her mother when she was a child.

Over and over, when her mother's mood swings would stabilize, Rachel had found herself believing that this time, everything would stay normal. Over and over, she'd been fooled.

Growing up with a mother who'd been bipolar, she'd learned a hard lesson. *Nobody was going to rescue her.* They hadn't then and they wouldn't now.

So she'd rescued herself. She'd become a psychiatrist, determined to defeat the type of disease that had deprived her of a normal childhood. Rachel straightened her back and prepared to do battle with Caleb's illness.

Just as she was about to speak, Caleb stiffened.

A look of anticipation crossed his face. "He's here." He jerked her up by her abraded wrist, causing her to cry out in pain.

"Who's here?" Rachel hadn't heard anything. Was Caleb having auditory hallucinations, too?

He wrapped his forearm around her neck, pulled the gun from his pocket and pressed the cold barrel under her chin, just like the night before. He pushed her through the swinging door into the dining room, where drapes as thick and dark as those upstairs shrouded the windows.

Beyond the archway that led to the living room, the front door opened and a silhouette blocked the bright sunlight.

Someone had come. Startled, Rachel squinted, but there was too much glare for her to make out anything about the person. Was it a policeman?

Caleb stopped cold, his breathing shallow and sharp.

The man stepped into the living room, away from the glare of the door. "Caleb?"

Rachel stared in disbelief at the sight in front of her. The man had Caleb's face. They were identical.

Her body tingled as if she'd been struck by lightning. Her brain worked to catch up with what her eyes saw.

"Eric," Caleb said. "You came. I knew you would."

Eric. Caleb was telling the truth?

The newcomer's face was pale, his eyes bright. He seemed as shocked by Caleb as Rachel was by him.

"Caleb. God, I'm so sorry. I didn't know—" His low rasp was very different from Caleb's harsh voice. "I thought you were dead."

Suddenly, Caleb released his hold on her. She stumbled and backed away, her attention divided between the two men.

Eric's gaze flickered briefly toward her, as if to make sure she was all right, then his attention turned back to Caleb.

"I know you did." Caleb laughed briefly, then his face grew solemn. "Grandmother lied to you. She lied to me, too, but I knew you weren't dead. You were always in my head."

Eric nodded, looking shocked, apparently trying to placate Caleb by agreeing with his nonsensical ramblings.

Caleb's breath caught in a near sob. "Eric, Grandmother died."

"Yeah. I know, bud." The tension emanating from Eric was palpable.

Rachel felt dizzy. She blinked, forcing her brain to accept what her eyes saw. The two men were practically identical: both around six feet tall, with wide shoulders and long, lean muscles. Their faces were beautifully structured, with high, prominent cheekbones, big dark eyes and strong chins.

But Eric's stance was watchful and expectant, and graceful, very different from Caleb's jerky stiffness. There were other differences, too. Eric was leaner, fitter. His face had more lines than Caleb's and he was more... Rachel couldn't put it into words.

Not more handsome exactly. Still, something intense and elegant about him stirred a response in her that went far beyond relief that at last a rescuer had come.

As if he sensed her scrutiny, he turned his full attention to her and a shiver ran up her spine. His gaze gleamed with a light that was missing from Caleb's. The light of reality.

Those chocolate-satin eyes assessed her, lingering on her hair and mouth before meeting her gaze again.

She shivered. She'd never been looked at like that in her life—as if he knew everything about her. As if he understood her.

"Dr. Harper, are you all right?" he asked.

She nodded, but Caleb waved the gun. "Don't talk to her. Talk to me."

Eric's smoky gaze held hers for a beat. Amazingly her body responded somewhere beyond the fear. She felt a deep, visceral awareness stretch across the space between them. A purely sexual instant out of time.

Eric's brows shot up and a faint spot of color rose in his cheeks. His gaze drifted down, sliding over her body like a caress.

He'd felt it, too.

He turned his gaze back to Caleb, as if compelled. Caleb's wild, dark eyes devoured his brother. Rachel felt the link between the two men who'd been born of one zygote, their bond closer than any physical bond on earth because they shared the same DNA.

Identical twins.

Caleb had been telling the truth. He did have a brother named Eric. Was Eric a secret agent?

A disturbing thought occurred to her. If Caleb's outlandish story of his brother was true, what about everything else he'd told her? What if Misty had died and the hospital had covered it up? What if Metzger really was conducting secret experiments?

Everything inside her rose up to deny that possibility. Metzger had been her idol since medical school. She couldn't allow a sick young man to sway her. Caleb was mentally ill, possibly dangerous. He had a history of delusional ravings.

"Caleb? Put down the gun." Eric's quiet, rough voice interrupted her thoughts.

"Eric, I killed him. Killed him." Caleb chewed on his thumbnail. "What am I going to do now?"

"We need to go back," Eric said softly. "We'll explain that it was an accident and—"

"No!" Caleb snapped, then shook his head. "No. No. No."

"Caleb—"

"I can't go back there. I can't take any more of his poison. I try to stay in control, so I can get better. So I can go to the ILC."

He wiped sweat out of his eyes. "Every time I get out—Frankenmetzger gets me back. He switches drugs, so nobody will know. The experimental drug makes me sick." Caleb's attention had turned inward. He breathed in shallow gasps.

"What's the ILC?" Eric's questioning gaze sought Rachel.

She swallowed, taken aback by Caleb's words. "The Independent Living Complex," she said. "If a resident does well there, he can move to a halfway house. Then eventually to outpatient treatment."

"And my brother?"

"Caleb copes well in acute care. So well, that about

every six months or so for the past few years, the board has approved his transfer to the ILC. But time after time, as soon as he's settled, he begins to relapse."

"Why? Isn't their medication still supervised, even in an outpatient setting?"

Rachel's shoulders rose in an automatic shrug "Yes. No one seems to understand it. Dr. Metzger is very concerned. Given Caleb's health and age, he should be an ideal candidate for outpatient treatment."

"And yet he's been locked up for twenty years." The pain in Eric's voice ripped at Rachel's heart. "So what about this new experimental drug?"

She shook her head sadly and met Eric's gaze. She spoke as gently as she could. "There is no experimental drug."

"Yes there is!" Caleb shouted.

Eric's eyelids fluttered and he turned pale. He was obviously still in shock over seeing his twin.

Rachel's curiosity was piqued. She resolved to find out the story behind the twins' separation. She knew Caleb's grandmother had died, but there had never been any mention of a brother. Maybe the trauma of being separated from his brother so young explained Caleb's volatility.

She stepped toward Caleb. "He's had no medication for almost twenty-four hours now. He's showing signs of—"

"Stop talking about me like I'm not here!" Caleb

swung around, waving the gun wildly. His frantic gaze landed on his brother's face. "I know what's real and what's not. Eric, I called you to help me. Tell the pretty doctor you're a secret agent."

"Caleb, listen to me."

"Tell her!"

Eric rubbed his temple and sighed. "I'm Special Agent Eric Baldwyn," he said to her. "With the FBI."

Rachel nodded, too stunned to reply. Caleb's brother was with the FBI. He *was* a secret agent.

"See," Caleb said. "I told you my brother can do anything. Eric, Frankenmetzger's going to kill me. You've got to stop him."

Eric held out a hand. "Nobody's trying to kill you, bud. We're going to take care of you."

He spoke to Rachel. "What medication is he on?"

Rachel felt as though she'd walked in on the middle of a play. She concentrated on answering his question. "Fenpiprazole, a brand-new atypical antipsychotic drug. The only known withdrawal symptoms are increases in negative schizophrenic effects. For instance, withdrawal, concrete thinking—"

Eric interrupted her. "I know what they are. So he shouldn't be having increased paranoia, right?"

She was surprised at his knowledge of schizophrenia. "That's right. Nor rigidity, nor hallucinations."

Rachel noticed a movement out of the corner of her eye, beyond where Caleb stood. Another silhouette darkened the open front doorway. This man was bigger, taller and carried an air of authority that emanated from him like a scent.

Eric acknowledged him with a slight turn of his head. Was he another FBI agent?

Caleb jerked his head toward the door and Rachel froze. She knew better than anyone how Caleb reacted to surprises. At the same time, Eric stepped forward, pulling Caleb's attention back to him. A smart move.

She took a deep breath. "Caleb," she said softly. "Remember I said I'd explain that the shooting was an accident?"

He shook his head. "I can't go back there. Frankenmetzger will never stop his experiments." He leaned closer to Eric. "He knows I know what he's doing."

Eric took another step toward Caleb. "I'll go with you, bud. We'll—"

Caleb narrowed his eyes at Eric. "No!"

Eric's head jerked backward.

The older agent glided silently into the room. Out of the corner of her eye, Rachel saw a gun in his right hand. A dizzying sense of fear-soaked déjà vu engulfed her. Darrell had come at Caleb with a gun and ended up in a bloody heap on the floor.

"Don't, pl—" she started, but the big man cut her off.

"Caleb," he said in a deep voice that resonated with calm authority. "Why don't we talk?"

Caleb whirled and pointed the gun toward the door. "Who are you? Eric, who is he?" He gripped the weapon in both hands, the barrel quivering.

Rachel shook her head at Eric, trying desperately to send him a silent message.

Don't let him make any sudden moves. Don't crowd Caleb.

Eric nodded slightly, his dark gaze riveting. It was as if he'd heard her thoughts.

"Caleb." His low voice was soothing. "He's my friend, and he's going to help us. You need to put down the gun." He sounded strained but calm as he moved slowly toward his brother, his hands extended slightly, his face white and pinched.

Caleb took a step backward and swung the barrel toward her. He doubled his other hand into a fist and beat it against his forehead over and over. "No, no, no! Stop!" he shouted at her. "You've fooled them, haven't you? You're on Frankenmetzger's side."

Rachel stared down the barrel, her chest pounding. Fear weakening her limbs. She swallowed. "Caleb, I'm on your side. Let's talk."

The agent at the door moved and his shadow streaked across the hardwood floor. Caleb stopped pounding his head and whirled, swinging the gun chaotically, one-handed. Then, with a strangled sound, he lifted the barrel to his own head.

The room went totally silent.

"I'm sorry, Eric," Caleb sobbed. "I can't go back there. If you won't help me—"

Eric's face mirrored the anguish in his brother's eyes. "Caleb. Don't, please." Eric held out his hand. "Let me have the gun. I swear to you I won't send you back there."

Caleb's attention was divided between Eric and the man at the door. Rachel took a small step toward him, then another.

The other agent straightened and his electric-blue eyes flashed a warning at her, but Rachel focused all her strength on holding Caleb's attention.

"Caleb," she said softly, gently. His head cocked toward her. That was what she'd been hoping for. If she couldn't get him to put the gun down, maybe she could at least distract him until Eric or the other agent got close enough to disarm him.

"You don't have to do this anymore." She hoped her voice would keep him calm. "I saw what happened. I'll tell them it was an accident. They'll believe me. Then your brother can take you away—far away from Dr. Metzger."

Caleb sent her a sidelong glance. The barrel of the gun tipped as his hand relaxed just slightly.

Beyond him, the agent moved. It took all Rachel's

control to keep from reacting. She held Caleb's gaze and smiled, hoping to keep his attention away from the lengthening shadow on the floor in front of them.

"That's right," she said. "You'll never have to see Dr. Metzger again."

The agent lunged, but before Rachel even registered the change in his eyes, Caleb twisted. The agent's hand merely grazed his shoulder, but he recovered quickly and pushed Caleb's arm upward.

A shot rang out and both men fell backward, the gun clattering to the floor between them.

"Caleb!" Eric yelled, leaping toward them.

Caleb scrabbled for the gun but Eric kicked it out of the way and hauled his brother up.

"Me!" Caleb screamed. "It should have been me!"

Eric swayed, but he held on. Veins stood out in his neck as he locked his arms around his brother from behind.

The agent lay still on the floor, blood spreading under his head.

Rachel stared at the bizarre scene in front of her. Two men, eerily alike, yet completely different, like distorted mirror images. And at their feet an FBI agent, lying in his own blood.

A chill spread through her. Caleb had shot another man.

Chapter Two

Decker was down. Eric's nightmare had turned into skewed reality. He was restraining the twin brother he'd thought was dead, his boss had been shot, and standing in the same room with him was the beautiful hostage from his dream.

Under his forearms, Eric felt his brother's coarse, heavy breathing, felt the dampness of his sweat-soaked shirt.

Eric's own chest was heaving. Caleb's outburst had affected him profoundly. It was an echo of their childhood, when his own brain would reverberate with echoes of Caleb's confusion and fear.

He glanced at Dr. Harper. She was real. The realization still stunned him. Her face, so like the face in his dream, was ghostly white, her hands clasped over her mouth.

As he watched, she straightened, pushed her silky hair back from her cheeks and started toward Decker.

"Dr. Harper."

She turned. Her blue eyes were still wide and panicked, but her chin was high.

"Can you handle Caleb if I cuff him?"

She nodded immediately and reached out to touch Caleb's shoulder lightly. "Caleb, let's go sit over here. Come on. It'll be fine." She looked at Eric. "Do you have to cuff him? He'll be quiet. He trusts me, don't you, Caleb?"

Eric felt the easing of the spring-loaded tension in his brother's limbs at Rachel's touch and shrugged involuntarily, imagining how her slender, capable hands would feel comforting him.

Caleb walked stiffly beside her to the straight-backed chair. She had to push on his shoulders to make him sit, but he complied without question. He stared at the wall, hardly blinking.

Eric pulled his attention away from his brother and the lovely doctor. Retrieving the gun, he tucked it into his belt, then knelt beside Decker, dread pooling in his stomach. He gingerly pressed two fingers on his boss's carotid artery.

Decker's pulse beat strongly and rapidly. A shuddering relief streaked through Eric, weakening his limbs. He blew his breath out in a sigh.

Decker moved.

Sitting back on his heels, Eric put a steadying hand on his boss's arm. "Careful, Mitch. You're wounded."

With a colorful curse, Decker sat up. "Believe it or not, I remember that." He put a hand to his head, then looked at the blood, grimacing. "It's just a graze."

"Let me take a look—"

"Hang on." Decker retrieved his cell phone from his pocket and pressed a speed-dial button. "Ford? It's Decker."

The sheriff.

"Yeah, stray shot, no problem. Hold back. Give us a few more minutes. Right. I'll call if we need anything. The suspect is under control and the hostage is fine."

Clicking off the phone, he pushed himself to his feet and dug a handkerchief out of his pocket. "They were ready to storm the house. How's your brother?"

Eric shook his head. *Sick. Disturbed.* And still capable of affecting Eric, even after all the years apart. "I'm sorry you got involved—"

Decker wiped blood out of his eye and pressed his handkerchief against the wound. "We've already had this discussion."

He glanced toward Rachel. "Dr. Harper. Are you injured? Did he hurt you in any way?"

Her black hair swung around her face as she shook her head. She never took her eyes off Caleb. "He didn't hurt me. He's not violent. Not really. He's afraid. And in need of medication."

Eric gaped at her. "What do you mean, not violent? He's shot two people within twenty-four hours. He's held you at gunpoint. We don't know if the security guard is going to make it."

Her wide blue gaze met his for an instant. "He's not dead? Caleb didn't kill him? Oh, thank God."

"What happened?" Eric asked. "How did the guard let Caleb get the better of him? He had Caleb by the throat."

She shot him a surprised glance. "How did you know that?"

Eric clamped his jaw. He'd almost said too much. He had to be careful to separate what he knew about the case from what he'd seen in his dream. "Some newscaster must have mentioned it," he said noncommittally.

Her gaze swung back to her patient as she talked. "Caleb woke while sleepwalking. He was agitated. I almost had him convinced to go back to bed, but the nurse called Security, even though I'd specifically told her not to."

Irritation flowed over Rachel at the memory. "The guard was too aggressive. He frightened him." She pressed long, graceful fingers onto Caleb's wrist, checking his pulse, her full lips flattening into a grim line.

She bent until she was in Caleb's line of sight. "Caleb, how are you feeling?"

Caleb continued to stare as sweat dripped from his chin. He started rocking back and forth and pounding his forehead again. Rachel took hold of his hand, but she couldn't stop its incessant movements. A shadow of worry and confusion crossed her face.

"What's wrong?" Eric asked.

"I'm not sure."

"Take a *guess*." He hadn't seen his brother in twenty years, but he'd seen him like this. It brought back all the protectiveness he'd always felt for Caleb.

"He's exhibiting classic symptoms of schizophrenia, the paranoia, the delusions."

"He did that when we were kids." Eric's voice rasped with bitterness as the memories surfaced. "I didn't know what they were back then. My grandmother called them spells. She'd lock him in the broom closet until he *calmed down*. Couldn't have the crazy grandkid embarrassing Olivia Stanhope in front of the help."

Rachel looked up at him, a dark pain in her expression that went beyond professional concern. For an instant she seemed to turn inward.

"He was locked in the dark?" Her voice choked on the last word. "How old were you?"

Eric couldn't tear his gaze from hers. He felt a strange compulsion to confide in her, something he'd never done—with anyone. He stepped closer, drawn by her empathy. "All our lives, until we were eleven. Until—" He'd almost said, *Until Caleb died.*

He rubbed his neck, his fingertips seeking the faint scar below his ear—the only visible reminder of that awful day. He glanced over at Caleb, whose fist pounded, pounded, against his forehead. Eric knew what Caleb was doing. He was trying to stop the voices.

"We were on the third floor, in Grandmother's sitting room," he said, barely even aware that he was speaking out loud. "Caleb's voices were loud that day. He pushed me and we got tangled up in the drapes and crashed through the window. The drapery cord caught me around the neck and kept me from falling. Caleb fell to the ground." He traced the scar with his fingertips.

Rachel's face drained of color as understanding dawned like the sun in her eyes. "Oh, my God. Your grandmother told you he died."

Eric nodded grimly. "She locked him away."

"How horrible for you. And you never knew?"

"I always wondered—" He stopped. He'd definitely said too much. He'd almost told this stranger his deepest fear.

He had to watch his every word. The shock of discovering that his brother was alive had lowered his defenses. Rachel Harper had nearly gotten inside his head, and that was something he could never allow. He blinked and turned toward Caleb, deliberately ignoring her question.

"If he's on fenpiprazole, he shouldn't be paranoid, should he? Isn't the usual reaction to withdrawal a catatonic state? The drug's half-life is only eight hours or so."

Rachel's disturbing gaze stayed on him for an instant, her blue eyes twinkling in surprise and admiration, immediately replaced by a puzzled frown. "That's right. You know a lot about fenpiprazole."

His lips curled. "Don't worry, I'm not taking it. I've read the literature."

Decker walked up beside Eric. "What's the problem?"

"Caleb seems to be having an adverse reaction to his medication. Even the shrink here agrees that his symptoms aren't typical of withdrawal from the drug he's on."

Decker looked at Rachel, who nodded.

"He's becoming increasingly paranoid," she said.

"Is that what caused him to panic and shoot the guard?"

Rachel took a step toward Decker and spoke in a low tone. "It certainly contributed. Caleb believes he's being used in some sort of experiments. He's been rambling about switched drugs and altered medical records. He has a history of paranoid behavior."

"So what Caleb is saying is not true?"

Rachel started to speak, but Eric cut her off. "Caleb does not lie. If he says there are secret experiments and altered records, I believe him."

"You believe—" She shook her head. "You haven't even seen him in twenty years. If you had experience dealing with mentally ill patients, you'd know you can't believe what they say." Her throat closed up. The terror and trauma of the past few hours had taken its toll on her usual detachment. She crossed her arms and clenched her jaw, pretending to study Caleb's jerky movements until she could compose herself.

Eric could not know. He'd been separated from his brother. He hadn't lived with the illness his whole life as she had.

Mental illness was cruel and greedy, sucking away at trust, at security, at love. Her mother's bipolar disorder had forced Rachel into the role of adult much too young. Her childhood had been a kaleidoscope of dark fear and brittle normalcy, spiked with blinding shards of mania.

She touched Caleb's shoulder. If Eric had been around his brother all these years, he'd be less inclined to trust him.

Caleb stirred at Rachel's touch, and her heart squeezed in compassion as his gaze sought his brother.

"Eric." Caleb's tone was filled with trust and love.

Eric stepped closer. "How're you feeling, bud?"

Caleb shook his head. "Hard to breathe. It's the drug. Had…this problem before."

He stood abruptly and grabbed Eric's arm. "You're going to…help me, right? You said I wouldn't…have to go back."

Eric's insides clenched at the fear in his brother's voice.

Rachel squeezed Caleb's shoulder. "It's okay, Caleb. We'll get you back to the Meadows, back on your medication, and—"

Caleb jerked away and shot her a wild-eyed glance.

Eric stepped protectively in front of Caleb. "Get away from my brother," he stormed, sudden anger pulsing through him like blood, his protective instincts overriding his professionalism.

Rachel stopped immediately and backed away. Eric had heard the fury and frustration that colored his voice. When he wasn't in total control, his throat muscles contracted and his voice rasped ominously, a legacy from the day he'd almost died, the day he'd lost his brother.

Behind him, he heard Decker talking to Rachel, making excuses for Eric's actions. "He's been under a lot of pressure with recent cases. He's exhausted and worried about his brother."

"Not a problem."

"Tell me about this Dr. Metzger."

"Let me take a look at your head wound first."

Eric shut out their voices. He stared directly into Caleb's eyes, steeling himself against the disorder he sensed inside his brother's head. "Hey, bud. Tell me about the experi-mental drug."

Caleb's breathing was labored. "It's Franken-metzger. He's…obsessed with curing schizophrenia. Has a secret—laboratory. Only certain people. Me. Misty. A few others. He injects us with chemicals—they're poison. Deadly." Caleb's ragged fingernails scratched Eric's arm. "I think he sucks the chemicals out of our brains. He's afraid I'll talk, that someone will believe me. He knows Misty and I found…proof."

"What kind of proof?"

"Eric." Rachel spoke from behind him. "Dr. Metzger is a world-famous neurologist, the foremost authority on schizophrenia in the country, arguably in the world. He's renowned for his research on the disease. But there are no research studies going on at the Meadows right now."

Eric bristled at the reverent tone of her voice. "It sounds like you're his biggest fan."

She blushed, but she lifted her chin and gave him back look for look. "I've always wanted to study with him. It's why I took this position. But my admiration for Gerhardt Metzger doesn't change the truth. There's no indication in Caleb's medical records that he has ever participated in a study, under Metzger or anyone else."

"That's because if he put me in a study, he couldn't do his private experiments on me. Don't you get it?" Caleb's voice rose.

"I'm afraid what you're seeing is classic paranoia. He needs his medication." She lowered her voice. "That's why we need to get him back there."

Eric clenched his jaw. "Don't say that again." His voice grated.

He placed his hand over Caleb's where it rested on his forearm. "What kind of proof did you and Misty find?"

Caleb's eyes darted rapidly back and forth before he settled his gaze on Eric. "I found a way to get into the basement without being seen. That's where the records are kept. We'd sneak down there…late at night. To be…together. There's a secret room. It's hidden behind the elevators. It's where Franken-metzger sucks our brains. He keeps the real records there."

Caleb's breath was coming in gasping bursts. "He kills people, Eric. Everybody pretends—the people just die, but Frankenmetzger kills them." Caleb's shoulders heaved with his labored breathing. "He has this big needle. It burns. And for a while every-thing seems beautiful—normal. But then it gets worse and you need more chemical. Dr. Green knew something was going on. Ask him."

Eric raised his brows at Rachel, who looked blank.

"I don't know Dr. Green," she said. "I may have seen his signature on some doctor's orders, but I've never met him. I don't think he's still there."

Eric turned to his boss. "Mitch, can we check out the Meadows? See if there have been any suspicious deaths, especially associated with Metzger?"

"I'll call Natasha," Decker said, punching a number into his cell phone.

If there were any information, Natasha Rudolph, the Division's computer expert, would find it.

"Eric—" Caleb gasped. He grabbed Eric's shirtsleeve, his mouth open, his face turning red.

"Hey, Doc," Eric called, suddenly alarmed. "He's having trouble breathing. Get over here!"

Rachel stepped over. "Let me take your pulse again, okay, Caleb?"

Caleb clawed at his throat. "I can't—" His voice died to a guttural rattle and he crumpled.

"Caleb!" Eric grabbed for him, but Caleb's limp body slid right through his hands to the floor.

"Move!" Rachel pushed Eric aside with surprising force. She bent over Caleb, her fingers at his carotid artery. Then she wet a finger and stuck it under his nose.

"What's wrong with him?"

"He's not breathing. Help me straighten him."
She pulled at Caleb's arms.

Eric quickly and efficiently laid Caleb's limp
body out, clamping his jaw against the lump that
sprang to his throat. He couldn't lose his brother
now. He'd just found him.

"Call 9-1-1," Rachel snapped at Decker, who was
just disconnecting from Natasha.

"I'll do better than that." Decker hit speed dial.
"Get that ambulance in here—now!" he ordered.

Rachel had quickly and efficiently positioned
Caleb for CPR and was breathing for him. "Respiratory—arrest," she said between puffs. "Doesn't
make sense—"

Eric felt the haunting guilt of helplessness. Caleb
wasn't breathing. He could die, and there was nothing Eric could do to save him.

Within seconds the house was swarming with officers and emergency medical technicians. A man
dressed in white with the letters EMT on his jacket
intubated Caleb and hooked him up to a portable respirator. Another quickly cleaned and bandaged
Decker's wound, while Decker filled in the sheriff
and the local FBI agent on what had happened. The
EMTs transferred Caleb to a gurney and started toward the front door.

Eric watched impotently, his brain on fast-for-
ward. His innate gift for processing a situation and

foreseeing the most likely outcome sent him on a virtual journey into the next few hours. Caleb would be rushed to the nearest hospital, admitted to the cardiopulmonary unit, stabilized, then transported back to the Meadows, where he'd be drugged again while he awaited arraignment on charges of attempted murder and kidnapping.

Then, like a poorly edited movie, images from the past flashed through his brain. Caleb pounding his fists against his head, screaming, begging Grandmother not to lock him in the broom closet. Him sitting next to the door, talking through the wooden barrier to his brother, promising to stay right there and protect Caleb from the monsters that clawed at his brain.

Can't go back there. I'm sorry, Eric.

"No! Wait!" Eric blurted.

"Sorry, sir, we've got to get him to a hospital. The portable respirator is only good for ten minutes."

"Mitch," Eric appealed to his boss, "I promised him he wouldn't have to go back to that place."

Decker clapped Eric's shoulder and squeezed. "It's probably the best place for him," he said kindly but firmly.

Eric shrugged off his boss's touch. "No. He's terrified. I'd go myself before I'd send him back in there."

Rachel's head snapped up and Mitch's eyes narrowed.

He met Rachel's shocked gaze, then look at Decker, who was already shaking his head.

Go himself. He hadn't even thought about it until he'd said the words. It made perfect sense. He'd go in there as Caleb—investigate what was really going on inside the Meadows.

"Mitch—"

"I know what you're thinking and the answer is no."

"It'll work. Send Caleb to the hospital with my identification. Put the word out that I collapsed, I was shot—whatever. Then after Rachel briefs me, I'll go in under- cover as Caleb and see what's going on."

"Slow down. Let's wait to hear from Natasha. There may be nothing going on at all."

Eric jerked his head at Rachel. "Ask *her.* She knows something's not right."

Rachel heard Eric's accusing words as she checked Caleb's oxygen levels.

When she lifted her gaze, she ran smack into Eric's intense brown stare. "Ask me what?"

The older man stepped forward. "What can you tell me about Metzger and his experiments?"

Rachel swallowed. In Eric's eyes she saw the reflection of doubt that had been planted in her brain.

"I—I'm not aware of any experiments. I've read Caleb's current file."

Eric silently challenged her to tell the whole truth.

She blinked and squeezed Caleb's limp hand. "But fenpiprazole doesn't cause respiratory problems."

Decker's blue eyes assessed her. "Never?"

She shook her head, her eyes still glued to Eric's. "Never. Of course he could have an infection, or this could be an allergic reaction…" Her voice died. She wasn't convincing anyone, not even herself.

"So what are you saying? Could someone be giving him the wrong drug?"

Rachel opened her mouth to deny it, but the word *no* wouldn't come out.

Eric's dark eyes snapped. "Caleb's right, isn't he? Someone at the Meadows is switching his medication."

The accusations were astounding. The idea that any physician would do such a thing went against everything she believed in as a psychiatrist. If what Caleb was describing was true, it was not only unethical and illegal, it could be deadly.

She moistened her lips and nodded reluctantly. "It's the only answer that fits all the facts."

Decker's phone rang. "Natasha, what have you found?"

Rachel stood next to Eric, uncomfortably conscious of his strength and determination. She still felt the brief thread of awareness that had stretched between them when their eyes first met.

The echo of the portable respirator provided a

low, rhythmic soundtrack as Decker listened with an occasional brief question.

"Okay, Nat. Stand by, and keep looking." Decker's face was grim when he pocketed his phone.

Behind Rachel, the EMT cleared his throat. "I've got one backup respirator, Dr. Harper. If we don't leave in the next five minutes, we might not make it in time."

She acknowledged the information with a nod.

Eric never took his eyes off Decker's face. "Natasha found problems, didn't she?"

"Nothing that would stand out, unless someone was looking. Apparently in the past five years there have been five deaths at the Meadows. Two suicides, one heart failure and two from natural causes."

"Heart failure. Natural causes." Eric's voice rang with irony as he turned to Rachel. "Interesting causes of death for a facility like the Meadows. Do you know the average age of the patients there, Doctor? Because I do. I looked it up."

Rachel gaped at him. She'd noticed, of course, that most of the residents were young people, but she'd never questioned it. She suddenly realized she hadn't questioned anything. She'd just been happy to have a job so close to her idol, Dr. Gerhardt Metzger. "The Meadows is not a nursing home."

Decker and Eric both waited in silence. She took

a deep breath. "The average age is probably thirty to thirty-five."

"It's thirty-four."

She cringed under the sting of censure in Eric's voice.

"Tell me, *Doctor,* how does a thirty-four-year-old die of natural causes?"

"Eric—" Decker's voice held a warning.

Eric rubbed his face in an obvious effort to hold on to his control. He sent a brief, worried glance toward Caleb. "How long have you worked there?"

She moistened her lips. "Two months."

"Two months." He laughed shortly. "So in your *vast* experience, has anyone referred to suspicious practices or odd incidents?"

She shook her head. "I'm a junior staffer. People don't talk to me a lot. And it's a private facility, catering to some extremely well-known names. It's impossible to access certain charts."

"Like Caleb's?"

She nodded reluctantly, her cheeks tinged with pink. "I had never seen a case of childhood-onset schizophrenia, and I've admired Dr. Metzger's work for a long time, so I requested Caleb's old records to study them. I was told they'd been archived. There was only three months of data available in his chart, less than six months on computer. His current administrative record makes no mention of a brother."

"No doubt." Eric's face was drawn. "So you've been refused a medical record. And from what you said earlier, certain employees disobey direct orders from physicians—or at least from you."

Rachel felt her face heating up. He was making her sound incompetent. She lifted her head, ready to defend herself.

"Eric," Decker broke in. "Natasha tells me that all deaths at the Meadows are investigated by a peer review board. The *official* finding in each case was that appropriate care was given and appropriate measures taken."

"Official finding?" Rachel spoke before she thought. She'd noticed Decker's inflection.

He nodded. "Were you aware that your predecessor was fired after he talked to the press about the last death, a suicide nine months ago?"

Feeling exposed and embarrassed, like a child caught unprepared for a test, Rachel shook her head. "My predecessor?"

"The information he gave the reporter was inflammatory, to say the least. He talked about bizarre responses to drugs, patients complaining that they were sedated and moved with no explanation, and odd activities by some of the staff."

The same things Caleb had been raving about.

Rachel's hand went to her mouth. From the grim look on the agent's face, she was deathly afraid he hadn't told them the whole story yet.

"We have to get that article," Eric said.

"Natasha's working on it."

"And talk to the physician. As soon as possible."

"That—" Decker took a breath "—poses a problem."

Rachel's heart thumped in her chest. A sense of foreboding weighed on her.

Eric's jaw muscle ticced and his fists clenched at his sides. "Don't tell me—"

Decker nodded. "Five months ago, Dr. Charles Green was found in his apartment, dead from an overdose of morphine and alcohol."

DR. RAJID PATEL considered his most famous staff member across the polished mahogany expanse of his desk. Gerhardt Metzger was almost certainly positioned to win the Nobel Prize in a few years if his research bore out his theories.

Right now, the famous neurologist was worried. And when his most valuable staff member was worried, Patel was worried.

Patel had been chief medical director at the Meadows for the past twenty-three years. He understood his job. A large and very important part of it was easing his staff's concerns. And of all his staff, there was not a one Dr. Patel was more interested in keeping happy than Gerhardt Metzger. The enormous sums of money Metzger had brought to the Meadows in grants, endowments and research projects in the past nine years since he'd joined the staff was worth any amount of humble bowing and scraping.

Metzger scratched his long sideburns and then removed his black-rimmed glasses and wiped them with a handkerchief.

"Will you have a brandy?" Patel asked, reaching into the bottom drawer of his desk.

Metzger nodded as he wiped his eyes then replaced his glasses. "When did the FBI say Mr. Baldwyn would be returned to us?" Metzger shifted in the brown leather chair. "They shouldn't be allowed to keep him this long. I want him back here, in his familiar environment, on his proper medications."

Patel handed Metzger the snifter of brandy, quelling the urge to run his finger around his tight collar. "I've been assured by the chief of staff at Walter Reed Hospital in D.C. that Baldwyn is doing well and will be transported back here tomorrow."

"Excellent."

"Gerhardt, he was very concerned about Baldwyn's symptoms. Suggested we double-check his medication history."

Metzger frowned. "I trust you assured him that the Meadows is entirely above reproach?"

Patel nodded quickly. "Of course. Certainly."

"I'm very distressed at this breach in security. Caleb Baldwyn is one of my most important subjects. His treatment should not be interrupted."

Patel ignored the small, worried voice inside him that kept asking what made Caleb Baldwyn so important. He'd agreed to give Metzger free rein in return for the money and positive publicity the famous researcher attracted to the Meadows, the recent pointed inquiries from the FDA about Metzger's last request for a new drug application notwithstanding.

He cleared his throat. "I've also been told that Dr. Harper was not injured and can return to work this week." Patel took a nervous sip of the fine brandy he favored, then sat back in his chair.

"Gerhardt, I'm prepared to fire her. Under the circumstances, there's more than adequate reason. After all, she failed to keep control of an inflammatory situation. With Grace Jones's statement that Dr. Harper tried to prevent her from sedating Baldwyn, there will be no problem making the case that it was Harper's negligence that caused the shooting."

Metzger scratched at his mutton chop sideburns, his gaze on the window behind Patel. He didn't speak.

"Really, it's no problem," Patel continued, setting

his snifter down onto the desktop with a tinkling rat-tle. "She doesn't even have to be given notice. I can terminate her on the spot." Patel's tie felt tighter and tighter.

He'd be much happier if the young psychiatrist were gone. The Meadows had never had an incident involving violence before she had come.

"No," Metzger said thoughtfully. "No. I have been impressed with certain aspects of Rachel Harper's performance. And she apparently has a rapport with Caleb Baldwyn. She could be useful."

"Useful?" Patel frowned. Metzger had de-manded the firing of staff for much less. Dr. Green for example.

Metzger harrumphed and tossed down the last of the expensive brandy. "Yes. I need information from her about what Baldwyn may have told her in his paranoid delusions to reacclimate Baldwyn to his surroundings. He's likely to be extremely confused and anxious when he returns. It will take him a while to recover. Perhaps I'll put him in isolation."

Patel drummed his fingers on the polished desk-top. "So you don't have a problem with Baldwyn remaining here until his arraignment for the shoot-ing? Because Walter Reed indicated they could keep him if we preferred not to have him around the other patients."

Metzger stood. "No. Not at all. In fact, when he

is receiving the right medication, Caleb Baldwyn is my ideal patient." He adjusted his glasses. "And now that Dr. Harper has spent so much time with him, it will be preferable to keep her here, where we can control her. Besides," Metzger continued, "it would be regrettable to have a repeat of the incident involving Dr. Green."

Patel wished everything the neurologist said didn't sound like a threat. "Believe me, I agree." It had taken all of Patel's accumulated favors, plus some serious groveling to keep the scandal over the loud-mouthed psychiatrist's death from a drug over-dose to a minimum.

Patel looked into Metzger's glittering eyes. "I would do anything to avoid another incident like that."

Metzger's thin lips stretched into a semblance of a smile. "Anything? That's good to know, Rajid. You may have to."

Chapter Three

"I can't do this." Rachel stood helplessly in the middle of the Washington, D.C., hotel suite where she was supposed to spend the night briefing Eric Baldwyn on everything she knew about the Meadows and Dr. Metzger.

She glanced at Eric, who paced back and forth in front of the large picture window, obviously troubled.

She couldn't blame him. He'd been so stunned when he'd first seen his brother.

Her heart squeezed with compassion as she imagined him as a little boy, trying to cope with his mentally ill twin. From what little he'd told her, his childhood must have been as bad as hers—if that were possible. His grandmother had wrenched his twin brother away from him when they were barely approaching puberty. The woman had lied to him all his life. Rachel couldn't even imagine such cruelty.

Yet Eric seemed very well adjusted, very normal. A fierce yearning grew inside her. If they'd met under different circumstances, she'd love to know more about this handsome, intriguing man.

But not like this.

She appealed to Special Agent Decker, who was preparing to leave.

"I can't be involved in an FBI undercover operation. If I get caught, it will be the end of my career."

FBI undercover operation. The words were incredible.

"Of course, I'm probably going to be fired anyway." She couldn't imagine the image-conscious Dr. Patel keeping her on his staff after she'd made such a mess of what should have been a minor incident.

She still wasn't sure how she'd lost control of that situation so quickly. Not to mention control of her life.

Had it only been a day ago that she was a junior staff psychiatrist at a peaceful, private mental institution with no more on her mind than catching up on her sleep after a long evening shift?

Now she'd seen two men shot, been kidnapped and was about to embark on a journey that could at best, ruin her credibility as a psychiatrist. At worst—if Caleb's ravings were true—it could get her killed.

"It's likely there won't be an investigation," Mitch Decker said. "We have federal investigators reviewing the information Natasha has gathered about the Meadows—patient deaths, any problems with accreditation, resignations or firings, as well as any information available on the death of Dr. Green. By tomorrow morning we may have found that there is nothing suspicious going on. Then you can go back to your job. But we must be prepared in case Eric has to impersonate his brother."

"Prepared." She wanted to laugh, but spending the night with Eric Baldwyn, teaching him how to be convincing as a mental patient—as his own brother—was anything but funny.

She'd always heard how quickly and efficiently the government could work when it wanted to. Today she'd seen it firsthand.

Within ten minutes of Decker's announcement of the apparent suicide of the doctor who had worked at the Meadows before her, an air ambulance had landed and picked up Caleb.

Rachel had explained the anomaly of Caleb's reaction to the onboard physician, and he'd written an order for a drug screen as soon as they got to the hospital.

"The chief medical director at the Meadows has been informed that both you and Caleb have been admitted to Walter Reed overnight for observation. The staff physician there is prepared to discuss Caleb's condition with the staff at the Meadows, if necessary." Decker glanced at his watch. "If our investigation turns up nothing suspicious, you and Caleb will be transported back to the Meadows as soon as he is able to travel. End of story. Otherwise, it will be you and Eric."

"But I don't know anything about the deaths, and I certainly know nothing about being an undercover agent."

"You know the layout of the hospital. You know the staff and the patients." Decker smiled at her and she couldn't help but feel his calm assurance wash over her.

"As Eric pointed out, I've only been there two months."

"You won't be expected to act as an undercover agent. Just be yourself. Help Eric. And by helping Eric, you can help Caleb and the other patients."

Rachel frowned, torn between her sworn oath to her patients and her loyalty to the other staff at the Meadows. "I don't like the idea of spying on my colleagues."

Decker's mouth tightened. "You only have one other choice. If you won't help us, we'll be forced to place you in a safe house until the investigation is over."

Rachel stared at Decker. "A safe house? You'd lock me up?"

He shrugged. "If we can't rely on you, we can't protect you. I can't have you going back to the

Meadows, putting yourself and my agent in danger, unless I can count on your full cooperation."

Rachel glanced at Eric, who hadn't spoken since they'd arrived at the luxury hotel near the Washington, D.C., field office of the FBI.

Like a caged leopard, sleek and restless, he paced from one side of the room to the other. He'd removed his sports jacket and his crisp white shirt hinted at the long, graceful muscles that rippled under his skin as he pushed a hand through his hair.

Caleb's ravings had sounded unbelievable. But he'd been telling the truth about his brother.

Eric stopped suddenly, as if he'd been interrupted. He frowned. "Have you heard anything about my brother?"

Decker shook his head. "Nothing yet. I'll let you know right away. I'm sure Caleb will be fine."

Eric's gaze slid to Rachel's, and she saw in his chocolate-brown eyes that he knew as well as she did that Caleb's chances of being "fine" were slim to none.

Mingled with concern for his brother was his suspicion of her. His expression, his very bearing, told her he didn't trust her. Nor did he think much of her abilities, obviously.

For her part, her impression of him had ratcheted up a few notches as Decker had explained Eric's job and outlined his background on their way to the D.C. hotel.

He was a special agent with the FBI's Division of Unsolved Mysteries. He served as the Division's profiler. He had a Ph.D. in Abnormal Psychology, and had done a fellowship on diseases of the brain at a highly regarded research hospital. No wonder he'd known all about the new drug. Rachel had heard in Decker's voice how much he cared for and admired the younger agent.

Decker's cell phone rang. Eric went rigid. Rachel held her breath.

After speaking briefly, Decker flipped the phone closed and sent Eric a slight negative shake of his head. "I've got to go. I'm testifying before the Senate early tomorrow and I'll be up all night myself, preparing."

"Mitch." Eric stopped pacing and rubbed his face wearily. "I apologize for getting you involved in this. Thank you for your help."

Decker shook Eric's hand. "I'll let you know as soon as I hear something. Rachel, what's your decision?"

Eric's troubled gaze called to her. Deep inside, she knew she'd already made up her mind. She moistened her lips and felt a small flutter under her breastbone as Eric's gaze lowered to her mouth.

She looked away and swallowed. "If patients'

lives are in danger, then I have no problem with co-operating. I will not be locked up. I won't abandon my job, or my patients."

"You have about seven hours to bring Eric up to speed on the hospital's layout, the names of nurses and patients he should know, and how Caleb would normally respond to specific situations, including his reactions to his medications."

Is that all? Rachel sighed. "I'll do my best."

Decker nodded. "Eric will explain the surveillance equipment." He indicated a nondescript black bag that had been delivered to the room just moments before.

With a last caution not to leave the room and to call the FBI agent stationed in the adjoining room if they needed anything, Decker shook Rachel's hand, thanked her for her cooperation, and left.

The door swung shut behind Decker, leaving Rachel alone in the room with Eric. His back was to her and he was staring out the hotel window, his legs braced apart and his arms crossed. He looked like a warrior, ready to defend everything he held dear. The strong bands of muscles across his back looked capable of supporting any burden.

Rachel wondered what it would be like to have someone like him at her side. Strong, fierce, willing to throw himself into danger to protect those he loved.

His body gave off tension like a fever. Although

his shoulders were straight and his head was high, corded muscles stood out in his neck.

He was hurting. She took a step toward him, drawn by his distress, longing to help him, but not knowing how.

So she retreated to a neutral topic. "Your boss is quite a guy."

Eric wiped both hands over his face, then slid them into the back pockets of his jeans and faced her.

His eyes glittered like brown glass. A faint dampness shimmered on his high cheekbones.

Her eyes welled in sympathy.

He shook his head, sniffed once and sat at the small conference table. "Yes, he is."

He picked up a meager stack of papers that Decker had left beside the black bag on the table. He tapped their edges against the wood, then shuffled through them like cards. "We'd better get started."

Rachel felt as though she was in a surreal play where everyone knew their marks and their lines except her.

"This is like every bad TV show I've ever seen about the FBI," she said with a little laugh. "How can you just go sneaking into a private mental facility with no evidence?"

Eric didn't react to her words as he examined one sheet after another. "We aren't sneaking in without evidence. Natasha and several other agents are working on the evidence right now. They'll spend all night gathering and verifying every fact available." He turned a sheet of paper sideways and studied it.

"Besides, Decker has contacted the local authorities and discussed our concerns with them. They've asked for our help." His gaze met hers. "That's how we do things in the Division of Unsolved Mysteries. It's a cooperative effort to solve cold cases."

"Cold cases?"

"Your predecessor's cause of death was ruled inconclusive. The case is not closed."

"So the FBI thinks he was murdered."

Eric shrugged. "It would be interesting to know what his colleagues think. Had anyone noticed anything wrong with him? Were they surprised by his death?"

"Nobody talked to me about him." She heard the note of disbelief in her own voice. How odd that no one had bothered to tell her about the previous psychiatrist's mysterious death.

"That's right. His death was six months ago and you've only been there two months. But I have to wonder, why didn't you ask why the job had become available? Positions at an exclusive facility like the Meadows can't be that easy to get."

His eyes pinned her and she squirmed. When he

looked at her with those brown eyes, he made her feel as if he knew all her darkest secrets. She clasped her hands on the tabletop and shook her head.

"I was stunned when I was offered the job. The Meadows is one of the most exclusive mental institutions in the Northeast." She hadn't wanted to seem too curious, hadn't wanted to do anything that would put her dream job in jeopardy.

"I was so happy to have the chance to work with Dr. Metzger."

"Metzger." Eric spat the name as if it were rotten meat. "Why him? Why a neurologist? You're a psychiatrist."

"He has a unique theory of mental illness. He believes that imbalances of chemicals in the brain can be corrected, possibly at the chromosomal level. He believes mental illness can be cured." She couldn't keep the excitement from her voice. "Some of the work that he and his mentor, Dr. James Farmer, have done is fascinating, and very promising."

Eric sent her an assessing look. "Maybe, given your high regard for Metzger, you shouldn't be involved. I heard you assuring Mitch that your patients are your first priority. But technically, I'm not one of your patients. How can I be sure you won't expose me?"

"I would never do that." As she said the words, she knew they were true. As much as she wanted Metzger's theories about curing mental illness to be true, she couldn't bear the idea that someone might be hurting the patients. It didn't matter who it was. She was a doctor. She'd taken an oath.

"Why not?"

It was a reasonable question. She thought of all the nights she'd cowered in her room as a child, praying that God would make her mother well again. She'd made it her life's work to conquer mental illness, to protect others from the helpless fear that haunted her. Her past gave her a unique understanding of Eric's need to help his brother, to protect him.

"You're going in there because of concern for your brother," she said. "I've agreed to do this because of concern for the patients I treat. I don't want anyone hurt—not even you."

Eric's inscrutable eyes, so like his brother's, searched hers. It was as if he could read her thoughts, as if he knew she had a deeper reason. She held his gaze as long as she could before she blinked and looked down at her hands.

"What the hell—?" Both of his hands shot across the table and grabbed hers.

"What are you doing?" She tried to jerk away.

His grip tightened on her fingers and he pulled. "Why didn't you say anything about these burns?" He bent his head and ran his thumb gently across a speck of adhesive that still clung to her flesh. Turning her hands palm up, he examined the angry red stripes across her wrists.

"You should have had one of the EMTs bandage these."

She'd almost forgotten the tape burns. Her skin shivered with sharply contrasting sensations—burning pain overlaid by the surprisingly tender stroke of Eric's soothing touch.

She looked down at the top of his head, his black hair that shimmered like silk, the ridiculously long eyelashes that cast shadows on his cheeks, the strong, elegant hands. A fine trembling started deep inside her.

When had she last been treated so gently? When had hands so strong and caring ever soothed her pain? She couldn't remember.

"You're trembling," he said, his voice rasping like soft rough cotton over her senses. He raised his head and his dark chocolate eyes lingered on her mouth for a brief instant before they met her gaze. "I didn't mean to hurt you."

Rachel couldn't speak. Her entire being was centered on the touch of his hands, the sound of his voice.

After another instant he sat up, letting his fingers trail down hers to the tips, as if he were reluctant to let go.

"We should wash those burns, get some antibiotic

ointment and bandage them." His voice was crisp, his gaze sharp.

Back to business.

She shook her head and hid her hands in her lap. "They're…fine. They hardly hurt at all." She pushed back her chair. "Excuse me for a minute, please. I have to—" She pointed vaguely toward the bathroom.

Relieved, Eric nodded stiffly. It would be good to have her out of the room for a few minutes. He needed to get his thoughts in order.

He couldn't stop himself from watching her walk toward the bathroom. She had on jeans and a snug T-shirt that read DREAM ON. She reached up to lift her hair off her long, graceful neck. The black strands slipped through her fingers like a fine silk scarf. The red marks on her wrists stood out against the blasé white of the hotel room walls.

When his thumb had glided over the delicate blue veins pulsing under her translucent skin, he'd felt the same thread of awareness he'd noticed the first time he'd seen her.

Something about her called to him, and he didn't like it. He didn't want to be drawn to her.

No one had ever evoked such a strong reaction in him. It was a mixture of empathic understanding and sensual awareness that went beyond anything he'd ever felt before.

He clamped his jaw. If he was going to protect his

brother, he had to guard against the odd, empathic connection between himself and Rachel. She could distract him, and he couldn't afford that.

As she disappeared into the bathroom, he leaned his forehead on his palms. The dull headache that had begun when Caleb collapsed had not abated. In fact, it was intensifying.

Eric massaged his temples, aware for the first time in twenty years that the dreams and thoughts and odd sensations he'd experienced all his life came, not from his own brain, but from his brother's. A shuddering relief clogged his throat with emotion. He'd lived for twenty years crippled by the fear that the sounds in his head were indications of schizophrenia.

But it was Caleb.

His eyes stung. Twenty years. God, he wished his grandmother was alive. He would take Caleb and confront her. He'd show her— What?

It didn't matter. If she'd cared about anyone but herself, she'd never have separated them, never have hidden Caleb away.

His hands clenched into fists at his temples. It was just as well that she'd died. At least he wouldn't have to fight her over his brother's destiny.

As Rachel returned to the table, Eric steeled himself against the effect of her presence and silently renewed his promise to Caleb.

I'll protect you, bud. Everything will be fine now.

He took a deep breath and composed his face and his thoughts before he leveled a look at Rachel. "Here we go," he said, looking through the papers that Decker had left.

"Looks like we have a sketchy blueprint of the main building at the Meadows, a fax from Natasha with a short description of each of the five deaths, plus a list of discharged patients and—" he held out a sheet "—the obituary of the doctor whose position you took."

Rachel couldn't make herself reach out to take the piece of paper. She glanced up at Eric, but his face was carefully blank. He flipped the sheet over and placed it on the table in front of her.

Daring her to read it.

She swallowed, then finally looked down.

"'Longview Physician Succumbs To Own Medicine.'" Her voice gave out. She skimmed the rest of the article.

"Complaints of loud music from an apartment Saturday sent police to Breckenridge Condominiums, where they discovered the nude body of Charles Green, a psychiatrist at the Meadows Psychiatric Facility. Cause of death was listed as a drug overdose. Dr. Rajid Patel, chief medical director at the Meadows called Green's death a tragedy. 'He was a fine doctor,' Patel reported. 'He was having some personal problems, but no one expected this.'"

She raised her head and met Eric's intense gaze.

"I never heard anything about this." Rachel's mouth was dry, her hands shaky. "Dr. Patel sounds like he's alluding to suicide."

Without taking his eyes off her, Eric handed her another page.

She took it with numb fingers. "Inquest Into Psychiatrist's Death Inconclusive." She took a deep breath and read on.

"At a coroner's inquest into the death of Dr. Charles Green, the judge ruled that the large amount of a prescription drug plus a high level of alcohol in the psychiatrist's system was consistent with overdose, either self-ingested or by person or persons unknown. A reporter's statement that Dr. Green had contacted him about 'suspicious goings on' at the Meadows was ruled hearsay, with no evidence to back up his claims."

Rachel stared at the last few words. "No evidence to back up the claims." She looked up at Eric. "Wouldn't the reporter have taped Dr. Green's statement?"

Eric raised a brow. "Maybe Green wouldn't let him. Maybe he was in fear for his job—or his life."

"His life?" She started as his cell phone rang.

He snagged it from his pocket. "Yeah?" He stood and turned his back on her. "Mitch, how's Caleb?"

The raw worry in his voice made Rachel want to

turn away. She felt like an eavesdropper. But she was as concerned about Caleb as Eric was. It made no sense that Caleb had just stopped breathing.

Remembering the agonizingly long seconds it had taken the ambulance personnel to get into the house and take over the CPR she'd started, she sent up a prayer that Caleb hadn't suffered any brain damage from lack of oxygen.

Dying to know what Decker was saying, she held her breath. Eric stood as stiff and straight as a soldier receiving orders.

"Yes, sir." His voice was steady, but his knuckles whitened visibly. "We'll be ready."

He turned to face her and the dull grief in his eyes sent horror shuddering through her. Had Caleb died? Had all their efforts not been enough?

As he closed the phone and pocketed it, Rachel stood and stepped toward him.

"Eric? What's happened to Caleb?" She touched Eric's forearm and felt the sleek muscles bunch under her fingertips.

His dark eyes burned into hers. "We need to get to work, Dr. Harper. You have a lot of information to share with me between now and five o'clock in the morning."

Rachel stared at him. She felt numb. "What about Caleb?"

"We'll be picked up in an unmarked van and

transported to Walter Reed. Then, as soon as possible, Dr. Rachel Harper and Caleb Baldwyn will be transferred by ambulance back to the Meadows." His gaze never wavered, his voice was steady, but Rachel saw in the depths of his dark eyes that something awful had happened.

"Caleb and me?" she whispered hopefully, bracing herself for his answer.

He shook his head. "You and me." He rubbed his hand over his face in a heartrending gesture that seemed designed to help him keep control of his emotions.

"Caleb can't go."

Rachel held her breath.

"The drug screen on my brother showed no fenpiprazole in his body."

"But that's impossible. Traces are detectable in the bloodstream for up to a month—" She stopped as the truth dawned.

Eric's gaze bore into her.

"So Caleb was telling the truth," she said, shocked. "It was withdrawal of the *substituted* drug that caused his respiratory arrest."

"I told you, my brother doesn't lie."

"Did they find out what the drug is?"

"They've found traces of a foreign substance in his blood, but they can't identify it."

From Eric's pallor and his white, pinched face,

she was afraid she already knew the answer to her next question. "How is Caleb?"

Eric rubbed his temples. "He's in intensive care. The doctors told Mitch he might not make it."

"Oh, Eric. I'm so sorry." She bit her lip, trying to hold back the tears, but they spilled over from her eyes anyway. "Poor Caleb."

"And that's not all. You might want to sit down for this one." His voice was tight, controlled.

Rachel's heart drummed in her chest as she lifted her chin and stood her ground. "What is it?"

"Our forensics expert, Laurel Gillespie, has been studying the M.E.'s findings in Dr. Green's death. She has concluded that his death couldn't have been accidental."

Rachel felt the room begin to spin. She forced herself to remain upright. A part of her brain registered the comforting feeling of Eric's hand on her arm, but all her strength was concentrated on understanding what he had said. For some reason her brain wasn't working well.

"Not accidental?" She heard the fear in her voice.

Eric's face was grim as he shook his head.

"Your predecessor apparently asked too many questions. He was murdered."

Chapter Four

As the ambulance delivering Rachel and Eric back to the Meadows pulled up to the front door of the old Georgian mansion that had been turned into a hospital, Rachel saw Dr. Patel and Dr. Metzger both waiting, along with a gurney manned by two men who looked more like weight lifters than orderlies.

"The tall, balding dark man is Dr. Patel. He's the chief medical director for the Meadows. Dr. Metzger has bushy hair and long sideburns," she whispered to Eric, who was lying flat on a gurney with Velcro straps across his chest, legs and wrists.

He glanced at her. His face was pale, his eyes edged with panic. Those eyes tore at her composure.

She had the urge to touch him, to assure him that everything would be fine. But she couldn't quite bring herself to do it. She was still reeling from her first sight of him this morning.

Somehow he'd managed to make himself almost indistinguishable from his brother. He'd cut—or bitten—his fingernails down to the quick. He'd gotten a haircut that matched his brother's and, worst of all, his eyes seemed to have lost their glow.

"Patel bald, Metzger bushy," he muttered.

"Right, although I don't know why they're both meeting the ambulance."

"I doubt they've ever had an escaped patient returned to them by the FBI." She heard the strain in his voice.

"Try to stay calm, Eric."

He clenched his fists and angled his head to glance at her. The silent plea in his eyes tugged at her heart.

She lay her hand on his shoulder. The muscles there spasmed and, for a brief moment, he strained against the straps.

"Be careful, you're going to bruise your wrists and arms."

He closed his eyes. "What would Caleb do?" His voice was choked.

Rachel's throat tightened to hear him so close to losing control.

"Caleb hates to be restrained. He fights it, but remember, he's—you're—weak."

The back doors of the ambulance opened, letting in a blast of sunlight. Eric cringed and lifted his head.

"No!" he snapped. "No!"

Rachel patted his forearm, which was rock-hard with tension. He jerked and glanced over at her.

The opaque blackness of his eyes cut through her like a dark laser.

"Don't let them take me. Rachel, stay with me," he cried, his body going rigid.

Her heart thumped. Tears stung her eyes. The tense, controlled FBI agent was gone and in his place was a sick, paranoid young man. She searched his face, desperately seeking the real, rational man beneath the undercover persona. But he wasn't there—not that she could find.

He could be Caleb.

The two weight lifters grabbed the end of the portable gurney, jerked it out of the ambulance and, with almost no effort, ripped the Velcro straps apart and transferred Eric to the hospital's gurney.

To her astonishment, Dr. Patel's long face appeared at the door of the ambulance, smiling self-consciously.

Not the reception she was expecting. He held out his hand to her. "Dr. Harper. We're so glad to have you back, safe and sound."

She tried to return his smile, but she was too worried about Eric.

"I trust your night in Walter Reed Hospital helped you recuperate from your ordeal?" he asked as he helped her down from the ambulance.

Rachel tried to watch Eric, but the orderlies were wheeling him away. She saw his torso arch upward as he struggled against his restraints, and heard him call out to her.

"Rachel! Don't let them—"

Dr. Metzger was walking alongside the gurney. He pressed on Eric's chest and Eric collapsed back.

"Dr. Harper?"

She couldn't pull her gaze away. "I should probably go with him. Help get him settled."

Patel shook his head. "It is truly unfortunate, but not unexpected that he would fight. Mr. Baldwyn is obviously much more unstable than we had previously realized."

"He's just frightened. I'd like to be with him."

Patel touched her bandaged wrist. "Dr. Metzger is with him. He's in excellent hands. What about you? Caleb injured you."

"Not on purpose." She glanced past him as the automatic doors closed, separating her from Eric.

Dr. Metzger walked up beside Patel. "Dr. Harper, I understand I have you to thank for getting our Mr. Baldwyn back to us."

His voice was pleasant, his face serene, but Rachel detected an undercurrent she couldn't quite identify. She looked at the doctor she'd idolized since medical school, then back at Dr. Patel. Their benevolent gazes unnerved her.

Taking a deep breath, she took a step backward.

"I really need to check on Caleb. Thank you for your concern."

She edged around Dr. Patel, but he caught her arm. "I'm afraid your presence might upset Mr. Baldwyn. You should take a day or two off," he said, "don't you think?"

She strained imperceptibly away from the chief medical director, acutely aware of the bulk of the miniature digital camera, the microcommunicators, and the other state of the art gadgets the FBI had given her. They weighed heavily in her pockets and she didn't want Patel or anyone else to notice them.

"No, I don't. I'm fine, really. I can't just sit in my apartment. I need to get back to work."

His beady eyes assessed her. "We can discuss that later. But first, if you don't mind, I would like to talk with you—in my office."

"Are they taking Caleb back to his room?" She felt close to panic. She'd gone over with Eric what would happen once they arrived back at the Meadows. She'd warned him not to fight the orderlies. She'd explained that he'd be restrained until they'd verified that he wasn't going to hurt himself or others.

He'd listened carefully and agreed with her. But after seeing him, struggling against the restraints, helpless fear contorting his face, she was doubly concerned. Was he that good an actor? Or was he really panicked? She had to check on him.

Dr. Patel ignored her question. Still holding on to her arm, he'd marched her toward the administrative wing. Dr. Metzger muttered something about making sure his patient was settled in and headed in the direction the orderlies had taken Eric.

Rachel followed Dr. Patel reluctantly. Mitch Decker had warned her about the inevitable questions. The doctors would want to know anything Caleb had told her. Mitch had cautioned her to tell the truth as much as possible.

You'll feel more at ease, he'd promised.

So far, he was wrong. She'd never felt less at ease in her life.

GERHARDT METZGER stepped into Caleb Baldwyn's room as Thomas, the tall, muscular male nurse, and an orderly wrested Caleb from the gurney to the bed. Caleb struggled halfheartedly.

"You want restraints, Doctor?" Thomas asked.

Metzger shook his head. "I don't think that's necessary. Caleb, do you know where you are?"

Caleb's face registered an odd, cautious look. "Yes," he croaked.

"Are you having trouble breathing?"

Caleb's gaze darted around the room. "Sometimes." He arched his neck. "Stings."

Metzger nodded. "I know, Caleb. We're going to take care of that right now. You trust me, don't you?

Remember, we talked about how if we worked together we could find a cure?"

"I remember."

"You know you shouldn't have run away, don't you?"

Caleb nodded and closed his eyes.

"Who did you talk to, Caleb? Did you have to answer a lot of questions?"

"Rachel. I talked to Rachel." He strained against the orderly's grip. "Where's Rachel?"

"She's fine. Who else did you talk to?"

"Government agents, but I didn't tell them anything." He glared at Metzger. "I should have. I should have told them what you did to Misty. I should have told them—"

Metzger breathed a sigh of relief. "But you didn't."

"They'd have put me in the loony bin." He laughed. "You can't believe crazy people."

Metzger nodded at Thomas. "Sedate him while the orderly is here to hold him."

Caleb's eyes rolled wildly as the orderly pinned him to the bed and Thomas injected the sedative.

Almost immediately Caleb took a sharp breath, then stopped struggling.

"Humph, that was fast," Thomas said. "He's usually more resistant than that to the drug."

Metzger stepped over to the bed and looked down at the most promising test subject he'd ever had. Caleb should have been sicker. He should have been in acute respiratory distress, at the least. Metzger hooked his stethoscope into his ears and listened to Caleb's breathing and heart rate. He seemed remarkably healthy, given the circumstances.

"You can go," he said to the orderly. "Thomas, stay for a moment, please."

He leaned over, and with thumb and forefinger, separated Caleb's eyelids to look at his pupils. "There's something wrong, Thomas. Your observation about Mr. Bald- wyn's reaction to the sedative was correct. Please keep an eye on him and report anything unusual to me."

"Yes, sir."

"It's possible we may be forced to accelerate our timeline. Be prepared. If anything happens, we may have to react within a few minutes."

"What can happen?"

Metzger scowled. "The FDA is questioning my latest new drug application. And now it's possible either Caleb or Dr. Harper may have said something to the FBI."

"What about the other patients?"

"Let's start weaning them off the drug. I'll leave them here if I have to, but Caleb Baldwyn will be going to Germany with us, no matter what."

RACHEL SAT IN A buttery-soft leather chair, waiting for Dr. Patel to finish a telephone call his secretary had insisted he take.

He hung up the phone and turned to her, his mournful face made even more melancholy by his halfhearted smile. "I truly regret the trauma you must have experienced."

She nodded. "I'm just glad I was there to help Caleb."

"Ah, yes." Patel leaned back in his chair, tenting his fingers. "How *did* you happen to be in the neurology ward so late at night, just in time to involve yourself in a patient incident?"

The question was innocent enough, but Patel's tone bore a note similar to Dr. Metzger's. An undercurrent of suspicion, as if he expected her to lie.

She answered honestly. "I always park my car at the side entrance to the neurology wing. It's near the hospital staff lockers, and the parking lot is well lighted there."

"Ah. And how did you find yourself in the sunroom?"

Rachel shifted in her seat. It didn't matter that she'd expected these questions. The piercing eyes shining out of that serene face made her nervous. Did he blame her for the shooting?

"Have you talked to the night nurse, Grace Jones? She stopped me on my way out and asked me to check on Caleb. He was sleepwalking."

Patel's dark slanted brows rose. "Mrs. Jones said that you asked *her* where Caleb was."

Rachel gaped at the doctor. "She said that?" Why would Gracie lie? She'd always been helpful and friendly. "No, sir. She's wrong. She stopped me as I was leaving."

Dr. Patel picked up a pencil and toyed with it. "Now see, Dr. Harper, this is where things become confusing. Mrs. Jones states that Caleb had agreed to go back to bed when you came in. Something about seeing you triggered his agitation."

Indignation swirled through her. "That is not true." She sat up. "Caleb was already awake and very agitated when I got there. Surely you know how sleepwalkers can be when they're awakened. Gracie wanted to call Security, but I told her not to. I'd handle it. But she called them anyway. Caleb was almost ready to go back to bed when Darrell showed up."

Patel shrugged. "Mrs. Jones has worked here for eight years."

"And I've been here two months. What are you saying, sir?"

"I just cannot imagine why one of the Meadows's most loyal and trusted nurses would lie about something like that."

"Neither can I."

Dr. Metzger appeared at the door. "I've given Mr. Baldwyn a sedative and ordered him placed on hourly bed checks throughout the night."

His words almost stopped Rachel's heart. She'd expected them to sedate him, at least the first day, but hearing Dr. Metzger confirm it sent terror shooting through her as she imagined Eric's intense, vital body limp with drugs.

"Hourly bed checks? You think he's suicidal?"

Metzger glanced at Patel, who leaned forward, placing his elbows on his desk, and scrutinized her. "He did shoot someone, Dr. Harper. Is there a problem with your level of emotional involvement with Mr. Baldwyn?"

Rachel felt as though the walls were closing in. Both doctors stared at her.

"I just need to be sure he's all right," she blurted.

"We have competent staff, Dr. Harper. Are you quite sure *you* are all right?"

"He's been through so much. He trusts me," she mumbled. "We have a good relationship."

"He actually became quite disturbed when I mentioned your name."

Rachel frowned at the neurologist. "What did you say to him?"

Metzger sent her a quelling glance, then raised a brow at Patel.

The look that passed between the two physicians told Rachel she was facing a united front.

Dr. Patel shook his head. "I'm afraid Dr. Metzger and I agree. Caleb needs constant observation right now, and we aren't sure what seeing you might do to him. He will be arraigned in two weeks for the shooting of Darrell Freeman, and until that time, we are treating him as potentially violent."

"Please," Rachel said desperately. "Let me be assigned to him. I can help him. I know I can."

Metzger glanced at Patel, then at Rachel. "Dr. Harper, we need to understand Caleb's state of mind. Why he became violent. What his reasoning was for kidnapping you." He scratched his bushy sideburns. "I'm certain that, as a psychiatrist, you observed and evaluated his behavior. I know you haven't had time to make a report, but give me an assessment."

"Time to—" Rachel almost laughed. Her feet had barely touched the ground before they'd rushed her in here to grill her.

Metzger watched her closely as he slid his fat, black fountain pen up and down in his lab coat pocket. There was a small ink stain on the bottom seam of the pocket.

"An assessment," she repeated. What did they want to hear? What would help Eric in his role as Caleb? "I don't believe Caleb is violent. When Darrell rushed him, Caleb felt cornered. All he'd wanted to do was to get back to his room, and Darrell was between him and the door."

Metzger shifted in his chair and a look of irritation crossed his face. "No, no, Dr. Harper. We know what happened in the sunroom. We have Mrs. Jones's account. I need to know his symptoms. Physical, neurological."

"But Gracie's account was not—"

"Please, Dr. Harper," Dr. Patel interjected.

Rachel swallowed the retort that struggled to escape her throat. She had to cooperate. If she were labeled difficult, it could hurt her chances of getting to Eric.

"Caleb was highly agitated. He expressed genuine remorse for shooting Darrell, and I had the definite impression that he grabbed me and ran simply because he was afraid of what would happen to him." She didn't mention his determination to find his brother.

"He knew exactly where he was going, so he wasn't out of touch with reality. He directed me straight to his grandmother's house." She paused, considering her next words carefully. "I got the impression that it may have been his grandmother's death that upset him. Wasn't she the last of his family?" She held her breath.

Patel's dark eyes flashed as he glanced at Metzger then back at her. "Ah, Dr. Harper. Interesting assessment. His grandmother's death as the inciting incident. What do you think, Gerhardt?"

"His physical symptoms, please." Metzger pulled off his glasses and cleaned them with a handkerchief, seeming completely uninterested in the mention of Caleb's family.

Rachel shifted in her chair. What was Metzger fishing for? The respiratory distress? His paranoia? How far could she go without mentioning Eric?

"I thought his physical symptoms were odd, considering his medications."

Metzger relaxed visibly as he pushed his glasses back onto his nose. "Odd?"

She nodded, pretending to fuss with the bandages on her wrists. "He grew increasingly paranoid and he seemed to have difficulty breathing."

"Please explain."

"He exhibited symptoms of shock—pale, clammy skin, heightened respiration, sweating. A couple of times I thought he might stop breathing altogether."

Metzger leaned forward. "He never did?"

She shook her head. "No, although he did struggle at times. I was worried that he might be having a severe allergic reaction."

"Indeed? How did you treat his symptoms?"

Rachel shrugged. "I was bound most of the time. I encouraged him to lie down and to breathe slowly and deeply. Luckily, the FBI had EMTs on the scene."

"Luckily." Metzger rose, sending a look toward

Dr. Patel. "I will make arrangements to talk with you later, Dr. Harper. I have rounds." He left the office.

"Dr. Patel? May I see Caleb?"

"Dr. Harper—Rachel." Patel shook his head regretfully. "If it weren't for Dr. Metzger's vehement defense of you, you would be facing termination. This is the first incident of patient violence involving a psychiatrist at our facility. It is grounds for immediate dismissal. However—" he shrugged and plucked a tissue from a box on his desk to blot his upper lip "—Dr. Metzger stepped in on your behalf. He apparently believes that you are a good doctor. He thinks you have a certain fascination for Caleb Baldwyn right now—because he kidnapped you and because you spent so much time alone with him."

Rachel stood, straightening her back and lifting her chin. "I'm not *fascinated* with him. I am a physician. The moment Caleb Baldwyn took me hostage, I became responsible for him. I took care of him. I know him now, and I should be with him. I'm a familiar face. He responds to me."

Patel's eyes shuttered and his expression turned stony. "The issue is closed."

"Issue?" she broke in. Her relationship with Caleb was viewed as an *issue.* "So you're telling me you don't trust my judgment?"

The chief medical director's face reflected his

irritation. "The next two weeks, while we wait for Mr. Baldwyn's arraignment, will determine that."

"I don't understand."

"How extensively were you questioned by the FBI? You have hardly mentioned that aspect of your kidnapping."

Rachel spread her hands. "Not very. The Special Agent in Charge was Mitchell Decker, who worked with the local agent as well as the county sheriff. They asked me about the shooting and about Caleb's illness."

"How much talking did Caleb do?"

"Caleb hardly spoke. He was in severe distress." Rachel's guard went up immediately. She'd been briefed by Mitch and Eric about what questions to expect. So far they were right on target. "What he did say was largely nonsensical. You know, talking about evil doctors and conspiracies and experiments." She smiled conspiratorially. "The usual paranoid delusions."

Patel nodded and Rachel saw a careful loosening of his tense facial muscles. She'd allayed his concerns. They would have been suspicious if she hadn't mentioned Caleb's accusations.

She suppressed a relieved sigh.

"Thank you, Dr. Harper. It sounds like you represented the Meadows in a favorable light. Until we can assess Mr. Baldwyn's state of mind, and find out what the charges against him will be, we don't feel it is in your best interests to be near him. You will be assigned elsewhere, for your own protection, of course."

Her relief changed to panic. "Elsewhere? W-where are you assigning me?"

"The Women's Dependency Center."

"Oh, no!"

The women's drug treatment facility was on the other side of the grounds from the acute neurological unit, near her apartment.

They were cutting her off from any contact with Eric.

LATE THAT NIGHT, Rachel walked across the grounds and into the main hospital. She'd checked the duty roster earlier. The security guard who'd taken the night shift after Darrell's shooting was new. She'd never met him.

She strode past him with a scant nod, keeping her expression carefully preoccupied, as if she were concerned about a difficult patient. As soon as she was past the security desk, she headed straight for the service hall.

When the Meadows was renovated and turned into a mental facility back in 1917, the builder had kept the aristocratic elegance of the original house. The carved mahogany woodwork had been stripped of years of paint and refinished. The doors through the main hallways gleamed with polish, accenting their high, ornate glass transoms. Long draperies hung to the hardwood floors and accented the rows of paned windows.

In contrast to the main corridors, the back halls were dull and shabby. They were used to transport meal carts and trash bins.

Stepping past bags of trash, Rachel headed west toward the neurology wing. Passing a cleaning woman pushing a mop and bucket, Rachel stopped at the elevator lobby, about twenty feet from the nurses' station.

She was facing the main hall of the neurology wing. It was after eleven. Most of the patients would be asleep. Gracie had just come on duty, and if she were following her usual routine, she'd be in the medication room, counting the narcotics.

Rachel slipped down the hall, trying to think of a plausible excuse for being here if Gracie caught her. Neither Dr. Patel nor Dr. Metzger had specifically told her she was banned from the neurology ward, but the implication had been obvious.

The counter in front of the nurses' workstation was deserted. The door to the medication room was ajar and the light was on. Rachel let out a careful sigh of relief. Gracie was right where Rachel had expected her to be.

Carefully, quietly, Rachel slipped up the hall to Room 3— Caleb's room. The door was closed.

With her hand on the door handle, Rachel considered the consequences of what she was about to do. If another nurse or an orderly were in Eric's room, Rachel would be caught. Considering what Patel had said, she'd probably be fired.

She took a deep, calming breath and pushed open the door. The room was dark, the only light coming from the night-lights above the bed.

Eric lay still and pale, the sheets tucked neatly around his bare torso. His eyes were closed and his hands were at his sides.

A pang of apprehension streaked through her. He looked so much like Caleb and yet so different. His dark lashes rested against his cheeks. His strong, stern mouth was relaxed.

"Eric?" she whispered.

He didn't stir. How much sedative had they given him? She stepped closer and touched his forearm. The muscle under his sleek skin quivered and his eyelids twitched.

She placed her mouth against his ear, trying to ignore the way his dark hair tickled her nose. "Eric. Please wake up."

Eric heard his name. Who was bothering him? The faint scent of something tart and sweet, something familiar, surrounded him.

The voice that rang like a bell in his head called his name again. He opened his eyes.

And blinked. Why was everything so hazy?

"Eric. Thank God, you're awake."

It was Rachel. He squeezed his eyes shut then opened them again.

"Damn," he whispered hoarsely. "What'd they do to me?" He coughed and tried to sit up.

"Don't move too fast. You've been sedated."

He fell back against the pillows. "Oh, yeah." A fog still clouded his brain, but memories began to surface. He flexed his left arm, where he still felt the sting of the injection. "Damn big needle."

He licked his lips. His throat felt raw.

Rachel picked up an insulated cup and held the straw for him to drink.

"I can do it." He reached for the cup but his fingers didn't want to work.

She put her hands over his and secured them around the cup.

It was an automatic gesture, one she'd probably used a hundred times to help her patients, but her touch streaked through him, straight to his groin, and he felt himself stirring. He raised his drowsy gaze to hers. The damn sedative had lowered his natural defenses. Oddly it seemed to have increased his libido.

Her eyes were sharp, assessing, but behind the

physician's scrutiny, there was something else. In the depths of her gaze was a sad look. Was it pity?

He took a long swallow of water, shivering as the cold liquid hit his empty stomach.

His head felt as heavy as a rock. He lay back against the pillows and closed his eyes. "What happened to that whopping dose of narcotic antagonist medication they gave me at the hospital? I thought it was supposed to counteract these sedatives."

"The antagonist is a long-acting drug. Its effects will increase as your body builds up its own resistance to the drugs. Remember, they think they're medicating Caleb, and his system is quite resistant to the drugs's effects. He requires larger doses."

"I can't operate like this. What else can you do?"

She didn't say anything. With a huge effort, he lifted his heavy eyelids and looked at her.

The sad look was gone and in its place was worry. "I can't do much, Eric. You're just going to have to fight it. Plus, you have to be careful what you say and do. The more out of control they think you are, the more they'll medicate you."

"Isn't it unethical to use drugs to restrain patients? Is this how they treated my brother? Is this how they treat other mentally ill people?" His senses sharpened as his anger grew. That was good to know. "Who gave them the right to control people's minds and bodies?"

"It's not as inhumane as it seems to you right now. Just try to work with it, and please, be careful what you say. They're watching you."

"Work with it." As the bite of fury pushed away the drugged haze, he sat up. "I'll work with it, all right. Just enough to find out what kind of heinous experiments are going on in this snake pit." He licked his lips and reached for the water. This time, using all his concentration, he managed to hold on to the cup. He took a long drink. He couldn't let Caleb come back to this place.

Caleb. His brother's name sparked a memory, or a dream. "I heard something." He took another drink of the refreshing water. "Right after the nurse gave me the shot." He rubbed his face. "Who was in here? An orderly held me down. The male nurse had the syringe. Somebody was talking. Was it Metzger?"

"Dr. Metzger went to check on you while I was talking to Dr. Patel."

Eric tried to force his brain to work, but a fog still clouded his thoughts. "Something about Germany."

"Germany? Were you dreaming? Maybe your brain was trying to place Metzger's accent."

"Maybe." He frowned. He'd have to think about that later. Right now he needed information. "Are they going to keep me sedated? Is this a locked ward? What should I expect?"

Rachel couldn't take her eyes off him. The sheet

had slid down as he'd sat up, revealing the sleek planes of his chest and shoulders. His long, blunt fingers encircled the plastic cup, their ragged nails jarring in contrast to his elegant body.

Her reaction to him disturbed her. Eric was Caleb's brother. With his torn fingernails and short haircut, he could *be* Caleb.

As far as she was concerned, he was her patient, just as Caleb had been. And as much as she cared about her patients, there was no way she'd ever be physically attracted to one, much less emotionally involved. Caring too much would only lead to heartache.

She'd been down that path, with her mother. When she'd taken her oath as a physician, she'd made a private vow to remain detached. She would do everything in her power to give her patients the best of care, but she would never, ever, involve her heart.

Chapter Five

Rachel swallowed as Eric's gaze met hers, his dark eyes flashing. For an instant she had the feeling he could read her mind.

She lowered her gaze and needlessly adjusted the position of the cup on the bedside table.

"Rachel? My daily routine?"

Composing her face, she gathered her cloak of professional detachment around her. "You're not on a lockdown ward, so your mornings will be fairly ordinary. You'll shower, dress, go to breakfast in the dining room. Tomorrow, you'll probably have a session with Dr. Metzger."

"So how do I act? How do I convince Metzger that I am Caleb?"

"Have you ever had any…experience with mental illness? Yourself, I mean?"

Eric's face closed down. His shoulders grew rigid with tension. The aura of safety and trust that emanated from him dissipated. "No. No, I haven't. Just dreams."

"Dreams? What kind of dreams?"

He shot her an ironic glance. "No psychoanalysis needed, Doctor. Just dreams."

Rachel's instinctive armor came up and her pulse fluttered with apprehension. She blew out a breath and immediately quelled the thoughts that had formed in her mind. Eric was not schizophrenic, like his brother. He was sane and safe. He was here to play a part.

"If you're right about Metzger—that he's giving Caleb drugs that make him worse—you may experience some dissociative episodes. You may feel alienated, disconnected from reality—"

"I'm familiar with dissociation."

"I'm just trying to warn you, to help you cope. It's going to take all your strength to fight the effects of the medication. If you've ever had any symptoms, I need to know that now."

His silence gave her the answer she didn't want to hear. The flutter of her pulse made her lips quiver. She tightened them.

After a moment he took a long breath. "Don't worry. I can fight the drugs."

His voice chilled her like a winter wind. She couldn't read his expression. Was he angry at her for asking about his mental health? Or was her first instinct correct? Was Eric in danger of succumbing to the mental illness that had stolen his brother away from him?

Suppressing a shiver, she stood. "I'd better go before someone sees me."

She hated the flash of unease that crossed his face.

"When will you be back?" he asked.

"I've been assigned to the Women's Dependency Center. They're watching me, so it's going to be difficult to get in here. I want to study the blueprints, see if I can find an unguarded door. This is the oldest building on the grounds. It was once a billionaire's mansion. There are probably several entrances."

"Call Natasha. She's going over the layout. If there's anything, she'll find it." He gave her Natasha Rudolph's telephone number.

Eric watched her as she jotted the number down on a small notepad. He realized how worried he'd been about her.

While he'd pretended to panic as they'd strapped him to the gurney and hauled him away, the chief medical director had waylaid Rachel. It hadn't occurred to him that Rachel's job might be in jeopardy until that moment. He'd been too worried about his brother.

His pretense of panic had turned terrifyingly real as the sedative had overpowered his brain. He'd feared he might never see her again.

"We need to plan how we'll meet."

Rachel's worried face tightened. "Eric, I can't figure out a way to do that. I'm being deliberately separated from you. Until your—until Caleb's arraignment, you'll be under suicide watch."

"Suicide watch!"

She nodded, dropping her gaze. "They consider you volatile, a danger to yourself or others. You probably won't be restrained, unless you misbehave, but your privileges will be restricted, and at night you'll be on hourly bed checks."

Eric cursed. How in hell was he supposed to find out anything under these conditions? A shard of doubt embedded itself in his chest. Maybe this had been a bad idea.

Frightening images popped into his brain. Dark corridors, rows of shelves, a secret passage. Was his drugged brain hallucinating? Or was he seeing things through Caleb's eyes?

Thanks for the reminder, bud.

He had to do this. He had to protect Caleb. And now he was responsible for Rachel's safety, too. With his brother's help, he'd come up with something.

Sending Rachel an assessing glance, he considered her actions while she'd been held captive by Caleb. She'd been brave, resourceful, clear-headed.

And tonight she'd managed to get in to check on him. "So, how did you get in here tonight?"

"I walked right in." A smile of triumph lit her face. "There's a new security guard at the front door."

"That won't work many times."

Her eyes darkened and her face turned solemn. "I know. That's why I've got to find another entrance." She checked her watch and sucked in a sharp breath. "Meanwhile, I've been here too long. Like I said, you're probably on hourly checks, and Gracie takes her job seriously. I'd better get out of here."

"Did you bring the microcommunicators?"

She retrieved two tiny silver cylinders from her pocket, turning them over in her fingers. "Do these things really work?"

He nodded, then rubbed his eyes and groaned. "Damn this drug." He sucked more water from the plastic cup, the cold shock hitting the roof of his mouth and the back of his throat, helping to clear the fog from his brain.

"As long as there's not too much interference, they can transmit within about a five-mile radius." He glanced around the room. "Does this place use wireless networking?"

"Yes. The nurses use laptop computers to record medication administration, and the physicians type in their orders and notes on freestanding laptops. They're all connected wirelessly."

"Hell. It would be easier if they weren't." He held out his hand and Rachel gave him the two devices.

"Do you have the safety pin Decker told you to carry?"

"Yes. Here it is." She unpinned it from the inside of her lab coat lapel.

Eric took the safety pin and manipulated something on one of the minuscule cylinder devices. Rachel could hardly believe there was anything large enough for the point of the pin to touch. He handed the cylinder back to her and worked on his.

"There," he muttered, closing the safety pin and giving it back to her. "I've activated the microcommunicators and set them to a channel that's restricted. The hospital won't have access to it." He fitted the device into his ear and indicated that she should do the same.

She looked at the tiny cylinder. "What if I can't get it out?"

"Don't try. Because of its size, it won't go any deeper than your middle ear. It can't get lost or stuck. And it can be extracted by a pair of tweezers or forceps."

She eyed it suspiciously, then slid it into her left ear. She shivered. "I don't like it."

He quirked his mouth. "You'll get used to it. Now, here's how you turn it on." He demonstrated. "Press on your ear, toward the eardrum. One time is receive. You should be able to hear my voice in your head."

Her eyes widened and she nodded. "I can. It's weird."

Suppressing a smile at her expression, he went on. "Press again and you can send. Say something."

"Testing, testing."

Eric heard the bell-like tone of her voice inside his head. "Good. Now press it a third time and the channels are wide open for send and receive. A fourth time will turn it off."

He counted on his fingers. "Receive, send, open, off. It's not voice-activated, so we need to establish a schedule for checking in. Don't leave it turned on for extended periods of time. It could be detected, or its battery might run down." He licked his lips and drained his cup of water with a slurping sound.

Rachel reached for it. "I'll get you some more."

He stopped her hand with his. For an instant his fingers curled around hers and, for that instant, she didn't move.

Something about the damned medication was playing hell with his usual composure. His footing on the tightrope he always walked between empathy and professional detachment was feeling precarious right now.

He was reacting to Rachel more strongly than he'd ever reacted to a woman. Her voice softly ringing in his ear increased the sensation.

Ironically, being turned on effectively countered

the drug-filled haze, too. Anger and arousal, he thought wryly. At least one of them could be useful. The other might prove to be too distracting.

He gritted his teeth and concentrated on his mission. "Where's the camera?"

She withdrew her fingers from his grip and patted her pocket. "Inside the tubing of my stethoscope. I hope I don't actually have to listen to anyone's chest."

Eric would have smiled, but the effort was too much. All at once, he was drained of energy.

Rachel's delicately arched brows knitted into a small frown. "Are you okay?"

Fighting the fog that enveloped his brain, Eric met her concerned gaze and nodded.

She relaxed visibly. "I'll get that water," she said, and picked up his cup. As she stepped into the connected bathroom, the hall door swung open.

Eric's pulse hammered in his skull. It was the petite night nurse. He let his eyelids drift closed as he fought not to look toward the bathroom where Rachel stood, rigid, the water cup clutched in her two hands.

The bathroom light was on. If the nurse took one more step into the room, she'd see Rachel.

The nurse frowned at him.

He held his breath, praying she wouldn't notice that his water cup was gone.

"Hi, Nurse," he slurred, lifting two fingers.

She sniffed. "Go to sleep. If you're still awake next time, I'll have to give you something." Then she exited, pulling the door closed behind her.

Eric didn't dare move. He cut his gaze over to the bathroom.

Rachel stood there, her hands white-knuckled around the cup, her eyes wide.

They stared at each other for a long moment, the silent shared danger like a shimmering thread connecting them. Finally, Rachel broke the spell with a long sigh. "That was close." Her voice quavered as she carefully crossed the room.

"You'd better get out of here. This is too dangerous. Besides, look at you. You're exhausted. You need a good night's sleep."

She shook her head and some of the color returned to her pale cheeks. "Not tonight. I'm headed to the basement—to the Medical Records room. We can't afford to lose any time."

Her words shot through him like a spray of ice water, clearing his head.

"The hell you are!" He grabbed her wrist. "Remember what Decker said? *I'm* in charge here. You are not to go snooping around by yourself. It's too dangerous."

Her jaw clenched pugnaciously and she tried to twist her wrist out of his grip. Rather than take the chance of hurting her, he let her go.

"Have you forgotten what happened to Dr. Green?" he asked.

"No, of course not. But there's no proof that he was murdered."

"Laurel thinks so, and she's one of the best forensics people I've ever worked with. She doesn't make a statement like that without evidence to back it up."

"What evidence?"

He shook his head. "I don't know the specifics. The Division is following up on it now. They're trying to contact the reporter Green spoke with, and Laurel is reanalyzing Green's autopsy results. Even if they find irrefutable proof, they won't approach local law enforcement until we can be safely extracted."

"That's great, but I can't just sit around and wait. You can't do anything with Gracie checking on you every hour. I'm stuck over in the Women's Center. Night is the only time I can search. If I have to, I'll do this alone. I *have* to find Dr. Metzger's records."

Her fierce declaration hung in the air between them. Eric stared at her, realization settling like a heavy blanket across his chest. He'd known the truth somewhere deep inside him, but he hadn't let himself think about it.

"You only agreed to do this to prove Metzger is innocent, didn't you?"

Her cheeks flamed. "I agreed to do it because your boss threatened to lock me up."

Eric stared at her. "Give me the cell phone. I'm having you extracted right now."

"No." She held up her hands, palms out. "Wait. Please. I didn't lie to Agent Decker. I just want the truth. I don't want anyone else hurt."

At that moment Eric couldn't read her. The sedative, combined with the fact that neither of them had slept in more than twenty-four hours, was playing hell with his usual innate ability. He dropped his head wearily against the pillows.

"You're lying. But as long as your agenda doesn't get in the way of mine, we're okay. I'm here to stop whoever hurt my brother and killed those patients and Dr. Green." He clenched his fists at his sides. "If that turns out to be your saintly Dr. Metzger, then too bad. He's going down."

RACHEL SLIPPED INTO the alcove that separated the main hall from the service hall. She pushed through the double doors, preparing her excuse if she ran into anyone.

She would just say she was on her way to Medical Records to catch up on her dictation and sign some charts. Every doctor always had charts to sign.

Gliding down the hall to the service elevators, she stepped inside the ancient car and punched B for basement. The elevator doors opened into a narrow, dimly lighted corridor. The walls were a dingy, depressing green, and the baseboards and door facings were thick with coats of paint. This was the old original basement of the mansion, which had not yet been renovated.

Rachel's tennis shoes squeaked on the mosaic tile floor as she hurried down the hall toward the door marked Medical Records.

And stopped.

The door was locked, its new stainless-steel knob connected to an electronic entry system. Rachel stared at the slot through which she would have to slide her badge to get inside. She'd done it before, when she was on duty and needed a returning patient's chart, or needed to access an old record.

Her entry would be recorded somewhere, on some security computer. Her neck prickled as she stood there, frozen by indecision. Who checked the records of entries? And how often? Finally, holding her breath, knowing if she were confronted, she would not have a believable explanation, she swiped her badge through the card reader.

After a frightening instant of silence, she heard a quiet, electronic click. Relief and apprehension warred inside her. She pushed open the door and slipped inside, feeling along the wall for the light switch.

She was in. Now what?

The front of the room was laid out for the convenience of the physicians. Banks of workstations with computers, telephones and dictation machines were lined up like office cubicles. Beyond them, in the back half of the room behind a work counter, were the stacks. The rows and rows of shelves that held archived medical records.

Rachel threaded her way around the workstations, wondering how long it would take her to find Caleb's chart in this maze of files. The records were probably arranged alphabetically or by social security number.

She pushed through the swinging gate and stepped behind the counter. There was an eerie perfection to the shelves. The folders were crisp and new and perfectly aligned. Not a single dog-eared sheet peeked out. It was almost as if the files were props in a movie. As if no real work had ever gone on here.

The thought made her uneasy.

Her gaze swept the counter. The usual office supplies and machines were lined up like toy soldiers. Even the unfiled charts were stacked neatly on a rolling cart, in order by ID number.

As she glanced through them, she made a startling discovery, something she'd never noticed before. There were no patient names anywhere on the charts. The colored tab on the outside of each chart held an eleven-digit ID number. She'd seen the ID numbers, but they'd meant nothing to her. She'd figured it was one of those things she'd eventually learn.

It occurred to her that every patient chart she'd ever handled had been encased in a binder labeled with the patient's last name. But what about the individual doctor's order sheets? They had to be identifiable by patient to avoid errors.

She flipped through a few charts, but there was not a patient's name anywhere—not on the doctor's order forms or any other forms. Each sheet was stamped with that blasted ID number and nothing else.

She needed Eric to look at the numbers, to see if he could figure out the code.

Rachel's gaze swept the spotless, pristine room, her jaw clenched in frustration. Somewhere there had to be unfiled records. In four years of medical school and two years of residency, she'd never seen a hospital that wasn't behind on records filing.

She searched under counters and in drawers. Nothing. Then in the back of a file drawer, behind beautifully coordinated, jewel-toned file folders, she hit pay dirt. A crumpled bundle of forms that had probably been hidden at the end of a shift, then forgotten.

Rachel's pulse raced as she grabbed the stack, and with a quick flip-through to verify that they were indeed doctor's order forms, she stuffed them into her backpack and zipped it shut.

She checked her watch. She'd been here for fifteen minutes. Longer than she'd intended. She wondered if Gracie had finished her bed checks. If so, she'd be back at the nurses' station near the side door.

As Rachel started toward the swinging gate, she heard an ominous sound: the faint swish of a name badge being swiped through the security card reader.

Her entire body went into fight-or-flight mode. Her heart rate tripled. Adrenaline pumped through her veins, heightening her senses. She was about to be caught.

As the doorknob turned, Rachel hurtled herself through the swinging gate and into the nearest computer chair. She pitched her backpack under the workstation as she grabbed the mouse and wriggled it, relieved when the monitor hummed and began to brighten.

The door swung open, revealing a man Rachel didn't know. He was medium height, stocky, dressed in teal-blue scrubs. A surgical mask hung loosely around his neck and his shirt was spattered with blood. When he saw her, he halted, startled, then glanced quickly around the room.

Rachel slanted a look at the gate through which she'd just lunged, relieved to see it had swung into place and stopped. Then she leaned back in the ergonomic chair and stretched. "Hi," she said with an exaggerated yawn. "I didn't know anybody else worked this late."

Eyeing her with frank curiosity, the doctor nodded. "Nobody does, unless there's an emergency or a new admission. This place is like the tombs at night. My bipolar patient tried to fly and took a chunk out of his knee earlier. Eleven stitches."

"Yikes. Sorry."

"Yeah, so since I was here anyway, I decided to clear out a few charts. It'll be hours before I can sleep."

"I know what you mean."

He sat down a few cubicles away from her.

She made a pretense of typing in an ID number. Of course, since she had no idea what she was typing, nothing came up.

She yawned again, aware of her companion's scrutiny. "Well, my eyes are crossing." She pushed her chair back and retrieved her backpack.

"Aren't you Rachel Harper?"

She let a small, rueful laugh escape her lips. "Yes, that's me. I guess I'm famous now, after the whole kidnapping thing."

He smiled. "Bill Dobson, Psychiatry. It was the most exciting thing that's happened around here in a while, well, since Chuck Green's suicide." He shook his head. "At least the guard is out of the woods."

"Darrell is going to make it? That's wonderful. I hadn't heard."

Rachel felt a profound relief to know that Caleb wouldn't be charged with murder. "How long have you been here, Bill?"

"Two years next month. I like it. I don't usually get called out in the middle of the night."

"Two years. Wow. You can help me then. Explain these darn ID numbers to me. They must mean something."

He laughed. "Yeah. It took me a few months to get them straight." He came over to stand beside her chair. "Who are you looking for?"

She gave him a name of one of her psychiatry patients.

He leaned over her, but she neatly slid out of her chair and snagged her backpack. "Go ahead and sit."

"Here we go. I've pulled up your patient by name, Marsha Middleton. There's the ID number. The first number is the number corresponding to the first letter of the patient's last name. For M, it's thirteen. For A it would be zero one. The next four are the last four digits of her social security number. Then the four-digit birth year. Then the first three digits of her social security number, then the birth day. And see, in her case, her birth day is the fifth, so it's zero five."

Rachel shook her head as she committed the

information to memory. "Wow. I'm glad it's not *too* complicated," she said sarcastically.

Bill laughed. "It'll make sense."

"Yeah, eventually. Thanks, Bill. I'd better head home. So, I'll see you around." She hooked her backpack over one shoulder and headed for the door. "'Night."

She felt the doctor's eyes follow her as she exited. Outside the door, she blew out her breath. She felt as though she'd been holding it ever since he'd opened the door. A shiver passed through her.

Now she had to get out of the building. Maybe she could walk back out the front door, past the new security guard. Or hide in the service hall until Gracie had to answer a call button.

She rode the service elevator back up to first floor, cringing at the groaning of the ancient wires and chains that echoed through the long narrow corridors.

When the doors creaked open, Gracie stood there. Rachel almost shrieked.

Gracie was obviously just as shocked to see her. "What are you doing here?" the nurse demanded.

"Gracie, hi. I was in Medical Records." *Tell the truth whenever you can.*

The petite nurse's black eyes snapped as she waited for Rachel to finish her explanation, but Rachel didn't say anything more. She wasn't used to lying, so she figured it would be best to keep her mouth shut. She tried to slip past Gracie, but the nurse stood her ground.

"You're not assigned here."

"That's right. I'll be working day shift over at the Women's Dependency Center."

Gracie's mouth pressed into a thin line. "Dr. Metzger told me to report to him if you tried to see Caleb."

Metzger was having her watched? A pinprick of betrayal stung her. "Look, Gracie. I know I'm not supposed to be here. Dr. Patel read me the riot act earlier. But I need my notebook computer. It's still in my locker."

Gracie frowned and opened her mouth, but Rachel took the offensive.

"Gracie—" She took a step closer and bent to whisper near Gracie's ear. "Did you tell Dr. Patel that I asked *you* about Caleb that night?"

Gracie's throat moved as she swallowed. A glimmer of guilt shone in her eyes and she backed away a step. "That's not what I said. I told him I called you when I discovered that Caleb was sleepwalking."

Rachel didn't believe her. "And then you called Security after I told you not to. None of this would have happened if you'd only listened to me. I had the situation with Caleb under control."

"You're blaming Darrell's shooting and your kidnapping on *me?*" Gracie's face distorted in anger.

"That's not fair. I was only following orders. Caleb is on the list."

"List? What list?"

Gracie bit her lip. "Never mind. I have to get back to the nurses' station."

"Gracie, wait—" Rachel reached toward her, but Gracie backed away. "I need to know about the list. Who else is on it?"

"Never mind about that. I have to give my one o'clock medications."

Rachel assessed the nurse. Rachel didn't intimidate her. She was worried about someone else. Dr. Patel? Dr. Metzger?

"All right, Gracie. I'm just going to get my things." She gestured in the direction of the women's lockers.

Gracie checked her watch. "I'll walk with you."

"No," Rachel blurted. "I mean, I'm sure you're busy. I'll just be a minute."

But Gracie walked with her down the hall past Caleb's room and through the double doors. And she waited, her arms crossed, while Rachel grabbed her laptop computer from the locker. Thank goodness she'd told the truth about that.

Her chest tight with frustration, Rachel slung her backpack over her shoulder and her laptop under her arm. She couldn't afford to open her backpack or Gracie would see the wads of paper from the

Medical Records room. Rachel headed for the side entrance.

It was obvious Gracie wasn't going to let her out of her sight until she'd left the building.

Rachel wondered if she dared to mention Dr. Green. It was obvious the staff knew about the hours she'd spent as Caleb's hostage. So it was reasonable to assume that Caleb had told Gracie of his suspicions, as well.

As they reached the exit, Rachel shifted her backpack and turned to Gracie.

"How well did you know Dr. Green? The psychiatrist who was here before me?"

Gracie's dark eyes widened in wary surprise. "Not well. He worked here in neurology sometimes."

"Do you know why he left?"

Gracie swallowed. "I think he was fired."

"That's what I heard. Why was he fired?"

"I believe it had something to do with him revealing confidential patient information to a reporter."

"What happened to him?"

"Didn't he have an accident?"

"He died. Of a drug overdose. Do you think he killed himself?"

Gracie hunched her shoulders and stuck her hands into her pockets. "I have no idea. We're not supposed to talk about the staff. It upsets the patients."

"There are no patients around right now. What happened to Dr. Green?"

The call button rang, startling both of them. Gracie glanced back toward the nurses' station. "You shouldn't be nosing around here. It's not safe."

"What do you mean?"

Gracie stepped around Rachel and opened the exit door, an explicit invitation for Rachel to leave.

Rachel had no choice but to step through the door. As she started her descent down the concrete steps, Gracie's voice followed her.

"You watch yourself, Dr. Harper. Dr. Green asked too many questions, and look what happened to him."

AT HER APARTMENT in the staff housing unit on the other side of the grounds, Rachel climbed wearily into bed. Her body ached with exhaustion.

After a quick shower, she'd retrieved the doctor's orders from her backpack and spread them out on her kitchen table. She'd stacked them, brushing out the wrinkles, and tried to read a few, but after squinting at several sheets, she'd been forced to admit she couldn't focus. The hot shower had drained the last of her energy.

It had been more than twenty-four hours since she'd had any real sleep. Tomorrow she'd get up early, study the papers and take another look at the blueprints. Surely, in a building as old as the main building of the Meadows, there was a way to get inside without alerting Security. Maybe through the basement.

She yawned and groaned quietly. She was almost too tired to sleep.

She closed her eyes and tried to relax, but Eric's face rose in her mind and her heart squeezed in compassion. She'd seen how hard he'd struggled to maintain control, despite the drugs. He was obviously unaccustomed to being helpless.

She turned over restlessly and plumped her pillow. She couldn't afford to let herself feel too responsible for Eric. He was a specially trained undercover agent. He could take care of himself. Her concern was for her patients.

And yourself, a tiny voice whispered in her brain. She'd only known Eric for a little more than twenty-four hours. But from their first eye contact, she'd felt a connection between them, an awareness that went beyond their mutual concern for Caleb. She saw his integrity, his commitment to his job, the protectiveness that was obviously a part of his makeup.

"Rachel?"

She froze, her breath caught in her throat. It took her a few seconds to realize she was hearing Eric's voice through the com unit. She'd completely forgotten about the tiny communications device. For an instant she felt exposed, as if he'd somehow lifted the covers and slipped into bed beside her and was whispering in her ear. Her skin tingled and she shivered.

"Eric?" she whispered.

"Are you in bed?" His voice sounded strained and drowsy.

She couldn't answer, could barely breathe. The significance of his question sheared her breath. The com unit had been on all this time. "You've been listening to me?"

"Some. I keep falling asleep."

"Dear God, why didn't you say something?" He'd heard her sneak down into the basement, heard her exchange with the other doctor, heard her confronted and escorted out by Gracie.

"I didn't want to startle you." His voice slid across her skin like sandpaper and silk, rough and soft.

He'd been there with her, listening to her frustrated tears and her palm slapping the steering wheel as she'd driven the short distance from the main building to her apartment on the other side of the grounds.

And he'd heard her in the shower. Her face burned and a deep thrill slid through her as her mind replayed the sounds he must have heard.

Her hand flew to the low-cut bodice of her little satin camisole.

"If you've been listening, then you *know* I'm in bed." She pressed her lips together and squeezed her eyes shut as a spear of desire brought a flush to her skin. He'd heard everything.

Rachel sat up and hugged a pillow. She felt exposed and a little invaded. A part of her wanted to pull the minuscule cylinder out of her ear and throw it across the room.

But another lonely part of her wished she could just cuddle down into the covers and let his low, raspy whisper wrap her in safety and comfort.

"You had no intention of going straight home, did you? Even after I warned you."

His words reminded her that he might be concerned for her safety, but only so far as it aided his mission.

"It was the perfect opportunity. There was no one around."

"It was dangerous."

"I was able to get out with some unfiled records."

"It wasn't worth the chance you took."

Rachel sighed in exasperation. "Caleb's current chart contains only about six months of records. The only place we're going to find any information about what caused his respiratory arrest is in the archived records. That's where we have to concentrate our search."

"The operative word is *we*. You don't make a move without my say-so, is that understood?"

"You're stuck in that room. Right now there is no

we. There's just me. By the way, did you hear me talking to Bill Dobson?"

"No, I must have slept through that."

"He's a psychiatrist who works here. He gave me the key to the patient ID numbers." She rattled off the information Dobson had given her.

Eric's weary sigh echoed in her ear. "Whoa. Tell me that again when I'm more coherent. Right now I'm half asleep. Meanwhile, you need to lie low."

"Eric, we don't have much time. How long do you think you can fool them? They're going to figure out that you're not Caleb. Plus, the drugs are going to start taking their toll. There's only so much I can do to protect you."

She was silent as she thought about the implications of what she was doing. What she'd already done. Breaking into an unauthorized area. Stealing medical records. She squeezed the pillow.

"Oh, God. I can't believe I'm doing this. I must have broken a dozen laws tonight. I'll probably lose my license to practice. Psychiatry is all I know."

"Everything will work out, I promise. You've got the FBI behind you. Don't worry about me. I can handle the drugs, and I'll figure out a way for us to meet. Meanwhile, your job is to study those blueprints and talk to Natasha. The cell phone you have is as secure as the FBI can make it, but it's not impossible to track. Use it sparingly."

"Has Gracie come by to check on you?"

"Yeah, at one-seventeen. That's Gracie? The same nurse that tried to forcibly sedate Caleb? The one who called Security?"

"Yes. That's her. Did you hear the last thing she said to me as I was leaving?"

"No."

"She told me to watch myself. She said Dr. Green asked too many questions, and look what happened to him."

Her com unit was silent for an instant.

"Don't trust her, Rachel. Don't trust anybody."

Rachel slid down in the bed and turned onto her side. "I'll be careful, I promise."

"Please do. You're under suspicion. Every move you make will be under scrutiny."

Rachel's eyes drifted shut. She stretched out, sighing.

"Rachel, did you fall asleep?"

"Close." Her insides quivered with a hunger she recognized. One that had never been satisfied completely. "I'm barely whispering, Eric. How can you hear me?"

She pictured him lying in his bed, his bare shoulders and chest golden and sleek against the snow-white sheets. They were in their separate beds, whispering to each other.

"Technology." She heard a trace of amusement in

his sleepy voice. It sent a thrill all the way to the core of her. She smiled in the darkness.

"Rachel, Metzger is determined to find out exactly what Caleb told you. You've got to be careful. Watch yourself every minute."

Rachel sighed. "I don't think you understand how closely *you're* going to be watched."

"I'll manage. It's vital that we stay in communication. Open your com unit at quarter past the hour, every hour, to check in with me. Start at nine-fifteen in the morning. Be quiet and discreet. You've already seen how easy it is to hear even a whisper. I may not be able to answer you, but I'll know you're okay."

"Eric? How will I know you're okay?"

"I will be."

She lay on her back, staring at the lights from the grounds of the Meadows reflected on her ceiling.

"Eric?" she whispered.

He didn't answer. He was gone.

Picking a Winner

Chapter Six

The sudden silence unnerved Rachel. Eric had been there, inside her head, talking, then suddenly he was gone. She turned over and glanced at her bedside clock. Two-eleven. Gracie had probably opened his door.

It was a scary feeling, to have another person's voice in her head. Was that how schizophrenics felt? After the first few seconds, once she'd gotten used to the sound, Eric's voice had soothed her like a healing balm. It was the most comforting sound she'd ever heard, even if it did stir longings she'd rather not feel.

Eric was not the kind of man she needed. He had an identical twin who was plagued with an illness as debilitating as her mother's. What did that say about Eric?

She knew that identical twins didn't always suffer from the same mental disorders. Still, a sliver of apprehension imbedded itself under her diaphragm. No, her interest in Eric was not personal. It was just her loneliness combined with the knowledge that they'd been whispering to each other in bed, barely clothed, an oddly intimate sensation. Even if she admitted to a physical attraction, she couldn't risk letting her heart get involved. What if Eric did succumb to the illness that had crippled his brother? The idea was disturbing.

"Hey…"

Her heart skipped a beat. Despite her thoughts, Eric's raspy voice sent a thrill through her. "Hey, yourself. I thought you were asleep."

"Gracie stuck her head in. Did I wake you?"

"No. I'm a little jittery."

"Yeah. I've slept too much today. Feel like talking?" His voice barely resonated in her ear. It was like having her own personal relaxation tape.

She closed her eyes. "Okay."

"Why did you become a psychiatrist?"

"My mother."

"Did she encourage you?"

A twinge of pain brought her wide awake. Deep pain, old pain. He'd caught her off guard. She had never talked to anyone about her mother. She rubbed her chest and sniffed wryly. "You could say that."

He didn't say anything. His quiet breaths were all she heard.

After a long silence, he spoke. "I'm sorry, Rachel."

The knowledge in his voice frightened her. Bravado forced an immediate response. "Sorry about what?"

"Your mother. She's ill, isn't she?"

Rachel sat up and pulled a pillow over to hug it. His question wasn't really a question. "How...I mean, why would you think that?"

"The hurt in your voice."

A painful lump lodged itself in her throat. She shook her head and pressed her lips together. "Don't try to psychoanalyze me, Mr. Secret Agent. You're out of your league, trust me." Her words came out too harsh. She hadn't meant to snap at him. Her shoulders began to ache.

"My turn," she whispered. "Why did you become an FBI agent?"

"So you're going to psychoanalyze me now?"

She chuckled softly. "Or I'm just making midnight conversation."

He was quiet for a couple of seconds. "I've always had a...talent for understanding people, and I'd read all of John Douglas's books about criminal profiling and the criminal mind."

"Oh, right. Mitch said you have a Ph.D. in Abnormal Psychology. I guess you chose that field because of your brother's illness."

Eric didn't answer.

She took his silence to mean she was correct. It

was ironic. His entire life's direction had been dictated by mental illness, just like hers.

"Do you ever wonder what your life would have been like if you hadn't had mental illness in your family?"

"Do you?"

The two words struck her like a slap to her face. "What—" Her voice gave out and she had to start again. "What are you talking about?" She hugged the pillow more tightly.

"Tell me about your mother. Is she schizophrenic?"

Rachel felt cornered. Suddenly, Eric was too close. His voice in her head gave her the creepy feeling he could read her mind.

"No. She's bipolar." Rachel shuddered. She'd never said that out loud to anyone other than the therapist she'd been required to see as part of her own psychiatric training.

"So you went into psychiatry to help her?"

Rachel laughed uncomfortably. He was turning the tables on her. "Ha. Not exactly. She's just fine with her life. I went into psychiatry to wipe mental illness off the planet. It destroys lives. Not just the person with the illness, but everyone around them. I care about my patients, but I hate the disease." She realized her fists were clenched around the pillow. She consciously relaxed them. She'd said more than she'd intended.

"You know you can't cure mental illness."

"Metzger's theories are solid."

"Yeah? What I've seen so far looks barbaric, like the old days when mental patients were tortured and restrained and treated like animals."

"You're prejudiced against him, because of your brother. Dr. Metzger believes most mental illness is caused by a process in the body similar to autoimmune diseases."

"The body fighting itself, like arthritis."

"Right. More accurately, certain brain chemicals fighting each other. He's done some research, but he's had trouble obtaining grants to test his theory."

"No doubt."

Rachel bristled at the sarcasm in Eric's tone, but she continued. Maybe if he understood what Metzger was trying to do, he'd be less hostile toward him.

"Dr. Metzger believes that injections, similar to allergy injections, can desensitize the brain's over-reaction to certain chemicals, and can, in essence, cure mental illness."

"That may be what he's been giving Caleb."

Rachel shook her head. "No. His theory is experimental. He can only use the injections in a research study, and he's not doing any research right now. He's waiting for approval for a new drug he wants to research. There's been a delay in receiving FDA approval."

"I thought you hadn't worked with him yet." Eric's tone sounded accusatory, and skeptical.

"I haven't. But I've read every journal article he's ever written and followed his previous studies in the literature." She sighed in exasperation and tossed the pillow she'd been hugging aside. "Why are you so determined to believe that Dr. Metzger is some evil scientist from a B movie, conducting awful human experiments on helpless patients?"

"Because I believe my brother, and I want to help him."

His voice carried a pain that Rachel could only imagine. If Caleb were her brother, wouldn't she believe him?

The lonely ache inside her intensified. Probably not. Her experience with her mother had cured her of believing people with mental illness. She would take care of them, but she'd never trust them.

"Don't you want to help your mother?"

Eric's question irritated her. "My mother doesn't need my help. Husband number three has that happy task now. She's better off without me around."

"Why is that?"

"Let's just say I find it easier to deal with people when I'm not so emotionally involved."

"So how do you do your job without getting involved?" His voice held a chill.

"I didn't mean I don't get involved at all. Of course I care for my patients. But it's not personal."

"So, Rachel." His voice echoed through her. "That sounds like a lonely way to live."

A deep ache settled under her heart and intensified with every heartbeat. She sank down into the bed and curled into a fetal position.

The seconds ticked by.

"I'm sorry," he finally said. "That was a thoughtless comment. I had no right."

"Don't worry about it," she mumbled. "I'm just sleepy, all of a sudden. I'm fading fast."

"Okay. Call me at nine-fifteen. And, Rachel—"

She didn't answer. Her lower lip trembled. Her eyes stung.

"Thanks for being there for me. And remember, I'm here for you, too, if you ever need to talk. Don't forget to turn off your com unit. Good night."

The noise in her head went silent. She fisted her hands in the pillow and lay quiet, trying to recapture the feeling of his low, sweet voice reverberating in her ears.

As she tried to relax and concentrate on clearing her mind, one question stuck in her brain like a compelling melody.

How would it feel to have Eric's voice enveloping her in its promise of protection all the time? To have his strong body stretched out beside her, shielding her, every night?

"Dream on," she muttered, pressing on her ear to turn the unit off. She rolled over onto her back.

Eric Baldwyn was here for only one purpose. He was risking his life for his brother. He was using her—the FBI was using her—as bait to track down a killer.

SOMEONE OPENED the blinds, letting in glaring sunlight. Eric groaned and squinted. In front of him stood a small, gray-haired woman in one of those silly jackets covered with cartoon cats and dogs and umbrellas that made her look as though she'd wandered in from the pediatric ward.

"Good morning, Caleb," she said, turning to smile at him. "It's nice to have you back. Are you feeling better?"

Eric blessed his excellent vision as he blinked and squinted at her name tag. MARIE SAMPLES. He assessed her as she pulled out her stethoscope and wrapped the blood pressure cuff around his bare upper arm. What had her relationship to Caleb been? She seemed to be sincere, and as far as he could tell, genuinely glad to see him—or Caleb.

She frowned slightly. "Your blood pressure is low. Are you on any different meds since you got back?"

Eric considered her question. He had very little

knowledge of how Caleb reacted to normal, every-day events. All he knew was that his brother was schizophrenic and paranoid. That probably made it easier, in a sense. If Eric said anything odd or out of character…well, what exactly was in character for a paranoid schizophrenic young man who might be receiving deadly chemicals?

"Not that I know of, ma'am. But you know what goes on around here. They could have snuck in and given me something while I was sedated."

Marie chuckled, but her smile didn't reach her eyes.

"What does it say in my chart?"

"You know what you're on. Ten milligrams of fenpiprazole by injection daily."

"Daily?" He hadn't meant to say that out loud. He cringed and suppressed a shudder. He was going to receive an injection every day. "I haven't gotten a dose today."

She slung her stethoscope around her neck. "No. Yesterday you received a sedative. Dr. Metzger doesn't like to mix medication. If you had been having trouble breathing, he would have ordered a dose."

"Maybe they should change my medication."

She patted his cheek with a motherly caress. "Try to do what the doctors tell you, dear. I hate to see you suffering. Dr. Metzger knows what's best."

"Does he?"

"Now, Caleb, you know we don't talk about the

doctors." She checked the clipboard hanging on the door. "Let's see what your day is like. Oh, you're supposed to see Dr. Metzger at ten o'clock. You'd better get up. I'll see you back here for lunch, then this afternoon you're scheduled for some tests."

"Tests?" Eric's pulse sped up. "What kind of tests?"

Marie waved a hand. "I'm sure it's just the usual. They probably want a follow-up brain scan, after everything you've been through the past few days. Now it's time to get up. You're going to miss breakfast if you don't hurry."

Eric glanced at the clock on the bedside table. It was a few minutes before nine o'clock. By the time he got dressed, it would be nine-fifteen. Time for Rachel to call.

Rachel. He'd dreamed about her. As he quickly showered, he let his brain replay the dream. She and Caleb were hanging by their fingertips from a cliff. Below them, fiery waves broke and sizzled against red glowing rock, and the tide was rising. Eric only had one rope, and it wasn't long enough. Even if he climbed down the rope himself, he could only save one of them.

He lifted his face to the warm flow of water, trying to wash away the startling images and the leftover drowsiness from the sedative. It didn't take a psychiatrist to interpret the dream. He felt responsible for both Rachel and Caleb, and he was worried that he couldn't protect them both.

It weakened his knees anew each time he thought about Caleb, locked away all this time. How could he not have known that his brother was alive?

He closed his eyes, searching for the connection he remembered from his childhood. The sense that he wasn't alone.

With a pain as sharp as a knife piercing his heart, he realized that he had never been alone. He'd spent his childhood trying to protect his brother. Then, when he'd been told Caleb had died, he'd felt ripped in two. To discover, twenty years later, that his brother was alive had been a brutal shock, but also a relief.

He'd spent all that time nearly paralyzed by fear that the whispers in his brain and the odd dreams were precursors to schizophrenia.

He shook his head under the shower spray. Now he knew. The odd formless whispers he'd always endured were from his brother.

Caleb had always been there.

He tried to search, to connect with Caleb in a more concrete way, as they'd occasionally done as children. But he was distracted, probably because of the medication.

Plus, his brain was suffused with Rachel's face. Her melodic voice in his ear last night had stirred him, even in his sedated state. By the time their conversation was over, her sexy bell-like murmurs had swirled around him like fine perfume and he'd ached with restless wanting.

Now, just thinking about her, his body sprang to life. What the hell was the matter with him? Suddenly he was reacting like a randy teenager. He hadn't done much of that, even when he *was* an adolescent. Those years had been spent in grief and guilt, missing his brother and traumatized by his death.

With a groan, he turned off the hot water and quickly finished under icy spray.

As he exited the bathroom, he glanced at the clock and pressed his ear, activating the com unit.

A movement in the mirror startled him. He looked up and froze. He hadn't realized how much he looked like Caleb. The new, shorter haircut made all the difference. He glanced down at his ragged fingernails, then back up. Deliberately he forced a dark, fearful glare into his eyes.

Paranoid. Angry. Haunted.

"Eric?"

The word hummed like a harp in his ears, breaking the spell. He glanced down at his nakedness.

The sounds he'd heard last night, the splash of water and quiet sighs as Rachel had showered, painted an erotic picture in his mind: Rachel, nude, her creamy skin glistening with droplets of water, her midnight hair plastered to her head, her brilliant blue eyes surrounded by wet, spiky eyelashes.

He watched himself grow hard.

"Yeah?" he croaked.

"What's the matter?"

"Nothing. Where are you?"

"At the Women's Center. I'll be here all day."

He tossed the towel aside and opened a drawer. Gritting his teeth, he pulled on underwear and jeans and grabbed a T-shirt. "I'm meeting with Metzger. What will he want?"

"He's probably fishing to see what you told me. What you—what Caleb—told the FBI."

"Is this unusual or does Metzger meet with his patients a lot?

"I think he has private sessions with his schizophrenia patients at least once a week. Eric, last night Gracie mentioned a *list*. I've never heard that before. She told me she'd had to call Security because Caleb is on the *list*."

"That list may be a group of special patients, the ones Caleb said Metzger experiments on. Have you talked to Natasha?"

"Not yet. I'll call her in a few minutes."

"Make the call quick. Tell her we need a recent aerial photograph of the building. Tell her to overlay the original blueprint, and then mark every single spot that doesn't exactly match. I don't care if it's a new window shutter. And tell her about the list."

"Okay. How will she get the information to us?"

"You may have to leave the grounds to meet someone. Pretend you're going out to dinner or something. I've got to go."

"Eric, your brother is a charmer and a smart aleck. Mezger will expect you to talk back to him and to question everything. He'll be watching you closely."

"Okay. Thanks. Open your com unit every hour on the fifteen-minute mark for about five minutes, but don't speak. I'll talk to you when I can."

He toggled the com unit off and wiped a hand down his face. There was no way he could concentrate with her voice in his head all the time.

Looking back at the mirror, he watched the haunted look return to his eyes. Deliberately he smiled, raising his brows in a sardonic slant. Did he look like a smart-ass?

He winked at his reflection, thinking that it would be easier for him to endure a slow, long torture than to be charming. He headed for the dining room.

GERHARDT METZGER scratched his mutton-chop sideburns and frowned as Caleb Baldwyn left his office. The young man's attitude had been one of irritation and wariness.

During the forty-eight hours Baldwyn had been away from the Meadows, something about him had changed. Metzger couldn't pinpoint the exact difference, but it was there.

Even though Baldwyn had eyed Metzger the same way he always had, as if trying to reverse their roles, his entire demeanor was different today.

For one thing, he was stiffer, more controlled. Metzger pulled a legal pad toward him and picked up his fountain pen.

The pen scratched reassuringly against the paper as he quickly wrote his assessment of Caleb.

"Alert. Calm. Appeared tired, but not ill. Respiration normal, color normal, no indication of schizophrenic symptoms, except mild paranoia. Less communicative than usual. Healthy."

Healthy.

Metzger stared at the word.

Too healthy. The young mental patient had been receiving the solution of extracted brain chemicals daily for seven years, making him Metzger's longest continuously running experiment. In all that time, there was only one documented incident of a missed dose—a nursing error during one of Caleb's transfers to the Independent Living Center. Within twelve hours, he'd become increasingly paranoid and had experienced several episodes of difficulty breathing. As soon as he'd been given a booster of the solution, his vital signs had returned to normal.

"No evidence of withdrawal from the mixture," Metzger wrote, then tapped the cap of his fountain pen against the paper.

He reached into his pocket for his cell phone, checked the time, then keyed in a familiar number, a number in Germany.

"James, my friend."

"Gerhardt, I was just about to leave for the day. Has your patient been returned to you?"

"*Ja.* And in good health."

"Really? How many injections did he miss?"

Metzger nodded in satisfaction. True to form, James knew immediately the source of Metzger's biggest concern.

"Two. He was gone for forty-eight hours. He should have gone into respiratory arrest." It was always satisfying to talk to the one man who understood the importance of Metzger's work and the gravity of the situation.

Dr. James Farmer, a Nobel Laureate in medicine, had been Metzger's friend and mentor for many years. It was Farmer who had discovered an important pathway in the brain that had led him to his controversial theory of mental illness as an autoimmune disease. A theory his protégé Metzger shared.

"Didn't you tell me he kidnapped a psychiatrist?"

"Yes. Dr. Rachel Harper. I had mentioned her to you before."

"Ah, yes, the young woman who is so devoted to you."

"To our theories. Her background and training combined with a personal crusade to cure mental illness made her a good choice to replace Dr. Green."

"And she was with the subject for how long?"

"Approximately twenty-four hours. They both were hospitalized at Walter Reed Hospital in Washington, D.C., for observation, then brought back here."

"What was her assessment?"

Metzger tapped his fountain pen. "She noticed what she termed 'slight' respiratory depression. Said it came and went. Essentially the same information I got from the hospital where he was taken. There's something wrong."

"I agree. Is it at all possible that Baldwyn has developed a resistance to the respiratory effects over the years?"

"I don't believe so. Only eighteen months ago, a nurse missed administering his daily injection and he reacted as we would expect. Difficulty breathing, increased paranoia, reduced oxygen levels in his blood."

"Ah. Have you continued experimenting with the refining process?"

"Yes. In fact, in the past three months, I've refined the process again. I'm comparing mass spectrograph tests of the current solutions to the prior ones."

"You still believe it could be a contaminant that is causing the respiratory effects?"

"I hope it is. If I had the time and the freedom to do the experiments I'd like to do, really push the dose up to the patient's maximum tolerance level, I'm sure I could isolate and eliminate the ingredient."

"So how soon will you be able to complete your plan to move your laboratory over here?"

Farmer had lived and worked in Germany for the past twenty years. Metzger had chosen to practice in the United States, hoping to be able to win approval of his refined drug from the FDA. But he had never been able to meet their stringent standards.

"I have more than one problem right now. As you know, the FDA has once again disapproved my application."

"You did not indicate that your chemicals were human in origin, did you?"

"Of course not. But apparently they have some significant questions about my process for manufacturing the synthetic drug. But that's not my biggest worry. Because the incident with Baldwyn was a kidnapping, the FBI became involved. I have no way of knowing what he may have told them."

"Your pet subject is getting uncomfortably close to the truth."

"Yes. It's been easy so far to blame it on his paranoia, but eventually someone is going to believe him. And this Dr. Harper is young and filled with idealism. A practiced manipulator like Baldwyn could easily convince her of his suspicions."

"And the FBI, have they questioned you?"

"Only marginally. They apparently consider the matter closed, since Harper was not harmed, and Baldwyn was brought back here. He'll be arraigned in two weeks for the shooting of the security guard. I'd like to be out of here before then."

"Are you still planning to bring Baldwyn with you?"

"Of course." He had already signed the necessary papers. "I've arranged for him to accompany me to a 'symposium,' then once we land in Germany—"

"What about his arraignment?"

"He's been released back into our custody. All the paperwork is in order for him to make a short trip out of the country."

"Good. I have arranged for you to disappear. All you have to do is get yourself and your patient through security and customs. Gerhardt?" Farmer paused for an instant. "What about Dr. Harper?"

Metzger pushed back from his desk and walked over to the window, looking out over the grounds, scratching his sideburns. Frustration ate a hole in his gut. "Ever since the incident with Baldwyn's friend Misty, he's become increasingly obsessed with the idea that she was murdered. He still raves about evil experiments."

"You're certain he told Dr. Harper of his suspicions."

"Yes. She alluded to his paranoia and delusional thinking. Still, it's unfortunate that she was involved in the incident. Now she's the unknown quantity in my plan. She's only been here two months, so I can't depend on her loyalty. That makes her a liability."

"Just like Charles Green," Farmer said.

Metzger sighed. "Right."

"How much do you think she knows?"

"Unfortunately, at this point, it doesn't matter. Anything is too much."

Metzger said goodbye and disconnected. He stood, staring out the window at the manicured lawn.

Rachel Harper was in his way. She had to go.

"ERIC?"

It was Rachel. Eric almost shouted in relief to hear her bell-like voice in his ear. He was sick of sitting in the beautifully decorated day room with recovering victims of stroke, brain injury and early onset Alzheimer's. Why had Caleb, a psychiatric patient, been housed on a neurology ward? And how many of these patients were being treated by Dr. Metzger?

"Hmm?" He didn't want to speak any louder than a quiet hum. The orderlies had been watching him all afternoon. One burly guy had even accompanied him to the exercise room and stood, arms folded in the classic these- are-my-impressive-biceps stance for the entire hour Eric worked out.

"I guess you can't talk. I'm in my apartment."

Eric stood and walked over to the wide paned-glass window, as if he were looking out over the grounds. He felt the eyes of the orderly on him. He made an affirmative sound deep in his throat.

"I talked to Natasha," Rachel continued. "I gave her your message about the aerial photo. She said they were already on it. She found something in the blueprints. There appears to be an old servants' entrance on the back side of the building. She said the basement is underground in the front, but the ground slopes downward toward the back."

"North?" Eric mumbled.

"Yes. The north side. Also, I was able to review the records. The ones I grabbed were older, six months or more. Some had Dr. Green's signature. But none of the actual records have names on them. Just those ID numbers. Remember what I told you last night?"

"Yeah. Let's talk about that later." Eric glanced to the side, to be sure no one was close to him.

"Okay. Eric? How did your session with Dr. Metzger go? Can you tell me?"

Her worried voice warmed him. "He's suspicious." He covered his words by reaching up and rubbing at an imagined spot on the sparkling-clean glass. "Can you get in past security tonight?"

"I'm going to try that basement entrance."

"No!" *Crap*. He'd spoken too loudly.

Before he could even turn, the big orderly was beside him. With an internal sigh, cursing his knee-jerk response to the thought of Rachel wandering the grounds alone, he prepared for a performance.

"No!" he said again, rubbing harder at the spot on the glass.

"Eric? What's the matter?" Rachel's voice sounded panicked. He wanted to say something to reassure her but he couldn't, and he certainly couldn't risk the orderly hearing the quiet hum of her voice. He reached up and pretended to scratch his ear as he switched off the com unit.

"Okay, Caleb," the man said, right behind him. "What's the problem?"

Eric glared at the guy's broad, tanned face. "What kind of housekeeper are you? There are spots on the window. Spots."

The orderly sent him a disgusted glance. "At it again, I see. I guess your little vacation didn't do you any good, did it?" He gripped Eric's arm with a viselike fist.

Eric jerked, but his strength was no match for the bigger man, and he didn't dare use the martial arts tactics that had been a part of his training for the Division.

"Brawn before brains," he said sarcastically, not really knowing where the compelling urge to taunt the orderly came from, but it felt right, so he went with it. "I guess you keep your brains in those magnificent biceps."

"Shut up, Baldwyn, or I'll give you another taste of what these biceps can do." The orderly jerked Eric toward the door. "You remember the last one, don't you?"

Eric had to clench his teeth at the orderly's reference to having used his muscle against Caleb in the past.

"I think you need to spend the rest of the afternoon in your room."

Fine with me, Eric thought. It would give him a chance to talk to Rachel.

The orderly pushed him through the door into Room 3. "I'll tell Thomas you need a little cocktail."

As the door slammed shut, Eric pressed on the com unit. "Rachel?"

"Eric, what happened? Why did you turn your com unit off?"

"What's a cocktail?"

Her soft intake of breath echoed through him as if she'd blown in his ear.

"Did they give you a cocktail?"

"No, but they're talking about it. What is it?"

"It's a mixture of drugs. Often a sedative, or an anti-psychotic. Despite the name, it doesn't have to be in liquid form. It can be tablets or an injection."

"I'm already getting one damn shot every day."

"I know. That's supposed to be the fenpiprazole." Her voice sounded worried. "Are you noticing any effects?"

"Nothing except that I'm learning to hate needles even more than I already did. Rachel, is there anything I can do to keep them from giving it to me?"

She was silent for a few seconds. "Are you in your room? Then this might work. Lie down. Pretend to be asleep when the nurse brings the dose in. Maybe she'll leave you alone if you're asleep."

"Thanks. Do *not* go wandering around alone. Promise me."

"But—"

"Promise!" he said fiercely.

"I'd better go. You've got to convince them you're asleep."

The seductive buzz in his ear went silent.

"Damn it, Rachel," he muttered. His muscles bunched with need for action. She had deliberately refused to promise him that she wouldn't go out alone.

Aware of the seconds ticking away, he stretched out on the bed, then turned over and used deep-breathing and biofeedback techniques to calm himself. He consciously relaxed each muscle, but nothing stopped his racing brain.

Somehow he had to get out of here tonight. He had to find the door on the north side of the basement. He couldn't let Rachel go down there alone.

RACHEL TRUDGED through the underbrush that lined the edge of the grounds of the Meadows, happy that the moon was nearly full, but worried, too, that its pale light was too bright. She hoped her black turtleneck sweater, black pants and hiking boots were enough to camouflage her.

The Meadows was located on six hundred acres of land in the southern part of Connecticut. The late-nineteenth-century mansion that served as the acute care center had deteriorated into disrepair by the time Dr. William Carpenter had bought it and turned it into an insane asylum in 1917. Today the renovated building was surrounded by four newer structures that housed the Women's Dependency Center, the Independent Living Center, an apartment building for medical staff and one for maintenance personnel. The main building included an acute care facility, a nursing home and the administrative offices.

Rachel hadn't dared to drive the short distance from her apartment to the main building. Her car would be recognized. So she'd shored up her courage with black coffee and headed out on foot.

She circled around to the north side of the building, trying to pinpoint where Natasha said she would find the servants' entrance. She felt guilty about literally cutting Eric off, but she'd been worried that the nurse bearing his drug cocktail would come in while he was arguing with her. And truthfully, she hadn't wanted to give him a chance to talk her out of it.

He was being watched way too closely. She couldn't sit by and wait for him to figure out a way to sneak out of his room. She wasn't sure he could.

That meant finding Caleb's records was up to her. She had given her word that she would do everything she could to find out what was really going on here. As terrified as she was, and as fervently as she hoped that Dr. Metzger was not involved, she would not back down.

As she approached the rear of the building, working her way through the shrubs and overgrown grass, an owl hooted mournfully and something skittered across her path. Suppressing a shiver, Rachel surveyed the rear of the building. A couple of anemic spotlights shone from the corners of the roof. Otherwise the rear of the building was cloaked in darkness, making it barely visible in the feeble moonlight.

Just as she tensed to make a dash across the expanse of carpetlike grass, she heard a noise.

Shadows moved on the east side of the building. A security guard with a German shepherd on a leash came into view.

Rachel froze and dropped her head, letting her black hair fall down to cover her face. She'd showered, but she'd used scented shampoo and body wash. How foolish of her! She should have thought about using scented products. What if the dog smelled her and barked? What if the guard swung his flashlight in her direction?

Her heart pounded, cramping her chest with the need for more oxygen. She opened her mouth and tried to breathe silently and calmly.

The dog's ears perked up and he yelped. Once. Twice.

Terror streaked through her, stealing the last molecules of air from her lungs.

"What's up, Babe?" the security guard asked, his deep voice carrying over the expanse of grass. "Is something out there?" He swung the flashlight beam in a lazy arc around the edge of the manicured lawn.

Rachel cringed as the edge of the light's halo swept across her black-clad shins.

"You gonna tree a squirrel? Is that what you want to do, Babe? Whatcha see?"

The dog was whining and straining at his leash. Sweat trickled between Rachel's breasts and dotted her temples and forehead. She didn't dare look up. Her pale face would shine like a beacon.

The guard's boots barely made a sound on the grass as he moved closer. The dog's whine got louder. Rachel heard leather creak as the animal strained at its leash. She scrunched her shoulders and tried to be as still as a tree.

Several feet to her left, an owl screeched. It took all of her strength not to gasp out loud. Her heart thudded so loudly, she was sure the dog could hear it.

The guard chuckled. "Settle down, Babe. There's your intruder. You don't want to mess with an owl. Let's go. We'll get a squirrel tomorrow night, how's that?"

Rachel didn't dare move until the affectionate banter faded. Finally the night turned silent again as he rounded the other side of the building, where a long drive angled up from a large loading dock.

How long did she have before he came around again? She should have checked on the guards' habits. But that might have aroused suspicion.

She crouched in the grass and studied the rear of

the building. About two-thirds along its length was a shadowy rectangle. Was that the door? It was approximately where Natasha had said it would be.

Certain the door would be locked, and feeling like a rabbit in a field of foxes, Rachel took a deep breath and darted across the manicured lawn. She watched her shadow race in front of her and felt the moon's light on her back like a spotlight.

Reaching the building, she flattened herself against the wall and studied the recessed doorway.

"Yes!" she whispered as she spotted a rusted doorknob.

Thank you, Natasha. It *was* the door. Now if it by some miracle it wasn't locked...Rachel had come armed with a fingernail file, a small screwdriver and a pair of tweezers, as well as a couple of credit cards, but she had little hope that she could pick the lock, even if it was an old one.

Carefully, quietly, she turned the knob. It protested with a small squeal, but the door didn't budge.

Damn. Was it locked or just stuck? Her money was on locked.

She turned the knob again and pushed against the door. Still nothing.

Digging out a credit card, she tried to slide it between the door and the door facing. She wriggled it carefully and jiggled the knob, but that effort met with failure, too.

So she dug in her pack for the fingernail file. Holding the knob with her left hand, she inserted the file into the keyhole with her right. As she carefully manipulated her makeshift tool, she turned and twisted the doorknob. Did she feel something click?

In the distance she heard a sharp whistle and a bark.

Her shoulders tensed and she froze in place. It was the guard, coming back. She muttered a curse. Didn't he have anything to do except circle the damned building all night long?

Curling her body inward toward the door, she redoubled her efforts with the fingernail file, gripping the knob, wriggling the file and pushing at the same time.

The dog whined. Rachel stood rigid as a statue, not daring to breathe. Her hand cramped around the doorknob.

"You still after that squirrel, Babe?" the guard asked, his voice splitting the night. "What did I tell you about that owl? Is that what you see?"

The dog barked sharply.

"What is it, Babe?"

The door flew open.

Rachel overbalanced.

Hands grabbed her and jerked her forward, into pitch black. She shrieked.

Chapter Seven

Eric pulled Rachel's slender body through the half-open door and pushed it shut. He wrapped one arm around her, pinning her arms to her sides, and clapped a hand over her mouth, barely in time to muffle her surprised cry.

"It's Eric. Shh!"

She went completely limp.

"Rachel!" Had she fainted? Had he hurt her? With his heart crashing against his chest, he lowered her gently to the ground.

His eyes had dark-adapted, but there was very little light. All he saw was the pale oval of her face. He cradled her cheek in his hand. She felt hot.

"Rachel. Say something. Are you okay?"

He leaned over her and almost got knocked over as she scrambled up to a sitting position.

"Dear God, I thought I'd been caught. You scared me half to death!" she whispered angrily.

Relief that she wasn't hurt turned into anger at her

for cutting off their only line of communication earlier. "Quiet. And turn on your damn com unit. Don't ever cut me off again."

She turned it on. "Why turn it on now?"

"So we can hear each other." He kept his voice controlled and stern, but the familiar, sexy hum of her voice in his ears soothed his fractured nerves.

He'd had to lie still for more than two hours during the afternoon while Thomas checked on him at odd intervals. He'd gotten the definite impression that Thomas was just waiting for the smallest excuse to medicate him. He'd even poked him in the shoulder once, but Eric had just half turned and glanced up with heavy-lidded eyes, then closed them again.

He could have used Rachel's voice in his ear then. It might have eased his cramping muscles, distracted him from the agony of pretending to sleep.

Now, more relieved than he dared admit to see her safe, he settled beside her and wrapped his arm around her.

"How did you know I was here?"

He pressed his fingers against her lips. "The guard," he mouthed, barely loud enough to be heard. But she hunched her shoulders and sat still.

The sound of footsteps and the whine of the dog leeched through the heavy wooden door. Eric waited, listening, until he was certain the guard had rounded the building, before releasing his hold on her.

As soon as he did she jumped up. "Where are we?"

Her voice swirled around him in stereo, echoing inside and outside his head.

"As far as I can tell, this is a small entryway below the kitchen of the original house. There are stairs behind us to my left. They lead up to the back hall, near where the nonperishable food items are stored."

Rachel's pale face peered at him suspiciously through the darkness. "How do you know all that?"

How did he know? He'd avoided asking himself that question. He couldn't explain the vague impressions that slipped into his brain at odd moments. Particularly when he was on the verge of sleep or as he walked through darkened corridors, times when his mind floated free. He had the very definite feeling that there was only one explanation for his acceptance of the sensations, for his belief that he was being led in the right direction. It had to be Caleb.

Avoiding Rachel's curious gaze, he shrugged. "I looked at the blueprints, too, when we were in the hotel room."

"Oh, come on. They weren't *that* specific."

Eric clamped his lips together. There was no way she would believe the truth. He was barely able to acknowledge to himself that it was his connection to his brother that had fed him the information.

If he told Rachel that, she would think he was crazy. So he improvised.

"I've been exploring."

Rachel sent him a glance filled with doubt. Did she suspect that he was not giving her the whole truth?

"Let's get away from the door. I'm pretty sure that guard makes two rounds an hour, but it could be three."

He pulled her close and wrapped his arm around her waist.

She stiffened. "I don't understand how you just happened to be here in time to open that door."

Eric heard the stubborn lilt to her voice. She wasn't going to give up. "You told me you were going to try to find a way into the basement tonight. You couldn't come through the main entrance again without causing suspicion, since you're not supposed to be here. You told me what Natasha said about this entrance. Shift change is at eleven." He paused. "You could have waited, but I didn't think you'd be able to."

She twisted and looked up at him with a frown.

He almost chuckled. She didn't like that he could read her so well. He didn't tell her that he'd been down here around nine o'clock, as well. Or that he'd planned to sneak back around midnight and every other hour until morning, if he had to.

He also didn't tell her how relieved he'd been when he'd heard her rattling the doorknob. He didn't even try to explain to himself how he was so certain it was she and not the guard checking the door.

"Wasn't there a flashlight among the tools Decker gave you?"

She dug out a tiny, stainless-steel tube.

"Great." He turned the light on, then adjusted the brightness of the beam. "This is a super-high-intensity bulb. Turning the lip will adjust the intensity."

He shone the light on her. Her small frame appeared fragile in the black clothes and her pale face was beautiful, even in the harsh light.

He forced himself to think about the reason they were here.

"What else did Natasha tell you about the blueprints? Was she able to identify any of the rooms on the basement level?"

"She said right inside the door there was a mudroom, with a washroom and a root cellar, and a couple of other unidentified rooms connecting it. Toward the front the basement becomes nothing more than a dirt-lined crawlway."

Eric swept the narrow light around the room. A few stained boxes and some broken bits of furniture were all he saw. Sending the faint light skittering along the walls, he counted three doors.

"Which way is Medical Records?"

"It's on the—" she paused "—west side of the building."

"Okay, let's go."

He heard her uneven breathing. "What are you going to do?"

He bent his head toward hers. "I only have a few more minutes until I have to be back in my bed."

"Oh, no! I forgot about your bed checks. Eric, you have to go now. How did you get out of your room?"

Eric guided her over to the door in the direction she'd indicated. He paused with his hand on the doorknob. "There was some excitement a little while ago. One of the patients had a seizure. Apparently a bad one."

Rachel placed her hands on his bare chest.

Immediately his body responded to the warmth of her fingers. He was standing in front of her in his nighttime uniform. All patients had to change into pajamas by ten o'clock. So he wore briefs and thin cotton pajama bottoms and nothing else.

She slid her hands across his collarbones and down his arms to clutch his forearms.

He shivered, knowing she wasn't trying to be seductive. Her face reflected her concern for the patient who had seized.

"Oh, no! Who was it?"

Eric felt her concern through her tight, hot grip on his arms. "I'm sorry, Rachel. I don't know. I just know it gave me a chance to sneak out of my room and across to the service hall."

With an effort, he turned away from her and twisted the knob. "Give me whatever you were using on that door."

"It was a fingernail file."

"No kidding?" He raised an eyebrow. *Practical.* "What else did you bring?"

"Don't laugh at me."

"Trust me, I won't." He couldn't tell her that laughing was the last thing he felt like doing. He'd already shocked himself a couple of times tonight by the way he kept finding excuses to touch her.

It was as if he couldn't keep his hands off her. He'd never experienced such a strong desire for a particular woman before. His adolescent years had been far from typical, and even as an adult, while he was no virgin, he'd always found it difficult to connect with women on a personal level. The emotional drain was too much.

Not with Rachel, though. He tried to put it off on the weirdly seductive intimacy of her voice in his ear, but he'd used these com units before, with Natasha and Laurel. Neither of them had ever turned him on by just whispering his name.

"I brought the nail file, a screwdriver and some credit cards." She shrugged. "I didn't know if I could pick the lock or not."

Inventive and resourceful. He stuck the file into

the keyhole. After a few deft manipulations, he felt the tumblers move.

"I think I've got it," he whispered. "Stand back, I'm going to open the door a crack. If anyone notices us, you hide, then as soon as you can, get out of here and back to your apartment."

"I'm not leaving you." Her voice slid through his brain as her hand closed around his arm.

"Have you forgotten who's in charge here?" He turned the knob slowly and gently pushed on the door. A dim sliver of light grew as he moved one millimeter at a time. And with each tiny movement of the door, Rachel's fingers tightened on his arm.

Finally he got a look at what was on the other side of the door. Shelves and shelves of folders, neatly ordered, impeccably lined up and brightly color-coded.

He slid the door closed and put his hand on hers where it rested on his arm. Ignoring the fact that through the com unit he could talk to her from five miles away, he slid his hand up her arm to her neck and bent his head toward her until their foreheads were touching.

"Good going, Dr. Harper," he whispered. "Behind that door are shelves full of files."

"Medical Records." Rachel's breath warmed his mouth. "This door must be in the rear of the stacks. I didn't see it the other night."

He nodded slightly. "You were smart to bring tools. You'd make a good partner."

"Do you really think so?"

"Yes. You were brave to come in here, given your fear of the dark."

"How did you know—"

Without considering the consequences, he slid his thumb under her chin and tilted her head up.

"You told me, by your reaction when I described how Grandmother locked Caleb in the closet."

Her lashes dipped to hide her eyes. "It's childish to be afraid of the dark," she said dismissively.

He brushed the backs of his fingers across her cheek and bent his head, allowing his lips to barely touch hers.

She took a soft, swift breath and her lips parted. In surprise? In invitation? He had no idea. With desire and curiosity surging through him, he brushed his mouth across hers again, a featherlike touch that left him aching.

She didn't pursue his mouth, but she didn't pull away, either. It was as if she knew how fragile and fleeting the moment was, just as he did. And, like him, she didn't want to do anything to break the spell.

Her lips trembled.

A thump and a scrape of metal on metal sounded above them.

Eric jerked his head up and tensed. He took a step closer to Rachel, shielding her with his body, though what he could do in pajama bottoms and nothing else, armed with a nail file and a flashlight, he didn't know.

"It's the service elevators," she whispered nervously.

Voices sounded on the other side of the door. Someone had entered the Medical Records room.

"I thought your doctor friend said nobody came down here at night." He felt her shrug.

"He's not my friend. And what he said was 'unless there was an emergency or a new admission.'"

The com units made it possible for them to talk with hardly a sound. Rachel's breathy voice tickled inside Eric's head.

"Do you recognize the voices?"

She shook her head. "I can barely hear anything."

Eric tightened his fingers around her neck as the voices rose. "Shh. I'm going to slide the door open a crack."

Beside him, he felt her stiffen.

Carefully turning the knob, he pushed on the door and held his breath, listening.

"Here it is."

It was a male voice, not far from the door.

"I knew this chart had to be misfiled. So how'd your job interview go?"

Eric couldn't make out what the other person was saying.

The voice near the door began to fade as the man headed toward the other end of the room. "Did you hear about the FDA investigation?"

"Investigating the Meadows? No. Tell me."

"I heard Metzger's latest new drug application was—"

Wooden chairs scraping on concrete floors drowned out the rest of the words.

"They're sitting down at the computer workstations," Rachel said. "They're going to be here for a while, and it's getting late."

He nodded as he slowly pulled the door closed and carefully released the knob. He held up the fingernail file, but as Rachel reached for it, he palmed it.

She sent him an alarmed glance. "You can't keep that. If they find it they'll lock you up."

"I'll take my chances," he muttered, slipping the file into the loosely sewn drawstring waistband of his pajamas.

Then he caught Rachel's arm and led her quietly over to the exterior door.

"What was that about an FDA investigation?"

"I don't know anything about that."

"It would have to be linked to a research study, wouldn't it?"

"I suppose so."

"Call Mitch when you get back to your apartment. Tell him what we heard and ask him to contact the FDA about anything concerning the Meadows, Metzger, Green or anyone else connected with this case."

He gripped her shoulders and placed her, back to the wall, next to the door. Then he eased the heavy wooden door open with agonizing slowness, finally peering out across the lawn.

"It looks clear. Run back the way you came. And for God's sake, be careful."

He took her face in his hands. Her blue eyes were barely visible in the inky darkness. He pressed his forehead against hers and spoke quietly. "Don't cut me off again. Keep up our check-in schedule. Talk to me. And I swear, if you ever pull a stunt like this again, I'll contact Decker and get you extracted immediately. Do you understand?"

She nodded and put her hands over his. "Go. You're going to get caught."

He knew she was right.

He pressed on the small of her back and urged her out the door. "Run!"

When he was sure she was safely across the open lawn and hidden in the underbrush, he locked the door, wound his way through the corridors and vaulted up the stairs.

By the time he got back to the first floor service

hall, Gracie was six rooms away, making her rounds. He listened as she opened a door and peered in, then continued on to the next room, where she did the same thing.

He waited. At the third room from his, he heard a patient's voice call her name as she pushed open a door. He angled his head around the corner in time to see her step inside the room. He slipped across the hall and into his room, heading straight for the bathroom.

Checking the mirror, he saw cobwebs in his hair and smudges on his shoulders. His breath hissed out through his teeth in relief that he'd thought to duck into the bathroom. Grabbing a washcloth, he brushed it over his head and down his shoulders. He exited the bathroom just as Gracie opened his door.

Squinting against the bright hall lights, he smiled at her. "Hi, sweetheart. Come to kiss me good night?"

Gracie frowned. "What are you doing out of bed?"

"Call of nature, my dear."

Gracie harrumphed, but she didn't leave. "Stay in bed, Caleb."

Eric climbed into bed and turned over, feeling the sharp tip of the nail file pressing into his side. Its cool metal sharpness was reassuring. As soon as Gracie was done with bed checks, he planned to use the file to bend the metal flashing on the doorjamb so it creaked and dragged when pushed open. He couldn't afford to have anyone walk in on him unannounced.

"Say good night, Gracie," he whispered.

With another sniff, Gracie closed his door.

Chapter Eight

When Rachel got back to her apartment, she saw the message light on her phone blinking. The call was from Dr. Metzger's secretary, informing her of an appointment with Dr. Metzger in his office, the next afternoon at 4:00 p.m.

Rachel stood staring at the phone. She'd been so thrilled to be accepted at the Meadows. Ever since she'd first heard of Gerhardt Metzger, it had been her life's dream to work with the famous neurologist. He was closer to a breakthrough on the treatment of schizophrenia than anyone had been in the past fifteen years.

In the two months she'd been at the facility, she'd seen Metzger maybe three or four times. She'd never had the chance to speak to him.

Now, because Caleb had kidnapped her, suddenly he was interested in talking with her.

Why? To consult with her on Caleb's condition? Or to find out what Caleb may have told her?

Rachel fervently hoped it was the former. Her goal from the time she was old enough to understand what was wrong with her mother, had been to become a doctor—to defeat mental illness.

Dr. Metzger was her idol. She had read all his articles and papers on schizophrenia and brain chemistry. She could not believe his intent was evil.

She unloaded her pockets and saw that the cell phone the FBI had issued her had a missed call on it. She read the text message from Natasha.

SpAg N. Rudolph: Dr. Harper, need to arng mtg to tx bps to u. UnID'd ctrl area in bsmt may be lab. Poss bmb shlt in 60s.

"Eric?" she whispered into her com, but she heard only dead air. He'd turned his unit off. When it was on, she heard and felt the connection between them.

"Eric, damn it!" He'd *ordered* her to keep her com on, but he'd turned his off? She wanted to growl in frustration, but then the implication hit her like a blow.

What if he hadn't made it back to his room? What if he'd been caught? Fear for his safety gripped her.

"Eric, answer me!" But she knew it was futile. If Eric had been caught sneaking back into his room, Gracie would probably write it up as another episode of sleepwalking. Caleb had been known for sleepwalking through the halls at night. From what he'd told Eric, he hadn't always been asleep.

She looked at her watch. It was after one o'clock in the morning. She considered going back over to the main building to check on Eric. But her appearance would just cause more suspicion. And if he'd been caught—fear crawled up her spine. She couldn't afford to take the chance.

Her skin itched with frustration and sweat. She showered quickly and climbed into bed. She was going to be exhausted in the morning.

Reluctantly she turned off her com unit. She stared at the ceiling, worry firing her nerves. With the com unit off, she felt more alone than she'd ever felt in her life. She clamped her jaw, deliberately closed her eyes and turned onto her side.

She could not depend on Eric being there. Because once the FBI found the evidence they sought, he would be gone.

LATE THE NEXT NIGHT, Rachel crouched in the tall grass, waiting for the guard and his dog to round the west corner of the building. Her nerves were raw. The entire day had passed with agonizing slowness, made worse by her dread of the afternoon meeting with Dr. Metzger. She'd marked each hour by turning on her com unit and trying to contact Eric, according to their plan. But he never answered.

As the day had dragged on and on, her nerves had stretched as taut as a rubber band, until she'd felt as if she would snap. She'd found it almost impossible to concentrate on the problems of the women in the two group sessions she'd conducted and a routine clinical assessment on a new admission.

Then, in the middle of Dr. Metzger's office, as the receptionist had explained that Metzger was involved in an emergency and couldn't see her, her com unit had come alive. Somehow she'd managed to suppress her relief at hearing Eric's voice until she'd exited the office.

Eric had instructed her to bring the FBI-issue cell phone with her and meet him at the back entrance at eleven o'clock. He'd cautioned her to hide in the grass and wait until he contacted her. Then he'd turned his com unit off.

So here she was, waiting. She was worried about Eric. As relieved as she'd been to hear his voice, he'd sounded odd—stressed and tired.

"Rachel? Are you here?"

She jerked. The shadow that was the secret doorway shifted and she saw a pale figure.

Eric. Her eyes stung with relief. There he was, whole and unharmed.

"I can see you," she said on a sigh.

He lifted one arm.

"Come on, hurry."

She glanced around to verify that no one was around, then dashed across the velvet carpet of grass straight into his arms.

"Whoa," he whispered as he pulled her inside and closed the door. "I'm glad to see you, too, but be careful."

For just a second she pressed her face into the hollow under his collarbone, until the urge to cry went away.

Something was wrong. His body was hot, with fine tremors rippling through his muscles. She pulled back and looked at him in the almost non-existent light. There was a hollow, haunted look in his eyes.

"Eric, what's the matter?"

He shook his head. "Did you bring the cell phone?"

"Of course." She was angry with him for not contacting her all day long. "You had no right to leave me for almost twenty-four hours with no contact. You were the one who insisted on regular check-ins."

"I was a little busy today. Now give me the phone. We don't have a lot of time."

His voice was tight, his movements jerky—almost awkward. Something had happened to him. Judging by his demeanor, something bad.

She dug the phone out of her jeans' pocket and handed it over.

"I need you to look at it anyway. There's a text message from Natasha," she said.

Rachel watched his strong, elegant hands as he quickly manipulated the keypad. They trembled slightly, but he didn't fumble.

"'Dr. Harper, need to arrange meeting to transfer blueprints to you,'" he read. "'Unidentified central area in basement may be lab. Possible bomb shelter in the sixties.'" He looked up. "That's interesting. You need to get those blueprints as soon as possible. Set up a meeting."

Rachel was taken aback by his abrupt tone. He sounded as if he was barely holding himself together.

He raised his head. "Did you bring the flashlight?"

"Yes, of course."

"We need to search for Caleb's records."

He turned and headed for the door to the Medical Records room. He pulled the fingernail file out of the narrow seam of his drawstring pajama bottoms and picked the lock, listening for a few seconds before slipping inside.

Rachel followed him, her heart in her throat. What if one of the doctors was down here, like last night? Or an emergency situation required a chart?

"How is this area laid out?" Eric asked quietly.

"These are the stacks. There's a counter up there,

about twelve feet from the door, and beyond the counter are kiosks with computers, telephones and a dictating machine."

"Are the charts computerized?"

"It's a double system. The doctors can either use the computer or they can write or dictate notes the old-fashioned way, and transcribers enter the information. The Meadows keeps computer records and hard copies. You saw last night how perfect the files are. It's hard to believe they're real. Charts are usually pretty beat up, especially old ones."

"What did you tell me about the patient identification system?"

"The first two digits represent the number of the first letter of the patient's last name." She explained the rest of the ID number.

"Okay, got it. I can give you most of Caleb's ID."

"You can?"

He smiled wryly. "My birth date is the same as Caleb's. And our social security numbers were issued at the same time, so his is bound to be close to mine."

"Of course. So your ID number would be 02— what?"

He rattled off the number.

Rachel repeated the number to herself. If Caleb's number was close, it should be easy to find Caleb's chart, as well as any of his unfiled records.

Eric nodded toward the stacks. "I'll keep watch

while you retrieve Caleb's file. We won't take the chance of trying to hack into the computer. I'll leave that to Natasha if it becomes necessary."

Rachel turned on the high-intensity flashlight and began searching the stacks for Caleb's chart.

She heard quiet beeps as Eric keyed a number into the cell phone and walked a few steps away from her.

"Mitch."

Rachel stopped, shamelessly eavesdropping.

"Yeah. Kind of rough. Today, especially. No, she's doing great. Not totally convinced that she's doing the right thing, but she's committed. Keeping her promise to help. Pretty resourceful, too."

Rachel raised her brows as warmth flowed through her. *Doing great.* She had no doubt that if Eric thought otherwise, he'd say so.

She directed the light across the tabs until she came to the section of ID numbers that began with the number two for B, the second letter in the alphabet. They were on the far side of the shelf nearest the back wall.

"No, I'm okay. What about Caleb? He hasn't woken up, has he?" Eric's tone changed when he asked about his brother. It was at once hopeful and disheartened, as if he already knew the answer to his question.

"Yeah. I could tell. I'm getting some help. A sense

of direction that helps me get around. A vague understanding of where things are. An instinct about how to act. Nothing specific, but then I never was able to hear—" His voice faded to silence.

What was he talking about? An oppressive blanket of unnamed fear and caution enveloped her, similar to how she felt when she visited her mother.

She shivered.

"I know. We're in the Medical Records room now, looking for his records. Apparently, Metzger has a few specific patients he uses for his experiments. Natasha contacted Rachel. Have arrangements been for Rachel to meet an agent to get the blueprints? Good. I'll talk to you when I can. Meanwhile, Rachel's got the phone if there's any change in Caleb's condition. Thanks."

Rachel scanned the folders in the section marked B, but she didn't find Baldwyn anywhere. There was a Baldwyn, first name Anne. She pulled it out and glanced through several pages, just in case.

"Rachel, have you found anything?" Eric asked.

"No. The chart isn't back here."

"Are you sure?" He walked over to her side. She felt the trembling in his limbs. "Could it be misfiled?"

"I doubt it. He's about to be arraigned for attempted murder and kidnapping. His chart is probably in police custody, or at the very least in the chief medical director's office."

"There has to be something here that we can use." His voice was harsh. "Look again."

"Eric, what's wrong with you tonight? What did Mitch say? Is Caleb no better?"

He shook his head.

"I'm so sorry. I wish I could be more help. I can't believe we're having such a hard time finding anything."

"Obviously someone has gone to a lot of trouble to hide the evidence."

"If there's anything down here referring to Caleb, it would have to be in that bin of unfiled forms."

"Great. Where is the bin?" He wiped a hand down his face.

She grabbed his muscled wrist.

He looked down at her and his throat moved as he swallowed.

"First you tell me what's wrong. What happened to you today?"

"I'm fine. We don't have a lot of time here, Rachel."

"I deserve to know why you didn't contact me all day."

He took the flashlight from her, rechecking the shelf she'd just looked at. She knew his action was just something for him to do to keep from looking at her.

"This morning, the big registered nurse, Thomas,

who seems to have it in for Caleb, came in with an orderly. He gave me my regular daily injection." He paused, wiping a hand down his face. "Then he told me I was going for a 'procedure,' and the orderly held me down while Thomas gave me a second injection. I guess they thought I might fight it, but I didn't." He took a shaky breath. "It was a strong sedative."

Rachel took a sharp breath. "What had you done?"

He sent her an irritated glance. "I hadn't *done* anything. About five minutes later, Thomas returned with another orderly and they strapped me to a gurney and took me—somewhere." He rubbed his hand over his eyes. "I tried to keep my bearings, but I was too drowsy. I know I was taken on an elevator."

Rachel thought about what he'd said to Mitch.

A sense of direction. An instinct. Dread washed over her.

"I faded in and out of consciousness, but I tried to pretend I was asleep the whole time. They obviously thought I should be. I guess the antagonist medication they gave me at Walter Reed is kicking in."

The flashlight beam wavered.

Rachel's heart went out to him.

"I remember a syringe—a needle. A stinging at the base of my skull." He blew out a breath. "I remember a burning sensation in my head, like it was on fire. It was hard to stay still." He sent her a quick glance. "I remember seeing Metzger."

He turned to face her, the flashlight's halo lighting his face. She saw the feverish panic in his eyes. "I think Metzger extracted something from my brain. Remember Caleb talking about Metzger sucking out his brains?"

She remembered, but her instinct was to protect Metzger. He was a fellow physician. He'd taken the same oath she had. "Dr. Metzger's first priority is to help his patients, not hurt them. We both know Caleb has delusions. I never saw anything like that in Caleb's chart."

Eric's face darkened in anger. "And you think I'm having the same delusions?"

"You're receiving the same drug. That's got to be affecting you. It was probably a routine procedure."

"I'm telling you it was not routine. I believe Metzger's using the fluids he extracts to create the injections I'm getting every day. The ones that are recorded in the chart as fenpiprazole. You said yourself that Metzger's theory is based on immunizing patients against their own brain chemicals."

"You were drowsy. Maybe you dreamed—"

"I did not dream anything," he snapped. "Damn it, Rachel—"

A noise behind them froze them both in place. A sliver of light shot across the worn tile.

Eric's arms encircled her and lifted her off her feet. She wrapped her arms around his neck as he propelled her silently backward, into the far corner of the stacks, then lowered her to the floor.

He whispered through her com unit. "Shh. They won't see us if we stay perfectly still."

Rachel lay beneath Eric, his hard, lean body pressed along her length, sending erotic signals to her brain. Her breasts tightened, her breathing quickened.

How did they keep ending up in these dangerous situations with their limbs entwined, so close they were practically breathing as one person?

The lights came on. Rachel cringed and Eric's body tensed. The corner where they hid was shrouded in shadow, but anyone who got close enough would be able to see them.

The swinging gate that separated the front of the room from the shelves creaked.

He's in the stacks, Rachel mouthed.

Eric nodded once. His breath was hot against her cheek. His arms sheltered her and his bare chest pressed against her breasts. She was hyperaware of him, of his barely controlled breathing, of his steel-hard muscles, of his growing hardness against her belly.

She swallowed and tried not to think about how quickly and easily she responded to him.

Beyond them, soft footsteps marked the approach of the person who might turn the corner at any second and find them. Rachel heard the unmistakable sound of papers rustling. She held her breath as adrenaline pumped through her veins like her blood.

If she were caught in such a compromising position with a patient, she'd be fired. Moreover, she'd probably lose her license to practice medicine forever.

Eric's chest rose and fell against her sensitive breasts.

The gate creaked again and the quiet footsteps moved away. Then the light went out and the door's click echoed in the sudden quiet.

For several seconds neither of them moved.

Rachel felt Eric's rapid heartbeat as it synched with hers. After what could have been one second or an eternity, he lifted his head.

The darkness was so complete after the harsh shock of light, that if it hadn't been for the glow in his eyes and the secure strength of his body, she'd have screamed in terror.

Her breath shuddered out. "I thought we'd be caught."

"Me, too."

"Eric—" She shifted and he made a low, pained sound deep in his throat.

Then he pulled away. "Sorry," he whispered.

"Oh, please, don't—" she whispered.

Eric tried without success to calm his out-of-control desire. He filled his mind with their risky close call, but that only fueled the hunger that surged through him.

He'd never felt like this. It was the danger, his rational brain calmly asserted. Nothing like almost getting caught to add to the excitement.

Rachel's hands slid around his bare waist and up his back. "Don't move away. It's so dark," she whispered. "I'm scared."

Her hands burned hotter than the damn needle this morning. He shivered with instant reaction. The heat of her hands and the warm caress of her breath engulfed him.

"I feel your heart pounding. Are you scared, too?"

He nodded, hearing her need for reassurance in her voice.

"Not of the dark." He was afraid of her. Of her ability to make him believe he could have a normal life. Of the hold her strong, delicate body had over him. Of the part of himself he'd never shown to anyone, but that he knew she deserved to see.

The part that would frighten her away.

"Of what then?"

Her words echoed in stereo in his head. Here in the dark, alone with her, could he tell her the truth? "I'm afraid of you."

She stiffened.

"Of this." He closed his eyes and pressed himself against her, laying his cheek against hers so that her silky hair tickled his nose. "I have a hard time opening up to people."

Her lips touched his ear and something happened inside him. A dam broke between his heart and his body, and the pent-up passion he'd never allowed to surface flowed over him. It took all his self-control to keep from coming right then.

He clenched his jaw and braced himself to stop this foolishness before it went any further.

But Rachel's lips moved against his ear. "Don't leave me yet," she begged.

He turned his head. She turned hers at the same moment and their mouths met in a careful, slow kiss. He didn't move a muscle, holding on to the last frayed strand of his restraint with all his might.

She leaned in, giving more, seeking more. Without meaning to, he found himself giving her what she sought. His tongue touched her soft, full lips and her moan slid through him, a potent aphrodisiac that left him rigid and pulsing.

He turned, pulling her fully against him, kissing her with an abandon he'd never even allowed himself to imagine. His prior experiences with women were reduced to adolescent memories as he gave himself over to the incredible feel of her supple, shapely body. She felt like the finest satin, wrapped around him.

And he knew, he *knew,* what she was feeling. Her hesitant movements, her trembling limbs, told him she was as surprised and overwhelmed as he.

He slid his hand up under her black sweater, craving the feel of her bare skin against his fingers.

"Do we have time?" she whispered, her fingers tracing his biceps up to his shoulders.

Ah, hell. Her words hit him like a bucket of ice water. He took a sharp breath and rolled away.

"What is it?"

"I have to get back." His voice reflected the intense control that he had to dredge up from within to quench the fire that had almost consumed him. He groaned as he sat up, his arousal aching.

"I'm on two-hour bed checks now, but I've been gone a long time."

He stood, his legs unsteady, and held out his hand.

Rachel let him help her up, using her other hand to straighten her sweater.

"Rachel, we need to talk. Come upstairs with me."

She stared at him. "And do what? Hide under your bed?"

He shrugged. "There are things we need to discuss."

He felt her tense.

"May I have the flashlight please?" Her voice was carefully controlled.

He handed it to her and followed her as she

found her way back to the door that led to the basement.

"We can talk through our com units," she said crisply. "I need to stay here and search through the unfiled records. I know your ID number, and of course I'll only be looking at records that begin with the number two. That will eliminate a lot."

"No."

"Yes." She propped her fists on her hips. "Didn't Mitch tell you that Caleb is not getting better? The longer he remains unconscious, the higher the chances he'll contract an infection or go into a coma."

He knew she was right. He had to trust her to be careful. "Stay in constant contact with me. Tell me where you are every second, and if I turn off my com, it will only be because I'm being watched. I'll turn it back on as soon as possible." He wrapped a hand around her neck, feeling her resist his touch.

"Keep your com unit on. Promise me."

Her chin went up, but she nodded. "I promise."

"I'll try to get into the sunroom. That way I can see the guard and can warn you when he's headed around the building."

He caressed her cheek with his thumb. *God, he hated to leave her down here alone.*

"Be careful," he whispered, then he headed for the service stairs.

Chapter Nine

The next night Rachel met with the FBI agent. Despite their close call, the search the night before had yielded nothing about Caleb. Rachel had spent a restless night, tortured by the memory of Eric's body against hers.

Then Mitch had called her first thing in the morning to let her know of the meeting. All day, she'd had to force herself to concentrate on her patients instead of the clock.

Now, she drove through the darkness, rain falling much too fast for the windshield wipers to push it out of the way. Rachel drove carefully, turning up the defroster to keep the windshield clear. Up ahead, she saw the small road sign that read Meadows Lane.

A shaky sigh escaped her lips. She was almost home. The meeting at a restaurant in the next town had been uneventful, if one considered a clandestine rendezous with a secret agent to exchange documents uneventful.

It occurred to her how different her life had become in less than one week. All her life, she'd pursued normalcy with the zeal of a religious convert. It had taken her a long time, after her chaotic childhood, to learn that it was actually possible to live quietly and safely.

But now, suddenly, she was caught in a bizarre world where murder investigations and secret meetings and danger were everyday events.

She hadn't realized how nervous she'd been about the meeting until now. As she made the turn, she noticed the stiffness in her fingers from clutching the steering wheel.

She took the long circular drive around to the staff apartments and pulled into her parking place, right outside her apartment door.

Before she braved the pouring rain, she made sure the copies of the blueprints the agent had given her were secure inside her backpack.

Then she jumped out of her car and dashed toward her door without an umbrella, key in hand.

She turned the key quickly and ducked inside, sighing in relief as she closed the door behind her and reached toward the light switch.

She wasn't alone. The thought skittered through her brain as if someone had whispered it to her. Her com unit was off, though, so it couldn't have been Eric. She froze, her gaze sweeping the kitchen area to the left of the door.

The night-light she always left burning over her sink bathed the room in a pale blue glow. But the green and purple screen saver that started up after twenty minutes of no action on her computer wasn't on. Instead she saw an open file. Someone had recently touched her computer.

Suddenly a dark shape blocked the computer's glare. Before she had time to react, the shape slammed into her, shoving her out of its way and into the kitchen counter. She hit hard, knocking a glass onto the floor, then fell, her palms and right knee crunching on broken glass. She cried out in pain and surprise.

The door flew open behind her. Rachel whirled, but all she saw was a big shadow disappearing into the haze of rain.

She sat up, her hands and knee stinging. Frantic, she groped for her backpack, wincing when her hand touched the rough canvas.

Gulping air in huge terrified sobs, she hugged her backpack to her chest and scrambled to her feet. She pushed her door closed and threw the latch. Her rational brain noted that the lock still worked and the door hadn't been forced, which meant that whoever had invaded her apartment had used a key. The security guards probably had master keys to every room on the grounds. That thought did not make her feel safe.

She put the chain on with shaky fingers, feeling silly. If someone wanted to get in, a hardware store chain lock wasn't going to keep them out. But it made her feel a tiny bit safer to hear the reassuringly solid rattle of metal against metal.

For a panic-stricken instant, she considered running out to her car and driving away—but where would she go? To the FBI?

No. FBI agents probably dealt with situations like this all the time. If Mitch Decker thought she was incapable of handling a simple break-in, he'd probably jerk her out of there so fast her head would spin, and make good on his promise to lock her in protective custody until the investigation was over.

She shook her head, feeling dwarfed by the powerful presence of the stately building on the hill and intimidated by the magnitude of her task. Yet she couldn't leave. Not while Eric was still here. She had to stay, for his sake.

She put her hand over her mouth, trying to control her spasming lungs. She was about to hyperventilate. Someone had been in her apartment, touched her computer. Who? What else had they touched? And what were they hoping to find?

She looked down at the navy-blue backpack she carried with her everywhere. The backpack that had held the doctor's order forms until earlier this evening, when she'd turned them over to the FBI agent. Then she peered at the computer. What had the intruder been searching for? The open file was titled Journal. Rachel had been typing a little each night since she'd been at the Meadows, recording her experiences here. Her last entry had been five days ago on Tuesday, the day she'd been kidnapped.

Luckily, she'd been too busy, or too tired, to journal since she'd been back. Staring at her mundane words only emphasized the bizarre nature of her life since her kidnapping. And it had only gotten more bizarre since Eric had gone undercover as his brother. At first, all the sneaking around, dodging guards and dogs and taking secret messages had been exciting, even titillating.

But all at once, within the space of a few seconds, she no longer felt safe. Her world, which she had worked so hard to make structured and secure, had turned fragile.

She pressed the button that turned on her com unit. She heard the dead quiet that meant Eric's unit wasn't on. But still she tried. "Eric?" she said.

Glancing at the clock on the kitchen wall, she saw that it was 8:35p.m. It would be forty minutes before Eric turned his com unit on for the last time tonight. At eight-fifteen, she hadn't tried to contact him, because she'd been out of the five-mile range.

"Damn it, Eric," she whispered, her voice cracking. Why didn't he ever feel the need to turn the unit on as she occasionally did, just check to see if she was listening or might need him.

"I need you," she whispered.

She bent to pick up a shard of glass and her knee screamed in protest.

"Ow!" Tears sprang to her eyes. She limped into the bathroom and looked at herself in the mirror.

She was a mess. Her hair was soaked and plastered to her head. A wide streak of red stained her forehead and left cheek where she'd wiped them with her bleeding hands. Her eyes were red-rimmed with tears. She reached up to wipe the blood off her cheek and her stinging palm left more red than it wiped away. She turned her hands over. Her palms sparkled with slivers of glass.

She spent some time digging it out of her hands and knee, then washed the cuts and splashed water on her face, rinsing off the blood. She combed her wet hair back. The streaks of blood were gone but she still looked like she felt.

One heartbeat away from panic.

A faint ringing sound reached her ears. It was the FBI cell phone. She stared at her wide-eyed reflection in the mirror, wanting to ignore the call. She did not want to talk to anyone except Eric.

But the ringing persisted. She slung a terry-cloth robe she kept hanging on the back of the door around her as she hurried to her backpack and fished the phone out of the side pocket.

"Rachel? It's Mitch Decker."

"Oh, Mitch. Hi."

His deep, steady voice made tears well in her eyes. She swallowed, afraid he could hear her distress.

"I spoke to Agent Simmons. He said the exchange went smoothly this evening. Are you all right?"

"S-sure." She grimaced, certain he could tell she was lying. She had to get control of her emotions. Mitch had threatened to lock her in a safe house once. If he thought she was too emotional, he might actually do it.

She would not be taken away. Eric needed her.

"Where are you?"

"I'm in my apartment. I just got back. It…it's been raining, and these roads are not well marked." She bit her lip as hard as she dared, struggling to control the trembling sobs that kept trying to escape her throat.

"Are you saying you had an accident?"

"No." She pressed her fingertips against her mouth for an instant. "Close enough to scare me, but no. No accident." She cleared her throat. "I'm fine."

"Rachel—" Mitch's kind, authoritative voice penetrated her fragile self-control.

She couldn't lie to him. "There was someone…in my apartment tonight."

"Who?" Mitch's voice didn't change timbre.

"I don't know. I surprised him and he ran out. He'd been on my computer, but he didn't find anything." She took a deep, shaky breath. "Mitch, don't take me away. I can handle it. I need to stay here."

"Could he have found anything pertaining to the investigation?"

"No. I keep everything with me."

"Good. Someone is suspicious of you. Be extra careful. Don't give them any reason to be. I'm going to put together an extraction team, in case you need to be pulled out quickly."

"Mitch, I swear, I can handle it. Please don't extract me."

"I'll leave you in as long as I can. You're my only link to Eric. You've got the blueprints, right?"

"Yes. And I handed over the physicians' orders to Simmons." She sounded pathetic. She took a deep breath and closed her eyes with relief. Mitch was not going to extract her. "One page, a progress note written by Dr. Green, refers to respiratory depression in a young white female. I couldn't identify the patient, but I think it may be Misty Norwood, the girl Caleb mentioned." As Rachel talked, her fluttering pulse began to calm and her voice sounded stronger.

"Good. Natasha will contact you as soon as she has verified any of the information. Rachel, I need to talk to Eric. Tonight if possible. Can you get the cell phone to him?"

"Yes." Her pulse raced as she thought about going back out into the darkness. "Is something wrong?"

"I have some information for him." His tone discouraged questions.

"Should he call this number?"

"Yes. Thanks. How long do you think it will be?"

"No more than an hour."

"Okay. I'll be waiting."

Mitch disconnected.

The tears Rachel had held at bay during the conversation overflowed.

Wiping her hot cheeks, she pulled on the first thing at hand: stretchy yoga pants and a little T-shirt that read UNBEND.

She didn't have time to feel sorry for herself. She had to get the phone to Eric. It worried her that Mitch had evaded her question, that he hadn't just given her a message for Eric. Something must be wrong with Caleb.

It was a dark, miserable trek across the grounds to the main building. The rain had stopped, but the ground was wet and slippery and the unsettling noise made by water dripping from the trees frayed her nerves.

By the time she got to the rear of the building her watch read three minutes after nine. In twelve minutes, Eric would turn on his com unit. She activated hers, but all she heard was the flat silence that meant his unit was off.

Hearing that absence of sound was worse than anything that had happened tonight. Because it meant Eric wasn't there.

She felt isolated, claustrophobic, as if she were trapped in a sound-proofed room. She'd gotten too accustomed to having his voice in her ear.

She wanted to switch the unit off, to cut out that awful deadness, but Eric might try to reach her at any moment, so she left it on.

Without Eric's help, she couldn't get in through the back door, so she circled around to the front entrance and looked through the glass doors at the security desk. The guard was leaning back in his chair, talking on his cell phone.

She debated walking in past him, but given her state of mind right now, she was afraid if the guard stopped her she wouldn't be able to give him a coherent answer, much less a plausible excuse for being in the main building this time of night.

She checked her watch. It was seven minutes past nine. She'd wait and get Eric to sneak down and open the rear door.

Just as she was about to sneak away, the guard pocketed his phone and stood, stretching. He picked up his two-way radio, and walked away from the desk.

Her pulse sped up. Was he going on a break? Or to make his assigned rounds? It didn't matter. All that mattered was that she had a tiny window of time to get inside without being caught.

Hurrying up the steps, she pushed through the glass doors and strode past the desk as if she were late for a meeting. She passed two physicians on their way out, but she pretended to fiddle with the strap of her backpack to avoid looking up as she headed through the lobby toward the neurology wing. Her wet hiking boots squeaked on the tile floor and the nape of her neck prickled, as if a hand hovered just close enough to reach out and grab her.

The main corridors were empty, except for an occasional housekeeper mopping floors or a pharmacy technician wheeling a cartful of medications to one of the wards. On the other side of the doors that separated the main corridors from the service hall, Rachel heard the rattle of metal and glass, the sound of evening food trays being transported to the main kitchen.

She paused outside the double mahogany doors that led into the neurology ward, taking a moment to push her fingers through her wet hair and to wipe her face. Considering what she would say if Gracie confronted her, she eased open the doors.

The com unit in her ear came alive. Her pulse jumped.

"Eric," she whispered.

"Did the exchange go smoothly? Where are you?"

With a glance down the hall, she darted over to Room 3 and pushed on the door. It squeaked as it opened.

"Right here."

He whirled. He'd been standing at the window, already dressed for sleep in the standard, light blue, drawstring pajamas issued to all the male patients. Like Caleb, Eric didn't bother with a T-shirt.

"Hi." She smiled as her eyes filled with tears. A long shuddering breath rippled through her. She was okay now. She was with Eric.

His lean body, silhouetted against the window, had the fluid grace and easy confidence of a lion. But as his soft dark eyes scrutinized her, his face creased with worry.

"What the hell happened to you?"

Before her brain registered his movement, he was beside her. He wiped his thumb across her cheekbone, then rubbed his thumb and fingers together. "This is blood. Did you have an accident on the road?"

To her dismay, Rachel almost broke down. She put her hands over her mouth, fighting to control the sobs that tried to escape from her throat. She shook her head.

"Damn it, Rachel. Look at your hands." He pulled

them away from her mouth and bent his head to examine them. When he looked up, concern darkened his eyes. "What happened?"

She shook her head and swallowed. "The meeting with the agent went fine. I got the blueprints and I turned over the medical records."

He nodded, his face grave. "Good." Holding her hands gently in his, he waited for her to explain.

"When I got back to my apartment, someone was inside. He knocked me down."

Eric's grip tightened. The cuts burned and she flinched. He let go and grasped her shoulders.

"Tell me."

She sucked in a deep breath. "When I unlocked my apartment door and went in, I must have surprised him, because he knocked me down and ran. I fell onto some glass."

He cursed under his breath, but through her com unit she heard every word.

"What was missing?"

"Nothing, as far as I could tell. He'd checked my computer, but nothing seemed out of place."

"They were probably looking for anything that might connect you with the FBI."

Her breath shuddered out. "Do you think they know?"

"No, but I think Metzger suspects, based on some of the questions he's asked me. So there was nothing in your apartment that would confirm their suspicions?" His gaze burned into hers.

She shook her head. "The Meadows provides a cleaning lady once a week. I didn't want to leave anything around that she might find."

"That's good," Eric said absently. He began to pace, grazing his knuckles with his teeth. "Something doesn't add up. Breaking in doesn't sound like Metzger's style. If Metzger was suspicious of you, I'd think he'd just have you killed."

Rachel went white as a sheet. Eric immediately wished he could jerk back the words.

"I'm sorry," he said.

Rachel lifted her chin. "No. You're right. Dr. Metzger is very results-oriented." Her throat moved as she swallowed.

He frowned. "I'm beginning to think it's too dangerous for you here."

Her eyes snapped with blue fire. "I can handle it."

Eric eyed his beautiful, stubborn partner. *Yes.* He believed she could handle it. "That's not the point," he said, folding his arms and staring down at her. "The point is, you've been hurt twice already and I have no intention of allowing you to be hurt again. They suspect you, that means we need to get you out of here."

She shook her head and a strand of hair fell across her forehead. "If I leave now, won't that seem even more suspicious? And what will you do alone? You need me."

Eric's eyes roamed hungrily over her, taking in her snug pants and figure-hugging black T-shirt, the graceful slope of her neck, the black hair that, even wet, curved under her chin, and those amazing, brilliant blue eyes. His body reacted to just the sight of her.

Yes, he needed her. But what he needed from her he couldn't have anyway. And he certainly wasn't going to put her in danger just because with her at his side he felt complete for the first time in his life. He'd always thought Caleb was the other part of him, and he was. Eric had a connection to his identical twin that had transcended their separation. But he was beginning to realize just how important Rachel was to him.

"Give me the phone. I'm calling Mitch and telling him to get you out of here before you get really hurt."

"Oh, Eric." Her face turned pale. "Mitch called. That's why I came. He wanted to talk to you personally."

Eric went still. "Why didn't he just give you the message? Was it about Caleb?"

Her fingers looked pinched as she held out the phone. "He didn't say."

As Eric took hold of the phone, his fingers brushed hers. She held fast and looked up into his eyes. "I told Mitch what happened. He agreed to let me stay."

He started to speak, but she interrupted him.

"Please, Eric. Don't ask Mitch to have me removed. I need to do this. I need to help Caleb and... and you."

There was a passion in her eyes that he couldn't ignore. He knew that passion. He understood it. She needed to prove to herself that she could make a difference in someone's life. He even knew where it came from. The same place as his need. The feeling that in the past, she'd failed the one person in her life who'd depended on her. For her, it was her mother. For him, it was Caleb.

Eric pulled the phone from Rachel's unsteady hand. She was obviously shaken by her experience. He had to admire her for being so determined not to give up.

As he keyed in Mitch's number, Eric wondered who was growing suspicious, and how much they had figured out. He knew if Metzger gave him a physical exam, the doctor would immediately realize that he wasn't Caleb Baldwyn. The scar under his ear would prove that.

Mitch answered right away.

"What is it?" Eric didn't waste time with niceties.

"We obtained the complete autopsy report and evidence box on Charles Green. Laurel reran some tests, considering the possibility of murder. She found extremely high levels of morphine, but she also discovered a lethal level of potassium."

"Potassium? A tox screen wouldn't normally test for that, but what about injection sites on the body?"

"According to the autopsy report, the morphine and alcohol were found in his stomach contents. So the blood tests were run on those. The medical examiner didn't test for other substances."

Eric lifted his gaze to Rachel. "I'll bet he didn't check for hidden injection sites, either, like under the tongue or in the scalp."

"Nope."

"So Dr. Green was fired for talking to a reporter, and he apparently died of a drug overdose. Yet now it appears that someone dosed him up with morphine and booze, and injected potassium into his bloodstream. That's murder."

Rachel pressed her knuckles against her mouth.

"We're obtaining permission to exhume the body. Laurel says it's theoretically possible to find an injection site on an embalmed body."

"I hope she's right." Eric gripped the phone tightly. "So is that what you called about?"

"I have information from Natasha. She found a Misty Norwood. It turns out the young woman was admitted to the Meadows by her parents following a suicide attempt, and stayed there for several months. She was discharged at her parents' request, after they became concerned by some of the things she told them. She's now living at home with them. We're making arrangements to interview her."

"Mitch, Rachel could have relayed all this information to me."

The instant of silence on Mitch's end told Eric why his boss had wanted to speak with him personally. He'd already felt that something was wrong.

From the moment he'd heard his brother's name on the television newscast, he'd been slowly accepting the truth. The sensations and dreams he'd always feared, the images and odd thoughts, and now the heightened awareness and instinctive knowledge of how to navigate the halls and corridors of the Meadows, were a part of the link he shared with his twin brother. But in the past twenty-four hours or so, those thoughts and sensations were becoming less and less coherent.

Sometimes he had to fight the disorder in his head just to think and act rationally. What he couldn't figure out was if the increasingly chaotic sensations were from the daily injections he was forced to endure or from Caleb's deteriorating mind.

"What's wrong with Caleb?"

Oh, no, Rachel mouthed as Eric heard Mitch take a long breath.

"Your brother is having seizures. Right now they're only lasting a couple of seconds, but they're getting worse."

"So that's it. I knew something was wrong."

Rachel reacted to his words. Her brow pulled tight in a tiny frown and she hugged herself.

"Obviously there's no time to waste. Natasha has gone over the blueprints with a fine-toothed comb," Mitch continued. "Rachel has them. Take a look. There's an unexplained area in the basement. It appears to be totally blocked off. That could be Metzger's lab."

"We'll check it out tonight. Thanks."

"Eric, how are you holding up?"

Eric rubbed his eyes as he assured his boss he was doing okay.

"What about Rachel?"

He lowered his hand and looked at her. "Rachel? She's fine."

"Are you sure? I'd hate to have to extract her, but we can't afford any mistakes."

"She's doing great. I don't know how I'd have managed without her."

When he disconnected, Rachel was studying him, that little frown still in place. She'd reacted when he'd told Mitch he knew something was wrong with Caleb.

Was she concerned about his brother's health? Or *his* sanity?

"You have the blueprints?" he asked her.

It took her a fraction of a second to react. "Yes. In my backpack."

"Let's have a look at them."

Rachel glanced toward the door. "What about Gracie?"

"She's off tonight. The substitute nurse came around just after nine, right before you got here. It'll be at least eleven o'clock before she checks the rooms again. She was complaining about how busy she was, and bed checks are way down on the list of priorities."

He unfolded the blueprints on the tiny desk that sat under the window. "Look at this."

Rachel approached, and Eric pulled out the chair for her, then leaned over her as he pointed out the area that Natasha had marked.

Her hair smelled of rain and sun and gardenias. He gripped the back of the chair until his fingers cramped, forcing himself to remember that he was here because of Caleb.

His reminder didn't help. Rachel's closeness tortured him with unslaked need. Still, he knew how she would react toward him if she had any inkling of the bond between him and his twin. For her, any hint of a psychic connection would smack of insanity.

He couldn't stand it if she looked at him with the hurt and betrayal and aversion that had darkened her eyes when she mentioned her mother.

As long as he stayed in control around her, he could keep her near him. He could ensure that she was as safe as he could possibly make her.

He concentrated on their shared goal.

He pointed with his free hand. "There don't seem to be any doors." The area Natasha had highlighted was located toward the south side of the building, near the dirt and stone crawl space. The north wall of the highlighted area appeared solid, and formed the back wall of the banks of service elevators, and the east and west boundaries looked like nothing more than corridors.

"Natasha thinks this may be Metzger's secret lab." Eric traced the boundaries of the mysterious room with his finger, working hard to ignore Rachel's dark hair tickling his lips and cheek. "I see why she thinks it may have been a bomb shelter. This blueprint is dated 1970. And look, the walls of this room are thicker than any other room in the basement. They're probably made of some sort of metal."

Rachel nodded her head, torturing him with the feel of her silky hair.

"Eric? What did Mitch say about Caleb?" She turned her head.

Eric's heart turned upside down. Her face was millimeters from his, her lips soft and inviting, her eyes wide and filled with concern. A shuddering desire ripped through him like a knife through old silk, shredding his defenses, leaving a ragged edge of hunger that could never be soothed except by her kiss, her touch.

Her gaze traveled from his eyes down to his mouth. As he watched her lashes dip, and her chin lift until her lips were almost touching his, he came dangerously close to giving in.

But it wasn't fair to her. If he made love to her, it would be a lie. He owed her the truth about himself, about his connection with his brother. But he couldn't tell her yet.

Because when he told her, he would lose her. She would view his confession as an indication of a mental problem, and she'd already stated with stark certainty that she would never get personally involved with anyone like that.

He could tell her the connection he and his brother shared was not a delusion, but that wouldn't be the whole truth. The truth was, he wasn't sure.

He scooped up the blueprint and folded it. "Come on. I'll tell you what Mitch said on the way. If someone can get into your apartment, then we need to wrap this up. You're in danger, and we're running out of time."

Despite his promise to tell her about his conversation with Mitch, Eric remained quiet as they sneaked down to the basement. Once there, he seemed distracted as he studied the wall beside the elevators.

He stepped over and flattened his palms against the wall.

Rachel couldn't take her eyes off him. The shadows cast by the faint emergency lights lining the corridors lent a harsh beauty to his features. Her gaze played over his short, straight nose, his high cheekbones, his wide mouth.

"What are you doing?" she asked, watching him move sideways along the wall.

Without slowing his examination, he spoke quietly. "If there's anything behind here, there has to be a way to..." His voice trailed off and his brows lowered into a frown.

"I can't quite—" he whispered.

Rachel watched in fascination and growing apprehension as he continued his methodical search, occasionally muttering to himself. He frightened her when he acted like this. She had the sense he was listening to something or someone she couldn't hear.

It reminded her of her mother's delusions, when the mania would take over her mind.

"Eric, tell me what Mitch said." She had to know that he was grounded in reality. Plus, she was also worried about Caleb.

Eric closed his eyes. His hands continued to roam over the plaster. "He said one of the IDs you gave Natasha turned out to be Misty Norwood."

"Misty! She *is* real."

He angled his head toward her. "I told you my brother doesn't lie."

"Is Misty okay? What happened to her?"

"All we know so far is that her parents placed her in the Meadows after a suicide attempt. They became concerned by some of the things she told them, and took her home."

Helpless anger burned through Rachel. "Dr. Metzger told Caleb she was dead."

Eric's jaw ticced. "He wanted to observe Caleb's reaction."

"What about Caleb? Did Mitch say he was worse?"

The tic in Eric's jaw flared into a clench. He nodded. "He's having seizures."

"Oh, no." They *were* running out of time. Seizures could be a symptom of several problems, but they definitely indicated that Caleb's condition was worsening.

"They're becoming more frequent."

"Mitch told you that?"

Eric didn't answer. He walked around the corner, into a dimly lit corridor.

Rachel followed him. The odor of dirt and mildew increased as they grew closer to the front of the building. Down the corridor, beyond the circle of the last lights, she saw the end of the finished portion of the basement and the beginning of the crawl space.

In the middle of the west wall was a recessed area.

She shook her head. "There was no alcove indicated on the blueprint."

He closed his fist and lightly rapped on the wall. She heard the metallic sound.

He sent her a triumphant glance. "This is it."

Rachel's heart hammered in her chest. "The secret lab?"

He shrugged. "Let me have the flashlight."

He swept the bright light methodically across the entire surface of the alcove. "See the seam? It's barely visible."

Rachel squinted. "All I see are the inside corners of the alcove."

"That's it. That's the door, I'm sure." He looked around. "This section of the basement is almost totally deserted."

He closed his eyes briefly. "One of the service elevators comes down inside here."

"Inside? Why do you think that?" she asked.

He sent her a sharp glance. "Seems logical."

"So let's go in." A thrill fluttered in Rachel's throat. Was she about to find out that her idol, Gerhardt Metzger, was really the monster Caleb had said he was? She clutched the straps of her backpack until her fingers ached.

"I don't think we dare, until we know where Metzger is."

"But we have no way of knowing that."

"And if we open this door and he's in there, what are you going to say to him then?"

Chapter Ten

Metzger could be in there.

Rachel pulled her lower lip between her teeth. She had no answer for Eric. If Metzger was in there, then everything Caleb had said was true, and the dream that had sustained her since she was a little girl—the dream of helping to find a cure for mental illness, would be crushed.

"We could wait until after midnight. Maybe even two o'clock. When we can be relatively sure the doctor's asleep."

Eric nodded grimly. "What time is it now?"

Rachel looked at her watch. "Oh, it's almost eleven. I had no idea we'd been gone so long. You'd better get back to your room."

"Right. Let's go."

"I'll stay here. I want to search the Medical Records room again. I have to figure out what's in the injections. For Caleb's sake."

"No." Eric was adamant. "You're not going anywhere in this building without me. We have to be doubly careful."

"It doesn't make sense for you to be with me every second. It's not even possible. You know we're running out of time. By myself, I can search longer. I wouldn't have to watch the clock so closely."

"I said no."

Irritation flared within her at his flat refusal to discuss the matter. "You know I'm right—"

The look on Eric's face stopped her. His jaw was set. His eyes were as dark and hard as obsidian. She'd never win.

She glared at him. "What's your idea, then? Like I said before, are you going to hide me under your bed until two o'clock?"

"If I have to."

That sounded like a threat. Her ears burning with frustration, Rachel glared at him. "I know what this is about. You don't trust me."

Eric blinked and turned away, heading for the stairwell. "Not as far as I can throw you," he said flatly. There was a part of him that worried about how she'd react when she had proof that Metzger was using innocent patients for his vile experiments. For Metzger, obviously the end justified the means.

He'd seen in Rachel's eyes how passionate she was about finding a cure for mental illness. Would the end justify the means for her, too?

He'd only known her for five days, but her tenderness with his brother and her fierce protective attitude toward her patients made him believe she would never intentionally hurt them.

His biggest concern, however, was for her safety. He couldn't bear the idea of her sneaking around alone in this snake pit full of secrets.

After slipping up the service stairs and back to the neurology ward, Eric held out a cautionary hand to stop Rachel as he angled his head around the corner. The substitute nurse was checking rooms at the other end of the hall.

"The nurse is making her rounds. We can get across the hall if we hurry. I'll go first, then let you know when you can follow. Your com unit is working, right?" he said under his breath.

"Right." Her voice in his ear carried a note of irritation, maybe even anger. But that didn't bother him. Let her be angry with him. Let her think he doubted her competence. Let her even believe he didn't trust her.

As long as she was safe.

He checked the hall again, then dashed around the corner and down the hall to his room.

"Are you ready?" he asked after he slipped inside. He opened the door a crack and met her gaze.

"Yes," she whispered.

He nodded and carefully pushed the door shut.

When he was right beside her, he sometimes forgot the sensation of hearing her voice inside his head. It made him feel as if they existed deep within each other, as close as lovers. Closer.

The thought sent blood rushing through his veins. He felt himself become aroused. Gritting his teeth, he forced his thoughts back to the danger of their situation and the real reason he was doing this. It was for Caleb.

He checked the hall. The nurse stuck her head in another door. "Now! Hurry!"

She raced across the hall, her blue eyes flashing with fear. As she reached the doorway he jerked her inside and pushed the door closed. It creaked lightly.

"I saw the nurse." Rachel's body radiated tension. "Do you think she saw me?"

"We'll know soon enough." He felt her shiver.

"I should have stayed downstairs."

"Shh," he whispered, holding up a hand. He closed his eyes and stood completely still, his entire concentration on the sounds outside his door.

Rachel watched Eric in fascination. His face was calm, as if he was meditating, but his body was poised, alert, ready for anything. She listened, but she couldn't hear a sound.

He held a finger to his lips and pointed toward the bathroom. He wanted her to hide in there, like she had the other night.

She nodded and started around him.

All at once, Eric caught her waist. Before she could process what was happening, she flew through the air and landed on his narrow bed. He flipped a blanket up and over her, and plopped down beside her, his body between her and the door.

"Shh." His warning hissed in her ear as he slid under the edge of the blanket and bent one leg over her thighs. He curled his long, broad-shouldered body around her, rested his head on top of hers and lay completely still.

The door to his room squealed as it opened.

Rachel's heart pounded so loudly she was sure it echoed off the walls. Her muscles screamed with the effort of lying still. She was afraid to breathe.

Eric's body shielded her, heavy and hot. He appeared deceptively relaxed, but his limbs were as tense and tight as coiled springs.

Rachel made herself as small as possible. She couldn't see anything, with the blanket and Eric's body between her and the door, but she had an impression of a sliver of light growing brighter. Cringing deeper into the mattress, she held her breath and waited. If she were caught, both of them would be locked up. Not for the first time since she'd agreed to help the FBI, Rachel pictured her career going up in smoke.

"Caleb?"

Rachel felt Eric tense, felt his heart beating strong and fast against her palms.

"Hmm?" he murmured, lifting his head just slightly to acknowledge the nurse.

"Did I see you sneaking into your room?"

"No, ma'am. I'm in bed."

"Do you need a sleeping pill?"

He sighed. "I'm fine. Dreaming about you." His voice was slurred and drowsy.

The nurse chuckled softly. "All right then. Go to sleep," she said kindly. She sounded like a nicer person than Gracie.

Rachel lay rigid, holding her breath, as the light narrowed bit by bit until it disappeared and she heard the scrape of metal against metal, and knew the door was closed.

She breathed and realized her nose was tucked into the hollow of Eric's throat. Her nostrils filled with the smell of soap and clean linens and warm skin. She felt him swallow, felt his relieved sigh against her forehead. She knew when the sigh turn into a shudder of desire. Against her thighs she felt the heavy growing proof that he wanted her.

Each time they were close, each time she felt his fiercely controlled desire, she grew more curious, more bold, and less able to control her own response to his strong, sexy body.

She moved slightly, turning her body fully toward him, placing herself between his legs, an invitation, if he chose to acknowledge it.

His strength, his obvious attraction to her, the imminent danger of discovery, all combined to fill her with a need for release that she would never find in verbal assurances or even the promise of safety his closeness gave her.

She had to have more.

"What are you doing?" he whispered through her com unit, his breath barely noticeable against her cheek.

She put her fingers against his lips. "Don't talk. Just hold me."

He strained away and his lips moved against her fingers as he spoke. "We can't afford to do this. It's too dangerous."

With a shock, Rachel admitted to herself that the danger was part of the reason she wanted to. Her limited experience had been with safe, ordinary, even dull men— men whose every action was carefully thought out, planned. Men she'd chosen because their structured lives seemed the exact opposite of the way she'd grown up.

Eric was by no means ordinary. And although she felt safer with him than she'd ever felt, she knew he was a dangerous man in a dangerous profession. And that excited her, too.

"The nurse won't be back," Rachel whispered,

tracing the outline of his mouth with her index finger. "And we have two hours to kill." Her finger teased his lower lip.

He caught her hand. "Please don't. I don't have the strength to stop you."

"I don't want you to stop me. I want you to take me away from this insane place, even if it's for just a few minutes. Make me believe that this isn't reality." She lifted her head and sought his lips.

With a shaky sigh, he gave her what she wanted, a kiss to die for. His mouth explored hers—gentle, questioning, then suddenly—as if he couldn't stop himself, fiercely desperate. He kissed her deeply, sliding his hand around her neck in a protective caress, holding her close, holding nothing back.

Rachel felt drowned, drugged. Her head swirled with his quiet moans, her body felt at once languorous and alive. She pulled his head closer as his mouth left hers and trailed to her jaw.

"This can't happen," he said against her neck. "You don't want me. You just want comfort."

"Shh. I do want you. Please. I swear I won't ask you for more than this."

He lifted his head, and Rachel saw the anguish in his eyes.

"Oh, no, Eric." She cradled his face in her hands. "Don't think—"

He touched her lip with his thumb, silencing her.

"I understand. You're asking for normal. For an escape from the madness." He shook his head. "I can't promise you that."

His tone struck fear in her heart. She ignored the question that rose in the back of her mind, the question that asked why he wouldn't even give her the illusion of normal. Instead she pulled his head down so her mouth brushed his. "Don't promise me anything. Just love me."

He sighed raggedly. "I can do that," he whispered.

He kissed her again, sucking away her fear and feeding her some of the control that seemed so much a part of him. He slid his hand under her top and lightly traced her waist, then spread his fingers along her ribs as he deepened his kiss.

His lips and teeth nibbled at her tongue, then he trailed kisses down to her neck and shoulder as his hand encircled her back and he flattened his palm against its hollow curve. He pressed her close, fitting her to him.

Rachel's breath caught in a quiet moan as her sensitive breasts pressed against his bare chest, her belly and loins and thighs molded against his as his hand slid downward, over the swell of her hips to her bottom.

His body grew hard and hot, his breathing rough. Their bodies melded together. Rachel felt boneless. Eric's gentle, questing fingers traced the contours of her body until he skimmed the underside of her breast.

Her nipples tightened in a response that echoed through to her core.

He cupped her small breast in his palm, his thumb coaxing its tip into aching erection as his lips and tongue and teeth drained her of doubt and fear.

Magically, their clothes dissolved, and like a sculptor with fresh clay, he reshaped her to fit him. His arousal pulsed against her, flesh against flesh.

His head bent and he took the tip of her breast into his mouth, grazing it with his teeth and sending rhythmic vibrations streaking through her body. She strained against him, seeking release.

"Be still," he rasped, pressing his forehead against hers, gulping air in shallow bursts, his heart thudding through his whole body. Its cadence called to hers. "I'm not…much good at this."

His words shocked her, pulling her back a bit from the edge she'd almost tumbled over just seconds before. Taking a long breath, she shook her head slightly, rubbing her nose against his. "Not good?" she whispered. "I've never felt like this before. You've barely touched me and I'm so close—"

He lifted his head and stared into her eyes. A look of awe transformed his face. "I've been told I'm too closed off, too detached."

Rachel sucked in a sharp breath. "Not detached,"

she breathed, shifting to feel his hard length more intimately against her.

He grimaced. "Rachel." He practically in her ear. "Please."

A little laugh bubbled through her. "You make me feel sexy," she whispered, sliding her hand across his chest and down over his lean, taut abdomen.

"You make me feel out of control."

"But that's good, isn't it?" She flattened her palm against his taut belly.

"Ah, don't—"

He stopped, his breath hitching as her fingers brushed the rigid arousal that strained between them. His hoarse voice sent a thrill of triumph and passion coursing through her.

She did this to him. "Oh, Eric."

He shuddered and his arousal pulsed against her hand. "Rachel, be careful," he begged.

She lay back and he rolled over her, his fingers trailing down her belly, seeking assurance that she was ready.

She was. She knew it. Moisture flowed and gathered as he touched her more intimately than anyone had in a long time. As he discovered the proof of a longing that had never been so strong inside her before.

He caressed her gently. She sucked in a breath between clenched teeth. "It's too much. I can't hold back any longer."

"Good." His voice grated. "Now you know how I feel."

His biceps bulged as he raised himself above her, penetrating her slowly as she strained upward to take him, her hands clutching at his forearms to steady herself.

He eased in, agonizingly slowly, as she held his gaze. He grimaced and closed his eyes.

Wrapping a hand around his neck, she pulled his forehead to hers as he sank into her, arched away, then pushed in again, and again, increasing his speed as she caught up and matched him, thrust for thrust.

Her whole being burst to life with intense, knife-sharp pleasure. Moving, she accepted him more deeply.

Eric muttered something as he sank to the hilt and groaned.

Rachel's entire body was on fire, blazing with a heat like nothing she'd ever experienced. She felt the pulsing contractions build deep, deep inside her.

Then stars exploded, inside her and all around her like an endless fireworks display, and much later, the world went still and dark.

ERIC LAY AWAKE, staring down at the sleeping beauty beside him. He was still reeling from the intensity of his response to her. He breathed deeply, working to quiet his pounding heart.

If she'd taken the time to notice, she'd have been able to see all the way through to his soul. And that scared him. He'd never opened up like that to a woman before, hadn't intended to this time.

But Rachel, with her wide, trusting eyes, her strength and vulnerability, had slipped beneath the protective shell he kept over his emotions.

She'd exposed his heart, and now it ached.

He wanted to let her sleep for a few more minutes, before they had to return to brutal reality. She'd asked him to take her away from the insanity, but in truth, she was the one who had given him a taste of what normalcy meant, a glimpse of what he'd never hoped to have.

His world had been a lonely one. He'd been isolated by the fear of madness that had lurked inside him, by his grandmother's obsessive yet detached hold over him, and by his gift—the odd empathy that made him so good at his job.

Rachel turned slightly and the dim recessed light over his bed lit her face. He traced the air near her mouth, her nose, her soft cheeks. She was so beautiful.

And he was lying to her.

A knife blade of pain ripped through his raw heart. She wanted a normal life. He couldn't blame her. Considering what she'd told him, and what he'd discovered about her during these past few days, he knew how desperately she clung to the structured, conventional world she'd created for herself.

That was what he admired about her. The bravery that had enabled her to turn away from her fragile normalcy and brought her to this place that embodied everything she feared most. She'd come here for the most noble of reasons—to seek a cure for mental illness, to help people—only to have her trust betrayed.

He studied her face, the innocent delicacy of her parted lips, the black lashes that lay like raven's feathers against her cheeks.

He was as guilty as Metzger, in his own way.

He'd warned her. But damn him, he couldn't take that last step away from her. He should have been the strong one. But he'd given in. He'd made love to her.

His fingertips skimmed the line of her jaw, a millimeter from actual contact. The fine shape of her face was something he wanted to commit to memory. Something he could remember, when he was alone again.

She opened her eyes.

The startling crystal blue took his breath away. A tiny frown wrinkled her brow and she touched his face. "Are you okay?"

The quiet screech of metal broke the silence. The door!

He yanked up the blanket and threw his arm over

her. He bowed his bare back to hide her. His skin prickled as the sliver of light crawled across the bed.

He forced himself to breathe slowly, rhythmically. After a couple of seconds, the door eased shut.

Eric cradled her for another few seconds, until she moved. His body responded, but he pulled away, hoping she hadn't noticed.

She laughed nervously. "That squeaky door is handy. Was that your doing?"

"Yeah. Thanks to your fingernail file. Now we need to get dressed," he said gruffly. "We've got breaking and entering to do."

ERIC EXAMINED the wall of the alcove with the high-powered flashlight, acutely aware of Rachel standing at his elbow. The instinct he hardly dared to name told him the door was here.

"I still can't see anything but solid wall," Rachel whispered through his com unit. "Even if the door is here, how are you going to open it?"

"There's a trip somewhere. I know it. Hold this." He handed her the flashlight. He pressed both palms flat against the recessed wall and closed his eyes.

Come on, bud. How'd you get in?

Rachel couldn't figure out what Eric was doing. She couldn't see anything where he said there was a seam. The recessed wall appeared to be solid.

He stood, balanced on the balls of his feet, his

arms propped against the wall, his head down. "Too dangerous…"

Rachel started. "What? What did you say?"

He shook his head without raising it. "Nothing," he muttered, sounding distracted.

He spread his fingers and the long, elegant muscles in his arms knotted with effort under the short sleeves of his white T-shirt.

"Are you trying to push the wall in?"

He ignored her and slid his hands a few inches to the right. He muttered something under his breath.

She thought it sounded like a plea for help, or a prayer. Apprehension flared inside her.

"Eric, you're scaring me. Maybe we should wait."

He slid his hands another inch to the right and with a soft swish, the wall slid open a crack.

"Oh, my God," Rachel breathed. "It *is* a secret door."

She started forward, but Eric stayed her with his hand.

"Hold it. Let me go in."

"While I wait out here exposed? No way."

He turned his head and looked at her, his eyes glittering like gems. "It's too dangerous. You should leave."

"You can't find the records by yourself. You need me. I thought we were in this together."

He blinked and rubbed his temples, then glanced

around. "I'll go in first." His voice sounded odd, almost strangled. "Let me have the flashlight."

She lay it in his outstretched palm as if it were a surgical instrument. He pushed the door a little wider. Beyond them, nothing but darkness. After a moment of utter stillness, he held out his hand to her. His strong, safe, elegant hand. She took it and with a deep, shaky breath, followed him into the abyss.

When he turned on the flashlight and swung it around, Rachel saw that they were standing in a stainless steel room.

"This is where they brought us," Eric whispered. "Isn't it?"

His question seemed directed inward.

"I don't know. Do you remember being here?"

Eric turned around and pushed the sliding door closed.

"Is that a handle on the inside of the door?" she asked, seeing the shape in the small circle of light created by the flashlight.

Eric shone the light on the door. "So we can get out." His voice was tinged with irony.

Rachel stuck right by his side, keeping her body inside the flashlight's aura as he searched along the silver walls for the light switches.

"Get ready," he whispered in her com unit.

Rachel hardly had time to take a breath before the lights flashed on, nearly blinding her.

She squinted against the startling brightness. As her eyes adjusted, she saw a plain, stainless-steel table in the middle of the room, surrounded by carts that held boxes of operating room equipment.

A bank of low-hanging lights hung over the table and in a corner, near the foot-operated sink, was the only splash of color in the room, a bright red crash cart, in case of cardiac arrest.

She'd been in operating rooms dozens of times, even done her share of sewing up patients. On her brief surgical rotation, she assisted with a couple of gall bladder removals, a repair of a compound fracture of the thigh and several minor surgical procedures. Surgery didn't bother her.

But this room did. There was an oppressive, claustrophobic sensation in here, as if it were alive, an evil beast's mouth just waiting to clamp shut and trap them alive.

"I don't like this room," she said, hugging herself.

"I know what you mean." Eric walked over to the operating table and touched it. "I was here. I remember the lights."

"Eric, all operating rooms have these type of lights." Her words didn't sound convincing, even to herself.

Then Eric looked up at her and she went cold with fear.

His eyes burned with the same mad intensity that

she'd seen time and time again in her mother's eyes, the same intensity she'd seen in Caleb.

"Are all operating rooms like this?" He gestured. "Don't you feel it? There's evil in here. Why else would this place be hidden in a secret area of the basement?" His voice was hard and cold. "In a room that is accessed only through a *secret* door? Are all ORs like that? I was brought here, and needles were stuck into my brain. Just like Caleb, and Misty, and who knows how many others."

Rachel gaped in horror at his face, which had turned a sickly green.

"Eric, I know you're angry," she said shakily, "but I'm on your side. Not against you."

This is Eric, she reminded herself. Safe, competent, sane. She trusted him. Didn't she?

He fingered the thick Velcro straps attached to the table. Turning, he examined the anesthesia apparatus and a machine that looked like an EKG, with wires and leads sprouting from it like octopus legs.

"What's that?" With a nauseating dread knotting her stomach, Rachel stepped closer.

"It's for electroshock therapy," Eric muttered. "Haven't you seen one of these before?"

She pressed her palm against her belly. "No."

"Caleb has."

Rachel's eyes swam with tears. She couldn't bear

Eric's pain any longer. She felt as if she was losing him to the horror the room conjured.

"Eric." She touched his arm, trying to bring him back to the present. "We have to hurry."

For another seemingly endless moment, he stood immobile. Then finally he dragged his gaze away from the table and wiped both hands down his face.

"You're right."

Rachel let out a relieved breath. He sounded more like the man she knew.

He looked around the room. Rachel's gaze followed his. They both saw the door at the same time and started toward it.

"Maybe it's an office," Rachel said. "Metzger has to keep his real records somewhere."

"So you're doubting your famous mentor now?"

She replayed what she'd just said, surprised at how easily the words had come. "I don't want to doubt him." Her throat ached as the truth forced its way out. She'd never told anyone her deepest fears and hopes.

Stopping, she turned to look at Eric. "I have to believe there's a cure. Otherwise everything I've worked for is gone. Everything I've believed is a lie." She swallowed the tears that threatened to well up in her eyes. "How can I face my mother, or Caleb, or my other patients, and tell them I can't help them?"

Eric's sharp gaze burned away her tears. He stopped one droplet with his thumb, then cupped her cheek. "You underestimate yourself, Dr. Harper. You help people every day." His stern mouth lifted in a little smile. "And knowing you, you'll never give up. Just stop fighting so hard."

She nodded, worrying her lip with her teeth. "I guess we'd better go in." She turned the knob. "It's locked."

"Is the screwdriver still in your backpack?"

She dug it out and handed it to him.

He manipulated the lock. It took a while, but the door finally opened.

Eric swung it wide. "You go in. I need to—" He gestured vaguely back toward the OR table. His gesture was halfhearted, his thoughts were obviously elsewhere. "I'll be over there…" Eric's voice faded as he walked away.

The office room was small, one wall lined with file cabinets. There were boxes on the floor, some sealed, others partially filled with records. Shipping labels were stacked on top of them.

Rachel picked up a label. It had Dr. Metzger's name on it. "'Germany,'" she read in the address block on the label. So this *was* Metzger's office. And it looked as though he was about to ship all his files to Germany.

She crouched and quickly skimmed through the papers in the unsealed box. Most of them were handwritten notes, in Dr. Metzger's sprawling script. It would take hours to decipher them.

She moved to the next box. In it were bound notebooks. Rachel picked up one. When she opened it, her heart leaped with excitement.

The notebook was a day-by-day journal of Metzger's experiments. The last date recorded was three months ago. Rachel paged through, noting the names. There were six, including Caleb's. Flipping to the back of the notebook, she took out her cell phone and stored the names and their ID numbers in a text message. Then she studied the information.

Each patient's name appeared over and over. Just as they'd already discovered, each patient received a daily injection of something that was not recorded correctly in their charts. And once a week, they were sedated and taken to what Metzger termed "The Laboratory," where fluid was drawn from their brains.

Eric had mentioned the needle and the stinging in his head, just as Caleb had.

What was Metzger doing with brain fluid, unless… Rachel shuddered as the answer hit her. Eric and Caleb were right.

Dr. Metzger's theory centered around an autoimmune reaction. The patient trying to reject his own brain chemicals. Metzger must be taking the chemicals from his patients and purifying them, then reinjecting them. The numbers beside each injection log probably indicated batch numbers.

How was he doing this without arousing suspicion? She'd have to ask Eric, but Rachel bet that one day a week, the individual psychotherapy sessions were actually conducted down here, and consisted of extracting chemicals. The sedative he gave the patients to prepare them for the procedure was probably recorded in the chart as a facilitator for regression therapy or some other psychoanalytic procedure.

Rachel needed to find out what was in the daily injections, the ones that were listed on the patient's chart as the antipsychotic drug, fenpiprazole. Then maybe she could figure out the reason for Caleb's reaction after only two missed doses.

Metzger's formulas and testing logs had to be down here somewhere. It was the only place in the hospital that Metzger could be sure was safe.

Well, not anymore. Rachel turned back to the boxes.

Eric stared at the polished metal walls of the operating room. He clenched his fists and shook his head, trying to rid his brain of the terrifying images the cold, stark room evoked. He knew this was where he'd been brought on Friday, after the nurse had sedated him.

His recollection was hazy and distorted, but he

remembered the cold table, the round, bright lights, the unbearable pain and stinging at the base of his skull.

But his own memories weren't all he was seeing now. He was also seeing through Caleb's eyes.

Metzger's face, other faces, needles and tubes and lights and colors, all swirled around him like a living kaleidoscope.

So many times. So much pain.

"My God, bud. How did you stand it?"

He knew the answer to that before he'd even formed the words. His brother was strong-willed and brave. He'd managed all these years against impossible odds, and he would prevail.

Eric's eyes stung and his throat tightened. Now he and Rachel had found Metzger's lab. Soon they'd have the proof they needed to stop Metzger's heinous experiments.

He closed his eyes and dragged his thoughts away from his brother. He had to check on Rachel. She'd been in the office a long time.

He started toward the office and then the shock hit him—like slamming into an invisible wall. He lifted his head. He couldn't see. He touched his eyes, then his temples. His skin, his hair, felt the same, but inside, everything had changed.

"Caleb!" he whispered, his lips numb with fear.

Stark horror crawled up his spine. He reached

out with his mind, with his hands, but there was nothing there.

He was alone.

For the first time in his life, he was totally alone. His mind was a dead, cold place.

Caleb was gone.

Chapter Eleven

Rachel heard Eric say something through her com unit just as she put her hands on the document she'd been seeking. It had been stuck in the back of one of the logbooks.

"This is it! Eric, I think I've found the formula."

Forgetting everything else, she quickly scanned the handwritten notes, then frowned and read them more closely. Dr. Metzger's swirled handwriting plus the fountain pen he favored made the notes near illegible.

It appeared that he used fluid extracted from the brains of healthy and schizophrenic patients, and sterilized and filtered it to remove contaminants, then added a local anesthetic. As she deciphered the formula, she keyed it into a second text file on her cell phone, so she could send it to Mitch.

Rachel's stomach knotted in growing horror as she slowly made sense of Metzger's handwriting. Somehow, naively, she'd had the idea that his theory of schizophrenia as an autoimmune disease was just that—a theory.

She'd had a mental picture of him cooking up chemicals in a laboratory and testing the results on mice.

But now, reading his description of the process he used to obtain and refine the chemicals, dread certainty settled in the pit of her stomach, making her feel nauseated.

Caleb had been telling the truth. Metzger was conducting evil experiments. More evil than Rachel could have imagined.

He was using his patients as test subjects, giving them a home-cooked concoction taken from their own brains. It was a diabolical plot worthy of an old black-and-white horror film.

Caleb's description of Rachel's idol as *Frankenmetzger* was amazingly accurate.

The paper slipped from her fingers. She stared down at it, her mind struggling to take in the full implications of what she had discovered.

She reached down to retrieve the sheet and her eye was caught by one of the shipping labels.

Germany. She'd forgotten about the mailing labels.

Why was Metzger packing all his notes and documentation of his heinous experiments to send to Germany?

She straightened and glanced around the office.

He was moving. He wasn't just shipping his papers to Germany, he was planning to go himself. And with Caleb's arraignment coming up, and the FDA breathing down his neck, she'd bet it was soon.

They had no time to lose. She had to get the formula to the FBI. Not only was it Caleb's salvation, it was also proof of what Metzger had been doing.

"Eric." Rachel rose, paper in hand, and headed for the door. "Eric, what are you doing? Look at this. It's the formula."

As she came around the edge of the door, the sight that greeted her almost knocked her to her knees.

Eric stood rigid beside the OR table, his face drained of color, his eyes rolled back in his head and his arms stretched out in front of him like a blind man.

As she watched, he threw his head back and grimaced. His jaw was so tightly clenched that cords stood out in his neck.

A choked, guttural cry erupted from his throat and echoed in her ear. "Caleb!"

He swayed and crumpled.

"Eric!" Rachel stuffed the formula into her pocket and ran to him.

He crouched on the floor, squeezing his head between his clenched fists and whispering, "No… no…no…" over and over.

Rachel stood above him, unable to move, as she stared in horrified fascination at the man who, just minutes earlier, had held her and kissed her and made love with her.

All she could think now was that he looked and acted just like his brother. Like Caleb.

She took a step backward, her entire body crawling with the urge to flee. Terrors she hadn't encountered since childhood overpowered her.

Helplessness, fear, the sense of abandonment and betrayal. The knowledge that no matter how hard she prayed, or how quiet she was, nothing she did would ever be enough to stop the madness.

She took another step backward, the child in her wanting to run away until he'd worn himself out and fallen asleep, like her mother always had—eventually.

But she forced herself to think rationally. She wasn't a child anymore and this wasn't her sad, beautiful, insane mother.

Rachel was an adult. A psychiatrist. Unlike that scared little girl, now she knew what to do.

If Eric had somehow cycled into an acute schizophrenic episode, he needed to be sedated.

She glanced across the room at the bright red crash cart. There would be an injectable sedative in there.

She looked down at his bowed head and blinked to rid her brain of the double image that floated in front of her eyes like a two-faced mask. Stepping around Eric's crouched figure, she headed for the crash cart.

Eric heard a movement behind him. He blinked the tears away and tried to move. He found himself hunched down on the floor, his fists clenched so tightly they hurt.

Hurt.

Carefully he stretched his fingers, relishing the cramping pain. At least he still hurt. He must still be alive.

But Caleb was dead.

Anguish tore at his insides, as if a giant hand had reached in and ripped his heart out.

His throat rasped as a choked cry escaped. "I'm sorry, bud," he whispered brokenly.

Something metallic hit the concrete floor behind him and the sharp sound pulled him out of himself and back into reality.

He was in Metzger's secret lab, where Caleb had led him. His eyes burned with new tears. He couldn't help Caleb now, but he could stop that monster from killing anyone else.

He stood and turned.

It was Rachel. For the few awful minutes when he'd first recognized the absence of his brother, when he'd experienced for the first time in his life the feeling of being alone inside his own head, he'd forgotten about her.

Just the sight of her soothed his loss. He wiped his face with both hands.

"Rachel." His voice croaked. He swallowed and tried again, forcing himself to think about their purpose for being here. "Rachel, did you find anything?"

She raised her gaze to his and what he saw there staggered him. Her usually sparkling blue eyes were dull and sad, and she watched him with a narrow wariness that nearly broke what was left of his heart.

She lifted her right hand and he saw the syringe.

Alarm shot through him. "What the hell are you doing?"

Her lip trembled, but she lifted her chin and held out her other hand in a placating gesture.

"Eric—"

Then it hit him. He replayed in his head what she must have seen.

In that indescribable moment when his awareness of his brother had disappeared from inside him, he'd collapsed. The sudden emptiness had been like a light going out, plunging him into dark, nightmarish isolation for the first time in his life.

She must have thought he'd gone mad.

He took a deep breath and said, "I'm not insane."

She blinked and bit her lip, but she didn't move. "Do you remember what happened just now?"

He took a step toward her and spread his hands in a gesture of surrender.

She stiffened.

"Of course I do. Put down the syringe and let me explain it to you."

"Why don't I give you just a little bit of this and then we can take you back to your room. It will help you sleep."

"Rachel, damn it. Stop talking to me as if I were one of your patients. I'm not crazy."

She nodded and smiled, a bright, beautiful smile that he was certain made her patients feel comfortable as she assessed them and treated them.

But he knew her, and he knew her smile was fake.

"Of course you're not. You've been under a tremendous amount of stress. You just need a good night's sleep."

He stepped closer and saw the apprehension flare in her eyes. "Ah, Rachel, don't be afraid of me. I need to talk to you, and I can't with you brandishing that thing like a weapon." He dared another step.

Rachel recoiled, bumping the crash cart, sending the rattle of metal and plastic echoing around the room.

"Damn it. Would you stop acting like I'm some kind of monster? Come on, we're in this together." He held out a hand, well aware of the significance of what he'd just said.

He read her mind through her frightened eyes. She'd trusted him to be sane. She'd trusted him with her body, and with her emotions. Right now, to her, he *was* a monster.

And just a few seconds ago she'd discovered that, once again, just like with her mother, just like with all her patients whom she was so determined to help, she'd had her trust betrayed.

Eric knew he could never make up to her for what she'd seen. But he did know that there was something between them. He couldn't—he wouldn't—name it, but he knew it was there.

The question was, would the thread that connected them be strong enough to hold, no matter how hard she pulled away? If it wasn't, then he'd lost more than his brother. The sadness and sense of loss that he'd thought would kill him doubled. It took every ounce of strength he had not to collapse under the pain.

Knowing he was gambling with not only their safety but possibly their lives, he pushed aside his personal feelings and forced himself to play on hers.

He dropped his gaze to her lips. If he couldn't convince her one way, he'd try another.

"You haven't forgotten how good we were together, have you?" He whispered so softly that he knew she would only be able to hear him through her com unit. Did his voice inside her head affect her the way hearing hers did him?

"Making love with you was the most amazing experience of my life. You know that, don't you?"

She shook her head, but he knew he'd gotten to

her. In his deepest heart he felt a bitter self-loathing as dampness gathered in her eyes.

"For the first time in my life, with you, I felt safe enough to be myself. To hold nothing back."

"Please, don't say that. I know what you're doing. You're playing on my emotions." She blinked, dislodging a single tear that slid down her cheek.

He shook his head. "I'm telling you the truth. Nothing I've ever seen compares with you."

The tears overflowed, leaving glistening trails down her cheeks. "Please stop trying to get to me. It's not working."

Oh, yes it is.

He lunged forward and grabbed her arm, pressing his thumb into the inside of her wrist at a point guaranteed to make her fingers lose their grip. As the syringe hit the floor, he flipped her around and wrapped his arms around her, rendering her unable to move.

As Eric's strong arms pinned her, Rachel panicked. "No! Let me go!" she cried, fighting him.

A terrifying sense of déjà vu washed over her. It was the same as when Caleb had grabbed her, except that Eric's hold wasn't punishingly tight. Nor was his forearm cutting off her air as his breathing sawed unevenly in her ears.

This was Eric, not Caleb. Eric's hold was more of an embrace. He had his arms wrapped around hers, his hands covering hers. He bent his head and pressed his mouth against her temple and whispered to her.

"It's okay, Rachel. Didn't I promise I'd take care of you? You need to calm down so I can explain. I know what you saw. What you heard. I know it scared you. I'm scared too."

She felt him shudder.

"I need you right now. So much it terrifies me. I'm about to be lost, if I can't count on you." His voice quivered, sending a hum of apprehension through her. "Please don't be afraid of me. I don't think I can stand that."

"What—" She swallowed. "What happened?" She took a deep breath, her breasts pressing against his forearm. Despite her fear and worry, her nipples tightened.

He loosened his hold just slightly and pressed his cheek against hers. "No more syringes? No more screaming?"

Eric's voice in her ear, soft and reassuring, as it had been since the beginning, slowed her pounding heart and eased her panic.

He'd been through so much. The daily injections. The constant observation. Worrying about his brother.

Who knew what all that was doing to him? He deserved a chance to explain. She suppressed the vision that rose in her mind, of him with his fists against his forehead, his body rocking back and forth, just like Caleb.

She nodded and took in a huge breath, torturing her sensitized breasts, then blew it out slowly. "I'm okay."

When he let go, it took all her strength to stay put. Every molecule inside her screamed at her to make a break and run. She looked up at him and saw in his eyes that he realized that.

He stood, arms out, palms up, his dark eyes huge in his pale face, his lips pressed together and white at the corners.

"Tell me," she whispered, her pulse hammering in anticipation.

"I've lost Caleb," he said flatly, his gaze never leaving hers. Tears gathered in his eyes and his throat moved as he swallowed. He lifted his chin and took a swift breath.

Rachel stared at him. "I don't understand."

He blinked. A single tear balanced, glittering like a diamond, on his inky lashes. Rachel stared at it, watching as it finally fell and slid down his cheek.

Slapping it away like an irritating bug, he cleared his throat and squeezed his eyes closed for an instant, then brushed at them with his palms.

"I'm sure you've read accounts in the literature of unusual empathy between identical twins. Caleb and I always had something. Caleb's was stronger than mine, maybe because of his illness. He could—" He took a shaky breath that caught at the top, like a sob. "He always knew where to find me when we played hide-and-seek. And if he wanted to, he could let me know where he was."

He stopped, then laughed shortly. "It sounds crazy. You sort of had to be there to understand."

Dumbfounded, Rachel listened.

"When he—when we were eleven and Grandmother told me he had died, I didn't believe it until she showed me his grave. I still got sensations, feelings. For twenty years I fought them, thinking—" He smiled and shrugged, dropping his gaze to the floor. "Thinking I was going insane myself. Then when you were kidnapped—" He pursed his lips and blew out a breath. "It was a shock, but it was an amazing relief, to find out that Caleb was alive."

"You heard his name on the news."

He glanced up at her through his dark lashes. "No. I dreamed I took you hostage."

Rachel felt the blood drain from her face. "You *dreamed* about me?" She remembered Caleb's words, there in his grandmother's house.

I called him. He's a secret agent.

She folded her arms and took a tiny step backward. "You said Caleb could let you know where he was. Is that how you knew we were at your grandmother's?"

Eric's eyes grew dark with an apprehension she'd

never seen in him before. He seemed to brace himself. "Yes."

The word echoed off the walls, reverberated inside her skull. "And how he knew you were coming. He told me you were a secret agent."

"I suppose. He always knew things I never told him."

"How could he—?"

"Since we've been here, the reason I've known my way around, the way I found the door in the basement, is that Caleb has been helping me."

"Helping you—" Rachel knew she sounded like an idiot, parroting what Eric said, but she was having a hard time absorbing what he was telling her. "Caleb is unconscious. He's been on life support all this time. There's no way—"

Eric's face changed. His mouth tightened, his skin looked drawn and pale across his cheekbones, and his eyes darkened in a terrible grief.

"Just a few minutes ago, my brother died." His voice cracked on the last word and his head bowed.

"Oh, Eric." Rachel's throat closed in shock and sorrow. "How—"

"Do I know?" He lifted his head. "Because for the first time in my life, I'm completely alone." He rubbed his temples. "Caleb's not here anymore."

Everything inside Rachel told her that what Eric was saying wasn't possible. Sure, she'd heard the sensational stories. Twins separated at birth who went on to live eerily similar lives. Twins who experienced each other's pain. Even cases of a twin knowing when his sibling died. But Rachel had never personally seen a case, never even known anyone who'd seen one.

It took every ounce of her strength to stand in front of him and try to believe him. He had just found his brother after twenty years. It wasn't fair that he'd lost him again. If that was true.

She studied him. Her heart broke for him. He was kind and brave, and he wore his loyalty and integrity like a badge of honor. And he believed totally in what he was telling her.

He would die for Caleb. She had a feeling he might even die for her. But was he sane?

She honestly didn't know.

A blaring sound echoed through the room.

"Oh, dear God," she breathed.

Eric started. "What the hell is that?"

Rachel didn't even have time to explain before the operator's calm voice sounded through the paging system. "Code M, Neurology. Code M, Neurology. Please check your assigned areas."

"You've got to go. It's the code for a missing patient. You've been gone too long." She glanced at her watch. "It's 3:48 a.m. Half an hour after your bed check."

Eric cursed under his breath. "I can't show up now. Who knows what they'll do to me?"

Rachel bit her lip. "You have to. Get on the main elevators and go up to your room. Act like you're sleepwalking."

"Sleepwalking."

"Be stiff, unresponsive. When they confront you, act like you just woke up. Act surprised to find yourself standing up. Stumble."

"What are you going to do?"

"I'll stay down here until things calm down, then I'll slip out and go back to my apartment. I'll leave my com unit on. Contact me as soon as you can."

Eric gripped her shoulders, his eyes burning like dark flames. "No. You have to get out now. Metzger's liable to come down here or send one of his minions to check on his precious secret room. I'll walk with you to the rear door."

"You don't have time. It's already been a half hour. If they don't find you within the next thirty minutes, they'll alert the local police."

"That's enough time—"

"No it's not. Eric, you've got to trust me."

He put his hand on the door handle and looked back at her. "How can I leave you here alone?"

"You have to. The longer you're missing the worse it will be."

A hint of panic flickered across his features. He took a long breath. "They'll sedate me, won't they?"

Her eyes flickered, but she forced herself to hold his gaze. "Yes. Heavily. And they'll put you in lockdown."

He passed his hand across his face, then made a fist, grazing his knuckles with his teeth as he stared at the floor.

"Eric?" He looked so vulnerable, his shoulders bowed under the weight of everything he'd been through and everything yet to come.

"Then no." He raised his head.

Rachel was amazed at the transformation in him. Deep in his eyes she saw his grief, but now it was overlaid by a grim determination.

"I'll be damned if I'm going to lie in a damn hospital bed drugged to the gills while you put yourself in danger. We'll hide in here. Together."

Chapter Twelve

"It's obvious what Metzger's planning to do." Rachel sat on the floor of the small office, surrounded by papers.

Eric agreed, relishing the fury that flowed through him like hot lava.

He'd latched on to anger to keep himself from thinking about Caleb and the emptiness he felt without his brother's presence. He ground one fist into the other palm. "The SOB is taking his disgusting experiments to Germany, and from what it looks like, he's planning to do it soon."

"I know. Some of these shipping labels show a pickup date of next week."

"Did you contact Mitch?"

She shook her head, her expression reflecting sadness and pity.

He steeled himself against it by looking away, down at the logbook she'd given him. It lay open on the desk.

"No. I was coming to tell you about finding Metzger's formula when you—"

He made a dismissive gesture. "Give me the phone. I'll call him now. I need to find out about Caleb. I don't know why Mitch hasn't called."

She handed him the phone.

He glanced down at it and cursed. "There's no signal in this damn mausoleum of a room." He looked up at the metal ceiling. "We'll have to go outside to call."

"Eric, they're searching for you. The police are probably here by now. In fact, I'm surprised Metzger hasn't come down here."

"He's not going to chance being seen entering his hidden torture chamber while the hospital is crawling with police. He won't come near it until things have quieted down. He's probably in the middle of the search, terribly worried about his patient."

"Speaking of crawling with police, it's going to be dangerous for us to leave, as well." She started gathering up scattered papers. "What about using Metzger's desk phone?" Rachel asked

Eric shook his head. "We can't take that chance. It might be a private line. It's certainly traceable." He walked out of the office and into the main room. Something about the layout wasn't right. He remembered thinking that earlier, before the overwhelming pain of losing Caleb had hit him.

A wave of grief sucker-punched him. The thought had probably come from Caleb.

"What were you trying to tell me, bud?" he muttered.

Rachel's gentle hand touched his arm. "Are you okay?"

Still stinging from her wary revulsion, he shrugged off her touch and straightened, avoiding her gaze. "I will be."

He stepped over into the middle of the room, near the stainless-steel table. "What's wrong with this room?"

"Besides the spooky feeling that it's crawling with evil? I'm not sure what you mean."

"Just what I said. This room is different from the rest of the hospital."

"The walls and ceiling are metal. It feels claustrophobic, smaller than it looks."

"That's it!" He craned his neck, taking in the entire ceiling corner to corner. "The ceiling is lower in here."

Rachel looked up. "It is?" She measured his six feet of height with her gaze, then looked up. "You're right. It's only eight feet at the most."

"Right. And this old mansion's ceilings are at least twelve feet, maybe fourteen on the first floor."

"Right. All the doorways, even in the basement, are wooden and have big transoms over them."

"Grab the logbook and let's get out of here."

"What about the police?"

"I don't think they'll find us where we're going."

She glanced at him suspiciously. "Where *are* we going? Are you thinking about sneaking out of the hospital?"

"No."

"Eric, you've been through a lot. Maybe you shouldn't be making decisions right now."

He felt his anger heating up, felt the pressure of the last days stretching along his nerves like a rubber band. "You still think I'm crazy? Well, you know what, Dr. Rachel Harper? Maybe I am. And when all of this is over, you can make your little report and give it to whomever the hell you want to. But right now, right here, I'm still in charge. So are you with me, or are you going to go upstairs and turn yourself in?" His throat felt raw and tight, his voice scraping harshly, as it did when his emotions escaped the tight leash he usually kept on them.

Her eyes widened in surprise and apprehension. She took a half step backward.

Chagrined, Eric almost reached out for her, but he knew she wouldn't welcome his touch. He hated that she was afraid of him.

Closing his eyes, he reined in his anger and frustration and spoke calmly.

"I'm going to slide the door open just enough to

listen. We should be able to hear anyone walking on the concrete floors. Then, if the corridor is clear, we'll head south, toward the crawl space."

"They're probably going to look there. They know you—Caleb—has explored down here."

He glanced up. "I wonder if anyone will look up there."

Rachel followed his gaze. "Above the ceiling?"

He nodded.

"You can't know there's anything up there."

Yes he could. He didn't say it out loud. "I already gave you your choice. What's your decision?"

She paled, but her chin lifted. "I'm staying with you."

"Good answer." He turned on his heel and strode toward the door.

METZGER PLAYED WITH his fountain pen, sliding it up and down in his breast pocket. He was itching to get downstairs to check on his secret lab, but he couldn't leave Patel, not until he managed to calm the chief medical director down. He fantasized about calling Thomas to restrain Patel while he sedated him. No one would fault him. The man was one breath away from a total breakdown.

Patel hung up the phone and slapped his palms against his desktop for about the fifth time. "This is intolerable. Gerhardt, I must insist that we call in the local authorities. It's been over two hours. That was Wilson again. How long do you think I can stall my own chief of security? He's a retired police officer. He knows the procedures. We are required by law to report missing patients."

Metzger held up his hands. "I can assure you, if Baldwyn is in this hospital, Thomas and his team will find him." He gave a huge sigh and shrugged. "I can't be responsible for what Caleb will do if he's confronted by police. Not to mention that the damage to his psyche, after the events of the past week, could be devastating. And of course, there is always the possibility that he is sleepwalking and will turn up anytime."

"I never liked having him here." Patel shoved his chair back as he stood. "Not from the very beginning. He was too young. Eleven years old. He should have been treated by a children's specialist."

He paced, muttering to himself. "But Olivia Stanhope was adamant. She *said* she wanted the best of care. In over twenty years in this business, I've dealt with other people like her. All about social position—appearances. She wanted to hide the child. The taint of mental illness in her family was intolerable, an embarrassment."

Metzger stared out the window, only half listening to Patel's rambling. He glanced at his watch. Thomas should be reporting any minute. That was good, because Metzger wanted to send him to make sure nothing was amiss in the secret lab.

"Who in their right mind would turn down a multimillion dollar endowment?"

Metzger heard the creak of leather as Patel sat and leaned back in his executive chair.

He groaned inwardly. When Patel settled back in his chair, it was a sure sign that he felt the need to discourse. He'd been known to talk for hours. Metzger had to get out of here.

As soon as Thomas called, he would excuse himself to speak to the nurse in person.

"But nothing is ever free, Gerhardt. Nothing. I knew there would be a price to pay one day. Then after Olivia died, I actually expected Caleb's brother to show up, even though Olivia assured me a dozen times that the brother thought his twin was dead."

Metzger almost dropped his fountain pen.

Brother? Twin?

It took Metzger a few seconds to absorb Patel's meaning. Once he did, his entire body began to buzz with shock. Had he understood correctly?

"Twin? Did you say twin?"

When Patel frowned in puzzlement, Metzger realized he'd spoken in German.

"Are you telling me that Caleb Baldwyn has a twin brother?" he repeated in English. "Why was I never informed of this?"

Patel's dark face turned a sickly yellow. "I shouldn't have mentioned anything. I'm distraught."

Thoughts were crowding into Metzger's brain too fast to process. He took a long, shaky breath and tried to consciously slow down his racing heart. He shoved his fisted hands into his lab coat pocket.

"Rajid, you cannot unsay what you have said. Now explain. Caleb Baldwyn has a twin? Why was none of this information in his medical records?"

Patel dug a handkerchief out of his pocket and mopped his face. "I just t-told you. The endowment his grandmother gave the Meadows was more than enough to build and maintain the Women's Dependency Center. The stipulation on the money was that no one was to ever know that Caleb Baldwyn was alive, much less that he had any family. As far as his brother knows, Baldwyn died in a fall twenty years ago. Gerhardt, you must promise me that this information will go no further."

Metzger didn't even respond to Patel's plea. He leaned forward. "Where is the twin? Are they identical? How can you be sure the twin is unaware of the existence of his brother?"

Patel stood and rounded his desk, looking down at the shorter man. "You must forget what I have said. Please. Olivia Stanhope wanted the other boy to believe Caleb had died. That was her decision to make, not ours." He fingered his tie. "I don't think you understand the gravity of the situation. We could lose the monies she entrusted to us for Caleb's care. It is a *very* large amount of money. And Eric Baldwyn is now Caleb's legal guardian. And if that happened, the Meadows would be ruined. We could not possibly liquidate that amount of cash."

"That's an administrative problem. My interest is clinical. Do you have any idea how important this information is to my—" He'd almost said, *my research.* "To Baldwyn's treatment? Knowing he has a twin brother makes all the difference."

Metzger rose. Ignoring Patel's plaintive voice ringing in his ears, he left the director's office. He had to find Thomas. Now he knew why Caleb's behavior had been so abnormal since his return to the Meadows.

The answer was so simple, now that he understood.

It was because he wasn't Caleb Baldwyn.

RACHEL TOOK ERIC'S hand and used it to leverage herself up and over the wooden break wall that had been built to stop erosion of the dirt crawl space at the front of the basement.

He gripped the waistband of her jeans and hauled her up as she fought for a foothold on the packed dirt.

Finally she was sitting beside him in a cavelike hole that smelled of earth and mold and rats.

"This is not a good idea. Anyone with any sense who's looking for a missing patient would look up here."

"We're not staying here."

She coughed and wiped her face, then dusted her hands together. "I can feel spiderwebs," she complained, shuddering, even as she admitted to herself that she'd rather lie in a vat of spiders than go any deeper into the darkness.

Unfortunately she was afraid that was what Eric had in mind.

In the distance, muffled by walls and dirt, she heard the familiar creak of the service elevators. "Oh, no," she breathed. "They're searching down here."

"Come on," he whispered, hardly loud enough to reach her through her com unit. She barely made out his outline in the darkness as he put out his hand. "Watch your head."

They crawled several feet in, away from the light. Rachel's lungs burned. Every breath was torture. Her chest and throat were squeezed so tightly that she felt like she was suffocating.

The top of her head brushed the heavy wooden beams. She imagined the weight of the entire building above her. She groped to her right, until she touched and gripped a handful of Eric's T-shirt. "Eric, I can't do this," she gasped.

He took her hand in his, dirt and grit scratching

the skin of her palm, and pressed it quickly to his lips. "Trust me."

His low voice humming through the com unit held a promise she wished desperately she could believe in.

Voices echoed down the corridor below them. Eric's warm fingers pressed lightly against her lips.

"Just a little further. Hurry," he whispered, and pulled her forward.

Her breath caught as she felt something solid in front of them. "What is this?"

He pushed a piece of wood aside. "Put your hand out. Feel that opening?"

She ran her hand along what felt like a plank of wood, until her fingers slipped off the ragged edge. "Y-yes."

"Crawl through."

Terror ripped through her. "It's too little."

"No it's not. Come on, duck your head." He pushed gently.

She balked, her breath coming in short sharp gasps, the heavy darkness more and more oppressive. She glanced behind her, hungrily seeking the faint glow of light that was much farther behind them than she'd realized.

"You've got to trust me, Rachel."

The voices below them were getting louder.

"I'm afraid of the dark."

"I know."

Taking a deep breath of musty air, and reminding herself of what Metzger would do to Eric if he found him, Rachel slithered through the tiny opening and into a large open space. She felt air moving around her and the smells of dirt and mold had faded. In here, the odor was more like the rest of the building—old wood with a slight smoky scent, probably from the fireplaces in the original house. It was pitch-black, but at least she didn't feel the walls closing in on her—yet.

Eric slid in behind her and she heard the quiet scratch of wood against wood.

"Where are we?" she asked, reaching out to touch him for reassurance.

"Shh. Scoot over here to the side and don't make any noise."

He pulled her against him and wrapped his arms around her. "Be still," echoed in her ear.

She buried her face in the hollow of his shoulder and pretended that the only reason there was no light was because she had her eyes shut.

He cradled her head with his hand and put his cheek against her hair.

Below them, a dog barked and a voice shouted.

Eric's arms tightened and Rachel hunched her shoulders.

"Back here!"

"Somebody check the crawl space," a deep voice called.

Tensing, she lifted her head and saw the brief flicker of a flashlight beam through a crack in the wooden planks.

Her heart slammed against her chest. Were they about to be discovered?

The absolute irony of her situation did not escape her. She was hiding with a missing patient in the crawl space of a mental institution, holding proof that an internationally famous physician was conducting illegal and dangerous experiments on helpless patients and may have caused one or more deaths.

If Dr. Green was killed for talking with a reporter, Rachel had no doubt that her fate would be the same. She shuddered.

"Can you see through to the hallway on the other side?" the deep voice asked.

A voice that sounded as though it was just on the other side of the wall from them spoke up. "Nope. Looks like dirt and structural beams are blocking it."

The man who had climbed up into the crawl space cursed. "Damn, I hate spiderwebs."

Rachel heard shuffling and dirt falling as the searcher backed out of the narrow space.

"I got an idea," he huffed as he landed on the concrete floor with a thud. "You climb up on the other side."

The other man laughed. "And get my uniform all dirty? I don't think so."

The dog barked.

"Hush, Babe. Let's go."

Eric held Rachel until the footsteps faded. Her body trembled against his. Her quick, panicky breathing seared the skin below his collarbone, even through the cotton of his T-shirt.

Once the corridor below them was silent, she shifted against him, sending an agony of desire surging through him.

"Don't move," he whispered. "Stay strong. They're not gone yet."

She nodded against his shoulder. "I'm sorry."

He buried his nose in her hair and caressed her head, putting his mouth to her temple and kissing it lightly. "Don't be sorry. I'm so proud of you," he said softly, knowing she'd be able to hear his slightest whisper through her com unit. "I know how much the dark frightens you. I wish I could give you light."

She tilted her head, until her mouth brushed the underside of his chin. Faintly, in the distance, he heard the searchers' voices. They were checking out the crawl space at the end of the corridor to the east.

Eric suffered her lips caressing his skin. He knew he couldn't bear to kiss her. It would lead to more, and more could put them in danger. So he turned his head.

She barely moved, but he felt her withdrawal. She thought he was rejecting her.

Finally, after what seemed like an hour, he heard the creak of the ancient elevator.

Rachel heard it, too, because he felt her tense against him. "Are they gone now?" she asked.

"I think so, but we still must be very careful."

"Can we—" Rachel paused and Eric heard the poorly disguised terror in her voice. "Can we turn the flashlight on?"

"Yeah. Let's see where we are." He sat straighter and Rachel eased up beside him. He noticed she never let go of him. She'd hooked her fingers through one of the belt loops on his jeans.

He flipped on the flashlight and aimed its beam into the darkness.

"We're in a room."

The ceiling was only about five feet high and the floor was unfinished plywood. Support beams had been placed every few feet.

"Yeah. This is what was left of the original basement room in which they built the bomb shelter."

Rachel's gaze kept coming back to the beam of the flashlight.

"How do you know all this—" She stopped.

He sent her a quick, guarded glance. "This is where Caleb and Misty came to be alone. Give me the phone."

She dug it out and handed it to him. He traded it for the flashlight and keyed in a number.

Rachel shone the light around the room. Not ten feet from where they sat was a hospital blanket and a battery-operated lantern.

She scrambled over and grabbed the lantern. With trembling fingers, she flipped the switch at its base and sighed in relief when it came on. It gave off a soft, muted light. She turned off the high-powered flashlight and stuck it in the pocket of her backpack.

"Mitch." Eric's voice was tight.

Rachel fooled with the lantern. There was no way to give Eric privacy for the heartbreaking conversation he was about to have, but she wasn't going to just sit and gawk at him.

"Yeah, we're okay. Mitch? Tell me about Caleb."

Rachel waited, but finally, after several seconds of silence, she had to look up.

Eric's face was ghostly white in the lantern's dim glow, his high cheekbones prominent above slight hollows, his mouth straight and grim.

"A…coma?" he muttered.

Rachel's heart leaped. Caleb wasn't dead? A lump rose in her throat and she had a sudden and inappropriate urge to laugh, the relief was so intense, so cleansing, she almost couldn't bear it.

"When did it happen?" Eric turned away and bent over the phone.

Rachel felt the enormous effort of will he was exerting to keep from breaking down. If he'd been devastated before, when he'd thought Caleb was dead, she couldn't even imagine the melee of emotions that must be swirling like a hurricane inside him now.

For herself, she was still trying to take in the fact that Eric really had known when Caleb's consciousness had disappeared from within him. The doctor's part of her brain thought briefly of what this case study could do for the understanding of communication between twins.

But her emotional side, the side that had been betrayed by the illness her mother could not control, wanted to pull back.

While the knowledge was stunning in a clinical sense, from her position as a woman who, in the past five days, had become much too emotionally attached to the man she was now watching, it was devastating.

Even if Eric were interested in her as anything more than his key to Metzger, she could never handle the emotional turmoil of being with a man whom a lot of people would call crazy if he told them about his connection with his brother.

"Sure," Eric said, his voice harsh with iron-fisted control. "Here she is."

He handed the phone to Rachel without a glance

and retreated beyond the circle of light provided by the lantern.

"Rachel?"

"Hi, Mitch."

"How are you holding up?" His kind yet authoritative voice was comforting.

"Okay. We're close to something. I have the chemical formula for the injections Caleb has been getting. Is he really alive?"

"He's slipped into a coma. The doctors don't hold out much hope."

"Get the formula to them. It should help them, if anything will. I didn't find anything on how to treat withdrawal. Do you want to take it down or should I text message it to you?"

"Text it and I'll send it on to Walter Reed."

"I also have a list of names and ID numbers of the patients Dr. Metzger has been injecting, but there was a problem with one of the patients on the list, according to Metzger's logs. I'm afraid that patient may be one of the people who died here."

"You have the logbook?"

"I have the latest one. Not the one with the patient who died."

"Can you get back in there? We need something linking Metzger solidly with one of the deaths. We haven't been able to connect him directly with Dr. Green's murder."

"Oh, my God! I saw a folder with the word Green written on it. I thought they were the progress note forms. Everybody calls them green forms. What if it was information about Dr. Green?"

Rachel glanced over at Eric's shadowy form. "I can get back in there and get the folder. But, Mitch, you've got to get Eric out of here. He's been receiving injections daily and they're beginning to affect him. Now there's a missing patient alert and they're searching for us. If they've followed procedure, the local police have been called in."

"They haven't. If the locals had been called to the Meadows for any reason, the FBI would have been notified. At around 8:00 a.m. I'll send a couple of agents in under the guise of needing to question 'Caleb' and you to finish some reports. That should interrupt the search and create a diversion. Can you two get out of the building?"

"Yes. As soon as I get the logs and the folder. We can go out the rear door. Natasha knows where the door is. Also, Natasha knows about the secret lab. It was a bomb shelter in the sixties. The alcove on the east side is a hydraulic door. There's a pressure point on the wall."

"Do not go back into the lab. Forget the logs and folder. Your priority is to get yourself and Eric out safely. The information you're sending may be enough for a warrant."

"But Dr. Green's—"

"That's an order."

"Yes, sir." The cell phone beeped. "I'm getting a low battery tone."

"Text that information right now. Then leave the phone on standby. You probably have about six or seven minutes left on it. When you're out, call me at this number and we'll extract you."

Rachel programmed the text she'd saved and sent it to Mitch's cell phone, then put the phone in her pocket.

Eric had come back over to sit beside her as she'd finished her conversation with Mitch. He looked as though he'd been shaken to his core, his face pale and drawn.

"I'm so glad Caleb isn't dead." She tried to sound upbeat, but Eric didn't seem relieved.

He rubbed the back of his neck and glanced at her narrowly. "You're still spooked because of my connection with him, aren't you?"

"Mitch is sending two agents to the Meadows, who will ask to question us about some details of the kidnapping. He wants us to use the diversion to get out through the rear door. Once we do, we're to call him and he'll have us extracted immediately."

"We can't leave yet. I heard you tell him that we don't have the log of the patient who died, or the information about Dr. Green."

"Mitch ordered us not to go back in there. He said it was too dangerous."

Eric sent her a stony look. "He ordered you, not me."

"Mitch is your boss. You *know* that order was for you."

"I am not leaving here until I have enough evidence to put Metzger away for the rest of his life."

"Mitch said what we have is enough for a search warrant."

"You're the one who said I know my boss. I'm sure what he said was it 'might be' enough."

Rachel's face grew hot. "It's the same thing. We've got the formula that proves Metzger is conducting illegal experiments, and the logs that show how often the patients received injections and what their reactions were."

"Right. That *might* get his medical license suspended." The sarcasm in his voice cut like a knife. "It's because of him that I lost my brother." Eric's face distorted in the lantern's glow. "You can't know what that means."

Rachel wanted to cry for Eric, but she knew that wasn't what he needed. He was reacting from emotion, from fear, and he needed logic.

"I can never know what you and your brother shared. I may never understand it. But I do know what it's like to be alone." She placed her fingers on her temples. "All of us are alone, in here. If you have really had a connection with Caleb all these years, then you have been incredibly fortunate. The rest of us have no idea what it's like. We have always existed alone."

"Are you saying I should just give up?"

"No, not at all. I'm saying you have to get out of here alive. There are more people that need your help. You can't just sacrifice yourself for your brother."

"I'm not doing this just for Caleb."

"Are you sure, Eric? Are you sure you're not trying to make up to Caleb because he was sick and you weren't?"

He wouldn't look at her. "I'm after Metzger. He killed people. We can't let him kill anyone else. The proof that he's a murderer is in that room, and I'm going to get it."

Chapter Thirteen

Metzger entered the office in his secret lab through the rear door of the service elevator, followed by Thomas.

The elevator's rear door was only activated by a key and Metzger and Thomas had the only keys. As far as the rest of the hospital staff knew, the elevator's rear doors hadn't worked in years.

As soon as he stepped into his office and turned on all the lights, he knew his fears were grounded in reality.

"They've been here." He pointed at the boxes he'd been packing. His neatly stacked papers were disturbed and the shipping labels had been moved.

"They must have gotten in through the hydraulic door in the alcove," Thomas said. He stepped around the boxes and out into the lab.

Metzger quickly glanced through one of the boxes. His most recent logbook was gone. He cursed. If that information got into the wrong hands, he'd be ruined.

"I found this," Thomas said, coming back to stand at the office door.

Metzger looked up. "A syringe?"

Thomas held up a vial. "And an opened vial of lorazepam. It appears Dr. Harper was trying to sedate him."

"He must be reacting to the injections—showing some aberrant behavior. They may have one of my logbooks. We have to stop them."

"They won't get far. I have two men hidden, watching the rear exit door, and two at the loading dock entrance. They haven't left the hospital, or we'd know." Thomas craned his neck to look upward. "I'm betting they're somewhere in the crawl space, or in one of the closed-off rooms down here. Once they try to leave the building, we'll have them."

Metzger collapsed into his desk chair. "I can't understand how the twin brother managed to get in here to impersonate Caleb."

"Maybe Caleb did go into respiratory arrest and die. Isn't that what happens to the patients if they don't get their regular dose?"

"But why would one of the most prestigious hospitals in the country play along? How did the brother get the FBI to cooperate? It doesn't make sense." He slammed his fist on the desk. "That idiot Patel. If he'd told me that Caleb had any family other than his grandmother, I'd never have used him for the experiments. It's so much easier to use patients with no family, no ties. Although Caleb did make the perfect subject."

He shook his head. This setback was devastating. He'd looked forward to continuing his experimentation on Caleb. In his own private lab in Germany, he'd have been free to increase the dose of the chemicals and to observe the effects without having to hide any adverse reactions.

"Luckily, I've already transferred the computer files to Germany. Get out there, Thomas, and find those two. Pull one of the orderlies to help you search. We don't have much time. If Caleb's brother is in contact with the FBI, then he will have alerted them that he's trying to escape. I'll gather up the chemical and destroy it, so there's no trace of it left anywhere. And, Thomas..."

The nurse stopped at the office door.

"Where are we in weaning the other three patients?"

"I've diluted their doses three times. Two more dilutions over the next week should be enough to avoid respiratory depression."

"What about the vials?"

"I never leave the real drug on the ward. The vials up there are fenpiprazole."

"Brilliant as usual, Thomas. Perhaps the patients won't become too ill. In any case we'll be on our way before their symptoms become obvious.

"Get Baldwyn and Harper in here." Metzger pointed with his fountain pen for emphasis. "Any way you can. We'll lock them in and seal off the room. By the time anyone can get to them, we'll be long gone."

ERIC HELPED RACHEL down from the break wall. Their clothes were coated with dust, and she had spiderwebs in her hair. He reached over and brushed a sticky web from the side of her face.

"Eric, please, don't make me leave without you. What am I supposed to tell Mitch?"

"He'll understand."

"Understand why you disobeyed him?"

He looked down, brushing at his jeans. "Mitch knows firsthand that sometimes you have to do what you know is right, even if it seems wrong at the time."

Rachel glared at him. "That sounds like rationalization to me. You know we have enough proof, especially if we have Caleb's testimony with it, to stop Metzger, to put him in prison. You're mounting a personal vendetta. Assuaging your own guilt."

"Don't psychoanalyze me. It's none of your business, anyway, what I do or why I'm doing it. You'll be safe, as soon as I get you out of here."

"Don't even presume to tell me what is my business and what's not. Caleb became my business when he kidnapped me. And you became my business when…when you brought me back in here."

"That's right. I brought you into this. And now I've decided it's no longer safe for you."

He took her arm and started up the corridor toward the door at the north entrance of the basement. The lights were very dim, and as they walked toward the back of the basement, the anemic bulbs became farther and farther apart.

"And I'll tell you another flaw in your logic," he whispered fiercely, his voice echoing through her com unit. "We *don't* have Caleb's testimony, because he's in a coma. And unless your colleagues can pull off a miracle with that formula you sent them, I need to get a vial of Metzger's prepared drug to give him, or he may never wake up." He paused. "He may not anyway."

"Then I'll go in with you."

"The hell you will. You're leaving this building now. Wait for the agents to pick you up. I'll be fine." He set his jaw. "I can handle Metzger."

"Maybe," she responded. "In a fair fight. But you've got who knows what kinds of drugs in your system. And what about Thomas? There could be others. You don't know how many people Metzger has protecting him."

"I'll manage."

Eric stopped, pulling Rachel against him. They were at the end of the corridor that opened into the mudroom where the small door was located. "Here

we are. As soon as you're safely across the lawn and
hidden in the underbrush, call Mitch, and I'll head
back to the lab. Tell him to bring that search warrant, and hurry."

"I don't like this. You're doing this for the wrong
reasons. You're needlessly risking your life."

He touched her cheek and wiped away a smudge
of dirt. He tried not to think about the look on her
face, tried not to listen to his empathic sense that
told him it was more than just professional concern
that glistened in her eyes.

She might have feelings for him. Lord knew how
much he cared for her. But she saw him as damaged,
like her mother, like his brother. Her feelings were
nothing more than attachment to a patient. And she
would never allow herself to feel more, not for someone like him. She'd told him that from the beginning.

But he couldn't resist a last indulgent moment.
The next time they saw each other, it would be as
professional colleagues, testifying about the case.

"You've got dust in your lashes and spiderwebs
in your hair, Dr. Harper. Have I told you you're the
most beautiful woman I've ever seen?"

She shook her head and her lip trembled.

He bent and kissed that luscious lip, sucking on
it gently, opening his mouth as her tongue hesi-
tantly nudged his lips. Then, for one desperate instant, he deepened the kiss before he raised his head.

"I can't stand to leave you," she whispered, her voice humming in his ear.

"I know," he whispered back. "I feel you here." He touched his chest, over his heart. "Thank you, Rachel."

"For what?" She lifted her brilliant blue gaze to his. Her eyes widened and she gasped. "No!"

Too late, Eric felt the presence behind him.

He whirled. Pain exploded on the side of his head and he went down.

Rachel watched in horror as Eric collapsed. She recognized the two orderlies who stood over him, one with a piece of wood in his hand.

Her heart pounding in her ears, Rachel, with a huge effort, tried to speak crisply and authoritatively.

"That wasn't necessary," she snapped, hoping the orderlies didn't hear the faint shakiness in her voice. "I had the situation under control." She put her hand in her pocket and palmed her cell phone.

The smaller orderly snickered. "Yeah, looked like you did. Hey, Bob—" he elbowed the other orderly "—isn't that called 'fraternizing with a patient'?"

Bob frowned. "Come on, Dr. Harper. You been hiding out with Baldwyn. We got orders to bring you to Dr. Metzger."

Rachel stepped back, afraid to take her eyes off the orderly for even an instant to check on Eric, who was still on the floor. He must be unconscious. How badly was he hurt?

"Don't come near me," she warned Bob.

Bob tossed the stick aside and stepped over Eric's body. He towered over her as he grabbed at her arm. She jerked backward.

Suddenly Bob was no longer looming over her. He thudded to the ground with a breathy grunt.

Eric had knocked his legs out from under him.

Bob rolled and came back to his feet as the smaller orderly braced himself.

Rachel took several steps backward, looking around. She didn't see the stick the orderly had tossed aside, but she did see a piece of metal rod several feet to her left. She eased toward it.

Eric was up, too, thank God.

He was balanced on the balls of his feet, waiting for a move from one or both of the orderlies. Rachel didn't know a lot about fighting, but she knew Eric was at a distinct disadvantage.

Not only was he trapped between the orderlies and the wall, but the blow from the wooden block was bleeding into his right eye. He kicked out at Bob, who dodged his foot, then he used the momentum of the kick to whirl and land a punch in the other orderly's face.

Rachel's whole body shook with shock and fear. She glanced at the metal rod, still too far away, then over her shoulder toward the door. She wouldn't have a chance in a fight. Even the smaller orderly had a good eighty pounds on her.

She'd do better running. She gauged her chances of making it to the door before one of the orderlies saw her. She slipped the cell phone out of her pocket, almost dropping it, her hands were shaking so badly.

Bob lunged at Eric, knocking him off his feet.

Eric yelled as he went down, and shoved at Bob, who howled. Eric must have connected with something.

Rachel looked at the keypad of the phone. It was still in text mode. She gritted her teeth. She could barely see. She forced her trembling fingers to key in what she hoped spelled SOS.

"Get her," Bob huffed.

The smaller orderly started toward her.

The low battery tone beeped, again and again.

Rachel took another step backward and pressed the Send key, praying there was enough battery to send the message to Mitch. Then she turned and ran for the door.

As her fingers closed around the rusty doorknob, a hand grabbed the neck of her T-shirt and jerked her backward. She lost her balance, but a strong forearm wrapped around her throat, holding her up. He squeezed.

She gasped and clawed at the arm, but it didn't let up. Choking, straining for breath, she used the last of her conscious will to toss the cell phone away from her.

Then everything went black.

BRIGHT LIGHT shone in her eyes, and something was holding her down. She coughed, and winced in pain. The last thing she remembered was the orderly's arm around her throat.

The lights hurt her eyes. Squeezing them shut didn't help. She saw big blue circles—the burned-in afterimages of the lights.

Suddenly, with alarming clarity, she knew where she was. She was on the operating table in Metzger's lab. She tried to sit up, and felt the straps binding her wrists and torso. She heard the unmistakable sound of the Velcro straps straining.

A shadow blocked some of the painful brightness and she recognized the silhouette of Gerhardt Metzger's broad face and mutton-chop sideburns.

"Dr. Metzger," she said, her voice nothing more than a croak. "What are you doing?"

"Hello, Rachel. I'd like to explain it all to you, but we don't have much time. Turn your head to the right." He grabbed her jaw and twisted her head.

Rachel blinked, still half blinded by the bright operating-room lights. She saw red and white.

She blinked again. The red was blood.

Eric. "Oh, my God. Eric!"

He stood with his head bowed. Two orderlies held him, each twisting an arm behind him. Thomas stood nearby.

Eric's face and neck were coated with blood. He stirred when she cried his name, and lifted his head.

She saw the damage that had already been done. It must have taken both of the orderlies to restrain him. His right eye was swollen and blood dripped from a cut over his brow. His lip was bleeding and a red mark marred his left cheek.

But his dark eyes held hers with a determined intensity that she knew.

Don't tell them anything. She heard his voice in her ear.

Metzger squeezed her jaw and turned her face back to him. "Now I'm going to give you an injection of midaz-olam, and you're going to answer some questions. If you get the answers wrong, then Baldwyn will suffer. Do you understand?"

His fingers squeezed her jaw. She tried to nod.

"Very good." He let go of her and held up a glass vial, pushing the needle of a syringe into it and taking up clear liquid.

"I'm sure you know what midazolam is. Not only will you feel hazy and be willing to talk about anything I ask you, you'll probably forget what you said later, because of its amnesiac effects."

Rachel knew the drug. It was used in surgical procedures. It had all the properties of the perfect truth serum.

She cut her eyes over to Eric. His head was down but she felt his eyes on her, she heard his voice.

Don't mention the FBI. Be brave, partner.

"I will," she whispered as she felt the prick of a needle in the crook of her left arm. The fluid burned as it entered her vein.

"What did you say?"

"Nothing." Instantly she felt the fast-acting drug swirling through her blood. She fought it, squeezing her fists so hard her fingernails dug into her palms. She concentrated on the pain.

"Now, Rachel, let's do a practice question."

She gritted her teeth and ignored the urge to close her suddenly heavy eyelids. She strained against the Velcro straps around her arms and wrists, and turned her head toward Eric.

Metzger grabbed her jaw. "Look at me when I'm talking to you. What is your name?"

"Rachel Harper." Her lips felt swollen and numb. She bit her lower lip. Pain helped her focus.

"Good. Who is that standing with my orderlies?"

Eric. No. They didn't know about Eric. She squeezed her eyes shut against the fuzzy confusion in her brain. Who? Not Eric. "It's Caleb Baldwyn," she said carefully.

Metzger scratched his sideburns and smiled at her. "I'm sorry, Rachel. That's incorrect. You may need more medication. We already know that Caleb has a twin brother. It was obvious to me from the moment you returned that there was something very different about my favorite patient." He looked up. "Thomas, we have a wrong answer."

"No," Rachel begged. She turned her head, dreading what she was about to see.

Thomas turned and buried his fist in Eric's midsection. Eric grunted and doubled over, kept from falling only by the two orderlies holding his arms.

Pain ripped through Rachel, momentarily clearing the haze from her brain. "No, stop," she cried. "I'll tell you. Caleb's brother. His name is Eric."

She heard a strangled cough from Eric and saw him painfully push himself back to his feet, straining weakly against the orderlies' hold.

"Eric. Caleb's brother. Very good, dear."

Caleb is dead. Eric's voice echoed in her ear. *Caleb is dead.*

"Now, since Eric is here, where is Caleb?"

Tears overflowed Rachel's eyes. The hold she had on her consciousness was so tenuous that she knew she was losing long seconds of time.

"Caleb is—" She stopped, her breath caught on a sob. "Caleb is dead."

Metzger's face swam in front of her eyes. He made a deep, frightening sound, like a growl. "Not a good answer, Rachel. I'm afraid that's incorrect." He nodded at Thomas.

"No!" she shouted. "No! Can't help it. It's true." She couldn't stop herself from crying. If they hurt Eric again, she couldn't stand it.

She strained with all her might against the restraints. A ripping sound filled her ears. She put all her strength behind her effort to free herself.

"He's dead. Dead." She repeated it over and over in her mind. *Dead. Dead.* It was all she had to hold on to, that and the knowledge that if she lost control they would kill Eric.

Metzger held up a hand. "Now, Rachel, it's obvious that your involvement with Eric goes far beyond the professional, but I really need answers. It's highly probable that Caleb is dead, but somehow, I just don't feel like taking your word for it. Thomas, let's see if Eric will be better at answering questions. It's possible he might be more willing to talk if Rachel were the one to suffer."

Eric heard Metzger's words and a terror beyond anything he'd ever known took hold of him. He couldn't let them hurt Rachel.

It was bad enough watching her strain against the

straps on the table. Through the red haze in his eyes he could already see dark bruises forming on her delicate skin.

"How much longer you gonna fool with these two?" Thomas asked. "We need to get out of here."

Eric lifted his head enough to watch Metzger's face.

"I must find out if they managed to give anybody the formula. If the U.S. government gets its hands on it, I'll lose credibility here. And if that happens, I'll never get the recognition I deserve."

Rachel whispered something. Eric wished he could hear her, but in the fight with the orderlies, he'd lost his com unit. He couldn't communicate with her.

"What, Rachel?" Metzger said. "I didn't hear you."

Eric saw Rachel's eyelids drift closed. She was about to succumb to the drug.

Don't tell them, Eric pleaded silently. *Don't tell them the truth.* He wanted to promise he would save her, but he wasn't sure he could keep that promise. Still, he would die trying.

Hold on, Rachel, a little longer. Distract them.

He was badly injured, he knew, from the repeated blows. And his blood loss was weakening him. He only had one chance, and he had to carefully choose his time.

"Formula is…in my pocket," Rachel said thickly. "Didn't get a chance…"

Good girl, Eric thought. She'd already transmitted the formula to Mitch. Hopefully they wouldn't find the cell phone.

Thomas reached over and pawed at her jeans.

"Don't touch her," Eric mumbled through the blood that gathered in his mouth.

Thomas grinned at him, then went back to digging in Rachel's pockets, touching her deliberately and inappropriately with his big hands.

"Which pocket, Doc?" He leered down at her.

Her arms corded with slender muscles as she strained. "Right front, you pig."

Eric's heart swelled with pride. *You are so brave. Dear God, I love you.*

"Pig, eh?" Thomas slapped her.

Eric felt the blow as a flash of heat in the center of his forehead. Fury gave him the strength that he hadn't been sure he could muster.

Shoving his elbows out to either side, he connected with the orderlies' ribs. He didn't damage them, but he did gain the element of surprise, and he used it to his advantage.

In the split second they took to absorb the fact that their quarry had hit them, Eric slipped out of their grasp, whirled with his hands up and cracked their heads together.

Roaring with rage, Thomas dove for him.

Eric neatly sidestepped him, tripped him and brought his foot down on the nurse's head.

He knew he had just a couple of seconds before the men recovered. His instinct told him Metzger was no fighter, so he used those seconds to dive onto the OR table and rip the Velcro strap from one of Rachel's arms.

"Get to the lights," he whispered to her, hoping she had enough control over her faculties to rip off the rest of the straps and make it to the door.

Rolling off the table, he grabbed the crash cart and sent it rolling toward Thomas, who was rising to his feet. Then he turned, hoping to grab Metzger, but the doctor had retreated to the drug storage cabinet, too far away for Eric to reach him.

Rachel was off the OR table. Eric braced against Thomas's onslaught. He shoved the OR table at the other two orderlies, who were climbing to their feet.

"Get her!" Thomas shouted at them as he lunged for Eric.

Rachel killed the lights as Eric threw himself to the right and hit the floor.

He rolled to his feet, light-headed and disoriented by the pitch-dark. Which way was he facing?

The sink was straight ahead. He should get the syringe gun that sat on the shelf above.

Without stopping to question how he knew which way he was facing or where a syringe gun was, he moved straight ahead.

He heard Thomas heading his way.

"Somebody turn on the lights!" Metzger cried.

Eric felt the brush of air that signaled Thomas's presence and ducked sideways.

He should veer to the right. Now.

He reached up. His knuckles brushed the front edge of the shelf. He stretched out his fingers and wrapped his hand around the pistol-shaped device.

Rachel shrieked. One of the damn orderlies had grabbed her.

The lights came on, blindingly bright after the total darkness.

Eric assessed his position, and his attackers. His pulse hammered in his ears. He adjusted the syringe gun in his hand, wondering what it contained.

Metzger was to his right, Thomas headed straight for him.

As Thomas barreled into him and crushed his lower back against the edge of the sink, Eric pushed the barrel of the syringe gun into Thomas's gut and pulled the trigger.

Thomas crumpled right in front of him.

He turned toward the orderlies who had grabbed Rachel.

Rachel's face was sickly pale, her blue eyes huge and round as she stared past him.

"Metzger! Gun!"

Eric turned as Metzger lifted his hand. He held a semiautomatic pistol.

"Metzger," Eric said, dropping the syringe gun and holding up his hands. "I'm FBI. If you stop right now, we'll offer you a deal."

Metzger shook his head. "It's all ruined. I worked my whole life to cure schizophrenia. Now I have nothing. Nothing."

Eric watched his face. He was going to shoot. Eric knew it, and if he missed Eric, then Rachel was directly behind him.

There was only one thing Eric could do.

He dove straight for the gun.

A roar filled his ears.

Rachel screamed.

Chapter Fourteen

Rachel pushed at the hands restraining her. "No, no! Let me go." She curved her fingers and tried to scratch. She had to get away. She had to get to Eric.

"Hey, hey, hey." A gravelly voice that should have been rough but wasn't rumbled through her. "Hold still, sugar. Leave me a little skin. Eric's fine." The voice reassured her, but the hands still held her like a vise.

"And stop kicking. You're making mincemeat out of my shins. Give him a minute to get cleaned up."

Finally the words sank in. "He's fine?" she asked groggily.

The man who held her carried her over to a chair and set her in it, then crouched in front of her, rubbing her hands between his.

"You need to open your eyes, sugar. You're about to go into shock. Question is, are you okay?"

It was hard to focus. Rachel blinked several times

and moistened her dry lips. She had to force her eyes open, and when she did, she met a gaze that was darker than any she'd ever seen. The face was too beautiful for a man, but at the same time it was decidedly masculine. Perfect cheekbones and midnight-black hair told her he was of Native American descent.

"Hi. I'm Storm. I'm with the FBI."

She looked past him. "Where's Eric? Metzger shot him." She tried to pull her hands away, but Storm held fast.

"No, sugar. Metzger shot himself. Eric's a little banged up, but he's going to be okay. I'll take you to him in just a minute."

"Where are the orderlies?" Rachel realized the metal room was full of people, but none of them was dressed in white.

"My men are taking care of them. Good job, sending that SOS to Decker."

Rachel took a shaky breath. "Are you sure Eric's all right?"

"Just like a woman. One-track mind." The man sighed and stood, towering over her and wrapping her hand in his. "Come on."

As soon as she stood, she saw Eric. He was sitting on the OR table, with two people working on him.

His eyes were closed, his head bowed as a nurse closed the cut with a row of Steri-Strip bandages.

The bruise on his left cheekbone was purple, the corner of his mouth was swollen and there were dark circles under his eyes. They'd removed his bloody T-shirt. His belly was red and there were bruises forming. His knuckles looked raw and streaks of blood ran down his jaw and neck. He was the most beautiful sight she'd ever seen.

As if he felt her looking at him, he lifted his head and opened his eyes. They were soft and filled with pain, but they lit up when they met her gaze.

Tears welled, blurring her vision.

"Ah, don't cry," he said, his voice raspy and strained.

She shook her head.

His gaze moved to the man beside her. "Storm, nice of you to drop by."

Storm reached over and touched Eric's knee. "I guess I'm going to have to quit calling you a desk jockey, Baldwyn."

A ghost of a smile crinkled Eric's eyes. "I guess so."

"Well, I'd better—" Storm made a vague gesture and looked at Rachel. "If you're okay."

She nodded at him without taking her eyes off Eric.

"Oh, by the way, Baldwyn." Storm held out a tiny cylinder. "Here's your com unit. One of the men picked it up in the corridor. I guess it got dislodged while you were chatting with those goons that messed up your face."

Eric reached out and took the tiny microcommunicator.

Rachel stared at the little cylinder, trying to figure out why it seemed so odd to her that Storm was handing it to Eric. Hadn't Eric had it the whole time?

Storm said something she didn't catch and the two people ministering to Eric's injuries disappeared.

"You have a bruise where that bastard slapped you." Eric frowned. He reached out toward her face.

"It doesn't hurt." She took a step forward and grabbed the edge of the table. "Sorry, I'm still a little groggy."

"Rachel, I'm so sorry. I should have been stronger. I should have protected you better."

She put her hand to his mouth. "Please don't. Look at you."

"I'm fine." He smiled carefully, catching her palm in his fingers. "Really fine."

Rachel stared at him. Had she ever seen him really smile before? He had a beautiful smile, even marred by the cut on his lip. That smile thrilled her and terrified her as she realized a truth that she'd been trying to deny since the first hours they'd spent together.

She loved him. So much. Too much.

Her heart slammed against her chest and her brain went fuzzy again.

She tried to smile back, working to process his words. "You mean—"

He nodded. "Caleb." He looked down, then up at her, wariness in his expression. "He came out of his coma."

Terror overrode all her other feelings. Clutching at her throat, Rachel fought the urge to back away. She didn't know what to think, much less what to say. One thing she did know—she didn't want to hear any more. Yet she couldn't help but ask. "You knew?"

He nodded. "I know."

Rachel gently pulled her hand from his grasp. She felt a tear slip down her cheek. Her head was beginning to spin. Her emotions were so mixed up that she couldn't think straight.

"It must be the drug," she said, her voice breaking. "I'm a little...tired."

Eric's gaze turned hard and he averted his gaze, but not before she saw the flash of pain in his eyes. "Yeah. Me, too."

Storm appeared at her side. He put his arm around her. "Sugar, you're looking pale. Come on. We're putting you two in an ambulance. Next stop, Walter Reed Hospital in D.C."

Rachel couldn't deny that she was glad for the interruption. Her knees were trembling and she felt sick to her stomach. But her physical symptoms were nothing compared to the pain in her heart.

She hadn't been able to stop herself from recoiling when Eric mentioned Caleb. Caleb was a part of Eric. And Caleb was so very ill. She didn't know how to deal with that.

By the time she got into the ambulance, she couldn't see for the tears. She closed her eyes and gave herself up to the drowsiness caused by the midazolam.

THE NEXT MORNING, after spending the night in an observation room at Walter Reed Hospital, Rachel went to the Medical Intensive Care step-down unit to see Caleb.

When she pushed open the door into the room, Eric was there. Her heart did a flip.

He was cleaned up and dressed in teal-blue scrubs, and he looked better—and worse. The swelling in his eye and lip had gone down, but the bruise on his cheekbone had gotten darker, and it looked as though he was going to have a black eye.

He obviously hadn't slept. His eyes were too bright and his face looked drawn and pale.

He sat beside the bed, talking to Caleb, who lay with his eyes closed, an oxygen tube running across his face under his nostrils.

Eric's head turned slightly, but he didn't look at her. "So, bud, Metzger's gone now, and I'm going to take care of you. With the proper medication, you should be able to live in a halfway house, maybe even get your own place."

Eric paused, knotting one hand into a fist and grazing his knuckles with his teeth. After a couple of seconds, he went on.

"And guess what, bud. Misty is coming to see you."

Caleb's eyes opened and he smiled. "Misty wants to see me?" he whispered. "I still can't believe she's alive."

"Yeah. She'll be here in a few days, when you're feeling better."

Eric patted his brother's shoulder and stood, glancing at Rachel. "You've got another visitor now, bud. I'm going to go find some coffee."

He walked around the bed and over to Rachel. "Be careful what you say," he warned her.

He left the room.

Rachel closed her eyes for an instant, hurt flowing through her, numbing her as the midazolam had. She knew she had hurt Eric. But how could she ever explain how utterly terrifying it was to consider trusting her heart to him? She hadn't slept much. She'd spent most of the night dozing fitfully, dreaming about Eric, standing in front of two facing mirrors. His reflection was him and Caleb at the same time, and it bounced back and forth to infinity.

She took a deep breath.

"Hi, Caleb."

Caleb turned his head. "Hi, pretty doctor. Eric said you were here. I'm sorry...sorry for what I did."

She sat in the chair Eric had vacated and patted Caleb's hand. "I know. You couldn't help it. It was Metz-ger's experiments."

"Eric doesn't understand. He doesn't understand why I never let him know I was alive."

Rachel's heart broke as she thought of Caleb, locked away by his grandmother for twenty years, and Eric, believing his brother was dead, believing he might be going insane.

"He missed you a lot."

"But you understand, don't you?"

She glanced sharply at him. "Understand what?"

"Why he was better off without me."

A shard of guilt embedded itself under Rachel's diaphragm. Caleb's words resonated inside her. What would her life have been like if she'd grown up somewhere else? Someplace where she'd never endured the fear and chaos of living with a mother who was bipolar.

She couldn't imagine it. When it came down to it, no matter what her mother had done to her, the fact remained—she was her mother.

"Oh, Caleb, Eric wasn't better off without you. He loves you. You two are connected. Without each other, you wouldn't be the same people." As she spoke, Rachel realized the truth of what she was saying.

She was here, now, because of her mother. She

was the person she was because of how she grew up. It was the way life was.

"Eric needs you, just like you need him. Your grandmother was wrong. She stole your lives from you. No one has the right to do that. Now you and Eric are together. He loves you, and you love him.

"I think you just taught me a valuable lesson, Caleb." She smiled at him. "Let me tell you about my mother."

Rachel told Caleb about her beautiful, eccentric mother, who had loved her and cared for her the best way she'd known how.

By the time Rachel finished, tears were streaming down her face and she was astounded at how many wonderful memories had spilled out of her brain.

She leaned back and wiped her face. "You must be sick of listening to me. I'll go find Eric. He's probably waiting for me to leave."

She got up and leaned over to kiss Caleb's forehead.

"Rachel?"

"Hmm?" She straightened and fixed his sheet.

"Eric loves you."

The words shattered her heart. With a quiet cry she flopped into the chair and put her hands over her mouth.

"How—" She had to start again. "How do you know that, Caleb?"

"He told me."

She shook her head. "I think you…must be mistaken."

"No. I'm not. I'm telling the truth."

My brother always tells the truth.

"When did he tell you that? Today?"

"No. When you were hiding in the Medical Records room. When you kissed him." Caleb laughed weakly. "He didn't exactly tell me. I just knew." He sighed. "I'm…I'm sleepy now."

"Okay, Caleb." She stood and touched his forehead. "Sleep well."

Outside the step-down unit, Rachel looked toward the coffee machines and didn't see anyone. She walked around the corner to the waiting room.

Eric was pacing back and forth, talking on his cell phone, a cup of coffee sitting forgotten on a side table. He looked up and saw her, and cut short his conversation.

"Waiting for me to leave?" she asked.

He glowered at her. "I figured you'd be more comfortable dealing with only one crazy person at a time."

She pressed her lips together as the hurt swelled inside her. She knew she deserved that. That and more. She wanted to run, but she stood her ground, her heart pounding in her throat. Her hands shook so much she had to fold her arms.

She nodded at the cell phone and spoke stiffly. "Information about the case?"

"That was Mitch," Eric said. "Metzger was dead at the scene. No surprise. Thomas is trying to cop a deal, spilling his guts. He has a lot of information about Metzger's experiments. There are three patients who will have to be weaned off the injections, but they appear to be in good health. None of them had been on it more than a few weeks, maybe a couple of months. Apparently Caleb was Metzger's only long-term experiment. There were plane tickets to Germany for Metzger, Thomas and Caleb."

"What about Dr. Green?"

"There are some discrepancies in the narcotics register at the Meadows. Missing morphine. Dr. Patel is answering questions from the Drug Enforcement Agency about that now."

Eric frowned. "What do you think about Caleb? How's he doing?"

Rachel smiled shakily. "Caleb is going to be fine. He's responding to the new drug the doctors have him on." She looked down at her hands, which were clasped at her waist. Her knuckles were white.

Eric studied her, his gaze hooded. "You're spooked by me, aren't you?"

She almost laughed. Spooked was only one of the

things she was feeling right now. Confused, sad, curious about Caleb's statement.

"This isn't easy for me…"

Eric's eyes softened. "I know that, Rachel. More than anyone. I don't mean to make it harder on you. When I told you I didn't have a lot of experience with relationships, I was telling the truth." He turned his back, looking out the windows.

She stepped toward him. "Eric, I heard Storm tell you he found your com unit."

"Yeah?"

"When did you lose it?"

"In the struggle in the hallway, when the guy hit me with the block of wood."

"But I heard you—" Rachel chewed on her lower lip.

"Heard me? When?"

"When I was on the table. You told me not to tell them anything. You told me—" She paused, looking at him oddly.

Eric stared at her. He felt flayed wide open.

Of course he'd been sending her thoughts, sending her strength, as much as he could. It had helped him stand the pain, to concentrate on trying to reach her.

But he'd been a dozen feet away from her, held by two orderlies, and his com unit had been lying on the floor two corridors away. She couldn't possibly have heard him. He shook his head.

"I guess it was the drug Metzger gave me. I guess I was dreaming."

Taking a long breath, he watched her carefully. "What did you hear—in your dream?"

"You said to hold on a little longer. You said—" She stopped, her eyes wide and scared.

"I said what?" he muttered. "Tell me."

She lifted her chin. "You said you loved me." Her lips trembled. "But I couldn't have heard you, could I? It's impossible."

His face grew hot with embarrassment. His flayed heart ached. How could she know? Was he that transparent? "I suppose you could have been dreaming."

"I suppose."

Was that pain in her voice, anguish shining from her blue eyes?

He turned his back. The things he was about to say he could not say to her face. He sighed deeply and bowed his head. "I've never been in love. Never thought I would ever be. It's always been difficult for me to connect with people. I guess I am too closed off emotionally, because of the way I have to work."

"Closed off?" Rachel sounded stunned. "Didn't I tell you how you made me feel?"

He turned and saw the confusion in her eyes. "When I met you, when I felt the connection between us, I thought…"

Rachel stared at him.

Eric would have given the world if he could have read her thoughts then, but of course he couldn't. She'd been crying, about Caleb probably. She had too soft a heart to be a psychiatrist. She took everything too personally, which was why she could never become emotionally involved with anyone who had a mental problem.

And Eric knew that she believed he had a problem.

"You felt a connection?"

He nodded, his throat clogging up. He couldn't say anything else. She had told him how she felt, at the very beginning. He'd gotten too involved, and now he'd lost her.

Rachel knew that Eric would never take that last step. And she knew why. He thought she could never love him.

She knew if she wanted him, she would have to cross the chasm that divided them.

"Caleb thinks—" she started, then lost her nerve.

"Caleb thinks what?"

She searched his face—the beautiful countenance she would never forget as long as she lived. The bruises and scars were a testament to what he had endured for her.

He had been so brave. She owned him enough courage to at least speak the truth. "That you love me."

His features twisted into a sarcastic smile. He

couldn't hold it, though, so he dropped his gaze, "Well, he *is* crazy."

The harsh words cut her to her soul.

She waited for him to look up at her, but he didn't. Sadness enveloped her. She turned on her heel.

"Maybe you're right and Caleb is wrong." She took a shaky breath. "Maybe everything you've been through has damaged you too much. Maybe you are too closed off to allow yourself to love. But when you said you felt a connection…"

She waited, but he didn't respond. "I'm sorry," she mumbled. "I guess I misunderstood."

She turned and walked out of the room, wishing—praying—that he would stop her. She held her breath, listening for the slightest whisper, the smallest movement. But she heard nothing.

Rachel made it all the way downstairs and out to her car before she broke down and cried.

Chapter Fifteen

Rachel put the last of her bags in the trunk of her car and checked to make sure her computer and monitor were secure. She walked back inside and made one last round of the apartment. The bed was bare of sheets, the closets open and empty. All the rooms with their institutional furniture looked as impersonal as a hotel room without her things scattered about.

She stood at the door and looked across the grounds at the main building. It stood stately and proud, hiding the evil that had dwelled within it.

The evil and the good.

Rachel sucked in a long breath as the memories crowded into her brain. Good and bad. The most wonderful moments of her life had happened inside that building, as well as the worst.

No, not the worst. All the torture and fear she'd endured at the hands of Gerhardt Metzger didn't hold a candle to the painful realization that she'd failed to get through to Eric.

An overwhelming loss filled her. Eric had taught her how to open up, how to love. He'd shown her that nothing is attained without compromise. And yet he'd been unable to meet her halfway.

He had given her a wonderful gift, the ability to accept others as they were, rather than trying to fix them. But he hadn't been able to accept himself. So she'd lost him.

"Damn it," she whispered. Now she was crying. She turned and went into the bathroom to splash water on her face. As she was patting her cheeks with rolled-up toilet tissue, she heard a sharp rap on the open apartment door.

"Don't be Dr. Patel." She'd already told him she wasn't interested in staying at the Meadows.

"Just a minute," she called, and wadded up the wet tissue and tossed it into the trash basket.

When she stepped out of the bathroom and into the hall, she saw a familiar silhouette outlined by the sun streaming in the open door.

She took a couple of steps toward him. "Eric?" she whispered.

He stepped inside, out of the sunlight. His face was still pale. The bruise on his forehead had turned an ugly yellow-brown in the three days since she'd walked out of the hospital in D.C. His dark gaze was guarded. "I was afraid you'd be gone."

She bit her lip. "Another ten minutes and I would

have been." Her voice sounded breathy, as if she'd been running. Not surprising, since her pulse was jackhammering.

He nodded, searching her face.

Could he tell she'd been crying?

"Where are you going?" he asked.

"My mother wants me to come and stay with her and her new husband for a while."

He looked down at his feet, then back up. "Caleb's being discharged today."

Rachel's heart leaped and she took a step forward. "That's wonderful. So he's okay? Where is he going?"

A hint of a smile lightened Eric's face. "I found a private facility near D.C."

"Oh, Eric, that's great. He's going to be near you. That will be so good for both of you." To her dismay, her eyes pricked with tears.

"Yeah." He walked over to the kitchen counter and leaned against it, looking down at his hands. "Rachel?"

"Eric, what's the matter? Is something wrong with Caleb?" She stepped from the hall into the kitchen.

He shook his head, then looked up at her through his lashes. "What if he's right?" he asked, his voice a shaky rasp.

A thrill of fear and hope skittered up her spine. "About what?"

"About what he told you."

Rachel could feel the tension radiating from him. But she knew he had to do this. She couldn't do it for him. He had to take that step alone.

"Is he?" She held his gaze.

He stood there for a second, then slowly he moved to stand in front of her, and cradled her face in his hands. He leaned over until their foreheads were touching. "You know me better than I know myself."

"I know that you are the only one who can answer that question."

His lashes dipped and he kissed her gently on the mouth, stealing her breath.

"You want a sane, secure life. You want normal. I'm sole guardian of a brother who is schizophrenic. And I definitely have issues myself. I can never give you normal, Rachel."

His breath fanned against her mouth—quick, sharp, nervous.

Rachel wrapped her arms around his neck. "Caleb and I had a very good talk the other day. He reminded me that we can't change who we are. All we can change is how we deal with it, and who we allow to help us. I've tried safe and secure. As you pointed out to me once, it's a lonely life."

She drew in a long breath. "I can live without normal. But not without love. Can you give me love?"

His soft dark eyes shone with the light she'd seen in them the first time he'd ever looked at her. The light of reality. And now the light of love.

"I can do that," he whispered against her lips. "Can you give me forever?"

Rachel laughed through tears. "Oh, Eric, I can definitely do that."